I bagged a couple muffins and headed to the Rubinesque booth. I let myself in through the main tent entrance and was beaten in the head with strobe lights like I had entered an underground nightclub. Not that I would know what that was like exactly, but I'd seen it on TV.

I held up my arm to shield my face from the flashing. As my eyes adjusted, I could see that the Rubinesque booth had been ransacked worse than ours. Boxes and tubes of skin-care products were strewn all over the place. Client postcards littered the floor like my sugar packets. And hot-pink paper had been shredded like Easter grass.

"Dr. Rubin, are you here?" There was no answer, so I followed the flashes to his treatment room and called him again. "Dr. Rubin?"

The treatment room smelled like someone had burned a ham that acrid smell that comes from boiling sugar until it looks like charcoal. I looked around to see where it was coming from, and that's when one of the creepy masks looked back at me. It was lying on a treatment bed, flashing through several colors, with smoke pouring out from the eyes. The bed was lumpy, and I had a sinking feeling that I knew what I would find under the sheet. I only lifted a corner, but I would recognize that blue star sapphire anywhere.

I reached for his wrist and didn't find a pulse.

This had to be Dr. Lance Rubin and he was most definitely dead. . . .

Books by Libby Klein

CLASS REUNIONS ARE MURDER

MIDNIGHT SNACKS ARE MURDER

RESTAURANT WEEKS ARE MURDER

THEATER WEEKS ARE MURDER

WINE TASTINGS ARE MURDER

BEAUTY EXPOS ARE MURDER

Published by Kensington Publishing Corp.

Beauty Expos Are
MURDER

LIBBY KLEIN

KENSINGTON
PUBLISHING CORP.

www.kensingtonbooks.com

KENSINGTON BOOKS are published by

Kensington Publishing Corp.
119 West 40th Street
New York, NY 10018

All Kensington titles, imprints, and distributed lines are available at special quantity discounts for bulk purchases for sales promotion, premiums, fund-raising, educational, or institutional use.

Special book excerpts or customized printings can also be created to fit specific needs. For details, write or phone the office of the Kensington Sales Manager: Attn.: Sales Department. Kensington Publishing Corp., 119 West 40th Street, New York, NY 10018. Phone: 1-800-221-2647.

The Kensington logo is a trademark of Kensington Publishing Corp.

First Printing: July 2021
ISBN-13: 978-1-4967-3313-9
ISBN-10: 1-4967-3313-4

ISBN-13: 978-1-4967-3316-0 (ebook)
ISBN-10: 1-4967-3316-9 (ebook)

10 9 8 7 6 5 4 3 2 1

Printed in the United States of America

For Tim and Gia
Love leaves a mark on our hearts forever.

CHAPTER 1

I don't care how good-looking a man is, somewhere there's a woman who's fed up with him.

"Bella, it's not what you think."

I dug my fingernails into the palm of my hand. *I bet Adam said the same thing to Eve in the Garden.* "It never is."

Was this a joke? Did Aunt Ginny and the biddies put him up to this? The pained look on his face said this was really happening. I had to fight my every instinct to run home and cry. I could still feel his lips on mine. His heart beating against my chest. I had just declared my love to Gia only to have him blow my world apart by being married. I scanned through my memory for any mention of Alexandra. *I thought she was dead. Didn't he tell me she was dead? I distantly remember asking him if he was married. And where is his ring! If there is no ring, this isn't my fault.*

I took a steadying breath and pulled out of Gia's arms to look at the statuesque honey blonde, my cheeks turning to lava. All these months working side by side, he'd been stealing little pieces of my heart. We'd talked for hours, revealing the most intimate details of our lives, how does *I have a wife* never come up?

A ripple of worry crossed Gia's face and he searched my eyes. He reached to stroke my cheek and I jerked away, giving Alexandra a look of triumph. The bell to the front door chimed. No one moved. A moment later Gia's sister, Karla, came into the kitchen, spun an about face, and made an immediate retreat.

Alexandra took a step toward Gia and put her hand on his arm. "Giampaolo, darling, who is this that I've caught you kissing?"

Tell me this isn't happening. I felt like I was moving under water. My heart was sinking like a shipwreck. If you put your ear against mine, you'd hear a tsunami.

Gia's eyes flashed hot disgust as he removed Alexandra's hand from his arm. "You lost the right to touch me a long time ago." He reached for me again and I arched away. "Bella, please. Let me explain."

I was almost gone. I had my hand on the door, ready to pull the trigger, when I felt a tiny pat on my hip.

Henry scrunched his face up and his glasses moved a fraction before sliding back down his nose. "Poppy, where are you going?"

I swallowed hard. I recognized that scared puppy look. So small and confused. I forced a smile and kneeled to face him. "Nowhere, buddy. Everything's fine." I tapped Henry on the nose. "Do you know how special you are to me?"

A grin split his face and he nodded.

Alexandra reached for him. "Henry, come back to Mommy now, darling."

Henry cut wary eyes toward her and he buried himself into my side.

Gia spoke through clenched teeth. "He has never seen you before today. Don't you think you are being ridiculous?" He squatted down to face me; his blue eyes were the gray of a coming storm. "Bella, nothing is as it seems."

Alexandra took two quick steps toward Gia and Henry, but before the words, "Darling please," had fully crossed her lips, Gia gave her a look so fierce and cold that it took my breath away. I didn't understand the string of Italian he spat at her, but I knew I never wanted him to look at me that way. Alexandra crossed her arms over her chest and looked away.

Gia took my hand. "Let's take Henry to Momma's and I will explain everything. Please?" His eyes pleaded with mine.

For months I'd kept my heart locked away to protect it from being hurt, and the very minute I took a leap of faith, I turned into Wile E. Coyote and plummeted. I'd always let my circumstances control me. I'd laid down under fear, shame, disappointment. I didn't know how this would end. Maybe it was a misunderstanding, or maybe I'd just repeated the biggest mistake of my life. But this time no one was going to choose my fate but me. One of these people was my enemy and I needed to find out which one. I glanced at Alexandra and told Gia, "You go. I'll wait here until you get back."

Gia looked uncomfortably from me to the strange blonde in the room. I could see a battle raging in his eyes. He spoke softly to Henry as he led him from the shop.

"Come, Piccolo. Nonna has chocolate milk and bomboloni."

I sized up Alexandra while she made an equally visible inspection of me. As soon as the bell in the front announced that Gia had exited the shop, she grinned like a cat with a cornered mouse. Then her eyes melted into soft pools that made her look like a Disney fairy. Her hair was the color of spun gold and she was willowy and pale and beautiful like a porcelain statue. She was the exact opposite of Gia, who was dark and broad and strong. Henry clearly got his coloring and features from his . . . *mother*. It was like finding the last few pieces to a puzzle you'd been working on, and now that it was finished you couldn't believe how much you had missed before. She reached for my hand, and a single tear rolled down her perfect peach cheek. *She even cries pretty.*

"Please don't think I am horrible. I don't know what you've been told about me."

You'd be surprised at how little I know.

"I can tell that you are very special to my son. Thank you for being here for him when I couldn't be." She sighed. "It's good to be home. I've missed everyone terribly." She brushed the tear away and her face brightened. "Oh, I am so ashamed. I don't even know your name. Did I hear Henry call you Poppy? Like grandpa?"

Her words dripped with honey but had a sting. Something about her made me unreasonably angry. I took a moment to swallow my terror. "Like the poisonous flower."

She smiled and nodded. "How pretty. And please, call me Alex. All my friends do." She took a step back and leaned against the granite counter, its flecks of silver winking under the pendant lights.

A memory flashed before my eyes of Gia holding me against that same spot, speaking careless whispers that he loved me. I swatted the memory away. "So, how is it we've never met before?"

Alexandra looked around the cobalt-blue kitchen. She traced the lines on the teal peacock of the KitchenAid stand mixer that Gia had given me when I first started working at La Dolce Vita. She sighed. "I've been away. I guess you know that I wasn't well after Henry was born. Gia and I were so excited to welcome our little one into the family, but then I became very ill. Gia said he would give me time to rest and get better, but he took Henry and disappeared."

"You're saying Gia kidnapped Henry?"

She twisted her hands together and hung her head.

What is that? Is that a yes or a no?

"Those were painful days. I didn't have any friends in Philly. No one I could talk to. I wanted to die, and I almost did without my little boy." She turned her face to be sure I saw the tear on her lashes before she wiped it away. Her smile was soft but reflected a hard shell beneath the surface. "I'm back now, and no matter what Gia tells you, I'm here to stay. I'm Henry's mother and no one can take that away from me. You understand, don't you? What am I saying, of course you do. You probably have children of your own. You are not exactly young."

Her words were like a kidney punch. Her eyes drilling into mine as she was waiting for me to give information that I refused to give. I held my poker face and waited.

She started to fidget with the tie dangling from an apron on a hook. "I'm sure my husband has been up to all kinds of games while I've been away. He is Italian, after all. But I finally have a chance to get my family back and

I'm going to fight for them. Gia is very angry with me, but soon he'll remember that he used to call me his treasure."

The front bell chimed again, and Alexandra swayed toward me and grabbed me by the shoulders. "Listen to me. I know you don't want to be a home-wrecker. You've just been enticed by the Italian charm. But you need to walk away for your own good. Trust me, Gia isn't who you think he is."

Gia marched into the kitchen, his mouth set in a grim line. In one fluid motion he put his hand on my back, broke Alexandra's contact, and led me out the back door with a slam.

We walked the block and a half to the beach in silence, the stress enveloping us like smoke at a medical marijuana clinic. I followed Gia up the ramp to the boardwalk and we found an empty bench overlooking the dunes. The sound of crashing waves drove my blood pressure down. *How did I ever live in Virginia without this? Oh yeah . . . Pop-Tarts.*

Gia draped his arm across the back of the bench and looked toward the ocean. "It must be high tide. The waves are close." His dark hair fluttered lightly in the breeze.

I expect the Valentine's Day massacre also began as a nice day. I rubbed my arms against the chill. I did not anticipate this turn of events when I ran out of the house to tell this man that I loved him or I would have grabbed a jacket. And maybe a Valium. I never expected a wife to appear after weeks of promises and innuendo. *I should have known he was too good-looking to be single.*

Gia sighed. "I didn't want you to find out this way."

Anger shot up to the roots of my red hair and a couple

new freckles popped out on my face. "Yeah. I bet not! But then, what is a good way to say, 'I'm married'?"

He turned to me, the picture of calm with just a hint of sadness. "I haven't been married since Henry was born and Alex took off with another man."

Oof. That was a punch in the heart. "She said you took Henry away from her and disappeared."

Gia's eyes narrowed. He breathed out a bitter little chuckle as he turned back toward the ocean. "Alex says a lot of things. Usually whatever she thinks will get her sympathy for the moment. I did not take Henry and disappear. After Alex left us, I moved to Cape May to be with my family, and she knew that. Momma's restaurant has been in the same spot for fifteen years."

My cheeks flamed and my eyes stung. "Why don't you fill me in on your side of the story?"

"Momma and Alex's father are from the same neighborhood. Vincenzo Scarduzio is a very powerful man. He helped Momma get us to America after our father died. One by one we got citizenship. So, when Signor Scarduzio said he wants his daughter to come to America, he asked our family to help. He does not want her to go to her cousins in Philly. Alex was different then. She lived with us. Momma gave her a job in the restaurant at night and she went to college during the day. One day Signor Scarduzio said he wants me to show Alex around. She was young and beautiful. She made me feel very smart and very strong. I fell in love with her and we got married. She wanted to move near her cousins, so we went. That was the beginning of Hell."

I was starting to feel like yesterday's pork roll left out in the sun after the beautiful, young Alex soliloquy when a couple of female Coast Guard cadets jogged past, giving Gia a long once-over. I sucked my stomach in and wrapped my arms tighter around me. I'd already felt enough jealousy for one day.

Gia shifted to face me. "I soon found out there was another Alex. Once she had a green card, the sweetness fell away and the real Alexandra came out. She would disappear for days and not tell me where she went. She emptied our bank account many times and I had to borrow money from Momma to pay the bills. I caught her cheating and she laughed in my face." He shook his head and watched a seagull dragging a curly fry down the boardwalk.

"Why didn't you leave her?"

"I was not the best husband. I work too much. I drink with my brothers too often. But I never cheat on her. I try to make it work. After two years I tell Alex I'm leaving, but she tells me she is pregnant. . . ."

I could see where this was going. I would have to be compassionate because he stayed with her for Henry and I did not appreciate it at all.

"Bella, Momma is very religious. She does not approve of divorce. She says I will dishonor God and the family if I leave Alex. Then things will not go well for us with Vincenzo Scarduzio. And we did not want to cross Vincenzo Scarduzio. But all I cared about was I had baby coming. So, I stay."

I listened to Gia closely and almost smiled through the pain. *The more upset he gets, the stronger his accent becomes.*

"I try to work on the marriage. I suggest counseling. Alex agreed, but two weeks after Henry is born, Alex is gone. She left a note that she felt suffocated and does not want to be tied down. If it were not for Momma and my sisters, I do not know what would have happened to us. I do not know how to take care of a baby. So, I move back to my family in Cape May. I swear off women. I am done with love. And then you come along." He ran his hand down my arm. "With your red hair and giant blue eyes, and that horrible pink feather dress. You wear your heart on the outside. I was caught. When you left my shop, I called Zio Alfio and told him to find Alex, whatever it takes, and make her agree to the divorce. I was ready to move on. It has taken him months, at last he found her."

"But why didn't you tell me? I thought she was dead."

Gia looked surprised. "Why did you think she was dead?"

"I asked you if you were married and you said no."

"I said she was gone. I didn't say she was dead."

"All this time I thought you were a widower. You sure flirt like a single man."

A crinkle of amusement crossed Gia's face. "I do not know what that means, but every moment with you was real. I love you. I've loved you from the very beginning. I should have told you I was trying to find Alex to get divorced, but I did not want to scare you away. I keep finding ways to be with you, but Tim is always close behind. If you were happy with Tim, I would walk away, but I see your heart in your eyes when you look at me, and I know Tim is not the one." Gia tentatively offered me his hand, waiting to see if I would take it.

I shook my head. "I'm still angry. And hurt. And honestly, I don't know who to believe."

Gia closed his eyes and took a deep breath. "After all this time . . . you still do not know me?"

"I thought I did, and then your wife introduced herself.

And what about Henry? I love him like he was my own. Where does he think his mother has been this whole time? What's best for him? Maybe he needs this relationship with his mother more than he needs me in his life."

Gia shook his head. "There are so many reasons why I know that is not true. Alex could have come home anytime if she wanted a relationship with Henry. She has only come because Zio Alfio gave her divorce papers."

"Did she sign them?"

Gia rubbed his cheek and his hand bristled against the stubble. He looked weary. "No."

"Then why is she here?"

He sighed. "She says she wants another chance. She is ready to be a family."

I felt hollow. Like someone had scooped me out and left my empty shell on this bench. No sadness. No anger. Just shutting down.

Gia put his hand on my back. "Bella, I am telling you. It is a lie. I do not know what she is up to yet, but I will find out. I promise you, she will not get between us."

She's already between us. "What if she's really changed?"

Gia took my hand and brought it up to his lips. "There is no room in my heart for two. I was alone for so long. You are my only love, and nothing will change that. I waited for you; I will not let you go. No matter how long it takes for you to trust me again."

He kissed my fingers. "Please, *mi amore.*"

I gave Gia some side eye.

"Do not listen to anything Alex tells you. She spins lies like a web. She cannot be trusted."

CHAPTER 2

I promised Gia I would think about what he'd said. I couldn't bear the awkward walk back to the coffee shop to get my car and I wasn't ready to face Aunt Ginny and the biddies. Not after that big pep talk they'd all given me just a couple of hours ago. *This is the lamest love affair ever.*

I didn't want to face my friends either. Why was I humiliated and ashamed? It's not like *I* had a secret wife I'd neglected to mention. Even if she'd run off and disappeared for four and a half years, I would still have had the courtesy to mention it. *Oh, by the way, still married. Thought you should know in case she ever pops 'round for a hello.*

Maybe I was being too hard on Gia. He'd been looking for Alex to get a divorce for months. I'd been stringing along two men because I couldn't get up the courage to tell one of them I didn't think it would work between us.

I walked a block down the boardwalk to Convention Hall. A workman was out front hanging a poster advertising the Spring into Beauty Expo coming in April.

He looked over his shoulder and caught me reading the description. "Ey, make sure yooze get your ticket a-sap. This one's gonna be uuge."

"What's so special about it?"

"They got a famous doctor coming in to do the BOTOX and day-boo some fancy new contraption that's being hailed as the beauty breakthrough of the century. The hens inside are all a twitter about it. He was on *Good Morning America*."

"And he's coming here Easter weekend instead of the middle of the summer? You'd think he'd go to New York or Atlantic City to draw a bigger crowd."

He closed the glass door on the display case. "Alls I know is, the county is over the moon that they got a big name like Dr. Lance Rubin to do a show at Convention Hall. Plus, they get to show the new building off. They're making a whole shebang outta the deal. Gonna set up booths selling juices and vitamins and stuff." He locked the glass cabinet and gave me a raised hand in farewell and went back in through the double doors.

I bet Karla would love this . . . Karla . . . pssh. I faced into the wind and started my march of grievances. *Gia's gorgeous sister. She knew about Alex the whole time and kept snickering behind my back like it was some hilarious joke. What kind of woman does that to another? What about girl code? Don't they have that in Italy? I don't care how long you've been in America, you need to learn proper relationship etiquette. At the very least her mother should have taught it to her. What am I thinking? Her mother probably dated Mussolini.*

I jolted to a stop in front of the five-story, red-and-white Sea Mist Resort, the tallest of the painted ladies on the strip. *Momma . . . pssh. Gia's very religious Italian mother who doesn't believe in divorce. No wonder she hates me. She thinks I'm here to lead her little prince into a life of adultery and depravity. How 'bout a heads-up, Momma! What's Italian for "adultery"? To be fair, she might have told me. I only understand a small fraction of what she says. I can tell that it's mean, then I tune her out.*

My shame and humiliation were being whipped back into anger. *I could just strangle Gia for putting me through this. How could I ever trust him again? If Alex is telling the truth, I'm the world's biggest idiot.* I steamed down the boardwalk like the Flying Scotsman, alternating between wanting to console Gia and wanting to choke him out.

I marched on, and when I finally looked up from my furious ramble, I was standing in front of the site that used to belong to the Christian Admiral Hotel. It had been beautiful and charming, but was sadly demolished anyway for being old, broken-down, and high maintenance. My thoughts mysteriously turned to Aunt Ginny, and I wanted to cry. What would I say when I had to face her?

I was so angry I could have walked all the way to the Coast Guard base, but the sun would be going down soon and when my fury wore off the ocean breeze would turn frigid. Part of me wanted to feel the pain so I could dwarf this hollow unrest that was rolling around my insides. I turned and started the slog back home.

The screen door banged against the frame behind me when I entered the house. Aunt Ginny came around the corner with the usual mischief in her eyes. "What are you doing home already? Well, how'd it go? Come on, I want details. What's the matter?"

I went into the library and threw a couple logs in the fireplace. "Did everyone go home?"

Aunt Ginny reached over and turned on a hurricane lamp. "Victory finished for the day and everyone expected you wouldn't return until late, so . . . Why do you look like you've been crying?"

I lit the fire and stood back to make sure it caught before I sat down. Aunt Ginny silently sat across from me and waited.

"Gia's married."

No expression crossed her face. Then she leaped off the couch and flew out the front door before I could stop her. A minute later, her vintage red Corvette backed out of the driveway.

Hmm. I should probably do something about that. Maybe warn Gia that Aunt Ginny is coming in hot. I spotted a *People* magazine on the coffee table and picked it up. I turned to the story about Dolly Parton and her libraries that was listed on the cover. *I really like Dolly. She's classy.*

About an hour later, I heard the Corvette run over our trash cans and knock my pot of pansies off the block by the walkway. Aunt Ginny banged in through the front door and slammed it behind her.

I put the magazine down and Aunt Ginny flopped back in her spot on the chair.

We looked at each other and didn't speak. She finally asked me, "Is it too late to pick Tim?"

I nodded. "I would feel slimy. I chose Gia because I love him, flaws and all. I just didn't know those flaws were gonna be wearing four-inch stilettos. And if it's not going to work out between us, I'd rather be alone than with someone who's not right for me."

Figaro peeked halfway around the corner before entering the room. He trotted over to the couch and jumped into my lap to begin taking a very inconvenient bath. I tried to pet him, and he swatted me. Apparently, this was not cuddle time.

"I knew in my heart things weren't clicking with Tim. We'd changed too much. I just couldn't face turning him down again."

Aunt Ginny sat forward on her chair. "I believe Gia that he wasn't trying to deceive you. Some men are just pigheaded like that. They think they need to protect women from the harsh realities of life in the name of chivalry. Idiots. *They* are the harsh realities of life. What are you going to do?"

"I don't know. I still love Gia, but I don't know if I can ever trust him again. Then there's Alexandra."

Aunt Ginny sat back and crossed her legs. "Yep. She'll be in your life as long as Henry is. But there's something phony about her. I don't trust her."

"She was still there?"

Aunt Ginny nodded. "With the mother and some old man who pinched my bottom."

"That would be Uncle Alfio."

"Whatever his name is, he's on to the girl, I'll tell you that. He was not buying her poor little victim act. Neither is Gia's sister. I think the only one on that girl's side is the mother."

"Oliva Larusso's a pretty big ally."

Aunt Ginny shook her head. "I don't think so. I think Gia adores you and if push came to shove, he'd shove the old battle-ax right out of the picture."

I'd had a long time to think while I raged down the boardwalk and back. And I knew the thorn that was twisting in my heart. "If I fight for Gia, am I being selfish? Maybe this is Henry's chance to get to know his mother. I don't want to break up a family."

Aunt Ginny gave me a long look. "What are you, some kind of nut? That isn't a family. And from what Gia said, it never was. As far as I'm concerned, you'd be saving Henry."

"I just know how I would feel if someone tried to keep me from my child. Alex says she wants another chance. While I know she was trying to manipulate me, I think I need to get out of the way and let the two of them work it out before I get involved. If she wants to reconnect her family, I won't stop her."

Aunt Ginny puffed out her cheeks and blew a raspberry. "She wants something—that much is true."

"But what could it be, and why now? Why has she come back after all this time?"

"Don't you worry, honey. The biddies are on this. We'll find out."

CHAPTER 3

The next morning I fed Figaro his tuna sardine surprise, made blueberry cheesecake French toast for the weekend guests we had staying at the B&B, then left to meet Sawyer at the Starbucks in Rio Grande before my current chambermaid, Victory, could do anything to make me crazy.

I fought my way through the packed room of uniformed Coast Guard cadets celebrating their weekend shore leave with venti Frappuccinos and free Wi-Fi and found Sawyer crammed at a table in the back corner. On my way past the long, polished wood bar, the barista—a boy who looked about twelve years old with a shock of purple hair—called out, "Venti Caramel Macchiato for Swanson and split-shot raspberry white mocha for Potsie."

Sawyer threw her arms out frantically and shouted for

me to grab the coffees. "That's us! Get them; I can't leave the table."

Three women in spandex workout wear who were either coming from, going to, or just fantasizing about doing Pilates immediately made a move toward Sawyer and tried to hijack the table.

Sawyer was tall and thin, but she was scrappy. She lay her chest down and spread her arms out to cover all four corners of the little table. "No! My friend is right there. We're staying."

I grabbed the drinks and pushed through the women. "I just got out of urgent care. The doctor says I'm contagious until this scabby rash clears up." The women twisted away like a Cirque du Soleil act. I giggled and handed Sawyer her Macchiato. "Here you go, Swanson."

"I'm sorry about that. I spelled 'Poppy' three times."

I shrugged and sucked the whipped cream through the tiny mouth hole. "Last time they spelled it 'Poopy' so, Potsie's a step up."

"I was surprised you wanted milk since you won't be able to breathe in about twenty minutes."

"Breathing's overrated." I took a slow sip of the creamy, sweet deliciousness and imagined a workman in my head changing the sign—Days on Diet Without Cheating: back to zero.

Sawyer leaned across the table and gave me a huge grin. "So. How'd Gia take it?"

I gave her a slow eye roll. "Have you ever heard of someone named Alexandra?"

Sawyer blinked a couple of times and furrowed her brow. "Uh . . . no, doesn't sound familiar. Who is it?"

"Gia's wife."

Sawyer slapped the table. "His *wife*!"

The room went silent for only a moment. This was South Jersey. Furious outbursts were a way of life. I took a sip of my drink and nodded slowly.

She had some choice words that I'd been thinking myself. "I've known Gia since he opened La Dolce Vita and I've never heard him mention a woman."

"Well, you had to know there was someone. Henry's only four."

Sawyer shook her head and shrugged one shoulder to her ear. "I thought his mother had died. Gia doesn't wear a ring, and you never see Henry with a woman other than Gia's mother or sister."

"So, I take it an ex-wife was never brought up in the conversation?"

"When Gia moved to Cape May I was having problems with Kurt cheating on me, so I wasn't very social, and Gia kept to himself. I could see him sometimes walking Henry up and down the mall, trying to get him to sleep. For a while I thought Karla was his wife, then Louise at the bath shop told me she was his sister. She said there was no wife. So, if Gia has a wife, where's he been keeping her?"

"She says Gia kidnapped Henry and disappeared while she had postpartum depression."

Sawyer's eyes narrowed and she cocked her head to the side. "Don't kidnappers go on the run and change their names so they can't be tracked? Gia opened a coffee shop fifty feet away from his mother's restaurant. His picture is on the website. How did it take her so long to find him? And why haven't the police been after him? It's not like he fled the country."

I'd been so shell-shocked that I hadn't thought of any of those things. I shrugged.

"What does Gia say happened?"

"He says Alex ran off with another man right after Henry was born because she didn't want to be a wife and mother."

Sawyer's face was a combination of shock and outrage. "Why is this coming out now? Did he tell you he couldn't commit to you? What happened when you went over there?"

"Well, first he kissed me, and I almost lost consciousness. Then his wife introduced herself."

Sawyer slammed her cup down and foam shot out of the lid and landed on my nose. "She was there?! Start from the beginning!"

I wiped my nose off and filled her in on my introduction to the other woman, realized *I* was the other woman, and had to take a minute to inject myself with raspberry and white chocolate to regroup. Then I told her about Alex's warning and the conversation on the boardwalk.

She kept her mouth shut with a steady intake of Caramel Macchiato and her venti was gone by the time I finished my tale of woe. "So, Alex said Gia kidnapped her baby, disappeared, she hasn't seen him in four and a half years, he's dangerous, but she wants to reconcile, to be a family now."

"That's about it."

"If that were all true, then why does she want him? She should call the cops, give him the divorce, and get on with her life."

"Aunt Ginny said the same thing."

Sawyer spun her lid on the polished espresso wood table while she thought. "Gia's been an anchor of this community since he moved down from Philly. With all the gossip in this town, I've never heard a bad thing said about him. In fact, the only rumor I've ever heard is that he's gay, but that's because he's turned down every woman who's tried to catch him. I think you should give him the benefit of the doubt. Why did you pick Gia over Tim?"

I dug deep into my heart for the answer. "Because he's the kindest, most patient man I've ever met. We talk about everything . . . except his marital status . . . I thought we talked about everything. I love how he is with Henry and how he makes me feel when we're together. No matter what skinny thing throws herself at him, I feel like he's only interested in me. I've never felt this way before."

"Mm-hmm, and why didn't you pick Tim?"

"I fell in love with Tim when I was fifteen. All these years I held on to that, feeling like I missed out on being with my soul mate. And being back here with him, I thought we would pick up where we left off. But I didn't realize how much I'd changed in twenty-five years. While Tim stayed on the same path, I've lived a whole 'nother life. Every trial I've been through, every pain, every scar, every choice has changed me a little. Tim thinks we're both just older versions of our high school selves, but I'm not. I don't even recognize that person anymore."

Sawyer tried to tap the caramel out of the bottom of her cup. "I think you romanticized your relationship with Tim into being more magical than it was. I mean, the reality is, there were a lot of problems that first time around. If he was the love of your life, you would have fought to stay together. There's no way you would have gone to college five hundred miles away from him. You'd have followed him to the ends of the earth, even if it meant working in some sketchy diner while he went to cooking school just to be together. And he sure didn't put up a fight to hold on to you."

She had foam in her eyebrow and caramel on the bridge of her nose, but she was a genius.

Sawyer frowned at the empty cup and threw it in the trash can behind her. "Did you tell Tim you're rejecting him for the second time around?"

Oof. It was the very reason I'd agonized over admitting I was in love with Gia in the first place. What kind of terrible person throws a man aside twice? Tim had practically proposed marriage—again. And once again I was meeting his proposal with a breakup for another man. I was a walking country music song. Even if things didn't work out with Gia, Tim would never forgive me. I wasn't sure *I* would ever forgive me. Maybe Gia being married was the karma I deserved. *Momma was right. I* am *the Whore of Babylon.*

"Poppy." Sawyer was staring at me with raised eyebrows. "When do you talk to Tim?"

"This afternoon."

"Why so soon? You're not exactly in a rush anymore."

"I don't want to string him along when he could be happy with someone else."

"Like Gigi."

"If Tim ends up with Gigi after everything she's put us through, I will lose my flipping mind."

Sawyer let out a deep sigh, then held her hand up to the barista. "Another round for Swanson and Potsie!"

CHAPTER 4

I'd tried to get Tim to meet me someplace neutral so we could talk away from Chuck and Juan and the kitchen staff. This was going to be hard enough without having the entire line be my audience. No matter how many suggestions I threw out there, Tim was too busy to get away. It had to be Maxine's. The giant, wooden Gigi crab glared smugly as I pulled into the parking lot, gloating that she'd always known this day was coming.

Tim was waiting for me at the back door. "Here she is." He leaned down and kissed me. "I'm sorry I couldn't get away, babe. It's Friday afternoon and we have a decent amount of reservations for tonight. The *South Jersey Dining Guide* has brought in so much business, I may need to hire another chef. We're just starting the dinner prep."

My throat closed up and I felt the noose tighten. I looked around the kitchen, all chrome and white subway tiles. Steam poured from stockpots, Troy was peeling potatoes, and the room smelled of caramelized garlic and onions. This was the quiet before the dinner storm. Chuck and Juan were currently in a competition to see how far they could toss a shrimp between two sauté pans without dropping it. Tyler was elbow deep in a bucket of blue crabs getting tonight's special ready. He waved a crab at me. "Hey Poppy!"

Tim put his hand on my back. "Come on, let's go to my office before these idiots do something I have to yell at them for."

I smiled to myself as I followed Tim down the tight hall to the little room where he planned menus and kept receipts and employee records. He moved a pizza box off the second chair for me to sit down. I picked up a pink, fuzzy scarf and handed it to him. He tossed it on the desk. "That's probably Linda's. So, what's going on with you? You sounded like this was pretty important."

I swallowed hard and opened my mouth, willing the words to come out on their own. The office door opened, and Chuck stuck his head in with a cappuccino. "For Chef Poppy."

"Aww, Chuck, you didn't have to . . ."

Tim made a face at Chuck. "Will you get out of here?"

Chuck slinked back out the door. "I'm goin'."

Tim yelled after him, "There better not be shrimp on my floor." Tim rolled his eyes at the door. "Sorry. What were you saying?"

I sipped my cappuccino, and it seared my throat like lava. That was fine. I deserved a first-degree burn. I put the cup on the edge of Tim's desk and folded my hands back in my lap. "Well. You know you've been asking me to make a commitment."

Tim's door flew open and hit the back of my chair. I pitched forward, and Linda stuck her head in. "Oh, sorry, Poppy. I didn't know you were here. Chef, we just got a ten res for seven over OpenTable. Where do you want me to put them?"

Tim closed his eyes. "Oh crap. Move that four res to thirteen and set up twenty-six through twenty-eight and give them the fixed menu. I can't have that large of a group order the blue crabs. I don't have enough."

Linda shut the door behind her, and Tim stood up. "I'm sorry, babe. Can we speed this up? Tonight just tipped from comfortable to hustle and we'll still have walk-ins."

I stood up and tried to step behind the chair. "You know what . . . let's do this another time."

Tim was looking at a chart on his desk and only half listening to me. He looked through me. "Can this wait until after work? I think I have to call Laura in tonight after all."

"Of course. Maybe we should talk when you have some time off."

I had my hand on the doorknob when Tim reached for my arm. "No. I'm sorry. You came all this way. Now is good. Besides, I'm probably not going to have any time off until October. Unless you want to spend the night and we can talk later." Tim gave me a seductive grin.

I swallowed hard. "I should come back. Maybe after-hours."

"Mack. Will you just spit it out already?"

I shook my head to myself. There was no way around it. It would have to be his way or not at all. "Okay. You know how we've both changed a lot since high school?"

Tim shrugged. "Yeah, I guess. So . . ."

"I just . . . we aren't the same people anymore. Not really."

"What are you talking about?"

"I'm talking about you and me and our relationship."

He smiled at me. "What's going on? You know I love you."

A fat tear welled up in my eye. "I will always love you too, but I think you're in love with a memory of how we used to be and that isn't enough to make a relationship work. When I'm with you it's like I'm seventeen again. All the memories and feelings come rushing back. But somehow we've grown in ways that don't click anymore."

"How don't we click? I'm the same person, Poppy."

"You're amazing, but you have to admit . . . when we're together there's something missing. Unless we're discussing food or cooking or old times, we have nothing to talk about. I've tried to get it back. I thought working here with you would get it back, but it's not happening. I just don't think it will work for us. Not in the long run. You deserve more."

Emotions rolled over Tim's face. Shock, confusion, hurt, sadness, then anger. The red crept up from his chef whites to his blond hair and his eyes flashed fire before losing all emotion. "Are you kidding me, Mack? Are you really doing this to me again?"

"I'm so sorry."

Tim was leaning down against his desk and he was yelling now. "No! You don't get to say you're sorry. Not again!" Tim turned his back to me, and I wasn't sure if we were finished or not. Then he spun to face me again. "Everyone warned me not to trust you again. You don't know what you want. Why am I never enough for you?"

"It's not you. We want different things in life. You're married to Maxine's." *Oh god, both of my men are married. Cape May sucks.*

Tim flung his hand out and swiped the papers off his desk. "You are a part of Maxine's. Don't you get that?"

I wiped my eyes. "But Tim, that's what I'm trying to tell you. I'm not. Maxine's isn't my dream. I have Aunt Ginny and the B&B. My life is not on the same course as yours. I think you still see who I was in high school, when we both wanted this more than anything else. I'm not there anymore. You work eighty hours a week. If we were together, I'd never see you. Resentment would grow between us. If we tried to force this, before long we'd both be miserable. I never want us to lose our friendship."

Tim was clenching his jaw so tight his cheek was quivering. "I knew you spending so much time with Gia was a bad idea. Somehow, I thought you'd be able to see that I was the one who's always loved you, and you'd make the right choice. You'll regret this, Poppy. And there is no coming back this time. We're done."

"Please, Tim, I don't want to leave things like this."

He looked down his nose at me and laughed bitterly. "What? Do you think we'll be friends? Maybe the three of us will have dinner sometime? I have enough friends. Friends who don't stab me in the back every time I begin to trust them again. And I don't need your desserts either. Pastry chefs are a dime a dozen in this town. You're done here. If I owe you anything, I'll send a check to the coffee shop."

I nodded. A rattlesnake had curled up in my belly and was striking my insides to the beat of my heart. I turned my back to keep Tim from seeing me cry. I reached for the door handle and tried to muster my dignity. I just had to get down the hall and through the kitchen.

It wasn't meant to be. The relationship or the dignity. As soon as I crossed the threshold of the kitchen, Tim yelled after me, "You made the wrong choice! Now you're going to regret it. When the day comes that you get tired of him, watch your back! That's not a family you want to cross."

I looked up into the faces of the kitchen chefs. They'd heard everything. Juan's shoulders slumped. Chuck gave me a sad finger wave. I knew it was the last time I'd stand here as one of them. My dream of being a restaurant chef had breathed its last breath, but this time it felt right. This time it was on my terms. My heart would eventually heal from Tim's words. If anything, today reinforced that I'd made the right choice. I'd rather be alone than be together and unhappy. I stepped out the kitchen door and the clamshells crunched beneath my feet. I breathed in the salty air. This pain would pass. I just had to keep moving forward.

And the first thing I was going to do was find out why no one warned me about Gia.

CHAPTER 5

"**D**o you want me to tell Gia you took off with a sexy Canadian?" Aunt Ginny took the pan of leftover blueberry cheesecake French toast to the kitchen table. She plunged her fork into the middle of the casserole. "There was a bunch of them in Speedos at that Polar Bear Plunge over the weekend. It's a good cover story."

"What? No. Why would I do that?"

"Why would anybody do that? There's not enough peppermint schnapps in the world to get me to jump in the ocean in my altogether in March."

I stared at Aunt Ginny and shook my head. I was going to need more coffee for this conversation. I picked up the French press and the last little bit sloshed around. "No. Why tell Gia I took off?"

Aunt Ginny hoisted her coffee cup over her head. "Well, you haven't so much as said boo to him. He's going to think you skipped town. Wouldn't you rather he thinks you took up with another man than that you slinked away with your tail between your legs because he broke your heart?"

I filled her cup and started the kettle to make a fresh pot. "I don't want him to think either. It's only been three days. Besides, I'm going to the coffee shop today to make some muffins."

Aunt Ginny snorted. "Three days is long enough for a man to go from sign the divorce papers to how do you unhook this girdle?"

"Well, if that's how he feels about it, Alexandra can have him. I'm not running after any man whose love is divided. Either you want me or you don't. Sawyer suggested I take the weekend to think about things and I agreed. So, I put us in a time-out."

Aunt Ginny dug around the casserole to get to the cheesecake layer. "That figures. This has Sawyer's fingerprints all over it. I remember when my ex, Morris, wanted to take a time-out."

"Morris? Which husband was Morris?"

She waved my question off. "I wasn't married to that one . . . don't focus on that. What's important is that he found all his clothes in paper bags covered with the word 'cheater' written in red lipstick sitting in the driveway when he came home from the dog track."

"I'm not trying to punish Gia. I just need some time to get my emotions under control."

Aunt Ginny snickered. "Delilah's Revenge. That was the name of the lipstick. I think it was Avon. I wonder if they still make that color. It went really well with my leather catsuit. Why don't they come to the house anymore?"

"Are you listening to me?"

Aunt Ginny poured a stream of syrup over the edge of the casserole. "What?"

"I said, Sawyer has had lots of experience with this kind of thing after being married to Kurt for fifteen years."

Aunt Ginny gave me the look that she usually reserved for teenagers bagging groceries at the Acme. "He cheated on her repeatedly throughout their marriage. She didn't need a time-out, she needed arsenic and an alibi."

I rolled my eyes. This is why we had to get rid of the Echo. If that thing ever reported Aunt Ginny's conversation to the authorities, she'd be hauled out of here in a wagon. I made a fresh pot of coffee and changed the subject. "Listen, I was thinking about what Mrs. Buckley said last weekend about the afternoon tea she had at the Chambers Mansion."

Figaro trotted into the room with his flat nose in the air, trying his best to get a sniff.

Aunt Ginny held her fork down to him. "There's no bacon today, but you can have some syrup. Was Mrs. Buckley the one with the mole or the one in the brown eyelash sweater that made her look like Snuffleupagus?"

"Snuffleupagus. She went on and on about that tea, and I was thinking we could do that here."

"You want to serve potted ham sandwiches and Mint Milanos to rich ladies?"

"Well, I was thinking we could do it a little nicer than what she described. John and I had afternoon tea at The Savoy in London once, and I still wake up craving those scones. Why don't we try it out for Easter weekend? It's still a month away, so I have time to advertise in all the papers. There's a beauty expo coming to Convention Hall the same weekend, so there will be lots of tourists in town."

Aunt Ginny's eyebrows disappeared into her side-swept red bangs with platinum roots. "You do have more time now that the ingrate fired you from making his desserts. What'd you have in mind?"

"I don't know. Definitely scones with clotted cream and strawberry jam. And maybe some hot cross buns for Easter."

"What about putting your chicken salad inside the hot cross buns?"

I grabbed my laptop and moved to join Aunt Ginny at the table to take notes. "I love that idea. We should make Grandma Emmy's egg salad, and every tea needs cucumber cream cheese sandwiches."

"I had a cheddar chutney in the Catskills one summer that I'd love to get you the recipe for." Aunt Ginny tapped her coffee cup. "You know, I think you should do some dry runs of these sandwiches before we present them at afternoon tea. Just to be sure they pass muster."

I looked up from my laptop where I was typing out an idea for a dessert sandwich. "You do, huh? You afraid I might mess them up?"

"You know . . . you can be cocky when you're full of yourself. . . . It pays to be prepared. Why don't you practice at the coffee shop? Maybe you can ask the mother for some family recipes."

"Like biscotti and amaretti?"

"I was thinking about Al Capone's secret spaghetti sauce."

I stifled a laugh and choked on my exasperation. "You think I should ask Gia if he's in the Mafia just because they're Italian? Isn't that racial profiling?"

Aunt Ginny got up to put the French toast back in the fridge and patted my hand. "Of course not, honey. We don't judge people in this house based on their skin color or ethnic roots. You know that."

"That's a relief."

"I think you should ask him because everyone in town says his family is in the mob."

CHAPTER 6

I paced back and forth in the alley, tapping a dirge on my tote bag. All the bravado I'd gained from my weekend time-out evaporated the minute the back door to La Dolce Vita was in sight. I'd taken special care with my hair and makeup this morning, just in case any resurfaced wives would be there. I put on a turquoise sweater dress I'd bought because Sawyer's eyes popped when she saw me come out of the dressing room in it. She said it made me look like Jessica Rabbit at a PTA meeting. Just because I wasn't getting in between Gia and Alex, I still had my pride. If I was going down, I was going down wearing heels and smoky eyeliner.

I deserved to feel good about myself whether I had a man or not. For all I knew, my efforts were in vain. Especially after Aunt Ginny's supportive discussion on how easy it was for a man to move on and why a woman needs an exit strategy. I could barely swallow my coffee after that rally.

I grabbed the doorknob, took a breath, let it out to the count of five, and cranked it open. Gia appeared instantly from his little office. How had he gotten better-looking in three days? I'd never seen him in tailored khakis before. His dress shirt was a sharp cornflower blue, the same color as his eyes, and they were searching my face for signs of forgiveness. *I feel like I swallowed a beehive.*

"I wasn't sure I would see you again."

I took off my coat and my insides turned to melted chocolate when I saw his eyes roll over me. "I'm angry, and hurt, but I still made a commitment to bake for you."

Gia stepped toward me and I put my hand up to stop him. I had something I wanted to say and I needed to get it out fast. "You should have told me you were still married before you kissed me on Henry's birthday. And you should never have asked me to make a commitment to you when you weren't able to make a commitment back."

He ran his hand across his chin. "You are right, I should have told you. I have not always been free with information, but I promise to do better . . . for us." Gia's eyes burned into mine. "Do you forgive me?"

Looking into his eyes was like being mesmerized by the snake in *The Jungle Book*. *What are we talking about?* "Yes. I mean no. I don't know. I'm trying to forgive you, but I can't just turn off how I feel."

He took a half step backward and I saw an ache behind the sexy smolder. "Yes. You need more time. I have all the time in the world if it means you won't leave me."

I tried to give him a brave smile and pulled my apron from its hook.

"Don't cover everything up."

I gave him a look of chastisement but made a plan to buy this dress in every color as soon as possible. "You need to behave yourself. There will be none of that until things are settled with Alexandra. Plus, I haven't baked for you in four days. We must be out of everything."

He leaned against the counter and crossed his arms. His eyes drooped like a puppy who'd just been bopped on the nose with a newspaper. "Momma gave me some cannoli from the restaurant, but people are asking when the gluten-free muffins will be back."

I took out the building blocks for muffins and sugar cookies and started an inventory of ingredients. "How did things go with Alexandra over the weekend?"

Gia handed me a carton of butter from the walk-in and made a face that said whatever patience for Alex he'd started with had run out long before I arrived. "She is still refusing to sign the divorce papers, but in New Jersey the spouse does not have to sign to get a divorce."

"Well, that's good."

"It would be, except she's filed to contest the divorce. No, no, no, don't look like that. It just means we have to go to court. Zio Alfio says not to worry. He might be on to something that will force her hand."

Aunt Ginny's Mafia warning flashed through my head. "Oh, like what?"

"He could not say over the phone, so he's coming in later to talk about it."

I started making a list of things I needed from the produce supplier. "What can't he talk about over the phone? Is he going to make her disappear if she doesn't cooperate?"

Gia chuckled and his eyes crinkled making little fans at the corners. "You have such an imagination."

"That's not a no."

"I learned a long time ago not to question Zio Alfio about his plans."

The hairs on my forearm stood up and I had to rub them back down.

Gia leaned against the counter so close the sides of our hips were touching. "When you finish your list, I'll send Karla. It has been slow today."

I checked my inventory of eggs, then handed him a shopping list, and he called Karla to the kitchen.

Her usual look of superiority disappeared the minute she saw the unflinching rebuke on my face. I wanted her to know that her silence these past six months wasn't appreciated. Her eyes slid to the floor as she took the paper from Gia. I didn't back down. Things were going to be different between us from now on. There are some lines that shouldn't be crossed.

After the door closed behind her, I considered who might be out front. I hadn't heard the bell ring since I'd arrived. "Where is your wife right now?"

"She is not my wife. And she is with Henry at Mia Famiglia. Momma is supervising the visitation."

Isn't that like leaving the bank guarded by the inside man?

Gia must have felt my thoughts. "Momma knows I do not trust Alex to be alone with Henry—and Henry is very nervous when Alex is around. Momma would not betray me. She would be devastated if Alex disappeared with her polpetto."

"Your mother really likes Alex."

"I think they have more of a mutual understanding."

"Understanding about what?" I started creaming butter and sugar together for a basic sugar cookie dough. I'd go through a lot of it in the next month, between the St. Patrick's Day shamrocks, the Easter cookies, and the lemon and raspberry bars for spring.

Gia blinked like he was considering my question. "Momma has some business with Vincenzo Scarduzio that she would like to continue." Gia crossed his arms over his chest and gave me a slight nod.

Apparently, follow up questions would not be answered. I filed the information away and changed the subject. "I was thinking of doing an afternoon tea for the B&B Easter weekend. Would you mind if I made some hot cross buns and English scones for the coffee shop so I could work on the recipes?"

"Bella. You do not need to ask my permission to make anything." He wound my hair around his finger. "I will capture the stars if you want them. You tell me what you need."

What I needed was to catch my breath before I passed out on the KitchenAid. "Uh . . . some rai . . . sins."

Gia chuckled. "Good for you, dream big."

I stopped the mixer and swiped his hand. I gave Gia the same look I would give a four-year-old trying to sneak cookies off the cooling rack. I meant business about waiting for things to be settled with Alex.

Before he could plead his case, the front bell went off. There were some choice grumblings on his way out to the bar, but it gave me time to regroup. I wrote a list of recipes to make today and put together an order for our dry goods delivery.

I had just finished scraping my vanilla beans when Gia returned to the kitchen with a brochure. "What's that?"

"There is some beauty show coming to Convention Hall. The program director said he stopped by to talk to us the other day when I was out, but I did not get the message. They want us to have a booth selling your Paleo baked goods."

I took the brochure he was offering me. Spring into Beauty. A weeklong event devoted to healthy skin and healthy lifestyle. "I've seen this. Do you want to do it?"

"It is up to you. You also have the bed and breakfast and the desserts you make for the other man. Do you have time to do this?"

"Well, 'the other man' fired me when I told him it wouldn't work with us, so . . . It will be a lot of work, but as long as we keep the menu simple and use the same recipes at all three places, I think I can. . . ." I didn't get to finish my thought because I suddenly found myself pulled into a bear hug.

"You really told him it was over?"

"I did. Even if that means I'll be alone forever."

Gia tipped my chin up. "Do not give up on me. I will call Zio Alfio and tell him whatever it takes I want those divorce papers signed."

"Within reason."

"*Sì*. No price is too high."

"Whatever is legal."

"Mmm. Whatever he has to do."

"We're not saying the same thing."

"Bella, you are so funny."

I narrowed my eyes at him and he tapped me on the nose. "I will be right back." Gia went into his office and shut the door.

Had I just ordered a hit on Alex? I started my mixer again and measured the dry ingredients for the sugar cookies. I kept watching the office door, for what I don't know. The Godfather to appear? Gia to emerge with a violin case? My imagination was running away with me. I was bringing the cookie dough together into a ball on the counter when the bell rang out front. I could still hear Gia on the phone speaking in rapid-fire Italian. I wiped my hands on a towel and went out to see who it was. If they wanted espresso, I'd have to stall. Why didn't I know how to work the espresso machine yet? How different could it be from my little one at home?

Alex was standing in the dining room with Henry by her side. Momma was peering through the front glass window with her eyes pushed between her cupped hands. As soon as Henry shrieked my name, Momma bit her fingers and flicked them at me.

I wanted to respond that the Pope would not appreciate that kind of sentiment, but she had already headed back to the Italian restaurant across the courtyard.

Henry wrapped his arms around my neck and I hugged him tight. "Hey, sweets. You're just in time to help me make some cookies."

"Can I help taste them?"

"You sure can." I glanced up at Alex, whose pretty little face was in a pout.

"Is he here?"

"Yes, he's on the phone." *Possibly with someone named Vinnie or Fat Tony.*

"I need to see him." She pushed past me into the kitchen.

Henry and I sat down at one of the coffee-bean-colored tables in the dining room. "Do you want something to drink?"

Henry nodded. "Chocolate milk."

Chocolate milk for Henry meant special, dairy-free chocolate syrup and almond milk. I had just put it on the table when Gia came flying out of the back room with Alex in hot pursuit. She was begging for something. Gia was calm, but clearly frustrated. He turned to face Alex and spoke very slowly.

"You. Are. Crazy. There is no way I want to . . ." He put his hands over Henry's ears and whispered, "Renew our wedding vows. You did not honor them the first time."

Alex grabbed Henry and pulled him in front of her. She spoke in Italian, presumably so I wouldn't understand her. Nice try, but I definitely know the word *famiglia*.

Henry wiggled out of her grip and sidled back to the table and his chocolate milk.

Alex threw her arm out and pointed to Henry. She had several points to make, all of which were in Italian, and I understood none of them except that she expected Henry to instantly love her.

I tried to disappear into the coffee beans until I could make a break for it. I took a couple quiet steps toward the kitchen.

Gia crossed his arms over his chest. "Piccolo, it is almost time for a nap. Do you want to go home and watch your new movie?"

Henry nodded a double nod without releasing his straw from his mouth.

"Okay, why don't you take Mommy's hand and she'll take you home and tuck you in?"

Henry carried his chocolate milk around the counter and took my hand. He didn't understand the fear and the fury he had just unleashed.

CHAPTER 7

Throwing a surprise party for an eighty-year-old is a risky venture. You don't want "surprise" to be the last word she ever hears. Of course, when said eighty-year-old is sharp as a razor and nosy as Mrs. Kravitz from *Bewitched*, the danger is lessened significantly. Since Aunt Ginny had petitioned for this surprise party by leaving Post-it Notes all over my bathroom and found the receipt for the party supplies in my purse while searching for candy after I went to the movies with Sawyer, we were just going through the motions of the surprise part at this point.

It was Royce's job to take Aunt Ginny to the beauty parlor and distract her while we set up for the shindig. Aunt Ginny's recently returned boyfriend was dealing with advancing dementia, so we were just hoping he remembered he was back in Cape May and not in an off-

Broadway revival of *Anything Goes* when the time came to bring Aunt Ginny home.

Figaro streaked through the sitting room in a blur of gray fluff and silver foil. "Catch that cat!" A panting Fiona came waddling after him, her painted-on eyebrows drawn together like an angry orange crow. "That cat has stolen the ribbons off three presents. I tried to catch him in the act, but he's so fast. Ignatius! Help me get the ribbon curls back from the feline!"

A gravelly voice rumbled out of the dining room. "Sorry, Mama, I'd help if I could, but I just took my pain pill, and you know I'm not allowed to do anything strenuous while on narcotics."

I put my hand on Royce's sister's shoulder. "I've got this, Fiona. Why don't you go have a glass of punch and sit with Iggy?"

Fiona grabbed my hand and pulled me farther into the foyer. "About that. I'm not sure that punch is safe to drink. I saw Thelma pour a whole bottle of liquor in it."

That sounds about right. "Okay. I'll check on that. Thank you." Before I could do some quality control on Mrs. Davis and the other biddies, who thought that prohibition was still on in my house and they had to smuggle booze into every event, someone rang the doorbell.

"Royce? What are you doing here?" I looked around the debonair gentleman for Aunt Ginny. They weren't supposed to be back for at least twenty minutes.

Royce took off his hat and released a pouf of fluffy white hair like a magician's act. "I'm here to pick up Ginny for brunch."

I led him into the foyer and gently reminded him, "Royce, you picked Aunt Ginny up two hours ago, remember? We had to make her a special hair appointment with Mr. Charles because it's Sunday, and we waited for the B and B guests to check out and go home so we could have a surprise birthday party."

Royce looked confused, then recognition dawned. "Oh, right. 'Frailty, thy name is woman.' I left Ginny at the beauty parlor, didn't I?"

"Yes. I believe you did." Figaro streaked out of the library and back into the sitting room, dragging about three feet of pink ribbon behind him. Royce put his hat back on. "Okay, I'll go get her." Before he could open the screen door, Gia pulled up in front of the house in his silver Alfa Romeo with Aunt Ginny in the passenger seat. Aunt Ginny looked into the front door, shook her head, and made a motion for Gia to go around the block.

They sped off, so I brought Royce into the house and took his hat and coat and deposited him in the sitting room with his sister and nephew and the biddies, who were all giggling behind jumbo-sized cups of punch. I went to the kitchen and checked on Sawyer, who was taking a pan of apple and brie tarts out of the oven. "I think these are ready, but your cheesesteak egg rolls need a couple more minutes."

"Did you see Mrs. Davis spiking the punch?"

Sawyer grinned. "Don't look behind the trash can."

Stuffed in the corner under a paper bag were three empty bottles of pink champagne and a large Irish whisky. "What's the whisky for?"

"I'm not supposed to tell you . . . but the coffee is going to have a kick to it."

I could use a kick right now. The back door slammed open and my delicate chambermaid bulldozed her way over to the kitchen island to drop off Aunt Ginny's sheet cake. I was amazed that someone so tiny could create so much destruction. To bring my point home, Figaro galloped into the kitchen with his ears pinned down. He tried to turn the corner, knocked over his food bowl, and slid out the other side. Victoryna Rostyslavivna Yevtushenko—or, as we called her, Victory—jumped out of the way to avoid a crash and stuck her elbow into the cake. "Gah! Naughty Figgy!"

Victory had joined us from Ukraine for the summer season on a special visa just a few weeks ago, and I think her main purpose in life was to keep my sanity on the edge. Her ice-blue eyes were such a stark contrast to her pale skin and jet-black hair that she looked like an arctic wolf in a Cher wig. She and Aunt Ginny had become very close because of their mutual admiration for chaos and drama. Speaking of which, Chaos and Drama just threw the front door open and yelled, "Surprise!" to her roomful of party guests.

Sawyer and I snorted at each other and went in to greet the guest of honor.

Mother Gibson had queued up Sister Sledge's "We Are Family" for Aunt Ginny's big entrance and now they were all dancing around the room like the Holy Spirit anointing had fallen on the choir loft.

Aunt Ginny was sporting a new, rose-gold-strawberry-blond tint to her hair and a powder-blue halter dress that she was convinced made her look like Marilyn Monroe. She greeted everyone and tinkled her fingers to make sure we all noticed the faux gems she had painted into her manicure.

Gia hovered in the foyer, watching with a bemused

grin. He was looking a little drawn, and his usual five-o'clock shadow was more like a two-day blackout. The past three weeks had been very stressful. I had said that I didn't want any affection passing between us until things were sorted with Alex, and Gia reluctantly gave in to my request. We were both tense and frustrated, and the days were getting longer. But if it was meant to be that Gia and Alex could reconcile, I wasn't going to get in their way, even though it would kill me. As it was, I didn't have to get in the way. Alex was tearing her chances down with her own hands.

She showed up at the coffee shop every day to trickle a stream of poisoned sweetness. Flattery spiked with belladonna. Her words were always innocent and helpful, but her kisses of kindness left you with welts on your face. I had never seen Gia so miserable. I heard him use the words "restraining order" more than once while talking to Zio Alfio on the phone. I didn't know what Zio Alfio was saying, but Gia was never happy with the outcome.

If anything, he was looking for ways to spend more time with me. He had Karla running the front counter and he'd been in the kitchen baking. We'd been working tirelessly, making mountains of scones and cookies and every kind of muffin under the sun so we could fill the pastry cases at La Dolce Vita and the booth we were running for the expo. But I knew the real reason he was so worn out was a leggy honey blonde from Italy who had forgotten how to sign her name and was determined to remain the current Mrs. Larusso like there was a million-dollar will and Gia was on life support. As long as she was contesting the divorce, I had to hold Gia at arm's length, and the anguish behind his eyes was breaking my heart. "Aunt Ginny called you when Royce wandered off?"

Gia nodded toward the birthday girl. "She said I'm still on her list, but I could make some of it up by fetching her. She knew about the party. She had me drive her around the block until everyone was in place so she could make her entrance."

"Yeah, I think Royce is the only one who was surprised, and we told him three times."

Victory danced her way into the room to do the bump with Aunt Ginny in the center. When the music finally ended she hugged her. "How old are you todaee, Miss Geinny?"

Aunt Ginny dropped into the wing chair that was reserved for the birthday girl. "I'm seventy!"

Victory's eyes flashed. "Sefentee! I weill need manee some more candle." She ran back to the kitchen while Royce belly laughed.

"Ginger, you and I are the same age, and I'm eighty-two."

Aunt Ginny cut her eyes at Royce and through gritted teeth said, "Well, I'm seventy!"

Royce closed his eyes and chuckled to himself. "Okay, baby."

Then Aunt Ginny rolled her eyes at the ladies. "*That* he remembers."

Sawyer leaned into me and whispered, "If he only knew how many seventieth surprise parties she's had."

Mrs. Dodson handed Aunt Ginny a glass of punch. "You're over twenty-one, aren't you?"

Aunt Ginny giggled and took a sip. "Whoo! Poppy did not make the punch, did she?"

I gave a conspiratorial look to Mrs. Davis. "I think I had some help."

Aunt Ginny shot forward in her chair. "You'll never guess what I overheard at the beauty parlor. A gang of hooligans broke into Congress Hall and stole the supplies for the Twilight Egg Hunt. They're going to have to cancel the whole event."

Sawyer brought in two trays of hors d'oeuvres and everyone began to help themselves. "Oh, I heard about that. What a shame. I was really looking forward to it too."

Gia was getting himself a cup of coffee, so I leaned in to ask, "What's the Twilight Egg Hunt?"

He took a sip of his coffee and started to choke. "Good God, what is in this?"

Royce handed him the cream. "Here, try a little snort of this in there. It cuts through the fumes."

Sawyer answered for Gia, who was still trying to recover from his unintentional shot. "It's a Cape May tradition. It started out with just a few tourists up for Easter weekend. They painted eggs with glow-in-the-dark dye and hid them on the lawn of Congress Hall, where they were staying. When the sun went down they put the kids to bed and the adults made a competition out of finding the eggs in the moonlight."

Fiona twittered from her spot on the sofa. "It sounds like fun."

Sawyer giggled. "The whole thing has grown into a huge event. Now there's music and prizes, and all the proceeds go to charity. It started out just for adults, but now people even take their kids to it. It'll be such a shame to see it canceled."

I asked Gia, "Have you ever been to that?"

Gia smirked behind his Irish coffee. "Once or twice. Alcohol is definitely involved."

Mother Gibson was pouring herself a healthy cup of punch, and she caught my eye. "This will be your first tourist season as a business owner, won't it?"

"It will. Have any tips?"

"Child . . . Get more insurance."

Gia laughed. "Get used to seeing a lot of skin. Tourists think clothing is optional at the beach."

Mrs. Davis squealed. "And that's just the men!"

That opened a discussion full of advice and warnings. The gist was that tourists are crazy, demanding, and come to create anarchy, steal your parking space, and eat soft-serve ice cream three times a day. Which I thought was ironic, because that also described Aunt Ginny and the biddies to a T.

Aunt Ginny pointed out that whatever they could dish up, we could take it. And by we . . . she meant me. Because she had plans with Royce all summer.

I glanced toward Gia to give him a grin and caught him watching me. The look in his eyes stole my breath. My heart ached in my chest.

That was when Victory plodded her way into the dining room struggling under the cake, which was lit with enough fire to barbecue chicken legs. The dining room smoke alarm went off and Gia rushed over to take the cake from her while Fiona fanned a napkin at the ceiling.

A low growl came from the corner, "I'd get up and help ya, but I just took my pain pill and I have to stay here."

"That's okay, Iggy. We got it. Hurry up, Aunt Ginny! I think Victory put a hundred candles on the cake."

Aunt Ginny tried to get enough air to blow the candles

out while Royce and Fiona helped enough to keep her from passing out.

Victory gave me a sheepish smile. "I had sefentee candles on cake, but there was emptee square. Eet look seelly, so I add more."

Figaro galloped through the room with a swath of white down one side of his fur.

Victory wrung her hands together. "Oh, um . . . while I look for beeger lighter, keitty may have swatted cake."

That was when we noticed the frosting roses were missing from one corner, and Figaro was under the wing chair licking vigorously at pink frosting up by his ear.

Aunt Ginny threw her head back and laughed. "We may as well have a pet raccoon in the house."

The punch and coffee had been emptied faster than moonshine at a redneck wedding. Everyone enjoyed the food and cake, all except for one corner that no one wanted, given the evidence of the paw print, and eventually they ambled on home. Sawyer and I cleaned up while Aunt Ginny and Royce lounged on the sofa, holding hands and sipping "coffee."

While we carried dishes into the kitchen, I went over my afternoon tea idea. "I'm doing two seatings. One o'clock and three. Do you want to help me? The advertisement has gotten more hits than I expected, and I've had forty-two reservations. I'm just about at capacity."

Sawyer bit her lip and wouldn't look me in the eye. "I would love to, but . . . I have a lot going on. Weekends are very busy from Easter to Memorial Day, and Through the Looking Glass gets a lot of traffic. And . . . and weekdays I have a lot of paperwork. . . . I just have a lot of extra chaos in my life right now. What? You don't believe me?"

I finished wrapping the leftover cake for Royce to take home. "Why wouldn't I believe you?"

"You're giving me a look."

"'Cause you're acting weird about it. It's okay that you can't help. What's the new chaos in your life?"

"What? Nothing. It's just . . . you know. Stuff. See, you're giving me that look again."

"You're being cagey."

"Well, I can't talk about it right now."

Aunt Ginny's inner scandal beacon sounded, and she rushed into the kitchen. "Can't talk about what?"

Sawyer's face went beet red and she looked like she was trying to find a hole to crawl into, so I went on a mission of mercy and diverted to the afternoon tea. "I think I'm going to set up tables all around the wraparound porch. I may need some extra hands."

Aunt Ginny waved her jeweled fingers. "I'll take care of it."

"Well, Aunt Ginny, I rather think it's too much for you too."

Aunt Ginny made a face. "What? No. Not me. I have plans. I mean I'll hire someone who can help."

Sawyer and I exchanged a look of concern. "You'll hire someone?"

"Yes. I've done it before."

That's what worries me.

In the hallway we overheard Victory giggling. "Seelly keitty. No more jelly bean for you."

"Don't worry." Aunt Ginny picked up the leftover cake for Royce. "I got you, Boo."

She left through the door to the dining room and Sawyer snickered. "Boo."

My stress level rose an octave as I worried that my event would turn into the Mad Hatter's tea party. I got a glass of water and dropped to the banquette to mourn all the snacks I could have eaten at the party but hadn't. The door to the dining room was still swinging, and I marveled at how similar Aunt Ginny was to the Cheshire cat. She loved to create chaos, then disappear.

CHAPTER 8

After another fitful night in a long string of insomnia and bad dreams, my alarm clock went off in the middle of the song "Tainted Love." I smacked the Snooze button and had almost fallen back asleep when I heard Figaro hurling on my throw rug. He had a room full of hardwood plus the ceramic tile in the bathroom if he should happen to get sick, but no. He preferred to keep his paws warm while doing his dirty business. "I told you that cake was going to make you sick."

Figaro lifted a paw and flopped onto his side as if to say *worth it!*

Today was our last day to prepare for the Expo. It officially opened on Wednesday, but we would spend all day tomorrow setting up. Kim had gotten us in touch with a printer who made custom napkins that said Paleo Treats, and Gia had ordered a ten-by-ten trade show canopy the color of espresso with La Dolce Vita scrolled across all sides in cream-colored letters. Everything was supposed to arrive today for final inspection before we carted it to Convention Hall in the morning.

I dressed in teal leggings and an ivory tunic and noticed that both had a little extra room from the last time I'd worn them. Apparently, the have-so-much-anxiety-you-rarely-eat diet was working wonders. Not for my hair, which was flat, or my skin, which was dull, but my pants were baggy, so who needs shiny hair and skin?

Aunt Ginny was already in the kitchen dressed in blue jeans and a black leather tank top. She had a matching black leather fisherman's cap, and her eyes were ringed with black eyeliner that I was 80 percent sure was on purpose. She was either ready for barhopping or joining a geriatric gang. "Where are you going so early?"

She grabbed the teakettle just as it was starting to whistle. "Going? I just got home."

"You've been out all night?"

"Don't be so surprised. I've stayed out all night lots of times."

"What were you doing?"

"Eating hot dogs."

"For eight hours?"

"No. Just one."

"Where did you find an open hot dog stand in the middle of the night?"

Aunt Ginny gave me some side-eye. "No one's open in the middle of the night."

I poured the ground coffee beans into the press pot, determined not to let this conversation beat me. "So, where'd you get the hot dogs?"

"What are you, the wiener police? A little fella named Skippy. No. Slappy. No, that can't be right."

I poured the water over the grounds and set the timer while Aunt Ginny held an argument with herself over the name of the random stranger who'd apparently sold her the dogs out of a bicycle hotbox. *I should find out how long it's been since she had a tetanus shot.*

"Anyway. We got the tickets!"

Okay, I zoned out too long. "Tickets for what?"

"Dr. Lance Rubin, silly. The girls and I waited in line all night. They just went on sale this morning. He's the New York plastic surgeon everyone's talking about. He was on *Good Morning America*? His seminar is Friday." She fished a stack of yellow cards out of the rim of her hat. "Here, we got one for you too."

Rubinesque Cosmetic Surgery. "What's so special about this that you waited in line all night?"

"The topic is 'Aging Invisibly.'"

I looked at the crooked lipstick in the creases around Aunt Ginny's mouth. *Isn't it rather too late for that?* "Thank you, but I'm not sure I can go. I'll be manning the La Dolce Vita booth."

"It would do you a world of good to get a consultation while you're there. I saw the way you and Gia were looking at each other when you didn't know the other was watching. But until that other woman is out of the picture, you gotta fight back. And I say there's no better way to fight fire than to fight fire with liposuction and a butt lift."

I poured her a cup of coffee and sloshed some of it on my wrist. "Aunt Ginny!"

"What?! That man is smitten. But that's today. You could use some tips to keep him interested in the long haul, so he sticks around."

Right now I wanted tips on how to be anywhere but here.

Aunt Ginny put her coffee down and took my hand. "There will be cutting-edge beauty products that aren't even on the market yet. Miracle creams. And after security hauled away that nellie with the protest sign, we overheard a rumor that Dr. Rubin is going to announce a breakthrough that takes ten years off your face after just a couple uses."

"So, if you use it for a month, will you look like a five-year-old?"

Aunt Ginny narrowed her eyes and took her coffee back. "Edith said you'd be a pill about this."

"What?" I laughed. "I'm kidding. I'll try to be there, okay?"

Aunt Ginny gave me a droll look, but I could see a hint of a twinkle behind the robin's-egg-blue eye shadow.

I tried the back door at La Dolce Vita, but it was locked. I had my own key, but I'd left it in the bowl by the front door when I stopped to clean up Figaro's masterpiece that was once an African violet. He watched me smugly from the library to be sure I recognized his signature move: potting soil flung up the wall.

I knocked, but no one answered. So now I had to walk down the alley and around the pretzel shop to the front of the walking mall. I passed Mia Famiglia and Sawyer's Through the Looking Glass across the way, an ice cream shop, a specialty bath store, and a shop selling rude T-shirts and kitchen towels that was always busy.

The bell chimed as I let myself in the front, and the

warm richness of freshly roasted coffee beans cascaded over me in a wave. My pastry case was full to the brim of lemon tarts, hot cross buns, and gluten-free muffins in pistachio white chocolate, pineapple macadamia, and chocolate cherry chip, which usually sold out first because they were half a step away from being cupcakes you could eat for breakfast. The line was several customers deep and Gia was working the espresso bar the way a concert violinist rocks out Vivaldi.

The hair on the back of my neck stood up as I saw who was handing out my precious baked goods. Alex gave me a delicate little wave while she passed a bagged pastry to the man who works in the T-shirt shop next door. *Get your hands off my muffins!*

Sierra, the cute little college girl Gia had hired to make me jealous, came out of the back room dragging an industrial-sized bag of roasted espresso beans and spotted Alex at the register. "Hey. What are you doing? I said I'd be right back."

Alex caught my eye and a victorious smirk crossed her face for only a moment.

The commotion caught Gia's attention and he looked up and saw the women squaring off. Then his gaze drifted to me. His expression was on lockdown, but I was sure I caught a flicker of exasperation.

I walked past Alex, who was insisting that she was just trying to help, and Sierra, whining that if Alex had wanted to help, she could have gotten the coffee beans from the storeroom. Then Gia calmly but firmly said, "Basta," and they both silenced.

My mind was whirling with important thoughts like, how did Sierra know "basta" meant enough? And was

Alex trying to push out all the women who worked for Gia? How did Gia keep surrounding himself with size twos when I'm a size—*not two*? And could I really hold his interest against all the sexy women who showed up here to get his coffee every day? There were a lot of ways to advertise that you were interested in a man, and I couldn't pull off any of them.

I unlocked the back door out of principle and went in the pantry to take out ingredients for some late-addition cookies for the Expo. A couple of weeks ago I'd cut out all the carbs to try to trick my body into losing weight. I didn't know if it was working or not; so far all that was happening was I had to pee all the time and I kept having dreams that I'd accidentally eaten a can of frosting while standing in the bathtub. But it did give me some new recipe ideas to fool around with.

I'd had a moment of inspiration while cooking breakfast and invented keto maple bacon chocolate chip cookies in my head. I was also going to make some Paleo lemon coconut macaroons and Paleo breakfast cookies with hemp, chia seeds, carrots, walnuts, and flaxseed. The Expo opened at nine every day, so they should be a big hit.

Alex had been kicked out of the dining room and came to wreak havoc in the kitchen. "So, you are here again today. Are you sure you need to make more cookies? We'll never sell everything you've made now." She smiled brightly, like we were long-lost best friends catching up over Nehi and oatmeal creme pies. It made me want to punch her in the clavicle.

I tried not to be obvious that I was scanning her from head to toe, but the woman knew how to work every inch of what she had. She looked like she was wrapped in one long bandage, with strategic bits of skin peeking out from the crisscrosses. I wrapped my canvas apron around my waist and noticed I'd spilled melted chocolate on my boob the last time I was here. *That's special.*

"Gia and I were up late last night talking about him taking some time off so we could get away to work things out."

My head shot up from my recipe and a muscle in my neck popped.

"He said he doesn't have anyone who could take over the shop while he's gone. I don't suppose you know anyone who could help, do you? We really need some time together. I think it would be wonderful for Henry to have a baby brother or sister."

Because having a baby fixed everything the last time.

Gia strode into the kitchen under a black cloud and went toe-to-toe with Alex. "Why are you here? You said you wanted to spend the day with Henry, not come to my business and get in the way."

Alex cocked her head to the side and turned on the most innocent tone of voice. "I wanted to see you while Henry was in preschool. Did you think more about what we talked about last night?" Alex slid her eyes to me to see if I was paying attention. I looked away and dropped a huge dollop of coconut oil into my mixing bowl. It splattered on my other boob. "I think Poppy would be perfect to run the shop on her own for a few days. She seems very capable and smart."

Gia practically had steam coming out of his ears, but his face remained calm. "I am not interested in going anywhere with you except court. Did you relock that door after I opened it this morning?"

Alex swatted him playfully on the arm. "Yes, silly. We

don't want just anyone walking in here. Like the time that drunk man thought our apartment was his house. Remember how you had to chase him out in your underwear because we were in bed?"

Gia looked up at the ceiling and groaned. "You need to go. I don't care where. Go to Momma's. Go to Karla's. Go sit in the alley. But you are not staying here. And I want you to leave Poppy alone."

He had more to say, but the tone in Sierra's "Gia, I need backup!" made him run from the kitchen back to the front.

Alex made a look that reminded me of Cruella De Vil when she first got the idea to make a puppy coat. "Did you see the fire in his eyes? Be careful. You never want to push a Larusso too far." Then Alex sauntered over to the back door, turned to face me, and clicked the lock back into place, so I was sure to know she was the one who had locked me out.

No wonder Momma loves her.

Alex hopped up on the counter and swung her legs back and forth. "I want to help out at the Expo."

"Mm-hmm."

"I was thinking you should probably stay behind the scenes and I should serve the diet cookies."

I gave her a sharp look. "And why is that?"

"I'm sure your cookies are very good, but I worry that people will not believe they work if they see you selling them because you are the fat."

I see. You want me to stick your hand in the Kitchen-Aid while it's running.

"If I serve them, everyone will run to buy them because I am so tiny, and they can find out how good a baker you are."

I leaned in toward Alex. "You need to leave my kitchen. Now."

She shrugged prettily, hopped off the counter, and headed to the dining room. "I just want to help."

Said the scorpion to the frog.

I was beating my coconut macaroons within an inch of their lives when someone started pounding on the back door. I went and unlocked it again to find Karla with her arms full from the Chef Supply shopping run I'd requested the other day. *"O dio mio, chi has chiuso a chiave questa maledetta porta?"*

I took a bag from Karla just as Gia came around the corner. He took my bag and put it on the counter. Then he pulled me close. "I love you. And I have something to ask you."

If he asks me to cover the shop while he goes away with Alex, I'm walking out of here right now and moving back to Virginia. Aunt Ginny can come with me.

Karla heaved her shopping bag up on the counter. "That's okay. I got it."

"I just had a visit from Momma."

Or, as I call her, the pale horse of death. "Go on."

"She wants you and your aunt to come to Easter dinner after church on Sunday."

Karla dropped the bag of gluten-free flour on the floor and a mushroom cloud of white enveloped us. She grabbed my arm. "For the love of all that is holy, save yourself."

Gia finally got Alex to leave the shop by using the words "immigration fraud." She countered with the phrase, "Papa would not like that." Then she said she was going to pick up Henry and left. Twenty minutes later, Henry walked in the front door. He was currently wrapped around my waist eating a maple bacon chocolate chip cookie and telling me everything he learned in preschool about frogs.

I tried to be casual as I asked Henry how he was doing. "Are you having fun with your mother?"

He didn't look away from his cookie, but his face scrunched up. "She's not my mother."

"What do you mean?"

He shrugged. "She says she is, but where was she?"

"That's a tough question. But she's here now."

Henry shook his head in dismissal and focused on his cookie.

I stroked his blond hair and thought for a minute. "Well. What kinds of things do you do when you're with her?"

"Mostly watch TV. She tried to give me cow milk. I told her it made me sick."

"We'll have to tell her about your special milk."

Henry looked at me, his eyes the size of quarters through his glasses. "I don't want to go back to Nonna's with her. Can't I stay here with you?"

My heart shattered into a million pieces. "Of course you can. As long as Daddy says it's okay. But at some point you'll need to give your mother a chance."

Henry eyed me like he wasn't buying what I was selling. "Can I have another meat cookie?"

Things slowed down for the afternoon and Gia spent most of his time in back with me and Henry while Karla worked the front of the house. We talked about his life as a child in Italy and Alex's family, while I taught Henry how to roll and cut out sugar cookies, and Gia washed the dishes in between customers. Karla took Henry home for dinner, even though he protested that he'd already had dinner because there was bacon in the cookies. Gia and I worked together into the night and packed everything up ready for transport tomorrow.

I left by the front door because I'd seen Sawyer's bookstore light still on through the dining room window and I wanted her to sample the coconut macaroons. I wrapped my coat around me to fight against the bitter drop in temperature. It was well past closing time and the store was empty. I knocked on the door, but no one answered. I called her on the cell phone to make sure everything was okay.

"Oh, hey. What's up?"

"Are you at work?"

"No. Why would I be?"

"Well, I'm outside and the lights are still on."

"You're outside my shop?"

"Yeeees. Is that okay?"

"What?" Sawyer strangled out a chuckle. "Of course."

"Why are the lights still on?"

Sawyer's words came out rushed. "Don't worry about that. It's nothing."

"Are you sure? I thought I just saw movement by your office."

There was silence for a moment. "It might be the cleaning people. They won't answer the door. It's okay if you just go home. I'll talk to you tomorrow."

"Okay. . . . See you at the Expo."

"Oh yeah. I'll see you there."

We hung up, and I looked in the front window again. I feared I was getting the brush-off. Sawyer didn't use cleaning people. And she'd been weird for days. As long as she was safe, it was her business. I was sure she would tell me when she was ready. She had a right to her secrets . . . Nope. These were the things I was telling myself, but I wasn't believing any of them. I could feel that something was off and I wanted to know what was going on. *Sawyer, are you in some kind of trouble?*

CHAPTER 9

Gia picked me up at six a.m. to drive to Convention Hall. He insisted. He said he wanted to spend as much time with me as possible before the Beauty Expo got ugly.

"You do understand that it's a two-minute drive, don't you? And that's if we catch the light on Beach. I could walk there in less time."

He gave me a cryptic grin and a one-shoulder shrug. "Best two minutes of my day."

Now I was waiting for him. I left Aunt Ginny a note that I had fed Figaro, because he wouldn't leave me alone until I did and he'd bemoan the lament of starvation in two hours when Aunt Ginny woke up. I didn't have time to make a French press, so I ran my baby-pink espresso machine and made myself a double shot. I had just downed it when I heard a light tapping on the front door. I checked the clock on the microwave. Gia was early.

I grabbed my purse and threw open the front door to one of the sexiest sights in the world: a man holding out a cup of coffee. "Ooh, thank you."

Gia was dressed for setup day in work boots, black jeans, and a faded, sky-blue T-shirt. I had also never seen his biceps uncovered. I was pretty sure I was spotting a tattoo, and I had to fight the urge to tug at his sleeve to check. He was fighting a grin. "Is everything okay?"

I shrugged and shook my head. "Yeah. Of course. I think maybe we should start casual Fridays at the coffee shop."

Gia raised one eyebrow and chuckled. He held the door open and I could see a large, white van at the curb that said Elite Imports on the side.

"Where'd you get that?"

"I have a connection."

It took longer to get my seat belt on than it took us to get to Convention Hall and pull up to the loading zone. There was a U-Haul and a van queued up to unload before us. After watching the U-Haul for a couple of minutes, I broke the spell and asked Gia if he'd seen anything weird happening at Sawyer's bookstore. I filled him in on how the light was being left on after-hours, and I thought I saw someone in there.

"And that is a problem why?"

"The first time I thought she was working late, but I was trying to help Kim with her winery problem, so I never got around to asking her. Now I'm afraid something's wrong. She's been deflecting my questions and being secretive—something Sawyer is not good at. And I really don't like it when someone is lying to me." I may have said that last bit as a subliminal warning.

Gia blew on his coffee and his eyes bored into mine. "Bella, I did not lie to you and I promise I never will."

So much for subliminal.

The silence was deafening. The air wound between us heavy and thick. After a couple minutes I couldn't take the pressure anymore. "Do you want to listen to music while we wait?"

Gia turned the radio on and the Eurythmics were right in the middle of "Would I Lie to You?" I choked on my coffee and he pushed the first Memory button to change channels. The song switched to Billy Joel, "Honesty." He pushed all the preset buttons from Patsy Cline, "Your Cheatin' Heart," to Leonard Cohen's "In My Secret Life." He punched the last button, and Britney belted out, "I'm not that innocent."

Neither of us were moving.

Gia spun the power off and looked out his window. "Radio is broken."

So, we waited.

The Mother Earth Market van finally pulled away and it was our turn to unload. Gia pulled into the loading dock. A young man with Event Staff embroidered over the pocket on his gold golf shirt met us with two wheeled carts. We loaded one with our containers of coffee beans, cartons of milk, paper products, condiments, and syrups. My cart was completely full, so I turned to check on Gia's progress and caught him on his cell phone. *"Ora."*

He hung up and shoved the phone in his pocket, and another van pulled up in the road next to us. Two dark-haired men in black hoodies got out and went to the back of their van. They were dark and scowling, like this was a major inconvenience. They brought out a bright-red professional espresso machine similar to the one at La Dolce Vita and placed it gingerly on the second cart.

Gia made no expression but waved his hand at me. "Go in and get warm, I will get the rest."

I looked around Gia at the two men, who were eyeing me quizzically. "Okay." I pushed my cart up the ramp to the boardwalk and over to the entrance to Convention Hall. There was a life-size poster of a very handsome African American man in a five-thousand-dollar suit with a million-dollar smile. In big blue letters at the top of the poster was *Dr. Lance Rubin*, and underneath it, *pioneer in cosmetic surgery*.

A woman in a gray suit and a brunette top bun approached me. She wore a name tag that said "Eloise, Guest Relations." "Why don't we come this way and I'll check you in." She consulted her iPad, handed me a vendor packet with laminated passes, and instructed another man in a gold golf shirt to escort me. "Kevin will show you to booth number three."

I followed him into the building, down a long hall, and into an enormous event space. The spacious room was painted the color of sand, with a two-story picture window taking up the entire back wall overlooking the ocean. If it weren't for the highly polished wood floor, you would never know this was where we used to roller-skate in junior high. I looked up for the mirrored disco ball, but it had been replaced with tasteful track lighting. "Wow. This is gorgeous."

"Yeah. Over ten million dollars to renovate it."

I almost tripped over my cart. "Get out of here!"

Kevin nodded. "Two amphitheaters. This one is set up for the vendors booths, and next door has the stage and seating for the demonstrations." We wound around other exhibitors getting ready for tomorrow. We were one of the first to arrive. "You have a really good spot, close to Dr. Rubin. You'll get a lot of foot traffic from people seeking Botox and consultations."

We reached our square in the back, right in front of the window. The lifeguard stand and white canoe with "Cape May" painted in red letters was on the beach right outside. A six-foot-wide, wooden counter with a butcher-block top was waiting for us. We unloaded the cart, and Kevin pointed out our extension cords and a water cooler with a five-gallon bottle to fill the tanks on the espresso machine. He showed me where to get more bottles, then he took off with the empty cart to bring in the next vendor.

I was admiring our view and wondering how we got so lucky to get oceanfront real estate when the two men from the second van appeared behind me with the big-ticket items. "Oh, thank you."

They gave me silent nods, then went to work setting up the custom canopy, pastry case, and the espresso machine. They worked together in eerie silence and I tried to stay out of their way. Every once in a while they looked at me and made curious eyes at one another. When you worry about being followed by strangers in a dark alley, these are the guys you're imagining. I kept watch for Gia, hoping he would be along any second—either to protect me or be a material witness. I was hoping for the former.

When they finished setting up the equipment they gave me a chin nod and took off with the empty cart.

What is taking Gia so long? I took out the coffee grinders and put them in place next to the cherry-red, two-pump, Italian espresso machine. It was definitely not new. She had some dings and scratches. This baby had been around the block a few times, but she was still sexy. I put the bags of espresso beans on the bottom shelf of the cabinet underneath, then unloaded the cases of boxed milk and stored them on the top shelf. The writing on the boxes was in Italian. Was this what Gia used at La Dolce Vita? I'd never noticed before since I only had the coconut almond milk he made special for me. *I wonder what he made special for Alex.*

"Ah, there we are." Gia finally showed up carrying the box from the print shop.

"Where in the world have you been?"

"I had to move the vans."

"Who were those guys?"

"They're family."

"Family as in you're related to them . . . or family as in *Family*?" I gave him a knowing look and touched my nose.

Gia's face was set in stone and his eyes bored into mine. Then he laughed a belly laugh. "This is a good spot, yes?"

Was I just blown off? "Right near the main event. There are posters all over the room advertising Dr. Rubin."

Gia walked up to the window. "I was talking about this view."

I went and stood next to him. "I know. Who'd you have to sleep with to get this spot?"

Without looking at me, he put his arm around my shoulders and pulled me into his side. He kissed the top of my head. "There is no one for me but you. We will get through this."

How does he see right through me? I don't like it.

"Hey, y'all. It looks like we're gonna be neeeighboors."

We turned around to see that singsongy southern twang coming from an Asian woman with wavy pink hair. She was wearing black leggings, UGGs, and a University of North Carolina Tar Heels sweatshirt. She put her hand out. "I'm Shayla Rose, Shayla Rose Skin Care. My booth is right between yours and this behemoth tent of Dr. Rubin's."

Gia shook her hand because I was busy hanging my mouth open. "Giampaolo Larusso. La Dolce Vita, espresso and Paleo-baked goods."

"Hi. I'm Poppy Larusso." *Oh god, why'd I say that?* "I mean McAllister, Poppy McAllister. Sorry. It's really early for me." *What the heck is happening to me?* I was making veiled accusations and now what was that? My ears burned. "We're not married."

Gia's eyebrows shot up and a grin broke across his face. He put an arm around me. "Well, not yet anyway."

"I mean one of us is married. But not to me." *Why can't I just shut up?* I tried a forced smile at Shayla. *An other woman is Mrs. Larusso.*

Shayla Rose smiled at us both but made no comment about my gaffe. She eyed the espresso machine. "I don't suppose that's up and working now, is it? I would kill someone for a latte."

Gia stepped away from me and turned the espresso machine on. "It will take a few minutes for me to fill the tank and warm her up, but we will have magic soon enough. No need to take anyone out so early in the morning."

"Thank God. You're a peach! Poppy, I have some fabulous goody bags for the first hundred guests who come to my presentation. Come and get one before the hordes arrive." She took my wrist and led me to her booth next door.

"It smells like roses in here."

Shayla laughed. "It's my last name, so it was a no-brainer making it my signature scent." She had two Asian men helping her set up a tent with blackout fabric on three sides.

"Aww, you won't see the ocean all closed up like this."

She opened a cardboard box and pulled out a dusky-pink-colored gift bag with rose-scented tissue paper springing from the top. "I know. What a shame. I love the ocean too. It makes me feel so peaceful. But I've developed a new age-reversal concentrate, and my secret ingredient needs to be kept in a cool, dark place and only applied at night."

"Oh, okay." I rooted through the bag and pulled out a very small black container with Shayla Rose written in pink script. Underneath the name it said Immortality. "What's the secret ingredient?"

Her expression melted like wax. "That's confidential. How could you expect me to tell you that? I will protect that secret with my life."

My chest got tight and I looked around for the nearest exit. "I am so sorry. I shouldn't have asked."

Shayla's face changed instantly to amusement. She grabbed my wrist again and laughed hard. "I'm only kidding. It's jellyfish. That's why it's called Immortality, for the immortal jellyfish. Oh Poppy, the look on your face." She went deadpan again. "No, but seriously. That formula is one of a kind, and it's not on the market yet. I'm technically not even allowed to sell it. I'm giving away samples Thursday morning after my stage demo, to create hype before the unveiling this fall. You'll come to my talk, won't you? It's about marine chemistry in the beauty market."

I wasn't sure what to do. I nodded and put the face cream back in its pink gift bag. "Well, thank you. I can't wait to try it."

"Just do me a favor, hon. Don't post about it on social media until the official release, 'kay?"

"I won't. I promise." I watched the men set up tiered boxes and start to load them with jars of moisturizer and tubes of creams. "Are these your brothers?"

"That's racist."

My mouth went dry and I felt like I was going to throw up. "I'm sorry. I don't know what's wrong with me today. I just thought it might be a family business." *I need to go home and go back to bed.*

Shayla waited a beat, then all three of them started laughing. "I'm kidding. These are my cousins, Leo and Jimmy. My grandmother made me hire them because she paid my college tuition."

One of the men made a face at Shayla. "Dude, I got band practice this afternoon."

She made a face back at him. "Then you better hurry up, huh? Oh my lord, there is so much to do to set up for this thing. Let's go see if your husband has that espresso ready."

My stomach did a drop and I felt myself overreacting. "Oh, he's not really my husband. . . ."

Shayla laughed again. "I know. I'm just messin' with ya. Talk about your Freudian slips, though. I don't blame you, he's hot!"

Gia had the bar up and running. Once Shayla had her cinnamon latte and Gia and I made test lattes for ourselves, it didn't take long for the smell of fresh-roasted coffee beans to spread. Gia was cranking out espresso drinks for the other vendors for hours while I managed to store all our supplies, hang the banner, and get the cream and sugar station set up for tomorrow's opening. Every time I tried to lift something heavy, he took it from me. "Bella, I got it." Once things slowed down and I could leave Gia alone to ring up the sales on the Square, I took a stack of our menus around to hand out to the other vendors and introduce our booth.

Shayla Rose wasn't the only skin-care line at the Expo. There was Naked Skin Care, Glow Skin Care, Lolly Korean sheet masks, and every kind of botanical perfume, organic makeup, and sustainable bath product you could imagine. The whole room was overwhelmed with essential oils, and the sickly sweet lavender and smoky sandalwood were competing with our coffee beans. The Radiance Day Spa was setting up a booth, and Mr. Charles had a station to show off his line of organic scalp treatments.

I turned down the third aisle and came across an unmanned booth over by the room entrance. The table was set up with a green canopy overhead that said Paleo Diva across the front, and on the green tablecloth were brochures promising the Shore's best Paleo baking. My first instinct was an itchy resentment that there would be two Paleo vendors. Then I told myself I was being ridiculous. What were the odds that we would have the exact same things? Besides, we sell a lot of allergy friendly items in the coffee shop that were not strictly Paleo because I loved butter too much to substitute for it all the time. I decided I would think positive and be excited to meet the other Paleo baker at the Shore. Maybe I'd get some good ideas that I could use in the B&B.

Gia had found me and was waving me over. "Poppy."
Ooh, that was weird. Gia almost never calls me Poppy.
"*Vieni, amore mio.* It is enough for today. Let's go."
Amore mio. My heart gave an extra beat that deflated
at the end. This time should have been full of romance.
Instead it was full of Alex. I didn't want to cry in front of
Gia, so I pushed that thought aside. At least our booth
looked cheerful, even if we weren't feeling it. Tomorrow
we'd be here bright and early with baked goods and brave
smiles. We gathered up the cash box and the iPad we ran
the payments on. Gia told the security guard we were
leaving, and we exited out onto the boardwalk. The cool
air coming off the ocean felt good after being on the
move all day. We stopped for a moment to listen to the
surf and the seagulls and let the salt breeze wash over us.

Gia searched my face. His eyes full of wanting mixed
with mischief. "Thank you for today. You are *una brava
moglie*."

"What is a *moglie*?"

"It means partner."

"Are you sure?"

"*Sì.*"

"Then why do you look so pleased with yourself?"

Gia winked in response.

I could tell he was teasing me about something and I
was working on a snarky follow up, but we were interrupted when a wiry little woman with corkscrews of
golden brown hair charged us and shoved a bright, pink
flyer into my hands. "You've been warned!" She scuttled
off like a hermit crab in purple Crocs, her orange sweater
flailing around her.

"What do you think that was about?"

Gia pointed to the flyer. "She does not like the doctor."

There was a grainy picture of Dr. Lance in front of the Rubinesque Cosmetic Surgery Institute that was probably taken from his website. Someone had added, "Dr. Lance ruins people's lives. Boycott the Expo."

"No, I would say not."

We took the ramp off the boardwalk and down to the crosswalk to wait for the light. I nudged Gia's arm. "Look!" Up and down Beach Avenue, car after car, every windshield, parking meter, and light pole had a bright-pink flyer flapping in the ocean breeze. "We aren't the only ones who've been busy today."

CHAPTER 10

A twenty-foot-tall, inflatable Easter Bunny had taken over my front yard. I stared at it from several angles, hoping that I was imagining things. I had been under a lot of stress lately. And I hadn't eaten anything all day except for a protein bar, and that was only because Gia insisted on it when I wouldn't get a salad from the hoagie shop. I was too sad to eat.

And I was tense. Being alone with Gia all day and not being with him had me feeling like I was being gently electrocuted. I thought I was being cool about everything that was going on with Alex. Then I would hear testy remarks come out of my mouth that I instantly regretted. And now this. *Maybe a big wind will kick up tonight and blow that thing down the street.*

Itty Bitty Smitty, my well-meaning handyman, came out of the garage carrying an eight-foot metal pole that was about three feet taller than he was. He gave me a salute. "Hey, Moe! Nyuck, nyuck, nyuck!" Smitty had a perpetual *Three Stooges* episode playing in his head. The biggest shock of my life was when I caught him kissing Georgina, my prissy and genteel, widowed, former mother-in-law last fall. Opposites attract and extreme opposites make out on the wraparound porch under the wind chimes.

"What's that pole for? And what's with Rabbitzilla here?"

Smitty dropped the T-pole in a hole that I had never noticed. "Ginny wants to hang a bird feeder and smarten up the place for Easter."

I pointed to the ground. "How long has that hole been there?"

"Thirty minutes." He wiggled his eyebrows.

I looked back at the menacing rabbit in a pink vest. "Is that thing tethered to the ground?"

"You know it, Boss!"

"Did *you* tether it?"

"Yes indeedy!"

So, there is hope it will blow away by morning. "Okay. What else does she have you doing?"

Smitty took off his Eagles cap and scratched his bald head. "I got a box of blue, yellow, and white bunting to drape along the porch and windows. And I gotta swap out the butterfly flag for one with Easter chicks and a cross on it."

I sighed. "That sounds tame enough. If she comes up with anything else, run it by me first, okay?"

Smitty saluted and I saluted back. When I stomped my feet on the welcome mat, Aunt Ginny came running down the hall. "Welcome home, my sweet girl. You look gorgeous today. Did you lose weight?"

Uh-oh. "What did you do?"

Aunt Ginny breathed out a laugh. "What . . . nothing . . . really."

I looked into the library and two older women waved at me.

One was short and trim and wore red designer glasses. She had auburn hair with a white-blond swish in the front. She was sitting on the couch reading a romance novel and eating a box of fudge. The other was a bit older, with a cinnamon-brown bob. She was large and broad, with an ample bosom that I imagined made it difficult for her to see the knitting in her lap or Figaro tangled up in the yarn at her feet.

I stepped into the library. "Oh, hello."

Aunt Ginny ducked in next to me to do damage control. "Poppy, this is Rita Bagshaw." The woman knitting smiled and nodded. "And her sister, Faelynn Archer. They arrived a day early, so I checked them in." Aunt Ginny gave me a toothy smile and I returned it with eyes so wide you could see my nightmares in them.

"Welcome, ladies. And how do you like your room?"

Faelynn answered for them. "Oh, both rooms are just lovely, aren't they, Rita? I have the Purple Emperor Butterfly Suite. The pillows are gorgeous!"

Rita cut in as a way of explanation. "I go to sleep early and she stays up all night with the reading light on, so we learned long ago we prefer our own walls. Ginny was able to switch me to the blue-and-yellow Swallowtail Suite. I prefer a tub."

I smiled and nodded to hide the panic I was feeling. "And what brings you two to Cape May?"

They answered in unison. "Shopping."

"Oh, fun. I have a stack of coupons for the Fudge

Kitchen and Morrow's Nut House I can leave on the table by the front door for you, plus a buy-one-get-one-half-off ornament at Winter Wonderland."

They both lit up and nodded vigorously.

"Well, if you need anything at all, let us know."

Faelynn put down her book on her lap. "Ginny told us all about the afternoon tea you have on Saturday. We'd love to get a reservation for that."

"Absolutely. I'll see what I can do."

Aunt Ginny and I backed out of the library. Once we were in the hall we mouthed a silent argument with each other. *What are they doing here?*

I don't know, they just showed up.

Why didn't you call me?

Because I knew you were busy and I thought I could handle it.

Victory came down the stairs dressed in ripped net stockings, a pink leopard-print miniskirt, and combat boots. She had on an oversize white T-shirt with a skull and roses tied in a knot at the hip. She walked down the hall without giving us a second glance. Figaro darted out of the library with some of Rita Bagshaw's yarn still wrapped around his middle and followed Victory into the kitchen.

"I'm not upset, but you put that lady in the Swallowtail Suite and someone else has requested it for the weekend."

"Well, maybe they'll leave early too."

"What will we do if they don't?"

Aunt Ginny shrugged.

Victory came out of the kitchen with a can of Dr Pepper and passed us again in the hall. "I am leeving for today. I have punk concert weith new friend. I weill not be here in morning because I weill have flu." She opened the front door and walked out.

I gave Aunt Ginny an exasperated look.

Her face brightened and she upgraded to a whisper, "Well, then, I have good news for you. I hired someone to help out in the kitchen."

I pointed to the front door. "Your last hire just called in preemptively hungover."

Aunt Ginny took my arm and led me down the hall. "This one will be fine. She's from around here. She has experience and she bakes like a dream."

Now I had ice water running through my veins.

"Plus, you already know her."

What have you done? I peeked around the corner into the kitchen and Oh. My. God.

Sitting at my banquette, casually drinking a cappuccino made from my precious powder-pink espresso machine, was my high-school nemesis, Joanne Junk. Figaro, the faithless rat, was sitting on the table in front of Joanne, purple yarn dangling from his foot, letting Joanne feed him crumbs from some flaky pastry.

I pulled Aunt Ginny around the corner before Joanne spotted me. "Have you lost your mind? No way am I working with her. She has always hated me. Don't you remember that time she filled my locker with jock straps? She has serious issues, Aunt Ginny. You know she still blames me for killing Barbie. Even though the killer had a psychotic breakdown on the stand and confessed."

Aunt Ginny rolled her eyes. "You. Are. An elitist snob. Plus, it's too late. I already hired her. She's making chocolate croissants for breakfast tomorrow. See, I told you I would help."

CHAPTER 11

That night I did some yoga to destress, followed by a long soak in the tub with a rainbow unicorn bath bomb. Figaro sat on the edge of the tub, trying to make up for his earlier shift in loyalties. I gave him a light splash, so he'd know I was still hurt. When I was done I dressed in Eeyore pajamas and wrapped my hair in rags so I'd have some curls tomorrow. Then I dug out my new Shayla Rose Immortality. I smoothed a little of the cream over my face. It smelled amazing. Like English roses. *I really hope that tingling means it's working and not giving me a blistering allergy. Don't I have enough going against me right now with Victory and Joanne and Alex?* Sirens blared down the street, followed by a loud *pop!* I ran to the window to throw it open. It was stuck. I set down the Shayla Rose container and banged the top of the sash with the palm of my hand. The window finally slid up and I could stick out my head and see the flashing lights. Down the street from the Sheinbergs, there were two police cars blocking the road like they'd screeched to a stop and were thrown into Park like an episode of *Wildest Police Videos*. I couldn't see any cops, but I was mostly relieved that for a change they weren't at my house.

My cell phone rang, and the home number flashed up on the screen. "Aunt Ginny? What's wrong?"

She cried out, "They shot him!"

I pulled the window closed and flew down the stairs to the front door. "Shot who? What's going on?"

Aunt Ginny was on the front porch with the cordless phone in her hands. "Benjamin Bunny. He's been the victim of a drive-by."

I stepped out onto the porch and looked into the side yard. The giant Rabbitzilla was deflating as fast as my ego when trying on bathing suits in a dressing room. I put my arm around Aunt Ginny. "That's all right. We can have Smitty come patch him in the morning. Don't be upset."

Aunt Ginny threw herself into me, wailing. "We're the victims of a hate crime!"

"I wouldn't say . . ."

"Do you really think Smitty can fix him enough to inflate again?"

I rubbed her back. "Yes, of course." My eyes slid down the street to the growing number of neighbors gawking at the police presence. "Why don't we go inside and I'll call him?"

Aunt Ginny nodded and tottered her way back inside, heading to her room. It was rare to see her this upset.

I speed-dialed Smitty. "We have a situation."

* * *

The next morning I moved Figaro off my face so I could check the time on my phone. The alarm was supposed to go off in forty minutes, but I'd been awake for more than an hour already. I lay there, awash with anxiety and shame. I couldn't tell you why; it was just how I felt. *I may as well get up.*

I was looking haggard. There were purple circles under my blue eyes that screamed insomnia, and one of my rags had come loose in the night so I would have a full head of curls minus one obvious flag of auburn limpness mocking me. I plugged in the hot rollers to try to punish the loose shock into a curl before Gia arrived.

I dressed in stretchy denim jeggings and a peacock-blue T-shirt that would go with the chocolate-colored La Dolce Vita apron once I arrived at the expo. I applied makeup more for damage control than ornamentation at this point. No amount of color corrector and concealer would hide that I hadn't been sleeping since Alex rolled into town.

Heavenly smells drifted up the back stairs. I picked out coffee and sausage and buttery pastry. When I popped out of the pantry, Joanne jumped and smacked the counter with her spatula. "Good God, how did you get in there?!"

I shut the door behind me and pointed to it. "Didn't you notice the spiral stairs in there?"

Joanne made a face much like I did when I found the jock straps in my locker. "No, I was only in there for a second to see the preserves."

"Well, they go up to my bedroom on the third floor."

Joanne gave a half shrug. "Whatever. I'm not going up there."

Figaro had followed his cake-sniffing nose down ahead

of me and was eating a few scraps of meat from his crystal pedestal bowl.

Joanne pointed the spatula toward him. "That is for him to eat out of, isn't it? It's nicer than everything in my house."

"Yes, that's his lordship's mush bowl. It's a long story, but let's just say he refuses to adjust back down to paper plates." I looked in the large sauté pan to see what she was working on. "Something smells good. What is that?"

I can't repeat what Joanne said she was putting "on a shingle," but suffice it to say we also call it creamed chip beef on toast.

"I also have pain au chocolat in the oven and a single-origin Brazil in the carafe. Hey! My eyes are up here."

I flicked my eyes up to meet hers, then back down to her chest again. "What the heck is on your shirt? It looks like a cat in outer space playing a giant taco piano with pizzas flying around."

Joanne looked down her neckline. "Yeah, so?"

She also had on gray sweatpants and neon-green sneakers, but all things considered, no one would notice those.

I poured myself a cup of coffee while keeping one eye glued to Joanne's shirt. The cat's eyes were following me. "So, we're going to have to discuss the afternoon tea. I've already got recipes for the scones and hot cross buns that I've been working on for days. And I'm thinking about a chocolate sandwich with sweet mascarpone cheese and cherry preserves. If I give you a recipe, do you think you could make me the chocolate bread if I run out of time?"

Joanne covered her cream chipped beef and gave me a sidelong glance. "If you give me a recipe, I'll quit. I know what I'm doing in here. And I already promised Ginny I'd make you petits fours and custard tarts."

"Will they be gluten free?"

Joanne screwed her eyebrows down. "No! They'll be good."

I didn't have time to get into an argument because Aunt Ginny busted through the front door. "You'll never believe what happened last night."

"Smitty's coming today to patch him."

"No. Not that. Gia! Come in here and tell them!"

Gia turned the corner into the kitchen and Joanne audibly gasped. I didn't blame her. He looked like a centerfold for Italian *GQ*. My heart gave a sad little flip to remind me he wasn't mine.

Gia smiled at Joanne and pointed to the carafe. "May I?"

Joanne dropped her spatula and grabbed a mug. "I'll get it for you. You just stand there."

Aunt Ginny and I watched in fascination as Joanne poured Gia a cup of coffee without taking her eyes off of him, then handed it to him like she was performing a Japanese tea ceremony.

Gia flashed her a brilliant smile, said thank you, put the coffee to his lips, and blew on it.

I was waiting for Joanne to pass out, but Aunt Ginny handed her a towel. "Here, honey, dab your chin."

I handed Gia the sugar bowl. "So, what is this news?"

Aunt Ginny charged ahead and spilled it before Gia could get a spoon out. "Somebody vandalized Convention Hall last night!"

"What! Did they damage our booth?"

Gia shook his head. "I checked half an hour ago when I got the email. Our equipment is fine. I think nothing was taken, but I want to do a quick inventory before we unload."

I looked at Aunt Ginny, who was known to have dubious sources. "Then how do they know it was vandalized?"

While my attention was on Gia for thirty seconds, she'd managed to get a plate of creamed chip beef and a piece of toast. She was about to take a huge bite, but she stopped mid toast. "Blue footprints all over the boardwalk in front of the door appeared last night."

"Are the footprints just outside?"

Gia shook his head. "They start in the main hall."

Aunt Ginny shrugged. "Whatever they were doing, they spilled something and walked in it."

Gia sipped his coffee and his eyes roved over me. "Probably just some kids on a crime spree for spring break. It happens every year."

I blushed under his gaze, but I didn't turn away. "What was the security guard doing when this was going down?"

Gia did a slow blink and rolled his eyes. "Getting a funnel cake. He said union rules demand he get a ten-minute break every four hours."

Joanne hadn't taken her eyes off of Gia and I realized they hadn't been introduced. "I'm sorry, Joanne Junk, this is Giampaolo Larusso. Gia owns La Dolce Vita, the coffee shop on the mall. Joanne is working for me to help run the front desk and the kitchen."

They shook hands and Joanne glanced at me. "I don't work for you. I freelance for Ginny."

"Oh. Okay." *Whatever you have to tell yourself to make me those petits fours.*

My cell phone dinged a message from Sawyer. **Can't make it. Something came up. Sry.**

I typed back, **U ok?**

Gia finished his coffee and put his hand on my back. "Are you ready?"

I said goodbye to Aunt Ginny and Joanne, who grunted in reply, and grabbed my tote bag. By the time I reached the Elite Imports van, Sawyer had answered my text.

I'm going to visit my aunt in the nursing home.

Sawyer's a really bad liar. Also, Sawyer doesn't have an aunt.

CHAPTER 12

It's amazing how many volunteers appear to assist when you have containers full of muffins and cookies. Once I'd rolled our cart up the ramp to the boardwalk, I looked around for the footprints. It was bright and sunny, but I didn't see anything. Maybe they'd cleaned it up. Or maybe it was a prank after all. You know how rumors start in small towns. Then, out of nowhere, I was pounced on by the same woman who'd handed me the bright-pink flyer last night.

"Go home! Don't be a part of this abomination. It's a scam!" She was holding a picket sign made out of heavy poster board glued onto a piece of splintered chair molding. It said, "Scared for Life!" I got a good look at her in the daylight. Something wasn't right. One eyebrow was cocked like she was about to make a comment with flaming sarcasm. I waited for it since I kind of like sarcasm, but nothing came. That was just how she looked. One eye was lower than the other and slanted a little. Her nostrils were two different sizes and the skin around her eyes was pulled so tight, I wondered if that was making the corkscrews in her hair.

"That's right. Get a good look at me. See what that butcher did."

"I'm sorry. I don't mean to stare."

"It's okay. My face says more than any protest sign can." She grabbed my arm. "Dr. Rubin should be given a botched face-lift to pay for what he did to me. A lawsuit isn't enough! He's a charmer, but don't let that fool you."

An armed security guard scooted over and stared her down. "I told you if you did this again, you'd have to leave."

She jutted her chin out. "I have the right to be here."

"You don't have the right to accost people. Now come on or I'll have to take you in for disturbing the peace."

I felt Gia's presence behind me. "What is this? Are you okay?"

I craned my neck to look at him. "Yeah, I'm okay." He gave me a hard look, and I could feel that he wanted to kiss me. I finally cast my eyes back to where the raggedy little thing conducting her one-woman protest had been. She was gone, and so was the guard. "That poor woman."

"What was she scared of?"

I chuckled. "I think she means *scarred* for life. At least judging from her unfortunate face-lift."

Gia turned me around and gave me an up-and-down look. Normally it felt very sexy, but this time it seemed like an inspection. "Why are you covered in glitter?"

I looked at my arm. "What do you mean?"

"You are sparkly."

I moved until the sun caught the glitter on my arms. "It

must be from this unicorn bath bomb I did last night. I think it's for kids, but it was pretty, so I wanted it. I guess I should have rinsed off in the shower."

Gia looked at his feet to try to keep from laughing, but he lost the battle. "I love you so much."

I laughed with him, then we both stopped and stared at each other with too many things to say, all of them blocked by our current circumstances.

Eloise from Guest Relations tapped Gia on the arm and interrupted our reverie. "I'm sorry, but we need to get these carts back for the next vendor."

We wheeled the baked goods to our station and unloaded. Kevin popped in to say hello and collected our carts just like yesterday. "I'm sorry about earlier, the crazy lady cornering you."

"She didn't hurt anything."

"Well, that's a relief. She's been harassing Convention Hall for weeks. Ever since the Beauty Expo was put on the schedule."

"Harassing how?"

Kevin made a face. "Angry letters, threatening emails. We had to block her on Facebook and Instagram." Eloise was waving him up to the front, so he started to move toward her. "Let me know if she approaches you again."

Gia prepped the espresso machine while I filled the pastry case with three kinds of Paleo muffins and two kinds of cookies. He left the booth and came back with a five-gallon bottle of water up on his shoulder. All of the women in nearby booths had stopped to follow him with lust in their eyes. Gia gave me a grin and a wink. *Look at him. He knows he looks sexy. I'm going to be beating these women off with a stick for the rest of the day.*

Other vendors were opening for the morning and we

overheard chatter about the protestor who Kevin had just been warning me about. Apparently, her name was Agnes Pfeister-Pinze, and she had an ongoing medical malpractice suit against Dr. Rubin. Some of the vendors had received letters urging them to boycott the Expo. No one was fazed by her protest, but most everyone felt sorry for her.

I handed Gia a blueberry muffin. "Did we get a letter from Agnes Pfeister-Pinze about boycotting?"

Gia swapped me a coconut almond latte for the muffin and nodded. "I didn't pay any attention to it. It looked like junk mail."

"What did it say?"

Gia took a bite of his muffin and blueberry oozed out the side. "'Do not come to the Expo and support the criminal doctor or bad things will happen to you. Something something.' I got a letter about Alex filing for joint custody the same day, so everything else is a blur."

I put my hand on his arm. "I'm sorry. How can she contest the divorce and file for joint custody at the same time?"

Gia picked up a demitasse-size paper cup and kicked back a doppio shot of espresso. "She is covering her bases. Alex is always scheming."

My hands were shaking. I could lose having Henry in my life if he went to live with his mom. And it would break Gia's heart to lose his son even part-time. I stepped over to straighten up the creams and sugars to keep busy. We weren't even officially open yet and our booth was just about wrecked from the other vendors getting their setup lattes. "Have you tried talking things out? To see if maybe she's sincere this time?"

Gia crossed his arms and took a wide stance to face

me. "Do you not understand? She digs her heels in because of you. She never wanted me or Henry, but now that we have you and we are happy, she must fight to take us back. She cannot lose to another woman. Especially to one as beautiful as you."

I snorted out a very unladylike laugh. I wanted to bask in the moment as long as possible, but a man wearing a bright yellow Sunshine Smoothies apron approached the booth and ordered a carrot coconut muffin and an Americano. I'd learned not to grimace when someone ordered an Americano even though I thought it was a crime to water down espresso. I handed him his muffin and was running his card when I heard a hubbub of activity coming down the aisle.

Dr. Lance Rubin was being led to his booth by Eloise of Guest Relations. Flanking him on all four sides were ladies dressed in white lab coats. They looked like sleek, white Arabian horses pulling a Hugo Boss pumpkin coach. He waved to every vendor as he passed them like a royal procession. All they were missing were the footmen blowing arrival trumpets.

They pulled up alongside La Dolce Vita, and he gave me a stellar grin. He was fit and attractive, with close-cropped black hair and a little gap between his front two teeth. He oozed charm and confidence. "Well, hello, gorgeous. Coffee and gluten-free muffins—I'll see you in a bit." He grinned, then set off to open the Rubinesque Cosmetic Surgery booth.

All righty then. I didn't know what to say. I exchanged a look with Gia. He wasn't as amused about it as I was, which only amused me more.

Once the Beauty Expo officially opened, hordes of people filled every space of Convention Hall. Throughout the morning, our booth was very popular. It was especially popular with the ladies. They were lined up the length of the event hall waiting their turn to see Dr. Rubin, and while they were in front of Gia, they flirted and giggled and cooed at him. They wanted coffee drinks but asked him to describe them slowly so they could listen to his accent. One of them asked if he was strong enough to pick her up. Gia said he didn't think so. He told them he was very weak, but Dr. Rubin had put fake muscles in his arms and chest so he'd feel better about himself. I had to hide my face behind a napkin to keep from laughing out loud. Not that anyone would have noticed me if I had.

One by one, they each bought whipped-cream-covered mochas and pastries on their way to discuss having their fat sucked out. I finally asked one of them what was so special happening in Dr. Rubin's booth. She told me he was having a raffle for free face treatments.

I looked at the Shayla Rose booth and wondered how she was faring with the large crowd. She was standing in the aisle handing out tiny little sample tubes of eye cream. She was dressed in a rose-colored, tailored dress with a black silk scarf draped around her neck. She definitely knew how to market herself. She caught my eye and waved.

Eloise marched past the line at our booth and cut to the front in spite of the loud protest. "Dr. Lance would like a large cappuccino and an assortment of muffins sent to his booth right away."

Gia and I looked at each other as if to say, *Who do these people think they are?* Eloise clapped her hands in my face. "He can't leave his booth."

I was really tired of being bossed around, and I was

emboldened by the ladies in line who had choice words for Eloise about her rude behavior. Also, I think South Jersey was rubbing off on me a little. "First of all, I don't have to do anything I don't want to do. And I'm especially not doing it for someone who lacks the courtesy to say 'please.'"

The ladies in line cheered, and Eloise's face grew a dark shade of pink. "I apologize; please take Dr. Lance some muffins." She leaned in and whispered, "I'm very stressed. This whole Expo revolves around his being here and it's my head if it fails. We've already had one disaster with the security company I hired. I can't take much more."

I considered her apology. It wasn't a good reason, but it was a reason. I handed her a maple bacon chocolate chip cookie. "Here, eat this and calm yourself down. I'll go visit his majesty." I bagged up a few muffins. Gia handed me a cappuccino and I headed over to the Rubinesque booth.

It took me longer to get through the impenetrable wall these women had formed to prevent line jumpers than it had taken me to actually make the muffins. "Please let me pass. I'm not signing up for anything. I'm not entering the raffle. I'm just here to deliver the coffee."

"No cutsies, Red! How do we know you won't take the last free sample?"

"Aunt Ginny? How did you get this far up the line without me seeing you?"

Aunt Ginny leaned in and wiggled her hand. "You got to bob and weave." Then she hollered, "Let her through, she's making a delivery for the doctor!"

The women, and a smattering of men, parted like the Red Sea for Moses, and I walked down the middle to the entrance. I had an unusual low drag at my back like I was toting a tugboat. I crossed the threshold into Dr. Rubin's booth and checked behind me.

Aunt Ginny gave me a cheesy smile and let go of the handful of my blouse she'd been grasping like a pilot fish. She caught the eye of one of the lab coat ladies. "Oh, hey. Where do I sign up for the free Botox?" And she was off.

Another woman in a lab coat approached me. "Is that for Dr. Rubin?"

"Yes, Eloise requested I bring it over."

Dr. Rubin stuck his head out of a hanging door that was framed into his expo tent. "Yes! Is that the muffin lady? Come on in!"

"Wow, you have a real door in here."

"This is the Mercedes of convention tents. The door is flimsy, it's attached on that support beam there, so it pivots, but at least I look like I have a private office." He took out the banana almond muffin and examined it. I got a good look at his blue, star-sapphire ring. You had to have a lot of confidence to wear a man ring. He popped a piece of muffin into his mouth. "This is so good. What's your name?"

"Poppy."

"Well, Poppy, do you want to see the treatment room?"

I looked around. "Sure. Why not?"

He jerked his head to the side. "Come on."

One of the women in a lab coat was passing us going the other direction. Dr. Rubin nodded his head to her. "Tally! Come with me."

Tally was a beautiful young woman with strawberry-blond hair wound up in some fancy updo that takes two people to maneuver. She spun around and immediately changed course to join us.

Dr. Rubin took me past the main entrance, where someone in line yelled that I'd better not get their raffle ticket, and down to an opening on the other side of the tent. He pulled the flap back to reveal a dark room with creepy, glowing mannequins lying side by side, and I jumped. They had identical blank faces, only some were glowing blue, some red, some green. They looked like something that would try to take over the world on the SYFY Channel. I thought I had the willies before, but when one of them sat up, ten years fell off my life.

"What is that!" My heart was pounding in my throat. I jumped behind Dr. Rubin, who doubled over laughing. One of the lab coats went to the mannequin and lifted the mask off a woman who'd passed our booth hours ago.

Tally put her hand on my shoulder. "They're just LED light masks. They're perfectly harmless but extremely beneficial for many skin ailments."

Dr. Rubin laughed again and pulled out the blueberry muffin. "My nurse is right. They're harmless unless you're acne, rosacea, or scar tissue. Then they're deadly."

I felt Tally stiffen. "Now, Dr. Rubin, you know I have a PhD in cosmetic chemistry."

Dr. Rubin was not fazed by the newly added tension in the room. He pointed to a treatment area that had been used recently. "Could you please set up for my next BOTOX patient? Thanks, Tally."

He led me back out the tent flap into the waiting area, where women were filling out paperwork on clipboards, signing up for consultations, entering the raffle, and asking about procedures. I heard a familiar voice ask about a

Brazilian butt lift and caught the eye of Mrs. Davis. She tried to hide her face behind a brochure, but I'd already seen her and her pink hair.

Dr. Rubin led me back toward his office and turned the charm up to eleven. "I hope you're coming to my keynote speech tomorrow night. I'm making a monumental announcement about a cutting-edge breakthrough that will transform the cosmetic surgery industry. You don't want to miss it."

"I think my aunt already has tickets for us."

He patted my arm while examining my face. "Good, good. You have gorgeous skin, you know that?"

Don't blush, don't blush, don't blush. "Thank you. I moisturize." *Real clever, Poppy.*

Then he said, more to himself, "Redheads. How would you like a private consultation?"

I was uncomfortable with what I thought was a bold advance, then he looked around to make sure no one was within earshot. "You could do with some liposuction, but everything else that I see is beautiful. Not everyone is built to be model thin."

Well, this can't get any more humiliating.

He walked over to a display of beauty products, took a brochure, and handed it to me. "Read this before our consult."

I looked at the slick paper in my hand. Remove Stubborn Belly Fat—Banish that Bulge. *I stand corrected.*

He nodded, then turned to head back to the front desk.

I was about to return the brochure to the display when my mind drifted to Gia and all the women throwing themselves at him. And Alex, with her tiny little waist and flat stomach. I folded the brochure into a square and tucked it into my back pocket.

Dr. Rubin's tent exited in front of an essential oil distributor and a bright-pink makeup booth. I was trying to get my bearings when I heard my name called. Alex was waving three tubes of lipstick at me from the Glam Lips counter. *Oh no.*

"Ciao, Poppy. I came to relieve you. You can go home now and work for your pensione. I am here to take Gia from you."

CHAPTER 13

The other day I'd seen Alex suggest to a heavyset woman buying a lemon tart for breakfast that she start Weight Watchers to keep track of her calories, so I doubted we were having a translation issue. "Shouldn't you be home waiting for Henry to get out of preschool? You have a lot of lost time to make up for. It's a nice day, why don't you take him to the zoo?"

Alex dropped the lipsticks on the counter and left the booth. "There will be plenty of time for that. I need to work on my husband too. He seems a bit distracted. I just bought the cutest little nightie. I can't wait for him to see it."

Maybe Italians don't have a word for "subtlety." "Well, the Beauty Expo closes in five days. He'll be back at La Dolce Vita before you know it."

Alex drooped her face into a pout. "That may be too late. He's different than I remember. He used to work all night and hang out at the sports bar until morning. Now he goes home early and he's not hungover. I think you've been a good influence on him."

I swallowed hard. "I think he goes home because he cares about Henry. Gia has dinner with him just about every night." *How do I get away from her?* I looked around to find an escape route back to La Dolce Vita.

Alex reached behind my head to feel a scarf on display in an eco-friendly booth supporting women in Africa. "I don't think you give yourself enough credit. I've heard him call you Bella. That means 'beautiful' in Italian."

"I know what it means."

"You may be beautiful to him, but I'm his wife. Don't you think you should cut your ties with Giampaolo to give us a chance?"

I was looking frantically for an exit. Alex had me trapped between Earth Mother Textiles and Facials by Peach. I spotted Shayla Rose by the main entrance in a heated discussion with Convention security. "I think you and Gia need to work out your own issues and quit using me as an excuse. I'm sorry, I see someone I need to talk to; I have to go."

I ducked through a display of woven handbags and took off down the aisle. I made eye contact with Shayla and she smiled in return. I was a few feet away from her when I was cut off by a perky blonde in a green apron shoving a tray of homemade protein bars in my face.

"Care to sample some Paleo Diva snacks? The best Paleo in Cape May County. Oh, it's you, Poppy. Come to check out the competition?"

I was stunned, so it took me a minute to register that I was staring into the face of the devil. "Gigi. You're the Paleo Diva?"

Gigi made a brilliantly smug smile. "No. We are."

I followed her gaze to Tim, glowering at me from the green-and-brown booth. I could feel his hatred from ten feet away and my hands started to shake.

"Tim told me what happened. I refuse to say, 'I told you so,' but I always knew it was just a matter of time before you stabbed him in the back. You were never right for him. Now he is sooo much better off."

I glanced back at Tim. He was talking to a customer and smiling like he wasn't affected at all by seeing me. I tried to keep my voice from shaking but failed miserably. "Whose idea was the Paleo Diva booth?"

Gigi handed a free sample out and turned her face up. "Hmm. I don't remember. I think we came up with the idea together, when we were waking up. Isn't that funny how two people have the same ideas when they're in love? Oh, sorry. I guess you don't know."

Tim was on his way over and I felt like I might throw up. I wasn't even hearing Gigi anymore. She was just white noise.

Tim put his hand on Gigi's back. "Babe, take the high road. She's not our enemy. Let her get back to her boyfriend."

She. Tim wouldn't even look at me. My eyes were welling up, and I did all I could to hold back the tears, but I knew I had to get out of there.

My rescue came in the form of Shayla Rose, who grabbed my arm. "Girl, I've been waiting for you. Come on. Let's go get those smoothies."

Gigi had one final arrow. She called after me, "Hey-ee, be on the lookout for the health department. I overheard that someone called them in to inspect the inferior food booths."

Shayla led my evacuation from humiliation, talking like we were best buddies. We wove around the brow shaping and past the bee pollen honey, and I could see La Dolce Vita just ahead. "So, what was that all about? Is that your ex?"

"How could you tell?"

"He had a vibe. Like he wants to punish you, but still look like a good guy."

"He is a good guy. He's just not the right guy. But the blonde came from the Underworld; don't be fooled. I think she turns into a bat when the sun goes down."

Shayla laughed, and we slowed to a meander. "Yeah. It's so hard to meet someone without them bringing a shedload of drama along. I had an amazing date last night with a man I met on Tinder. We like the same food—Indian; the same movies—chick flicks; the same music—Adele. We both want to travel the world and adopt Pomsky puppies—not at the same time. It turns out we both live in the same neighborhood and go to the same gym, but we've never met. Can you believe that? We've met for coffee a couple of times, but last night he drove up from Raleigh just to take me to a romantic restaurant in Stone Harbor. He was perfect."

"Be careful when they're perfect. Those are the ones who have hidden flaws that come out as soon as it's too late for your heart to turn back."

"Exactly! And this guy was too perfect. He had intelligent eyes behind these sexy glasses that made him look like Hugh Jackman. And he was interested in biochemistry and not intimidated at all by what I do for a living. But all I could think about was when the other shoe would drop, you know?"

"I do." Alex was standing outside the La Dolce Vita

booth, pouting. *There's my other shoe, and it's wearing a tight skirt.*

"And I asked myself, why am I so jaded that when I finally find the perfect man, all I can think about is, what's he hiding?"

"I don't think you're jaded. I think you're careful. If you give your heart away too early and he turns out to, say, still be married or something, you can't just turn off how you feel. Now you're stuck being miserable waiting for a divorce that may never happen and feeling like a lowlife for wanting it to."

Shayla went blank for a beat then recognition dawned. "Oh nooo. Sexy Coffee Guy really is married?"

I nodded. We were back at my booth and Gia made a face that begged me not to leave him alone with Alex. I got back there and handed Shayla a cookie. "Thanks for the rescue."

"Anytime. We girls gotta stick together." She raised a fist.

"Oh, by the way, I saw you yelling at Convention security. Is everything okay?"

Shayla leaned in close, and I could smell her rose perfume. "No. But there's nothing I can do about it now. If I have to kill someone, you'll give me an alibi, won't you?" She dropped her chin and raised her eyebrows, then she busted out laughing in that maniacal way again. "Oh, Poppy, you're too much." She gave Gia the finger as she passed us to get to her booth.

He saw it but had no idea what it was about. He was busy pulling shots for the two ladies in line.

I wanted to hug him so badly. I was one stab of jealousy away from running home and going back to bed.

Alex launched into a speech as soon as I hit the pastry

case to refill it. "Poppy, please tell Gia that you don't mind if I take over for you. I told him it was your idea that he and I work the Expo together so we could reconnect."

I choked on a bite of keto cookie and crumbs flew out of my mouth. I wasn't getting in their way, but I sure didn't want to tuck them into bed either. Then Henry's little face and giant eyes appeared in my mind. I turned to Gia to make a case for him to try with Alex and the black look on his face shut me down. I kept my silence, but I let my eyes rove around the other booths. I was trapped on every side by drama and spite. "I need a minute."

I exited the building to stand on the back deck overlooking the ocean. The sound of the waves silenced the noise in my head until I was at peace again. No matter what happened with anyone inside Convention Hall, I had a good life with Aunt Ginny. And a naughty Figaro, who was home waiting for snuggles. That was enough, wasn't it?

After a few minutes coffee appeared in my hands, and Gia put his arm around my shoulders. "I sent Alex off to help Momma. If you want to go home, I understand."

"I just needed a break."

Gia took my hand. "I wish we could run away somewhere—away from all of this. Just you, me, and Henry."

"Even if we did, Alex would be in our lives. She'll always be his mother."

"Maybe so, but you will eventually see the real Alex behind the act, and you won't be threatened anymore."

We stood out there for a couple more minutes, soaking up the sun, then I asked, "Did you close the booth?"

"No. Someone is filling in until we get back. I am not expecting it to go well."

I turned and looked through the window at the tiny, little, rose-gold redhead in the pink-velour loungewear brandishing a Paleo snickerdoodle like a saber. "We gotta go now."

Aunt Ginny was behind the bar snapping at a couple of teenagers. "You can buy cookies and drink water because I can't reach the controls on the espresso machine. That's it! Like it or lump it!"

I took the cookie from her hand. "Thank you, Aunt Ginny, I'll take it from here." I loaded her up with a few cookies and sent her to go pick out a salt scrub.

For the rest of the afternoon Gia and I worked side by side in relative quiet, hearing snippets of gossip.

All the talk around our booth was about how much better Paleo Diva's items were than ours. A balding man with a swayback and a paunch that made him look six months pregnant ambled over. He was wearing ladies' jeans and had them pulled up and belted over his belly. He looked around my pastry case and sniffed. "You know, the Paleo Diva has free samples."

"I've seen that."

"His stuff's a lot better'n yours."

"Oh really? Which ones?"

The man shrugged. "All of 'em."

"Wow. Even better than my maple bacon chocolate chip cookies?"

The man blinked and licked his lips. "Ayep."

"I'll have to give them a try. Thanks for letting me know."

He looked reluctantly at the cookie in my hand, then turned away. "Ayep."

Gia and I shook our heads.

About ten minutes later Maternity Jordache was in

front of my pastry case again. "That wadn't worth it. Gimme a maple bacon cookie."

I took the cookie out of the case with a pastry sheet and swapped it for his money. He shoved it in his mouth, and his eyes rolled back in his head. "Yeah. That's the stuff."

We'd completely sold out of everything about thirty minutes before the closing bell rang. We packed up the important things, like the iPad and the cashbox. Gia was making a list of things he'd have to bring tomorrow, like a couple cases of milk and a new vanilla syrup.

"Do you think our stuff will be safe? Security didn't exactly rise to the occasion last night."

Gia looked at the security guard drinking a Big Gulp while getting briefed by Eloise. "I'm bringing in my own security for tonight." We passed the green-and-brown canopy. It had been shut down early, and a closed sign was on the table. "Who is this Paleo Diva man?"

"It's Tim. He's here with his new girlfriend."

Gia came to a full stop. "He was here?"

"They both were. He's with Gigi now."

He led me outside Convention Hall, where the air was cooler, and pulled me into his arms. "I'm sorry. No one who loves deeply moves on quickly. Tim is a fool. I would be old and gray before I got over you."

Slow tears dripped from my eyes all the way home. Why is it when the pain doesn't get you, the kindness does?

Gia walked me to the front door to make sure I got in safely. He cast a wary look at Rabbitzilla, who was sprightly again, then ran his hand through the straight lock of my hair that had rejected its curl before lunch. No words passed between us, but our eyes filled in the blanks.

I checked the mail and the front desk. Joanne had left me a note that we needed more butter and cheese. Then, someone pinned up a receipt for butter and cheese, so I guess that crisis was averted. Figaro joined me as I went through email. He paraded back and forth in front of the monitor, and I had to work around him to confirm availability for several future guests. The summer was going to be very busy. It was getting late and I was about to turn out the lights when I heard a slight knock on the front door. I looked through the window to see who could be here this late. I expected Rita or Faelynn had forgotten their keys, but instead I saw an athletic little cop in a ponytail and blue jeans who usually just showed up to threaten me with incarceration. "Amber, what are you doing here?"

"I'm in trouble and I need your help."

"You need *my* help? What do you have like a baking emergency?"

"I think I'm being framed for murder."

CHAPTER 14

"It's not another cheerleader, is it?"

She gave me a sharp look. "This is serious, McAllister."

I wanted to ask her if there'd been a high-school reunion I hadn't heard about, but I refrained because she was already testy. I led her into the library, and we sat on the couch. "What happened?"

"At eight o'clock tonight I got a text from a CI. He said he needed me to rendezvous ASAP."

I cut her off. "Rendezvous? Like hook up?"

Amber made a face like she was already regretting coming to me. So Figaro decided to mediate by jumping up to her lap and staring at her.

She ignored him. She was past screaming when he looked at her, so we'd made progress in the few months she'd been showing up here. She pulled up the message on her cell phone and handed it to me. "A CI is a confidential informant. He needed to talk to me right away because it was an emergency. And could I come over after my shift ended at nine."

I read the message and handed her phone back. "Okay, I'm with you, but if it was an emergency, why didn't he want you to come immediately?"

"I don't know; he went dark after that. I thought he was pulling my leg because it's April Fools' Day."

"Oh, you're right. It is." *That almost explains the day I've had.*

"I arrived on the scene a little past nine. His front door was cracked open, which was already a bad omen, but I held it and knocked. There was no answer. I announced myself, drew my gun, and went in. All the lights in the apartment were off. I heard a hum and this weird, flapping sound. A window unit air conditioner was turned on High, making a frayed, yellow curtain billow out, and it kept sucking it back against itself. It was dark. I thought there was a pile of laundry on the couch. I called out to my CI again and checked the kitchen at my six." Her voice was tight, and she was looking straight ahead, reliving the moment. "When I came back to the living room, I switched on the light and realized the pile of laundry was my informant. There was evidence of blood on the wall and couch. He'd been shot in the chest."

Amber started petting Fig, and he shot me a look that said, *What do I do?*

"I reached down to take his pulse, but I was too late. He was ice cold and soaking wet. I checked the back of the apartment in case the perp was still there. Whoever had killed him was gone. Before I could call it in, Crabtree and Simmons arrived on the scene. They said they were responding to a 9-1-1 call reporting gunshots. Crabtree had me surrender my firearm while she called the chief to report the incident."

"Do they think you killed him?"

"Prudence Crabtree transferred down from North Jersey and she's trying to make a name for herself. I don't think she would have given me officer courtesy had Simmons not been there. My CI was an underage African American in the system, and I'm an off-duty cop standing over his body with my gun drawn. It doesn't look good. If this gets leaked to the press, all they'll say is that a white cop killed an unarmed black youth in his home."

"Don't you have that text from him to prove why you were there?"

"That text doesn't prove anything. And it won't mean a thing to a reporter trying to make a name for themself. They won't care about the facts. It'll destroy my career. I had to go to the station and file an incident report. Chief Fischer put me on administrative leave. He told me not to worry, but he's not the one facing jail time. I know he'll have my back if there's an Internal Affairs investigation. But I can feel it in my gut: something's wrong. My CI was just a kid. He doesn't 'rendezvous.' And why wait until after my shift? We talk to informants on duty all the time. I should have gone right over there. Somebody killed this kid and I need your help to find out what happened."

"Me? What can I do? Don't cops have rules in place for this kind of thing to protect officers? Can't they check your gun to see if it's been fired? This can't be the first time an off-duty cop found a dead body."

Amber flinched. "Homicide victim. And when they check my gun they'll see that it *was* fired because I spent an hour on the shooting range this morning and got called away before I could clean it. The crime lab can run ballistics on the bullets, but dirty cops know their way around the rules. Someone in my department is setting me up. Someone who knew my shift and my informant. I can't trust anyone. I need you. You have good instincts and you can get access to people and places I won't be allowed near. This is my whole life, McAllister. My career. If I'm not a cop, who am I?"

I gave Amber a look that said I'd rather eat worms than get involved in a police investigation. "I don't think I'm the right person . . ."

She tossed her head, and her ponytail did a three-sixty. "What would you do if the situation were reversed and you needed my help?"

"The situation *was* reversed, and you arrested me."

"I was doing my job."

"You had a chip on your shoulder, and you enjoyed it."

"Then how about helping me for old times' sake?"

"What old time? When did we have this time?"

"How about for that sleepover we had where Aunt Ginny tried to kill me. Can you do it for that?"

I reached back into my mind to find the playback on that memory. "You mean my Halloween sleepover in fourth grade?"

"She made me touch eyeballs, McAllister. I had nightmares for weeks."

"They were peeled grapes in a bowl of spaghetti and we were nine."

"I haven't eaten a grape since."

I gave her a look of mock pity.

Amber's cocky mask slipped for a moment. Her eyes were tense and darted away like a wounded bird. "I can't just sit back and let someone frame me for murder. Please."

I didn't want to get involved in this. The pain and hopelessness I went through when I was accused of murder was very traumatic. I still got nervous whenever I had to drive past the high school. But Amber was desperate if she was coming to me. Saying no to her would bring me a moment of relief followed by a lifetime of guilt and shame that I let her hang and didn't try to help. And once upon a time we were friends. "I'll do whatever I can. But I don't want to be put in a situation where I'm arrested, or shot at, or have to use that little toilet in the holding cell."

Amber stood and let out a tense sigh. "I'll call when I'm ready."

Amber was halfway through the door when she looked back, her eyes glistening. "His name was Temarius Jackson and he was just a kid."

CHAPTER 15

Figaro was lying on my chest, examining me. I'd been awake half the night thinking about Amber's request. I thought she might be making a big deal about nothing. She had her cell phone to prove Temarius had texted her. And isn't there some kind of ballistics the police can run to prove Amber's gun didn't fire the bullet that killed him? If I could pick up that much from watching *CSI*, she surely knew about it. This whole thing would probably blow over before the weekend. Unless the April Fools' joke was on me and she was at the police station laughing with Officers Birkwell and Consuelos right now.

I gave Figaro a couple of strokes and a head bonk, then moved him to the bed. A little yoga would help get the bricks of stress off my shoulders. But no matter how hard I tried, I couldn't get my breathing to calm. I blamed the cold lamb chop I ate over the sink at midnight for my insomnia. I had to eat something more than keto cookies and meat. I'd already had enough cheese to be concerned about my near future. People loved this keto diet, but after a month of it I would wrestle a bear for a blueberry. There was a protein powder booth at the Expo. I should try to visit it this morning to see if they had anything that could keep me from skipping lunch again. I was too stressed to eat.

I made it to the kitchen alive after several attempts by Fig to trip me going down the back stairs. We each had our morning routine and his started with snuggling, then moved to assassination.

Victory was at the table eating scrambled eggs and sausage.

"I'm glad you're feeling better today after your bout with the stayed-out-late flu."

She waved a fork at me and grinned. She had large pink splotches on her work pants from a Kool-Aid accident. Still, she was wearing pants and not booty shorts, so I kept my observation to myself.

I pointed to another plate of scrambled eggs on the island. "Good morning, Joanne. Are these for me?" I was also relieved that Joanne was less distracting today. She was wearing green sweatpants and a black T-shirt with an outline of a neon-pink pig.

Joanne snatched up the plate and dumped the contents into Figaro's crystal goblet. "That's for the cat. You can have a breakfast enchilada like everyone else."

I looked at Victory's plate and she tried to cover it with her arm. "Why does she get scrambled eggs?"

Joanne threw her hand to her hip. "Because she was here before I used all the eggs in the enchiladas."

Victory and Figaro both started eating faster, as if I would take their food away from them. *Silent fat-shaming.*

"When will the enchiladas be ready?"

Joanne's eyes glinted like steel. "Soon. There is juice, coffee, and some of those pineapple muffins you made in the dining room."

I gave her my best peeved expression. "Okay. Thank you." *You don't have to be so snotty.*

"Did you roll your eyes at me?"

"No-wah." *Geez.* "Where's Aunt Ginny?"

Victory looked up from her plate. "She ees swatting squirrels ein front yard."

Oh, well, this I have to see. Sure enough, Aunt Ginny was marching back and forth under her new bird feeder, brandishing a Swiffer.

"Get back, you beady-eyed rats! I'm not feeding the neighborhood!"

"What's going on?"

Aunt Ginny poked the Swiffer head at the empty feeders. "I just filled those up yesterday. Do you know how expensive bird seed is?"

"Yes, of course." *No idea.* I examined the setup. Two bird feeders hung on either side of the T-shaped pole Smitty had sunk into the ground.

Aunt Ginny smacked the pole with the handle. "What I can't figure out is how they're getting up there."

I pointed. "Probably jumping off the mailbox three feet away."

Aunt Ginny blew her hair out of her eyes.

A little red car came rumbling down the street going way too fast. Then we heard a loud *pop!* And Rabbitzilla was going down with a wheeze.

Aunt Ginny turned puce and waved the Swiffer over her head. "YAAAAAAA!"

I took her by the shoulders. "Okay, let's get you inside.

I'll call Smitty to repair Benjamin Bunny again, and we'll let the police know we have vandals who keep driving by shooting at the house." I led her into the foyer, and we ran into Rita and Faelynn coming down the stairs to breakfast. "Good morning, ladies."

Faelynn smiled at Aunt Ginny. "What was that exercise you were doing outside? It looked like fun."

Aunt Ginny's eyebrows flattened to a straight line. "Rage Chi."

Faelynn looked at Rita. "Ooh, I haven't heard of that, have you?"

I gave an uncomfortable laugh and pushed Aunt Ginny down the hall. "Why don't you go get a breakfast enchilada, Aunt Ginny? They smell like they're done."

I returned to the dining room and poured myself a cup of coffee while Rita and Faelynn got settled with muffins and juice. "So, where are you ladies from?"

Rita slathered soft butter on her pineapple muffin, and my mouth started to water. *Why didn't I make those low carb?* "I live in Manhattan. My husband and I have an apartment in Chelsea."

"That sounds amazing."

"It is. I've been there a long time." She was making that buttered muffin into a piece of art. "Lots of great restaurants and shopping, and I can walk everywhere. And, of course, Broadway is always fun."

"Do you go to the theater often?"

"I do. My husband is rarely home. He travels a lot for business, but Fae comes and stays with me sometimes when he's out of town. We make a girls' weekend of it."

I need a girls' weekend. I wonder if Sawyer can get her assistant manager to cover the bookstore so we can go to a spa or something.

Joanne brought out the enchilada casserole with Aunt Ginny hot on her heels. She announced that it was sausage and eggs with chiles and cheese wrapped up in corn tortillas, then smothered in her homemade enchilada sauce with avocado cream. Her presentation needed some panache—she pretty much dropped it on the table and ran—but the smells coming from that casserole dish were amazing.

Aunt Ginny offered the avocado cream to the ladies, but I noticed she kept her eyes on the enchiladas.

I sipped my coffee and tried not to feel sorry for myself that enchiladas weren't keto approved. "What about you, Faelynn? Do you live in the city?"

She dumped a hefty scoop of enchiladas on her plate and topped it with a dollop of Joanne's avocado cream. "Good lord no. I am not a city girl. I live in Connecticut. I keep myself busy restoring my eighteenth-century farmhouse."

"I bet that's gorgeous. Is that what you do for a living? Restore homes?"

"No." Faelynn made a face at Rita, like she was asking permission for something. Rita cocked her head a little and Faelynn's eyes bulged. "My husband makes a very good living, so I don't have to work. It's just a hobby."

Aunt Ginny was no slouch at catching furtive looks. She was eyeing both women warily. "Too bad your husbands couldn't come down with you. Cape May is beautiful in the spring."

Faelynn shoved a forkful of casserole in her mouth.

Rita daintily chewed and made mm-hmm noises.

A chime echoed through the house. It was a sound we heard so rarely that it took me a minute to figure out it was the doorbell. Figaro galloped down the hall to beat me to the front door. When I opened it there stood a man dressed in a snappy, blue-and-white, broad-striped suit and a straw, flat-topped boat hat. Next to him was a woman in a lilac dress and white kid gloves. *Is the local theater doing a revival of* Easter Parade?

"Hi, we're the Parkers. I'm Patsy, and this is my husband, Dale." She held up a cat carrier, and a smooshed white face pressed against the door and hissed. "And this here is our fur baby, Portia." Portia hissed again. Somewhere at my feet, I heard a thud reverberate off the wood floor.

Dale held out a card for me to take. "We have a reservation, but we're a skosh early. I hope that won't be a problem."

I looked at the card, expecting to see Dale's name, but it was a business card for Portia's Fancy, with a picture of the green-eyed, white Persian. *How long have I been working on this Expo? Have I lost complete control of the B&B?*

Patsy held up the carrier again. "Portia's a champion show cat. You may have seen her on the cover of *Cat Fancy* magazine. We're in town for the big show."

"The Beauty Expo?"

They stared at me blankly. "The what? Hmm?"

Joanne bustled down the hall all smiles. I looked behind her for the real Joanne, who would stab me with a shard of dry spaghetti for a nickel. "Hi, I'm sorry. You must be the Parkers. I made your reservation yesterday. Come on in."

"We're a bit early," Dale apologized again.

"Oh nonsense. We have the room. We've upgraded you to the Monarch Suite so Portia can have ample room to relax and prepare for the Pretty Kitty Cat Show at Congress Hall." That last bit was said for my benefit. I could tell, because it had a subtle bite to it.

Aunt Ginny had helped herself to the enchiladas and was sitting at the dining-room table, chowing down. She mouthed to me, *Swallowtail*, and I realized this was the couple whose Swallowtail Suite she'd given to Rita Bagshaw because of the tub.

Patsy grinned. "That's wonderful, isn't it, bay-bee? You'll have a suite."

I gave Figaro a look to warn him not to expect the kind of pampering he'd seen today, but he was too busy showing Portia how he could lie still and hang his tongue out the side of his mouth without blinking.

Portia hissed. She was not impressed.

The white Elite Imports van pulled up to the curb. "Well, welcome. I hope you and Portia have a wonderful stay. Joanne will get you settled. I'm just going to pop out for a bit." *Since I have no idea what's going on here.*

I was trying to reclaim some control of my dignity, but Aunt Ginny snatched it out of the air. "Don't forget, we have seats for that seminar tonight on butt lifts."

I gave her a double thumbs-up and ran out the door.

CHAPTER 16

I pushed the first cart of goodies down the aisle to the La Dolce Vita booth. I'd brought a different selection today to highlight some of the best items we carried in the coffee shop. I had the pineapple macadamia muffins we'd served at breakfast, along with pistachio almond and cranberry orange.

Gigi was passing out free samples again. And, apparently, giving an impromptu lecture that she may or may not have known was just to cornered vendors since the Expo didn't open for another half an hour. "The real benefits of the Paleo diet are what it does for your complexion and physique. I know 'Paleo' is a buzz word right now, and you may think it's just a fad, but you can tell who is passionate about clean eating and who is dabbling by what shape they're in. Here, Poppy, try a Paleo banana muffin. If someone says they eat Paleo, but they look like they live on Pizza Hut, chances are they aren't faithful." Gigi turned to look right at me.

I wanted to crush her muffin to powder and drop it at her feet, but I took the not entirely high road—but higher than Gigi road. "Your muffin is rubbery. A common problem when you overmix your batter and use too much xanthan gum." I handed her sample back and kept moving toward La Dolce Vita.

Before I crossed the threshold I saw Shayla Rose pacing in front of her booth, grimacing into her cell phone. I was going to check on her to see what was wrong, but she caught my eye and turned away from me.

I unloaded my cart and Kevin returned it. There was a line forming while I loaded the case with today's baking.

The smoothie guy, already in his bright yellow apron, pointed at my new, chocolaty, coconutty caramel bar cookie. "What in heaven is that, and how is it healthy?"

I grinned and took two of the bars out and cut them into sample pieces. "This is a Paleo version of a cookie my grandmother used to make called Hello Dollys. The caramel is made with coconut milk, the cookie crumbs are coconut flour and ground almonds, and I used dairy-free chocolate chips. They make a nice once-in-a-while treat."

The organic bath salts lady put her hand out. "I want my once-in-a-while treat for breakfast. I'll take two."

The samples disappeared, and I sold fifteen bars before I was able to load them into the case. People were shoving cash in my hands because I wasn't ready to run their cards. I looked across the room to see if Gigi happened to be catching the commotion at my booth. No reason other than professional curiosity. But I didn't catch Gigi watching me. I caught Tim looking my way. Standing in the middle of the aisle, hands shoved in his pockets, expressionless. The hemp jewelry lady walked between us carrying a box of bracelets, and when she had passed Tim was gone.

"What are you looking at so hard?"

Gia was standing at the threshold of the booth holding a case of milk, watching me, and for a minute I felt like I was caught doing something wrong. "What? Nothing . . . I thought Tim was just looking this way."

"Is he giving you a hard time?"

"No. He wouldn't. He's . . . moved on anyway." *Why is that so painful? He wasn't right for me, and it was my idea.*

Gia put the box down and put his hands on my shoulders. "I wish I could make Alex disappear. I wish I had never met her, but Zio Alfio is working on something that will take care of everything. Please give me some time."

"What do you mean, make her disappear?"

He popped his hands in the air. "Out of our lives."

"Are we talking like—make-it-look-like-an-accident kind of disappear?"

"Oh, it will be no accident. She will not bother us anymore."

"And . . . no one will ever find her again?"

He touched his forehead to mine. "I only know *I* will never find her again."

I wanted to beg him not to do anything that would be illegal, but Shayla slapped a brochure down on my counter. "I need a quad shot cinnamon latte with whip as fast as you can make it. Honey, I'm having a day to end all days."

"What's going on?"

She tossed her pink hair with her fingers. "It's a disaster. First, someone steals all the sample bags of Immortality, and then, last night, someone stole my laptop. I'm so disgusted I could pitch a fit right here." She threw her hands up. "Uhhh! Come on!"

Gia looked around the bar, his face full of concern. "You were robbed last night? Here?"

"Yeah. Now all I have to hand out at my big presentation are these brochures about my age-reversal concentrate, and my freakin' PowerPoint is gone because it was on my laptop." She pointed through the bakery case to the double fudge brownie. "I want that." I took it out of the case and went to slip it in a bag, but she took it out of my hands and shoved the corner in her mouth. "Oh, that's so good."

"So, they took all your gift bags?"

She nodded with her mouth full. "Of my new Immortality cream."

"Who knew what was in the bags?"

"Everybody. At least everyone who read the program. The schedule's been posted online for weeks. It says right there for today at eleven, 'Shayla Rose unveils a new breakthrough in anti-aging blah blah blah lifetime of research. Free samples for the first one hundred to sign up.' And there's a link to my website and the press release about my formula."

Gia handed her the latte. "On the house."

"You're too kind, thank you." She blew a hole in the whipped cream and took a loud slurp.

He put his hands on the counter. "Why did you leave your laptop here? You know we were vandalized a couple nights ago. Why wouldn't you take that with you?"

She closed her eyes and shook her head from side to side very slowly. "I feel like such an idiot. I walked from the bed and breakfast yesterday. Then I bought so much stuff at the Expo and had to carry back that I didn't want to take the laptop with me. I thought it would be okay. After my fit with convention security yesterday, they assured me they had everything under control. Besides, what are the odds we'd be vandalized two nights in a row? I didn't realize Cape May would turn into the crime capital of the Shore!"

The opening bell rang, and I grabbed my apron. "I can get you a laptop to use if you can get the file somehow."

Shayla grabbed my hand. "You are so great. But one of my cousins is bringing me a laptop, and the presentation is in Dropbox. As long as he gets here right away, I'll be okay on that end. I just won't have time to prepare and I don't have anything to pass out."

"I'm sure people will understand. They aren't just here for free samples."

Shayla pursed her lips. "Don't be so sure. People will stand in line for hours to get something for free that they could buy with pocket change. I mean, not my age-reversal cream." She laughed that loud, crazed laugh. "That's going to cost a fortune."

"Do you have any idea who would have done this?"

She leaned against the counter and whispered, "I'm sure it was one of the beauty execs in this room. There are at least five skin-care companies right here who would kill to have my formula. The beauty product world is full of backstabbing and jealousy. Everyone wants to unveil the newest breakthrough and be the first to invent a revolutionary product that actually works. Believe me, the Internet is flooded with fake miracle cures and counterfeit products that may as well be fifty-dollar tubes of mayonnaise for all they do for your skin. Some of them are full of poison, glue, even heavy metals. I can feel it down to my roots. This was corporate espionage."

I was frustrated for her. "Did you call the police?"

She backed away from the counter, suddenly very uneasy. "No. I can't do that, and I need you not to do that either. Okay?"

"Why not? If your samples were worth that much, this might be a felony."

Shayla kept shaking her head. "Some things you can't go to the police for. You have to handle them yourself."

Gia nodded. "That is true."

I gave him a probing look.

"What? Are you afraid I am vigilante justice?"

"I'm afraid you're a lot of things."

His eyes narrowed, but the slight grin gave him away.

Shayla took another gulp of her latte, and the line forming behind her was getting ugly. "Look. I already said too much. Please just keep this between us. Don't tell anyone, especially the police. Okay?" She tapped my hand and said thank you to Gia for the coffee, then returned to her booth.

I waited on several customers and had nearly sold out of the pineapple muffins when Eloise came up, excused herself, and handed me a box of vitamin chocolates and twenty dollars, then very sweetly asked me to take some muffins and coffee to "Dr. Lance" this morning.

Ohh, Dr. Lance, is it? "I can do that for you, but can I ask you something first? Didn't the Expo have security last night?"

She looked at the Sunshine Smoothie booth and whispered, "Only until midnight. The last guy was suspended, and this new company didn't have any guards available for the graveyard shift. So, from midnight until six a.m., the local police patrolled. You didn't have something stolen too, did you?"

"No. I was just wondering."

Then she accepted a free Paleo Dolly and was chased down by a juice vendor complaining about how far away their booth was from the bathrooms.

I took a selection of muffins and a cappuccino to Dr. Rubin's booth.

Tally was demonstrating the antiaging benefits of the Rubinesque skin-care line of potions and creams on her thirty-year-old face to a group of sixty-year-old women. She looked my way, and I held up the cup and bag. "Dr. Rubin has requested these."

One of the ladies in the group reached out to take them from me. "Hand them over; I'll give them to the nurse."

Tally's face went stony. "Again. Not his nurse. I'm a doctor here on staff."

The woman could not take a hint. "It's still his practice, though, ain't it?"

Tally gave a gracious smile that did not reach her eyes. "Yes, of course."

I handed off the goods and got the heck out of there as fast as I could. No amount of wrinkle cream would get that foot out of her mouth.

Someone stuck a blue flyer for Zen Mania in my hands as soon as I was back on the Expo floor. "We're doing a yoga class in the community room today at two. Why don't you come and join us?"

I recognized the woman. I'd even taken her class once, when I'd first returned to town. Her name was Skye and she'd banned me from ever returning, so I was surprised she didn't recognize me. Of course, this time I didn't have an eighty-year-old in a tie-dye turban on my arm. I smiled and nodded, and she shoved a flyer in the hand of the next person who passed by.

I pulled out my phone and called Sawyer to tell her what had just happened because I knew she would get a kick out of running into Skye again. Sawyer answered on the third ring, laughing wildly, and immediately hung up.

"Sawyer? Hello? Are you there?"

I dialed again, and this time there was no answer. I wanted to tell Gia what had happened, but he wasn't in the booth. His younger sister, Karla, was there.

"Oh hey. I didn't know you were coming today. Where did Gia go?"

Karla didn't look up from her examination of her nails. "He had some business to attend to."

"What kind of business?"

Karla shrugged. "I dunno. He just said business. You don't ask Gia too many questions."

A middle-aged man dressed out for yoga approached the booth to comment that Paleo Diva's muffins were not rubbery and they were better than anything La Dolce Vita had.

Karla gave him a turn-back-into-a-frog look. "I don't care. Then go buy from them."

The man was shocked, and I gave him an apologetic smile. "I hope you get something you like."

"Okay, but if she asks, will you tell her that I said hers were better?"

"I'll be sure to do that."

He smiled and hotfooted back toward Tim and Gigi's booth.

Karla pulled herself a shot of espresso. "What was that about?"

"I don't know yet. You'll hear it a lot, though."

Twenty minutes later the man returned. "She was wrong. They are rubbery. Can I have one of the cranberry orange ones?"

I rang him up and handed him the muffin, which he ate in three bites, then gave me a nod.

"Karla, if you don't mind, it's a little slow right now, so I'm going to go check out the yoga class."

"Go for it. You do you."

I skirted around the back of the room to avoid the Paleo Diva booth and exited out into the hall. The yoga class was down at the end of the long hallway, with floor-to-ceiling windows and views of the beach and board-walk.

I took a few steps toward the growing group of women in Lululemon and spotted Gia out on the boardwalk. He was talking to a shady-looking man in black jeans and a black windbreaker over a hoodie. I couldn't see his face, but he somehow looked familiar. Both men had their hands and arms flying about as they spoke, and the stranger kept checking for something toward the ocean. I pushed through the door, and Gia spotted me. He gave me a smile, but the man he was talking to immediately took off farther down the boards, away from me.

"Who was that?"

"That was Luca, but everyone calls him Stubby. You met him the other day."

"Met" is a strong word. I observed him while keeping a safe distance. "What was he doing here?"

"He did security for us last night. He watched our booth from that bench right over there. I asked him if he saw anyone at the booth next to ours."

"Wait, he did security for Convention Hall?"

"No. Just us."

"Oh-kay . . . did he see anything?"

"The doors were locked at nine. No one went in until the doors opened this morning at six. But . . ."

"But?"

"Someone came out the emergency exit right over there and hurried down to the beach a few minutes after midnight."

CHAPTER 17

The afternoon moved with the energy of a kid's birth-day party, and I watched for an opening to talk to Shayla, but both our booths were swamped. We sold so many cookies that it was hard to believe our success was tied to the lure of no more thigh jiggle. Dr. Rubin gave back-to-back consultations for hours. At one point, after an argument that ended with a broken bottle of sandal-wood essential oil and a shower of peach Bellini bath salts, the Convention Hall staff had to post crowd stan-chions to make a designated lane to his booth. A famous New York plastic surgeon offering free advice was a hot-ter ticket item than free bagel day at Buns and Beans.

Aunt Ginny and her crew came by to harass me before the keynote started. They were eating bags of gummy bears and being especially giggly, even for them.

"You all seem to be having a good time."

Mrs. Davis leaned heavily against the counter. "I want a fruitachinno latte with extra fruuuitachinno."

Gia and I looked at each other for a moment. Then he started pumping syrups into a cup. I had no idea what he was making because a fruitachinno wasn't a thing, but judging from Mrs. Davis's pink cheeks and glassy eyes, I didn't think it would matter.

Mother Gibson held up her bag of gummies. "Pretty boy. Can you whip this into a fancy coffee drink?"

The ladies squealed with giggles.

"Alright, what's going on?"

Aunt Ginny shushed everyone and leaned in very close. She crooked her finger at Gia to come down and listen too. "You two would make beautiful babies."

"Aunt Ginny!"

She cackled. "Well, you would. . . . We bought this Easter candy at the booth around the corner." She showed me her bag of bright green gummies bearing the label MyTHiC Teddies.

I turned the bag over in my hands while the ladies stood before me and snickered. "What exactly are these— OH MY GOD! Aunt Ginny!"

The ladies howled with laughter, then shushed one another and checked behind them.

I held the bag up. "How many of these have you had? This says a serving is one bear."

Mrs. Dodson examined her almost-empty wrapper. "But they come with five in the bag."

The biddies gave me stony expressions before busting into laughter again.

I hissed at them to quiet down. "What booth did these come from?"

Mrs. Dodson lifted her cane over her head and pointed

to the bright-green canopy on the far side of the room. "The CBD booth is right over yonder. See? Where Sawyer is standing."

"That's a pole with a hemp purse hanging from the top."

Aunt Ginny took the bag from me and tucked it into her pocket. "You're not going to narc on us, are you? This is the first time in ages my hip doesn't hurt."

Gia handed Mrs. Davis a drink with whipped cream and green sprinkles on top. "You might want to be careful, ladies. That stuff is not exactly legal in New Jersey."

Her face took on the expression of a Kewpie doll before she shoved her mouth into the whipped cream and snarfed it.

I looked past Gia at his collection of secret ingredients. "When did you get green sugar?"

"St. Patrick's Day."

Mother Gibson wiggled her fingers for Gia to make her a drink identical to the one Mrs. Davis had. "There's nothing illegal about CBD oil, pretty boy. And why didn't you tell our girl you were married? What's wrong wit you, child? Don't you got any sense? She's a good girl. She's already been through enough heartache."

I dropped my head down to my arms on the counter. "Lord help me. And there's more in there than CBD oil."

I heard Aunt Ginny say, "There's Sawyer."

"I told you it's a pole." I looked up to see Sawyer running up to us holding a nest of raffle tickets.

"I got them. And we need to hurry. He's setting up now."

I gave Sawyer a pointed look. "Hi. Remember me?"

She wouldn't look me in the eye, but she grabbed my hand. "Come on. I heard there're gate crashers who made fake tickets online. We have to get our seats before the squatters get to them."

Gia handed Mother Gibson her drink and gave my arm a squeeze as Sawyer pulled me from the booth to follow the Cheech & Chong Fan Club across the Expo floor.

We found our seats in the fourth row. The biddies would normally grumble about the fact that they'd stood in line all night for tickets, so they should be in the front row, but they were surprisingly docile about the situation. They were also nibbling on Paleo Dollys that I had not sold to them.

Sawyer dug through her purse. "Look, I'm sorry I haven't been around lately." She pulled out a bag of beef jerky for me and a chocolate bar for her. "I have a lot going on right now that I can't get into here."

The lights dimmed and loud intro music started to play, so I had to lean in to be heard. "'A lot going on' like what? Why can't you answer your phone when I call?"

Sawyer hissed, "That was an accident and my phone died. I can't talk about it now. This isn't the time or the place. And I don't want you to be critical of my choices."

The jaunty music swelled like the soundtrack to a game show. Aunt Ginny shook her head. "Amateurs. This isn't good entrance music." She reached over and grabbed a handful of my jerky.

I hissed back at Sawyer, "When am I critical? I always support you."

"I'm involved in something you won't like and I just don't want you to think less of me."

"Sawyer, I'll be there for you no matter what. Besides, I don't know why you'd think I'd judge you." The music stopped abruptly, right before I belted out, "My boyfriend is married!"

Eloise from Guest Relations had microphone in hand, mouth at the ready, but she zeroed in on me. "Oops, I think you're looking for the Marriage Expo. That's next month."

The crowd laughed while I slumped down in my seat and Aunt Ginny and the biddies tittered and pointed at me.

"It is my pleasure to introduce our keynote speaker. Normally, I like to give a little background information and list some of the accolades of our guest of honor, but Dr. Rubin is a surprisingly hard man to find on the Internet. I called his office in New York and extracted a couple tidbits to share with you. Dr. Rubin is certified with the American Board of Plastic Surgery, and he's one of the premier plastic surgeons in New York City. They wouldn't tell me who any of his famous clients are, and I really tried to find out."

The audience laughed appreciatively.

"But they did tell me that Dr. Rubin specializes in aesthetic surgery of the face, nose, breast, and body, and is considered one of the best breast augmentation surgeons in the world."

Sawyer looked down her shirt. "I should give him a call."

"And now join me in welcoming Dr. Lance Rubin of Rubinesque Cosmetic Surgery to talk about aging invisibly."

The crowd cheered and Dr. Rubin took the stage with his arms outstretched. He brought his arms in and patted his heart while giving a gracious smile. Then he took the mic and gave a slight bow to Eloise. "Thank you, everyone, thank you. It's a pleasure to be here with the beautiful people of Cape May."

The applause erupted again, but somewhere in the back of the room someone shouted, "You're a butcher!"

Dr. Rubin gave a chuckle, as if he hadn't heard the outburst, and patted his hand down to settle the crowd. "It's true, I am the last holdout from social media. I prefer to address people face to face. And because the discussion is often about altering their face, it just saves time."

More laughter.

Mrs. Dodson stage-whispered to the rest of us, "Oh, he's very good."

The biddies all nodded their agreement and chomped away on their cookies.

"You know I can make you feel good about how you look, but what you may not know is that I've done several tours with Doctors Without Borders, performing humanitarian surgery on children born with cleft palates. It's some of the most rewarding work that I'm a part of—and all your boob jobs pay for it." He giggled at his own joke and everyone joined in. "I also travel all over the United States to train other surgeons in rare surgeries for children with birth defects. I'm on the road a lot, but I have an amazing team at Rubinesque who have very capable hands."

He swept his arm out to our right, and a team of ladies in white coats and top buns stood and gave subdued waves. They reminded me of the Robert Palmer musicians in the "Addicted to Love" video.

"Now, that's enough about me. You want to hear about aging invisibly."

He went on for the next half hour, talking about different discoveries and breakthroughs in the scientific community that had potential for erasing wrinkles and dark spots. And a lot of things we already knew, like staying out of the sun, eating healthy, and staying hydrated. Then he made the announcement he'd been teasing for the past few days. "But I have developed something that is light-years ahead of all that." One of the lab coats got up and glided across the stage wearing the white, plastic manne-quin face and chest shield. It was the creepy device Dr. Lance had shown me the other day, when he was trying to solicit me to get the fat sucked out of my stomach.

Sawyer took a bite of her candy bar. "Can you imagine a whole fleet of those marching into town? Weird."

"Yup."

"This is a revolutionary LED mask. Now, I know some of you are thinking, 'You didn't invent this, Dr. Lance. We've seen these in magazines.' Well, that's true, but I've worked with scientists to augment the mask with a revo-lutionary new ultraviolet setting."

The crowd murmured.

"I know you're thinking I'm crazy now, but I just might be a genius. New research shows that various ultra-violet treatments of the skin are potential therapy options for psoriasis, acne, eczema, cutaneous T-cell lymphoma. Can you imagine a life with no more injections? No more foul-smelling medicinal creams? No more beauty potions and tonics that don't work? You used to have to make an appointment at a medical clinic, where health-care pro-viders would administer UV light therapy and charge you an arm and a leg. Now, in just a few minutes a day relax-ing at home, you can heal yourself, turn back the clock, and erase years of damage."

There was an energy in the room that was hard to de-scribe. There was excitement, but something else crack-led beneath the surface. I looked around, and there were quite a few people who made their living on those potions and tonics Dr. Rubin was disparaging. I spotted Shayla one row behind me on the end. She was making that face she makes right before she laughs like a crazy person, only the laugh wasn't coming.

Dr. Lance chuckled to himself for the audience's benefit. "And that is only the beginning. I'm working with my team of biochemists to develop a radical, light-activated serum that erases cell damage and rehydrates the skin, filling it with luminous proteins. You'll glow from the inside out! It's my very own Fountain of Youth. I hope you saved your money and didn't buy too many items promising miracles and delivering disappointment in the mirror. Throw away whatever you bought this weekend, because this replaces everything! I have the breakthrough you've been waiting for."

A woman rushed the stage from the wings. "You're a dangerous fraud!" Agnes Pfeister-Pinze, the lone protestor, jabbed at the doctor. His body shook violently, and he went down in a heap.

The rent-a-cop ambled to the stage and pulled her off. He pressed a button on the walkie-talkie fastened to his shoulder. "I've got her. She used a Taser. Get the paramedics." He dragged Agnes kicking and flailing offstage.

Mother Gibson let out a loud, "Girrrl, you best get ahold of yourself!"

Mrs. Davis munched on a piece of jerky. "The security here isn't very good, is it?"

Dr. Rubin held up his arm, and the audience gasped. "I'm okay. I'm okay." He struggled to his feet. "My mouth tastes like I just got a filling, but I'm alright."

The crowd applauded, which invigorated the doctor. "The lady is clearly disturbed. I just hope she gets the help she needs. Now, I believe we have some raffle tick-

ets to call for some lucky winners to try out my revolutionary UV mask."

The white coats took the stage with a fishbowl of tickets and started pulling numbers. Sawyer had both hands
up and her fingers crossed. "Pick me, pick me."

Aunt Ginny was on the other side of me, doing the
same thing. I thought they were both crazy. You couldn't
pay me to put that thing on.

Aunt Ginny's number was called and she squealed.
"It's me. It's me!"

"Well, lucky lady, you've won a UVaderm treatment in
our studio."

Aunt Ginny rushed the stage to collect her envelope.
"UVaderm? What is it? I don't care, I want it. When can I
have it?"

Tally led her offstage, presumably to make arrange-
ments, and I looked around the room for Shayla. She had
disappeared. The beauty execs from the Lolly sheet mask
booth and the Glow Skin Care people were having a furious tête-à-tête, and angrily watching Dr. Rubin posing for
pictures with fans onstage. Even the ultra-expensive
Qualicel Beauty team was huddled up with the hippies at
Naked Skin Care.

Sawyer and I wandered through the room, each waiting for the other to speak first.

After overhearing the words "slander" and "lawsuit,"
Sawyer snickered. "He did not make any friends tonight."

"You'd think he would play nicer while they were in
the same room. Those Glow ladies look like they're planning to jump him when he goes to his car."

We arrived at the stage, where Dr. Rubin was taking
questions. He spotted me and waved me over. He pulled a
card out of the breast pocket of his jacket and slipped it to

me with a wink before going back to the gathering. I turned it over. *Meet me tomorrow morning before the Expo opens. I want to discuss a treatment with you.*

Sawyer craned her neck to read my card. "What's that all about?"

I shoved the card in my purse. "He wants me to get liposuction."

"Why?"

"Because he thinks it will fix what's wrong with me."

"That's ridiculous. You're perfect the way you are."

"I don't feel perfect. I feel like a lone watermelon in a field of asparagus."

"Ew. Who wants to be an asparagus?"

"Do you think Gia would rather I look . . . like you?"

Sawyer stopped walking. "Truthfully? If Gia wanted someone who looks like me, he could have had me. I had a lot of lattes the first couple of months after Kurt and I broke up. He never made a move. I think he's interested in something unique to you, and it has nothing to do with your weight."

We started walking again and finished a lap of the room on small talk. When we made it back to our chairs, Sawyer sat down. "I'm sorry I wasn't here to help the other day."

"I didn't need your help, I needed you. I miss you."

I spotted Aunt Ginny scanning the room. I caught her eye, and she made a beeline for me. She held up a new bag from the CBD booth. "I went back and bought some more. I took a twenty from your purse on the floor."

I let that sink in, then held up my arm to show Aunt Ginny my purse hanging from my elbow.

Her eyes grew big and she looked at an open, brown

pocketbook on the floor in front of her chair. Then she squinted at the red purse hanging from my arm. "I gotta go."

Sawyer chuckled. "I'll walk her home to make sure she gets there okay. I parked at your house anyway."

"Okay, but when can we talk?"

Sawyer hustled after Aunt Ginny. "I'll call you; I promise."

I was heading back to the La Dolce Vita booth to help close down for the night when my purse vibrated. "That was fast."

It was a text from Amber. **Where are you? Meet me at the Marquis, now!**

Now? Geez, Amber, it's late. I texted Gia to say that I had an emergency and had to go. He sent me a heart emoji and said he'd see me in the morning. On my way out to the boardwalk, I spotted Stubby. He looked like he was having a deep discussion with a woman, almost intimate.

I was trying to work up the courage to say hello to him, especially since there would be an eyewitness if he felt I disrespected him and he wanted to whack me. A car honked, and the woman turned her face into the light. It was Alex.

CHAPTER 18

Like a fancy yacht bobbing in an ocean of bed and breakfasts, the Marquis de Lafayette was one of Cape May's oldest hotels. The ambling, six-story white building had rows and rows of oceanfront balconies awash in the neon-blue glow of the center tower scrollwork. I stood in the parking lot wondering what Alex was doing talking to the man who does security for Gia and waiting for Amber to mosey along with this emergency she had.

A lime-green car the size of a playpen pulled up and the horn squeaked out a *wheet whee!* The car had enough dents and dings to look like it played goalie for the Flyers, and there was a basketball-size doughnut of rust just behind the passenger-side door. I squatted down to look through the window, hoping to find a lost Canadian looking for directions. My heart sank when Amber waved me in.

Her car looked like it had been on spring break without her. I had to move several empty McDonald's bags to find the seat. Then a spring poked through the cloth and jabbed me in the butt, causing me to jump and hit my head on the ceiling, the lining of which was being held up by about a hundred red, white, and blue thumbtacks in the design of the Union Jack.

"Would you get settled? We don't have a lot of time for this."

"Good God, Amber, where did you get this car?"

"It's a hand-me-down."

"From who? Abraham Lincoln?"

"I've had it since college."

"I didn't know you went to college."

"Well, I did . . . for almost a whole year."

"Oh."

"Okay, give me a break. It wasn't for me."

"What, I didn't say anything." After several yanks I wrangled my seat belt in place. There was a lot of crunching happening under my feet, and discarded wrappers were sticking to my shoes. I started collecting the plastic bags and cellophane and stuffing them into an empty Slurpee cup.

Amber wove through the streets like we were being chased. When she flew through a red light in an empty intersection, I felt my stomach give me a tweak. "Are you allowed to do that when you're off-duty?" *Or on duty?*

"We're in a hurry."

"Yeah, I'll be sure to use that the next time I get pulled over." I felt like I was riding in a thirteen-year-old boy's bedroom. I didn't really get nervous until I noticed the lack of a passenger-side airbag. And the fire extinguisher behind the driver's seat. And the outline of the word Pinto above the glove box. I lurched, and my seat belt clutched me in a death grip.

"What's wrong with you?"

"Holy crap, Amber! Is this one of those cars that explodes when it's rear-ended?"

"Calm down . . . I have a fire extinguisher. It probably still works."

I twisted my head in circles and let my neck pop. "Where are we going?"

"I need you to do some recon. Things have escalated in the last twenty-four hours. This did not just blow over like the chief assured me it would. Internal Affairs is now involved, and they've sent Kieran Dunne. He's a hatchet man. If he's involved, someone up the food chain believes I'm guilty, and they sent him to take me down. I had a deposition today, and it was not just a formality."

I held on to the dashboard because it was the only area that didn't look sticky. "Are you worried?"

She snapped a look at me. "I've asked *you* to help me, haven't I? That's somewhere around my ninth circle of Hell."

I muttered peevishly to myself, "No offense taken."

Amber dug around under her seat and pulled out an open bag of nacho cheese Combos. She blew some dust out of the bag and offered me one.

"No thank you." *Speaking of ninth circles of Hell.*

She took a handful and popped them in her mouth. "I need you to search the victim's apartment. I have a box of latex gloves in there." She pointed her Combos bag at the glove compartment. "See what looks out of place to you. The cops will have turned off the AC and the lights, but they won't have touched anything else. That door doesn't open from the inside, so you can stop trying."

We had pulled up to a red light in North Cape May and I was yanking on the handle like Ted Bundy was in the driver's seat. "I didn't sign on for breaking and entering."

Amber put her hand on my arm. It would have been a nice moment, except she was pinching me like we were in fourth grade again. "I don't ask you for a lot, McAllister."

"Ow. You're hurting me."

"Look, when you're done with this, I'll owe you one, okay?"

I relaxed my grip on the door and she relaxed hers on the back of my arm. "I don't even know what I'm looking for."

"You have good instincts. Just look around and see what you think. And whatever you do, don't turn the lights on. The neighbor across the hall doesn't miss anything."

I dug out the gloves, along with a package of Chocodiles that had been discontinued during the Clinton administration, and held them up to the light. "You have a problem, you know that?"

Amber grabbed the chocolate-covered Twinkies. "Don't touch my snacks. I paid a fortune for those on eBay."

She gave me the rundown of where Temarius Jackson's apartment was in the HUD building, which housed a lot of senior citizens and people with disabilities, then rattled off a list of what not to do once inside. We pulled into a dimly lit parking lot behind the Bay Vista Apartments, a brown-brick building on the edge of the Villas. A plastic ShopRite bag skipped around a brown dumpster.

Iron bars guarded the windows on the ground floor and only two apartments on the upper levels had lights on.

I took a breath and willed my stomach to stop quivering.

Amber gave me a nod.

I nodded back. "You ready?"

"Ready for what? I'm waiting here."

"You're not coming with me?"

"McAllister, if I could go in there, I wouldn't need you. If you get caught, it's trespassing. You'll do community service, and honestly, with Aunt Ginny as a defense, it'll be time served. If I get caught, I'll look like I'm tampering with evidence. I could go to jail for that alone."

I gave a huff and manually cranked down my window, then shoved my arm out to open the door from the outside.

"Thank you. I'll be right here the whole time."

Ducky.

The lobby was nothing to write home about. I'd seen cheerier laundry rooms. I walked three flights up the dank stairwell to the fourth floor while I mentally prepared my defense about how I was on unofficial police duty for a cop on administrative leave and not really breaking into the apartment. I was met by a lone flickering bulb and the feeling that a set of creepy twins holding hands would be at the end of the hall. Amber had said that Temarius's apartment was number 412, the second door on the left. It was also the only one with a crisscross of yellow police tape blocking the entrance. I put on my latex gloves and tried the doorknob. Locked. I pulled my wallet out of my bra and took out my Torrid credit card, then reconsidered. *I can't live without that one.* I put it back and used the Home Depot card instead. There was a gap at the latch where the doorjamb was splintered, and wood was chipped away. This wasn't the first break-in the apartment had seen.

I wiggled my credit card around like I'd seen on *Charlie's Angels*, but all I achieved was breaking off a corner. *How did Farrah Fawcett do this in a miniskirt and go-go boots?*

I was getting irritated and about to go tell Amber I needed a screwdriver when I heard a click. I was able to force the latch aside and the door creaked open under its own weight. I climbed through the spiderweb of police tape, which in my mind looked just like Angelina Jolie climbing through a laser maze, and gently closed the door behind me.

It took a moment to find the button on the flashlight. There were a few evidence tags around the room. By the couch. On the wall behind the couch. On the air conditioner. The room smelled like wet dog and burnt hair. Someone had left bologna and cheese on the kitchen counter, and a half-eaten sandwich sat on the coffee table. The front door had a tower of dead bolts and a chain that were intact, so they must not have been set when the killer entered.

I walked over to the couch and scanned it. There was a very obvious hole in the back of the cushion, and the fabric around it was much darker and looked gummy and sticky. I peeked into the bedroom in the back. It was a mess. Not a somebody-tossed-this-room-looking-for-stuff mess, but a teenager-lives-here mess. Bed not made, basketball on the floor next to a pile of dirty laundry. A stack of graphic novels on the nightstand.

The only evidence in the bathroom was that this boy didn't do much cleaning, but there was nothing damning. Toothpaste, toothbrush, Scope, Axe body spray.

Across the hall was a second bedroom. The room was tidy, the bed was neatly made, and there was a Bible and a devotional on the bedside table.

I went back to the living room and looked at the couch again. I touched it. My glove was brown and wet—the cushion was soaked. For some reason that made my heart break for the boy who had died here. I didn't even know him, but everything in his apartment screamed *I'm just a kid*.

There was a pillow smooshed into the corner of the couch. Out of habit, I tugged it out to fluff it up, and something hard fell to the floor between the frame. I reached under the couch and fished out a cell phone. The battery was at 5 percent, but the screen displayed one text message at 5:27 a.m. I clicked the envelope. **"OMW."** I checked his call log to see if Amber's number showed up, but there was only one number in and out. No contact info. No name. Just a 647 area code. I stuffed the cell in my pocket to give it to Amber. It's not like she gave me evidence bags—although if you're someone who carries a box of latex gloves in the car, how far-fetched would some Ziploc baggies be? I just wanted to get out of there. This would have to be enough.

I flicked the switch on the flashlight and the room went dark. I froze with my hand on the doorknob as glowing blue tracks from the chair to the front door were brightening before my eyes.

CHAPTER 19

I peeled off my gloves and shoved them in my pocket, then raced down the stairs, preparing to run for the car. Blue lights bounced off the lobby walls. Why were the cops here? I wanted to find somewhere to hide, but it would only be a matter of time before they came inside. I slipped through the exit and ducked behind a giant box-wood with a sock sticking out of it. Two police cruisers were blocking the back exit of the parking lot. Amber was pushed up against a black-and-white by the dumpster. Her hands were being cuffed behind her back by the policewoman I'd heard Amber call Crabtree at the winery. We hadn't formerly met, so she probably didn't know I was the harbinger of death to Cape May County yet. It seemed wise to keep it that way.

Amber was pulled away from the car and her face turned toward the door. She was watching for me. Our eyes met and she shook her head no ever so slightly.

The officers were pointing to the apartment building. I had a sick feeling they were heading over here any second. I skirted the edge of the parking lot in the shadows and tried a couple cars until I found an unlocked Oldsmobile. I got in behind the wheel and pulled the door gently closed. I crouched down in the front seat and kept my eyes glued to the rearview mirror. They hadn't noticed me.

A very pale, blond officer with gloved hands held up a gun and dropped it into a plastic bag as Amber was guided into the back seat of the police cruiser. An attractive-looking, dark-haired man in a suit leaned down to her window and said something. Amber didn't answer; she turned her face and looked the other way.

Officer Crabtree climbed into the front of the cruiser and the suit patted the top of the car. She sped off, while the remaining officers continued their search of the dumpster and surrounding area. All the while the suit leaned against an unmarked black sedan with his hands in his pockets and silently watched.

My heart started to pound when the officer who'd found the gun headed my way, his flashlight bouncing off the mirror in the Olds. He moved toward Amber's car and poked around. After a few minutes of searching he rolled up the windows and slammed the doors shut.

After a quick powwow in front of the dumpster they all eventually packed it in and drove off.

My butt had glued itself to the vinyl seat, afraid to move even though the cops were gone. With all that activity surely some of the neighbors were watching the parking lot. I had to calm the pace of my heart. *What if they forgot something and they come back right when I open the door?* I held my breath to listen for tires on pavement.

I shook my hands out and sucked in a breath. I had to leave the safety of the giant car and put myself under the dim parking lot lights, exposed for all with really good eyesight to see. I rolled out to the pavement. I tried to play it cool but trotted more than walked over to Amber's death-trap car only to find the doors locked. And there was my purse. Dumped out on the passenger seat.

I looked around. Where is a metal coat hanger when you need one? How was I going to get home? I needed to call for help. I was several blocks away from a liquor store, and the low-end retail shops were all closed. I looked back at the two apartment windows with flickering lights indicating that someone was home and sighed.

Back inside and up to the third floor. I knocked on a few doors where I could distinctively hear the hum of a television, but no one answered. On up to the fourth floor, I worked my way back down the hall. The first apartment with light filtering out from under the door was directly across from Temarius's. The nameplate said Idel Rotnitzky. I used the knocker and waited. Muffled footsteps headed toward me, then paused. "Who is it?"

"Hi. I'm so sorry to bother you, but I'm a bit stranded. I've locked myself out of my car. Could I use your phone to call someone? Or could you call for me?"

After a few seconds a series of *thunks* and clicks worked their way down the other side of the door, and it cracked open the length of the chain. A watery blue eye peeked out over a wrinkled cheek, scanned me, and shut the door again. After a swipe of the chain, it opened to a little old lady in a pink-flowered housedress. She was wearing bright-pink Reebok cross-trainers, and the fifteen strands of gunmetal silver hair she had left were wound up in pink foam curlers. "I don't usually let strangers in except the Girl Scouts during cookie season. You don't have any Thin Mints, do ya?"

"I'm sorry, I don't."

"How about Tagalongs?"

"Uh-uh."

She shrugged and let me into the room. "What are you doing out here? You don't live in the building."

"I was visiting a friend."

She eyed me skeptically. "Then why didn't you ask your friend to use their phone?"

Wow, that's a good question. "Well, I came to visit, but my friend isn't home."

She narrowed her eyes. "Who's your friend?"

I had no doubt that Mrs. Rotnitzky knew the name of every resident and their exact schedule of comings and goings by heart. She would sniff out a lie like Figaro sniffs out that I'm eating lunch meat. "I came to see your neighbor, Temarius Jackson, but there's police tape barring his door. Do you know what happened?"

Her mouth turned down and she headed into the living room. "Oh me. That's a sad one. The phone's over there." She pointed to a cordless phone on top of a stack of crossword puzzle books on the coffee table. "Come on in and sit down, just not on the BarcaLounger—that's for Ed."

I looked around the studio apartment. "Is Ed your husband?"

"Was my husband. Ed's dead." She dropped into an upholstered, green rocking chair and picked up a glass. "But he still visits. Care for some Jack and Coke?"

I picked the phone up and dialed Sawyer. "No thank you."

"Good. I'm running low on Jack and my Social Security didn't deposit yet. So, you're friends with Temarius?"

I nodded. Sawyer's phone rang once and she picked it up.

"Any chance you can come get me in the Villas?"

"In the Villas? What are you doing there? Milky Way is closed."

Mrs. Rotnitzky was eyeing me closely. "My car broke down when I came to visit our friend Temarius and I locked my purse inside."

"What the . . . ? Oh-kaaay. Give me the address."

I walked over to the window and looked out to be sure I could see the parking lot from here. Amber's car was still sitting there like a lame green grasshopper, so it hadn't been towed yet. *I bet it could fit in the dumpster.* I told Sawyer where I was. "Honk twice when you're back there. And bring a metal coat hanger."

I smiled at Mrs. Rotnitzky and eased myself down to the worn moleskin couch. The cushions were clean but threadbare, as most things in the room were shabby chic without the chic. "Did you know Temarius well?"

She shrugged and took a swig of her drink. "Are you a social worker? Or maybe a hooker?"

I blinked a couple times, not sure I'd heard her right. "Am I a what?"

"You know, a streetwalker. Why would a middle-aged woman be visiting that boy this late at night?"

I looked down at my flowing, emerald tunic and black jeans. *Why do people keep asking me that?*

She shook the ice around her glass and shrugged. "People are into some weird stuff nowadays. Maybe they're into chubby prostitutes that look like soccer moms."

I'm gonna let the chubby part go on account of the mom part. "No. I've done some work with the Teen Center, baking cookies for their fundraisers, and I met Temarius there." Okay that was half true. I never actually met him, but I was pretty sure I'd seen him once or twice. How many kids named Temarius could there be in the Villas?

She put her glass down and reached into the pocket of her rocker to pull out half a bottle of Jack Daniel's. She poured herself a hefty shot of whiskey. "So, you bake?"

That's what you got out of that? "Do you want me to get you the Coke?"

She shook her head. "I'm outta Coke."

Sawyer better be on her way. "Do you know what happened across the hall?"

She kept rocking in her chair. "Someone murdered that boy."

"How do you know it wasn't suicide?"

She peered at me over her glass. "You don't seem surprised. Are you a cop? What am I sayin'? No cop would dress like that. Social worker, then. It's about time. You're too late, but then, I heard you all don't get paid much." Her mind had wandered off and I tried to bring her back.

"You were telling me you knew it was murder."

"I know it was murder because I pay attention. I keep my eyes on the window and my ear on the door all day. Nothing gets by me in my building. We take care of each other here. Plus, you never know when the Girl Scouts will come by. I heard the shots and called it in myself."

"You heard the shots?"

She pointed to the window behind me. "I heard the shots while I was watching my program."

"The shots came from outside? Not across the hall?"

She stopped rocking and gave me a long, watery look. "No, no, it was definitely across the hall." She took a swig of her Jack and Coke sans the Coke.

"Do you remember what time that was?"

She let the rocker propulsion nod her head for her. "Around nine. My program came on and I called 9-1-1 as soon as it went to commercial."

I leaned over my knees to look her in the cataracts. "Did Temarius have any enemies?"

She shrugged. "Don't think so."

"Did you hear him argue with anyone the day he died?"

She shook her head. "No. He was a good boy. He'd help carry the groceries in. And he never threw a loud party or tried to sell me magazine subscriptions."

"When the police arrived did they ask you if you'd seen anyone?"

"Oh yeah, sure."

"And what did you tell them?"

"The only one I'd seen all night was that little blond woman."

CHAPTER 20

Sawyer had finally arrived around the bottom of the bottle of Jack Daniel's. By then Mrs. Rotnitzky had changed her mind twice on where the gunshots had come from and exactly what time she'd seen the blond woman. The only thing she was sure of last night was that Temarius was dead and the Lotto Pick-3 number was 0-0-6.

I didn't get to bed until midnight because Sawyer and I were making a pros and cons list of whether we should trust Amber. My top pro reason was that the animosity had been at a manageable level lately. I was almost ready to say Amber and I had turned a corner on mutual hatred and were tiptoeing toward respected acquaintance. But Sawyer made such a good argument that if Amber was guilty, she'd be looking for a scapegoat. And what better scapegoat than a former murder suspect who had *unintentionally* made Amber look like a fool at a few crime scenes?

Around four a.m. I woke with my heart pounding and the fear that Amber had sent me into Temarius's apartment to retrieve evidence that I'd almost given to her. What if the only number in his cell was hers? There were no photos, no games, not even a password. Nothing to personalize the cheap little phone that must have been a burner now sealed in a sandwich baggie on my dresser. Isn't that what drug dealers and human traffickers do? Use burner phones? I Googled the area code; 647 was Toronto.

Once my adrenaline was peaked, I found myself waiting for the police to show up and arrest me as an accessory to murder. The wind blew a branch across the side of the house and I almost went into cardiac arrest. So, I'd gotten out of bed and done all the things. The yoga things, the beauty things, and the cleaning things. Then I went downstairs to clear my head and make a few batches of Paleo muffins for the Expo. The turnout had been better than we'd expected and I was concerned we would run out of food by tomorrow if I didn't supplement the stock.

I yawned and pushed the button on my espresso machine and pulled a shot. I was dragging this morning. I kept trying to pull out my phone only to be reminded that I didn't have it. It was either locked in Amber's car or confiscated by the police. My attempt to pull the lock with a wire hanger only resulted in a broken wire hanger.

I opened the laptop on the kitchen table to check my email. We had a couple reservation requests and some questions about amenities. One person wanted to know if our pet-friendly status included snakes. *Definitely not. And no birds, insects, or reptiles of any kind, just for future reference.*

I checked our page on Facebook and had to laugh. I

kept scrolling past ads for a website called Fraudster. Since Google tracks everywhere we go, my ads were usually for gluten-free flour and bras. *What in the world has Aunt Ginny been looking up?*

I checked the reservation book for tomorrow's afternoon tea and saw that all twenty tables had been booked for both seatings. I'd be up half the night making scones.

The sound of keys jangling at the back door caused me to turn my head.

"Hey, butt face. Why are you up so early? I thought you liked sleeping in while Ginny and Victory do the real work."

My mind was foggy from too little sleep, too much espresso, and the new silver hoop displayed in Joanne's nose, so all I could do was stare.

"You noticed my new bling. I just got it on the boardwalk last night. I'm not getting any younger, so I figured it's now or never."

"So 'never' was a sincere option?"

"Shut up. You don't have any taste."

"I also don't have Hep C, so I think that's a win."

Something furry was galloping overhead. It ran back and forth, then hurtled down the stairs. I expected Figaro to come sliding around the corner, but this floof was white and had a pink, diamond-studded collar around her neck. "Portia?"

Bright-green eyes watched me intently. "Merrooow."

"Wow. You are gorgeous. How'd you get out?"

The answer appeared behind her in a pair of bright orange eyes with a toy mouse in his mouth.

"What did you do?"

A shrill "Porrr-tiaaa," cried out above us.

"Uh-oh. Your absence has been discovered."

Portia sat pretty and raised a paw to me.

Figaro dropped the mouse at Portia's feet and eyed her expectantly.

She stepped over the mouse and sat on it, refusing to look at him.

He flopped over, and I nudged him with my foot. "She wasn't impressed, buddy."

"Porrr-tiaaa!"

Joanne tied a frilly, pink apron around her combat fatigues. "You better go tell that lady her cat is down here before she wakes up the whole house."

That was Aunt Ginny's cue to stumble into the kitchen from her bedroom. "What is that racket?"

I gently picked up the white Persian and carried her to the steps. "She's down here with us." Portia swatted playfully at my nose.

Patsy Parker appeared at the top of the steps in a silver silk robe with a matching eye mask pushed up on her forehead. "Oh my heavens." She ran down the stairs on Miss Piggy style feather pump slippers "You can't hold her like that. She'll get mats." She took the cat from my arms and held her like a running back carries a football.

"I'm sorry."

"Do you have any idea how she got out of her room?"

My own floof of gray fur rubbed up against my ankles. *I have a pretty good idea.* "Are you sure you shut the door all the way? The knobs are antique and they don't always latch right." *I suspect any paw could be shoved under the frame and pull the door open.* "You need to make sure you use the top lock."

She stroked Portia's head. "I guess we forgot to lock the door. Thank goodness Cape May has so little crime."

I tightened my mouth shut so I wouldn't blurt out

anything not tourism friendly, like my house being in the epicenter of murder. "Mm-hmm. Well, I'll see you at breakfast."

She cooed to Portia that she was a naughty girl all the way up to her room.

When I got back to the kitchen Joanne was taking my cherry brandy muffins out of the oven and putting in a pan of homemade cinnamon buns. "Ooh, are the cinnamon buns gluten-free?"

Joanne stuck her tongue out. "Eww, no."

Aunt Ginny held up a cup of coffee. "Bailey's is gluten-free."

"I'll keep that in mind."

"Oh, that reminds me. Gia called on the house phone last night. He said he'd been trying to get ahold of you and you weren't answering your cell."

"My cell phone was confiscated. I have to see if I can get it back or if it's been logged into evidence."

Joanne didn't look up from the shallots she was mincing. "Who'd you kill now?"

"It's a long story, but if the cops show up to arrest me, I was mugged by a pushy little blonde. What did Gia want?"

Aunt Ginny peered over her cup with a look that said she would demand details later. "He said he can't pick you up this morning. He has something he has to take care of."

"Did he say what it was?"

"Nope. I tried to get it out of him, but he was very shifty."

Voices carried in from the dining room. The guests were early for breakfast again. I filled the carafe with coffee and went in to greet them. Rita and Faelynn had mugs at the ready and they had already staked out their seats at the table.

"Good morning, ladies. How did you sleep?"

"Wonderful." Rita held her cup and I poured for her first. "Is it always so quiet here?"

My mind flashed to block parties during the season. "I think you're here at a good time. Things can get very rowdy in the summer."

Faelynn took off her glasses and polished them. "Well, I thought I heard a gunshot last night outside my window."

Rita gave her a look. "You imagine things"

"I do not. There was a loud pop, and then I heard someone crying in the yard."

I put the carafe down and went to check outside. Rabbitzilla was lying in another heap on my new pansies. *Aunt Ginny will be on the warpath.* I shut the door to buy myself some time from Aunt Ginny finding out and returned to the ladies. Patsy and Dale had just joined them. They were discussing what they had done yesterday. Patsy and Dale went to the local organic pet store in search of cat perfume. *Is that a thing?* And Rita and Faelynn went to a couple of art galleries, then art shopping on the Mall. They wanted to know what I had done.

I didn't want to ruin the magic by telling them I'd refilled all the toilet paper in their rooms. "Did anyone check out the Beauty Expo at Convention Hall?" I hadn't seen any of them, but I could have missed them while we were busy.

Rita blinked a couple times. "Honestly, I forgot all about it. How is it?"

"It's nice. There are a lot of vendors for skin care and cosmetics."

Faelynn looked at me. "I don't know. How have the crowds been? Is there anything there worth seeing? Anyone famous?"

"Well," I started, "there's a cosmetic surgeon who's supposedly been on *Good Morning America*. He gave a talk last night. I think everyone loved him."

Rita looked at Faelynn. "Interesting. What do you think, Fae? Should we check it out?"

Joanne brought in a tray of yogurt parfaits and a basket of cherry muffins. Faelynn had her hand on the basket before Joanne had a chance to put them down. "Beauty stuff is not my thing, Rita. You know that. I prefer to age naturally. I heard there's a colonial village that has a working farm. And there's a bakery nearby. Let's do that."

Rita took a parfait and placed it in the middle of her plate. "Honestly, Fae, if I ate like you, I'd have to wear a circus tent."

Faelynn took a scoop of brandy butter. "I know. Genetics aren't fair."

Dale snapped out a cloth napkin like a marine was going to bounce a quarter off his lap. "We have a preshow event with Portia this afternoon, so this morning will be her spa day. We want her to be relaxed and fluffy."

Patsy passed Dale the orange juice. "She's on a strict diet of salmon and kale with a little egg yolk so her coat will be glossy."

Joanne snorted and I cleared my throat to cover it. "Well, I hope you and Portia have a wonderful day."

I ushered Joanne back to the kitchen and waited for the swinging door to close. "You can't make fun of the guests, Joanne. At least not in front of them."

She rolled her eyes and pointed to the floor. "Look."

There, at Aunt Ginny's feet, was Portia snarfing down a bowl of Fancy Feast.

I grabbed Joanne's arm. "You can't feed her! They have her on a strict diet."

"Uh . . . I didn't feed her, butt face. I fed him. She just pushed him aside and he let her."

Figaro sat behind Portia, letting her have his breakfast while he watched on adoringly.

Portia, on the other hand, ate like it was the first day of fat camp and her bunkmate had sneaked in a layer cake. So I've been told.

I picked her up and she swatted my hand. Once I'd deposited her in the lap of her owners, I grabbed my purse and the four bakery boxes Aunt Ginny had packed and shot through the foyer. I almost tossed my muffins when I tripped over a paper bag wedged in the screen door. Inside was my purse and cell phone, with a note from Amber saying to wait for her call. *Pssh!*

I called Smitty to report another hate crime against Benjamin Bunny while I walked the two blocks to Convention Hall. He promised to come with another emergency patch kit, suggested we give Benjamin Bunny last rites instead, and gave me a nyuck, nyuck, nyuck before hanging up.

I was the first vendor to arrive for the day. The security guard clocked my badge and unlocked the door to let me in. It felt weird being in that giant hall all by myself. It was too quiet. Like being locked in the Mall after closing. You don't realize how safe you feel having other people around until they're gone. As I got closer, I could see that something was wrong. La Dolce Vita's booth was tossed, and someone had written "Paleo Fraud" on our banner and bakery case with black marker.

Tears stung my eyes, but I refused to cry. I took a few pictures with my cell phone and cleaned up the mess. Blue, yellow, pink, and green sweetener packets littered the floor like someone had used them for confetti at a Weight Watchers weigh-in. Straws, stirrers, and cup sleeves were tossed in the trash, unrecoverable. I cleaned up a stack of napkins, and a dime rolled to the floor. When I squatted down to pick it up, I spotted a brass button on the bottom shelf of the cabinet. It had CIA stamped on it. Culinary Institute of America. This was a button from a chef coat, but was it Tim's or Gigi's? *Why?* The tears slipped from my eyes while I was hidden under the cover of our booth. *Did Tim and Gigi do this together? Or was it just Gigi? But why now? She got what she wanted. Was she one of those people who couldn't be happy unless everyone else was miserable?*

I put the button on the shelf with the lids. I'd decide what to do with it later. Maybe it was because I was feeling extra vulnerable or maybe it was because I struggled to pull myself up after sitting on the floor for ten minutes, but I made a decision to have that consultation with Dr. Rubin this morning after all. Gia might like how I looked, but I didn't.

I bagged a couple muffins and headed to the Rubinesque booth. I let myself in through the main tent entrance and was beaten in the head with strobe lights, as if I'd entered an underground nightclub. Not that I would know what that was like exactly, but I'd seen it on TV. I held my arm up to shield my face from the flashing. As my eyes adjusted, I could see that the Rubinesque booth had been ransacked worse than ours. Boxes and tubes of skin-care products were strewn all over the place. Client postcards littered the floor like my sugar packets. And hot-pink paper had been shredded like Easter grass.

"Dr. Rubin, are you here?" There was no answer, so I followed the flashes to his treatment room and called him again. "Dr. Rubin?"

The treatment room smelled like someone had burned a ham—that acrid smell that comes from boiling sugar until it looks like charcoal. I looked around to see where it was coming from, and that's when one of the creepy masks looked back at me. It was lying on a treatment bed, flashing through several colors, with smoke pouring out from the eyes. The bed was lumpy, and I had a sinking feeling that I knew what I would find under the sheet. I only lifted a corner, but I would recognize that blue star sapphire anywhere. I reached for his wrist and didn't find a pulse. This had to be Dr. Lance Rubin and he was most definitely dead.

I scrambled out of the room and down the hall to the exit. No way was I getting caught at another crime scene. Not after the cops had seen my purse and phone and ID last night in Amber's car. I was getting out of there, and if anyone asked, I don't know what that smell is. I made it to the entrance and had my hand on the tent flap when someone knocked me off my feet and ran past me. I landed on my hip with a thud and hit my head on the front desk. "Hey! Come back here!"

CHAPTER 21

I considered bolting anyway, but whoever had just flown out of here could ID me. Plus, the Convention Hall staff knew I was in the building; security had logged me in the book. Vendors were setting up for the day on the other side of this canvas freak show. Surely someone would see me leaving the crime scene and report it. "Sugar! Sugar! SUGAR! Not again!" I pulled out my phone and called 9-1-1, then moved outside the tent to wait for the police.

Eventually, Kevin came by with a fancy-looking lumberjack carrying a case of beard oils. I waved him over and told him to get Eloise immediately. He asked why, and I said my booth was vandalized. I might want to sue. She showed up faster than it took Gia to pull a shot of espresso.

"Are you flippin' kidding me?" Eloise tried to push past me into the Rubinesque tent when I'd told her what had happened, and I grabbed her arm.

"You don't want to go in there. When the police arrive you'll be contaminating the crime scene, and trust me, you don't want to start off on that foot with them." *God knows I've never fully gotten past it.*

When Officers Birkwell and Consuelos arrived a few minutes later, they canceled the paramedics and bumped the call to the county coroner. Eloise and I were kept inside Dr. Rubin's tent to maintain some level of discretion from curious vendors who had slipped into Convention Hall before the building was locked down. We waited in awkward silence.

The coroner was a woman about my age, of medium height with an aquiline nose. She came wearing a black jacket that said CORONER across the back, and she seemed to be having one heck of a time examining the body. Dr. Rubin's revolutionary beauty mask was fused to his face and the power supply was crushed like it had been smashed with a hammer. She unplugged the device and the mask stopped flashing through its settings. When she peeled it off, his skin was badly burned, but the underside of the mask was glowing bright blue. "What the devil . . . ?" She took a scalpel and scraped glowing blue ooze from inside the mask and held it up to the light, where it faded, then away from the light, where it got brighter.

The police photographer was snapping pictures like he was working the red carpet at the Grauman's Chinese Theatre. Even Birkwell and Consuelos took a moment to rubberneck.

"I've seen a lot of things in my time on the force," Birkwell said to Consuelos, "but that's a new one."

Consuelos let out a low whistle. "What do you think it is?"

"I can't even begin to imagine."

The coroner packed up her tools and stepped away from the body. "I'm sorry, fellas, I need to get this one in the lab before I can determine the cause of death and whether or not it was murder."

Officer Birkwell looked at the treatment table in disbelief. "You don't think he did that to himself, do you?"

She pulled off a pair of goggles and removed her hairnet, releasing shoulder-length, rich brown hair. "I don't think anything yet. I'll call you when I figure it out."

Officer Birkwell pulled out his notebook, and we moved on to the statement portion of the morning.

"Why were you in Dr. Rubin's tent so early?"

"He invited me here for a private consultation."

Officer Birkwell gave me a suggestive look. "What kind of consultation?"

I was so humiliated. I'd rather let him think what he was thinking was the reason. "He suggested I have a simple procedure."

"What kind of procedure?"

"Lllpsushhh."

"I'm sorry, what was that?"

I felt a little piece of my pride die. "Liposuction. He suggested I should get my stomach done. . . ." I trailed off, feeling my cheeks get hot.

Officer Birkwell made a note on his pad.

"Don't write that down!"

He cracked a slight grin. "Do you have anything to back that up?"

"He gave me a card. It's in my purse."

"Go get it."

"Now? Do you need to come with me?"

"I know where you live."

I ran to my booth and pulled out my purse from where I'd stashed it behind the boxes of milk. I dumped the contents on the counter and fished around for the business card. It wasn't there. I was frantic now. That was my only alibi to explain why I was in Dr. Rubin's tent before the Expo opened. *Amber's car. It must be there.* I trudged my way back to the crime scene, ready to face the music. "I know this will sound weird . . ."

"I expected nothing less."

"I kind of lost the card, but I'm pretty sure I know where it is."

He made a note. "Okay. Call me when you find it. You still have my number?"

"Umm, yeah." *That was easy. Why was that so easy?*

Eloise wasn't doing as well with Officer Consuelos. Her top bun had completely unraveled and she was chewing on some of her hair.

The team from the coroner's department rolled the covered stretcher out through the tent flap and Officer Birkwell flipped to a new page in his notebook. "Did you see anyone else in the tent this morning when you arrived for your consultation?"

I could tell by the way his cheek quirked that he was trying not to laugh at me some more. "Someone was in Dr. Rubin's office and ran from the tent before I could get a look at them. They hip-checked me into the front desk."

"Can you describe them?"

"No. Only that they . . ."

"What?"

"Well . . . they smelled like roses. But there's rose-scented stuff all over the Expo, so it could be anyone who has been in here."

He stared at me for a moment, then let it go. "Did you

witness the deceased in any fights, arguments, or altercations this week?"

"He did get tased by an angry lady with a botched face-lift during his keynote."

That got a good eyebrow lift out of him.

"And he pissed off a lot of exhibitors with his speech. He said that his breakthrough would make all their products obsolete."

He made a few notes on his pad and it gave me a moment to overhear Eloise giving her statement to Officer Consuelos.

"You'd have to ask the security guard who did the precheck this morning. I was running late and arrived just before we were set to open. If Kevin hadn't told me we had an emergency, I would have opened the doors to the public."

"Where were you last night?"

"Last night? Why? Does that matter?"

"It might."

"I was home. Alone."

"How about convention security?"

"We had to fire our security company after a break-in. The new company didn't have anyone available for overnight. You guys were supposed to be patrolling from midnight until six a.m. Didn't you see anything?"

"Nothing was reported, ma'am. If there was a break-in, it may have happened between the patrols."

Officer Birkwell shut his notepad and slid it into his pocket, then he and Officer Consuelos told us to sit tight while they called the station.

Once they were out of earshot Eloise dropped her head in her hands. "We can't cancel. Dr. Rubin was the event backer. This whole thing was his baby, and we've only been given a deposit. I don't know if we'll ever be able to collect the balance now. Who do I call? His office? His lawyer? His wife? If we cancel the rest of the event, people will demand their money back. We'll go bankrupt."

I put my hand on her shoulder. "Let's not borrow tomorrow's trouble. The coroner didn't even rule it a homicide yet."

Kevin poked his head into the tent and scanned for Eloise. "Hey. It's getting ugly out there. The doors are still locked, and that rent-a-cop is standing guard at the entrance. He's not letting anyone in or out. Not even exhibitors who arrived late."

Eloise gave Kevin a sharp look. "You're going to have to figure it out. I'm stuck in here."

"Ticket holders are lined up down the block. They're getting antsy for samples and scalp massages. What do I do? They're starting to form an angry mob and demand free eye cream."

Eloise threw her hands up. "I don't know! Go get some of that lavender stuff from the essential oil lady and mist them with it. She said it's calming!"

He ducked back out, and Officer Birkwell approached Eloise. "I spoke with the chief, and until the coroner rules the death a homicide, we can't require you to postpone the event; however, that room is off-limits for the rest of the weekend. Officer Consuelos and I will stay today for crowd control."

Eloise crumpled into a heap. "Oh, thank God. I don't know what to do with all those people out there."

"It's fine, ma'am. We just don't want to create undue chaos while this is an open investigation, so I want you to go ahead with the event business as usual."

A shrill call of the wild pierced through the canvas

wall. "I don't care if you're the governor himself, I know my niece is in there! Now get out of my way!"

Speaking of chaos.

Aunt Ginny barreled through the tent flap with Officer Consuelos on her heel. He looked at Officer Birkwell and they passed a silent shudder.

Officer Birkwell stared down Aunt Ginny like a mountain troll looking at a rock gnome. "Mrs. Frankowski. I guess it was too much to hope you'd be home watching the Hallmark Channel, wasn't it?"

Aunt Ginny screwed her face up at the sandy-blond cop she'd tussled with more than once. "What are you, some kinda nut? I heard this one was in trouble again and I came to help."

I sat up straighter when I was mentioned. "You heard I was in trouble?"

Aunt Ginny planted her hands on her hips. "Well, news traveled fast about the coroner being here, so we just figured."

"Oh." *That wasn't worth sitting up for.* I slouched back against the chair.

"And I'll tell you something else." Aunt Ginny poked her finger at Officer Birkwell. "If you're not going to charge her, you'd better let her go. Her boyfriend is in a right state and I don't know if we can keep him calm for long."

Officer Birkwell turned to me. "Oh yeah? Which boyfriend?"

I hesitated a moment because in the boyfriend arena I was currently zero for two. I raised my eyes to Aunt Ginny. "Gia?"

"Yes, Gia! The man has been worrying himself to

death knowing she's back here. I'm surprised he hasn't torn this tent to the ground."

Officer Consuelos let out a little cheer for me. "Hey! You picked the Italian. Good for you. I like him."

Officer Birkwell took out his wallet and passed a twenty to Consuelos. "Aww. I was really rooting for the chef. There's just something about your first love."

"Yes, well, I know how emotionally invested you all were in my love life, but it is what it is." *And what it is sucks.*

A loud rip reverberated around the tent and a box cutter made a giant gash through the back wall. Gia jumped through, ready for a fight, and Officer Birkwell reached for his nightstick.

"She did not do it! You cannot hold her here! She's coming with me." Gia grabbed me by the wrist and led me to the front door. He pointed a finger at Officer Birkwell. "You will hear from our lawyer."

He led me through the tent opening and kissed me like he was a drowning man and I was the only air.

Behind us, I heard Eloise dreamily say, "Wow."

And then Aunt Ginny: "See. That's how you do that."

CHAPTER 22

I floated on air all the way over to our booth. *Why can't it be like this all the time?* Then I remembered why and doubled down my efforts to be above reproach until his divorce.

There wasn't a lot of time for me to fill Gia in on what had actually happened. He insisted we abandon the Expo and get me home where I'd be safe. I begged him not to worry. I tried to explain everything, but while he was letting himself in through Dr. Rubin's new back door, Kevin was opening the floodgates at the front. We had a line thirty people deep looking for gossip under the guise of coffee and Paleo muffins. Why were the police here? Why did the Expo open so late? Why are the cops guarding Dr. Rubin's booth? Did you know someone wrote "Paleo Fraud" all over your canopy? Does anyone else smell lavender?

I did manage to explain to Gia, in between milk frothing and bean grinding, that I wasn't a suspect. "They haven't even determined the cause of death yet. As far as they know, it could have been an accident."

He rolled his eyes down to me and made a face. "They think he accidentally melted his face?"

I shrugged. "You got me. I once heard of a man who was stabbed multiple times in the chest, and they ruled it a suicide."

Gia gave me a droll look that said he believed that as much as I did and went back to grinding espresso beans.

The Expo ticket counter had sold out of walk-in passes in the first hour. They had to start giving people timed entries because of fire marshal regulations.

Note to self: if I ever have an event at Convention Hall, put up police tape and have cop cars block off the street with their lights flashing. The crowds will come pouring in.

Whoever vandalized our booth only caused us to sell twice as much. Everyone wanted to know what had happened, and they bought muffins and coffee while we told them it was like this when we got here. Things were so busy that Gia called La Dolce Vita to send for backup.

Shayla hadn't been at her booth all morning. I didn't want to suspect Shayla; I really liked her. And I was really hoping she had a good reason for being late that didn't include getting rid of evidence and changing out of a hoodie.

The women in white coats floated out of the Rubinesque tent like a bevy of swans. They had surfed in on the wave of ticket holders this morning and had to find out about Dr. Rubin's death from security. Tally appeared especially distraught as she dabbed her eyes with a tissue and blew her nose. She stepped away from the group and pulled out her cell phone. She headed past our booth toward the exit, and I overheard her say, "We need to enact the Phoenix Protocol. Like yesterday."

That was weird. A few minutes later I heard her again, but this time she was crying outside the window behind our booth. I put a cherry muffin in a pastry bag and headed outside to check on her.

It was a little overcast and the wind was whipping up a frenzy. I put my hand on her shoulder and she gasped.

"Sorry. I didn't mean to sneak up on you."

Her eyes relaxed. "That's okay. I didn't hear you over the ocean."

"It's one of my favorite sounds." I held out the bag. "Here, I brought you this. I wanted to see how you're doing. I know Dr. Rubin was your colleague."

She took the muffin from the bag and sniffed it. "Thank you. That's very kind of you." She set the muffin on the railing.

"Oh, I wouldn't . . ."

Too late. Three seagulls dove like pterodactyls from *Jurassic Park* and grabbed the muffin while pecking feathers off one another. Within seconds shreds of wrapper dropped to the sand.

Tally burst into tears.

"It's okay. You're not from around here. You didn't know."

She wrapped herself around me, sobbing. "What am I going to do? Poor Lance. I should have gone with him last night. He must have come back here after he went to the police station."

"What did he go to the police for?"

"He had to fill out an official complaint to press charges against Agnes Pfeister-Pinze for attacking him with that taser. He didn't want to go alone, but I said I was tired and wanted to go to the hotel." She started to sob. "Now he's dead and I wasn't there for him. He knew someone was trying to kill him and I didn't listen."

I patted her back and tried to be comforting. "What do you mean, he knew someone was trying to kill him? How?"

"He was receiving these angry letters. At least once a week for months."

"That's a long time to maintain the urgency on a death threat. Did he report it?"

She pulled back from me and wiped her eyes. "He didn't know where they were coming from. He suspected one of the lawsuits, but I always thought it was that crazy Agnes. We tried to settle her case out of court, but she refused."

I suddenly felt a wave of relief that I hadn't had that consultation this morning. Then I remembered Dr. Rubin had died and I was ashamed of myself. I got over it quickly and moved right back to relieved. "How many lawsuits are there?"

"A few."

"Are we talking like on that TV show, with the uneven boob jobs and botched face-lifts?"

"Sometimes women come in with expectations that are unattainable. If you're five foot two and weigh two hundred and fifty pounds, liposuction won't make you look like a Victoria's Secret model."

I self-consciously sucked my stomach in. "No, of course not. That would be ridiculous." *So much for Operation Poppy Gets Skinny.*

"But people think that all the time. They think cosmetic surgery is a replacement for diet and exercise. We kept telling Lance he should turn some of them away because they won't be happy with their results. Even when we show them before and after projections, they still see what they want. But he never listens. He was always trying to fund another charity trip."

"Okay, so probably one of the lawsuits was sending the death threats, right? The cops should be able to track them down through the courts."

"Some of them are anonymous. The plaintiffs are using pseudonyms, so we don't know exactly who they are."

"You can do that?"

Tally hugged her arms across her chest. "Apparently, if you convince a judge your life is in danger, your identity can be hidden until trial. In six months we received news about so many lawsuits being filed and bad reviews on GreatDocs and other medical websites that Lance had to hire an IT forensic company to find out who was destroying his name and slandering Rubinesque online. I don't even know how to get ahold of them now that he's gone." Her face twisted in grief and the tears started again. "I'm sorry." She waved me off and ran down the boardwalk steps to be alone on the beach.

I felt like someone had stacked weights on my shoulders. Other people's grief hits you so much harder once you've experienced grief of your own. Tally had lost a friend she obviously cared deeply about. And without Dr. Rubin, it looked like the entire band might be out of a gig.

I looked through the window at the back of our booth. Gia had a long line of customers, and it appeared that Sierra had shown up for work dressed to lie on the beach. I knew I'd better get in there to do some damage control. Maybe we could wrap her in a yoga mat from Zen Mania.

The creak of a loose board came from my right and I caught the briefest glimpse of golden-brown corkscrew hair disappear around the corner.

CHAPTER 23

I tried to catch Agnes Pfeister-Pinze around the back of Convention Hall, but she was gone. If she went through that hole Gia had sliced into Dr. Rubin's tent, she'd have a surprise encounter with the cops waiting for her on the other side.

I went back around to our booth and assessed Sierra's outfit choice for the day. Cutoff shorts and a midriff tank top over flip-flops.

"What?" She looked from me to Gia. "Karla said the dress code was boardwalk casual."

Gia flattened his lips and looked at me.

All I could do was shrug. In another month everyone would be going to work dressed like Sierra. "Why don't we get you one of those skirts at the Earth Mother hand-woven booth?" I had Gia give her some money and sent her off.

My phone buzzed a text from Amber that said she was

working on a lead. **Stay ready.** *What is she getting me into now? Is she setting me up?*

My eyes fell on Officer Birkwell several feet away, dealing with complaints, which gave me an idea. I asked Gia to make me a cappuccino, and I cut up some of the cherry brandy muffins and piña colada macaroons to take around as free samples. I made a makeshift tray out of a plastic tote lid and I was off.

I didn't make it three feet before the seniors swarmed me and cleaned me out like a flock of seagulls. I looked back at the booth to see Gia laughing. I walked back over to the counter and put my tray down. "Very funny." I filled it up again and this time covered it with a napkin.

Round two, I made it to Officer Birkwell. "Hey there. I thought you'd like a cappuccino since you're stuck here all day." I handed him the paper cup in a sleeve and gave him a grin.

He had good instincts. He took my coffee, but with some noticeable hesitation and a little side-eye.

I lifted the napkin off the edge of the tray. "Try the muffins too."

He took a muffin wedge and gave me another look. "So, what's this all about?"

"What?" I laughed. "Nothing. I thought you might be hungry."

He popped the muffin wedge in his mouth but never took his eyes away from mine. "Thank you."

"You're welcome . . ."

"Shane."

"I'm sorry?"

He gave me a crooked grin. "My name is Shane."

"Are you serious?"

He narrowed his eyes, but he was still grinning. "Why wouldn't I be?"

"I dunno. I just figured you'd have a cop name. Like Joe. Or Mike. Shane is so cool-sounding." I realized my mistake the moment it left my mouth.

"You don't think I'm cool?"

"No, of course you're cool. You're very cool. I'm sure you're the mack daddy." *What am I saying? I hope that doesn't mean something dirty.*

He chuckled. "Alright. Can I have another sample?"

I held the tray up. "Of course. I really need to ask you about something."

A wary look crossed his eyes and they lost a touch of their playfulness. "You know I can't talk about an investigation."

"No, of course not. But that's not what I want to talk to you about."

He popped the muffin wedge in his mouth. "Okay, shoot."

I lowered my voice a smidge. "What do you know about Amber and Temarius Jackson?"

His eyebrows shot up and he looked around. "What's your involvement with that?"

I tried to choose my words carefully. "Amber and I have worked together in the past, and she's called on me as her CI before." *I hope that wasn't a secret.* "Temarius Jackson was also her CI. I just want to know if I can trust her."

Officer Birkwell had a grim look on his face. "I've known Amber for fifteen years. And there is no way she killed that kid. I don't care what evidence they have against her."

"Can't they run ballistics on the bullet that killed him?"

"That's what they're doing now." He lowered his voice to a near whisper. "She needs to be very careful. They brought Kieran Dunne down from Trenton to lead the IA investigation. He and Amber have had run-ins in the past that didn't end well. He'll try to take her down at any cost."

"How can that be ethical? Isn't it his job to be fair and find the truth? I thought that was what Internal Affairs did."

Officer Birkwell snorted. "Not all cops are the good guys. Some of them join the force so they can get away with violence and abuse. They're bullies with a badge and they make us all look bad. You learn who you can trust and who you need to stay away from."

That was all I could get out of him before a group of women showed up with free-treatment passes they'd won in the raffle, and he had to go to work defusing the situation.

I got a second cappuccino and refilled the samples, then walked to the end of the tent and found Officer Consuelos guarding the far side. An older couple was asking him if he could get them a handicap tag for their car.

"I'm sorry, sir, you'll have to apply for one at the DMV. The police don't handle that."

The woman grunted and led her husband away. "Come on, Earl. We'll go ask the American one."

Officer Consuelos and I shared a look, and I held up the paper cup. "Coffee?"

"Hey, thanks." He took it from me and removed the lid. "I'm so tired right now, this is great."

I lifted the napkin and offered him a muffin. His eyes lit up. "Yaas. You're a lifesaver."

"I was hoping I could ask you a question about the Internal Affairs investigation."

"How do you know about that?"

"Dude, you know misfortune follows me everywhere. I just want to make sure I'm doing the right thing."

"Okay. What do you want to know?"

"Is Amber a good cop? Can I trust her?"

He chewed thoughtfully before answering. "That depends on whether or not the rumors are true."

"What rumors?"

We had to wait a minute while three women came over and asked if I had free samples under the napkin. After they'd each taken something, Officer Consuelos took another muffin sample, and we waited for them to be out of earshot. "She was up for promotion to lieutenant a few months ago but didn't get it. Some people said it was department politics, but there were definitely whispers about something else."

"Like what?"

"Let's just say once you're on IA's watch list, it's just a matter of time before they make a move."

"So Internal Affairs has been watching Amber? Why? Do they think she's taking bribes or something?" *'Cause I would have wanted to know about that last September when my butt was in a cell.*

He shrugged and shook his head. "Like I said, it's just a rumor. She seems to close a lot of cases with very little evidence and there's speculation about her methods. Not everyone is happy to have a woman on the force, and they sure don't want her in charge. They'll look for any reason to push her out."

"If the chief suspected Amber was dirty, couldn't he just fire her?"

"There has to be evidence of misconduct to remove a cop from duty. If she did what they're saying, they'll have it."

"Thanks. I'd better get the rest of these samples handed out and get back."

He peeked under the napkin and gave me a grin.

"Take two."

I left Officer Consuelos happily eating cherry muffins and spotted the booth doing chair massage.

I ambled over to the sign-up sheet and lifted the napkin from my tray. It was like watching fish in an aquarium when the kelp flakes get sprinkled in. An entire school of shoppers thronged me, stripped my tray of its samples, and swam off again. I was even visited by the little man and his wife who'd asked about the handicap placard.

The woman reached in and took two macaroon samples. "One is for my sister. She's home sick and couldn't make it, but she has a ticket."

Her husband didn't get that memo. "Your sister's dead."

She glared at him and dragged him off toward the juice bar.

The sign-up sheet for the free chair massage had disappeared. I spun around to see if it was behind me and came chest to chest with Tim.

His expression was blank and yet somehow cold. I tried to say hello, but my throat had closed up on me. "Herm."

"Oh hiyee. Look, honey, it's Poppy." Gigi materialized from the abyss, holding a beautiful silver tray with twelve perfect paper cups of orange cakes. She also had the cutest little crystal decanter of olive oil. "Poppy, you can be the first one to hear our good news. Tell her, babe." Tim didn't answer, so Gigi carried on without him. "We've merged. I'm Maxine's new pastry chef. We're revamping the dessert menu away from the homespun muck it had fallen into, back into more chic, gourmet offerings. And we're running Le Bon Gigi together. I'm so excited. I can't wait to launch our new menu on Memorial Day."

"That's wonderful. I wish you both the greatest success." *Dear God, who is saying that?*

Gigi blinked and looked like she was trying to determine whether or not my well-wishes were sincere.

Tim's jaw worked overtime to keep his mouth shut. He gave me a nod. "Thank you."

Gigi held up her tray. "Our first new dessert is one of my specialties. It's an orange cake made with almonds, drizzled with the exquisite Morello DiSanto olive oil imported from Tuscany."

"It sounds amazing. Is it Paleo?" *Since you are the Paleo Diva.*

"Absolutely." Gigi grinned.

Something in the way she was looking at me made me fear for my safety. I looked Tim in the eye. Would he let me get sick just because he hadn't forgiven me?

He gave me a look that clearly said, *I don't weigh in on your life anymore.*

I took the tiny sample she was offering me. "Thank you so much. I'll just take it back to the booth with me and have it with my coffee."

Gigi smiled. "Byee."

I could still feel their eyes on my back as I took my sample of potential hives to La Dolce Vita.

Someone had been very busy while I was gone, and I don't mean Gia or Sierra. Our booth, and every other booth in our row, was covered with red-and-black bumper stickers that said Fraudster.

CHAPTER 24

"Who did this?"

Gia shook his head and shrugged. "What?"

"The stickers. How did you not see this happening?"

Gia and Sierra came out to the aisle and reared back in surprise. Gia peeled the sticker off the back of the espresso machine while muttering in Italian. "Do you know how much this machine costs?"

Sierra looked around the Hall to see if she could spot the culprit. "Someone must have been sticking them on while they were ordering. They weren't here when I came back with this butt-ugly skirt you made me buy."

Gia looked at the cup in my hand. "What do you have there?"

I held it up for his inspection. "Probably anthrax. It's something Gigi gave me. Orange cake with some fancy Tuscan olive oil. Morello DiSanti or something."

Gia twisted his neck. "Oh no. Uh-uh." He took the cake sample and threw it in the trash. "Trust me."

"Yeah. I felt the same way." *Except I was probably still gonna eat it.*

I was refilling the pastry case with more coconut macaroons and pistachio rose shortbread when Shayla tried to slink past my booth. "Hey! Where you goin'?"

She started walking faster, so I darted out after her. When I caught up to her, she spun around and caught me smelling her hair. "What are you doing?"

"What are *you* doing? My hip is bruised all the way down to my knee after you threw me to the floor."

"Girl. Are you on something?"

"Yeah. Tylenol. For my hip."

"Well, I have no idea what you're talking about." She started walking again and I followed her to her booth.

Her cousins had opened for her and they were trying to bluff their way through customer questions. When Shayla walked in they pointed at her. "See, here comes my grandmother now. She uses this stuff every day."

The woman took one look at Shayla and bought two of everything.

I tried to corner Shayla in the back of her booth by her boxes of stock. "Then where've you been all morning?"

She was dressed in a pink pencil skirt and a black silk blouse, but the wardrobe change wasn't enough to account for her being missing all morning. She took oversize pink sunglasses off and threw them in her purse. "It's none of your business, but I was waiting for Lance Rubin to meet me at a café down the street. I was going to confront him about stealing my antiaging concentrate and my laptop."

"Oh yeah? Did he show up?"

"No. He stood me up."

"Yeah. 'Cause he's dead." I watched her reaction carefully. She didn't flinch. She didn't seem surprised at all.

"Well, I wouldn't know about that, would I?"

"It doesn't take three hours to find out someone's not coming."

One of her cousins came over to us and asked Shayla if she could take over. People were streaming into her booth to buy miracle creams now that the plastic surgery tent was closed.

"Look, my booth is finally busy like it should have been from the start. I need to make the most of this." She started to walk away, then paused. "Lance Rubin was my biggest competition, but that doesn't mean I killed him. Okay? I've heard whispers that he stole that whole UV light mask 'discovery' from Dr. Shawn Hammerstein in Los Angeles. And I'm convinced he stole the research on my new line of age-reversal skin care. He's been accused of corporate espionage before. I almost pulled out of the Expo when I saw he was the keynote. You don't have to believe me. Ask around."

CHAPTER 25

My gut said Shayla was lying about not barreling into me earlier, and my nose agreed with my gut. When I sniffed her hair she didn't smell like her usual rosy-scented self. She smelled like Irish Spring. Someone like Shayla Rose doesn't use Irish Spring unless she has something to hide.

I did a lap around the room and chatted up a few of the skin-care companies. No one had heard the gossip that Dr. Rubin had stolen his UV mask from Dr. Hammerstein except the last booth I spoke to, and I had a sick feeling that by then, I may have been the one who'd started the rumor.

I turned the final corner and passed the Max Level Plant Protein booth next to ours. Part of their display was a life-size poster on a metal frame of a bodybuilder from his head to his oiled-up thighs. From the thigh down, he appeared to be wearing an orange corduroy skirt and purple Crocs.

"Hi, Agnes." The poster twitched on my way past.

Gia handed me a latte when I got behind the counter. "Taste this."

I took a sip. "That's interesting. It reminds me of cereal."

"We ran out of almond milk and Justin at the Sunshine Smoothies bar gave me some *oat beverage* to try."

"Oat *beverage*. So fancy. I wonder if you could add orange and raspberry syrup and call it a Fruity Pebbles Latte. Hey! That could be the fruitaccino!"

Gia laughed. "I like it."

Sierra sidled up in between us. "So, what's the deal with that lady with the messed-up face?"

"I think she's spying on us."

Gia kept his eyes forward. "She is not good at it."

Sierra pulled the folded-up Fraudster sticker from her shorts under her multicolored, woven skirt. "Do you think she's the one who plastered these all over the room?"

The bodybuilder poster moved a couple of steps closer to us, and one of the Protein guys yelled, "Hey! You can't do that."

Agnes Pfeister-Pinze darted from behind the stand and zigzagged down the aisle, her Crocs squeaking with every step.

Sierra scratched her head. "Never mind. I think I would have noticed her."

"What would you think if I told you someone killed Dr. Rubin? Would you believe it could be her?"

Gia and Sierra both watched Agnes run into the security guard, knock him back a couple of inches, and pivot to go out the other way. Gia shook his head. "She does not have it in her."

Sierra shoved the bumper sticker back in her pocket. "I feel like she'd have been caught by now."

They were both right. There was something very pitiful about the woman.

Two ladies came by pushing toddlers in umbrella strollers. They threw the familiar Paleo Diva sample cups in our trash. "Alright, let's see what you got."

Sierra stepped up and described our selections and the women each bought a piece of pistachio rose shortbread.

One of them held up her shortbread. "Are you sure this is Paleo?"

I nodded. "It really is."

"This is amazing."

I grinned. "That's what I was going for."

One of the women looked at the other while they chewed. "She can keep her coupon."

Her friend nodded her agreement. "Can I get a dozen of these to go?"

When they had moved on to Shayla's booth Sierra made an observation. "I think that Paleo Diva chick is saying stuff about you."

"Yeah, I got that."

"You know, she was here earlier. When you both stepped away."

I turned to Gia. "When did you step away?"

He put his hand on my back. "S'not important. What did she want?"

"To buy stuff. She bought one of everything and asked if I had any bacon cookies left."

Interesting. "Did she say anything else?"

"Just that my skirt smelled like cow."

I sniffed. "Yeah, li'l bit."

"See, there's Daddy." Alex clacked down the aisle toward our booth with Henry and Karla lagging behind looking miserable. Alex gave a finger wave. "Hello, Daddy."

Gia clenched his jaw. The kiss from earlier this morning came to the front of my mind and heat rose to my face.

Henry rushed around the women and into our booth to hug my legs. "Hey, Sweets. Whatchu been doin'?"

Henry's expression was made more exasperated by how giant his eyes looked behind his glasses. He groaned. "Shopping for hours."

I admit that I wanted to laugh. Just a little. He was so dramatic. All I could do was rub his back to try to comfort him.

Alex did a spin for Gia. "See. We got matching mother-and-son sweaters. Don't we look darling?"

Gia remained silent.

Henry pulled the collar of the pink-and-white argyle sweater away from his neck and stretched his face to the side. "It's itchy."

I saw a look pass between Karla and Gia. A look that said, *I can't stand much more of this*.

Gia sighed. "What are you doing here, Alex?"

Alex waved her hands. "I need some moisturizer. You don't stay this beautiful without a little maintenance." She looked my way. "Karla knows what I mean." Then she put her hand out. "Okay, Henry, come back to Mommy."

Henry turned those big eyes on Gia. "Daddy, I don't want to. Can't I stay with you and Poppy?"

Gia tousled Henry's hair. "Oh, Piccolo."

Alex barked, "Now, Henry!"

We were all stunned, including Sierra, whose eyes were as big as Henry's. I felt myself flinch and instinctively shifted Henry behind me to shield him.

Gia threw down the rag he'd been using to clean the frothing wand. "No. *Non parlargli in quel modo!*"

Karla jumped.

Alex narrowed her eyes. "If you aren't nice to me, I'm reporting it to Momma."

Gia did not back down. "I do not care what you tell Momma. My life will not be ruled by the family!"

Alex slammed her hand on the counter, then spun around and stormed out.

Karla slapped Gia on the shoulder. "*Idiota!* There are ears everywhere!" She turned and followed behind Alex.

I looked at Gia. "What did you say to her?"

"I said she was not to speak to my son that way."

"Well, she forgot to take him with her."

CHAPTER 26

Henry had been somewhat abandoned at the Expo, so I took him around the hall to see the booths and the makeup demonstration.

"Why do ladies put all that stuff on their face?"

"It makes them look pretty."

He scrunched his nose up. "She looks like a raccoon."

"Uh . . . yeah. Kinda." The makeup artist had used a very heavy hand with the eyeliner.

He looked at my face. "You're pretty without makeup."

I smiled. "Oh honey, I'm wearing so much more than you realize."

I took him over to the Sunshine booth and we bought a smoothie and a protein shake. We went outside to drink them on the deck, and Henry took my hand in his. I had to bat my eyes to keep from tearing up and ruining that makeup he didn't think I was wearing.

"Do I have to do more shopping for itchy sweaters?"

I knew what he was asking me and I wished I had a better answer. "Maybe Daddy can think of a way for this to be easier for you."

He pulled at the neckline of his sweater. "And less pink."

I stifled another giggle and put my arm around him. "I'll see what I can do."

Shadows shifted under the deck, and I could see through the slats that someone was lurking right below us. "Come on. Let's go inside and check on things."

Gia gave Henry a lesson in pulling espresso and I let him wait on customers. He had so much fun that an hour later, when Karla called to say that she was on her way to pick him up, he had a meltdown. I had to take him outside to sit him on my lap and rub his back until he fell asleep.

Gia watched me through the window, the look on his face a mixture of pleasure and pain.

When Karla arrived that was my cue to go. "I have to start making the food for tomorrow's afternoon tea. But I'll stop by in the morning to see how you're doing."

Henry gave me a long hug goodbye while Gia watched us with pain etched in the crinkles around his eyes. "Bring me a scone."

I laughed. "You got it."

I knew something was up when Karla wanted to walk with me to the exit. "You have something to say to me?"

"You need to watch your back. Alex has been hanging around Mia Famiglia and she's a schemer. Momma may go along with her tricks because of family connections in Italy, but the rest of us see through her."

"So, everyone else would be on my side?"

"I wouldn't say that either. Just because you're not Alex doesn't mean you're accepted."

Karla returned to the booth and I went down the ramp to cross Beach Drive. The crosswalk light turned green, and just as I was about to step off the curb, someone yanked my purse. I grabbed it with my other hand and threw an elbow toward my assailant.

She squeaked like a mouse. "I'm sorry. I just want to talk to you."

"What the heck, Agnes! I thought you were trying to mug me."

She held her hand up to cover her face. "I've been trying to talk to you all day, but someone was always around."

"Well, what do you want?"

"I've heard you asking questions and I'm here to warn you. You need to stay out of it."

"Stay out of what exactly?"

"Lance Rubin deserved what he got. Don't go nosing around where you don't belong or more people will get hurt."

"Is this your idea of a confession?"

She jerked away from me and her corkscrews bounced in every direction at once. "I didn't do it. I wanted my day in court to expose him for the fraud he was. I wanted to see him suffer the way I've had to suffer with this face."

"Can't you go somewhere and get that fixed?"

"Not until I get justice."

The light turned green, so I crossed the street to get away from her.

She called after me, "You're trusting the wrong people!"

* * *

Aunt Ginny's two-story, inflatable rabbit was starting to look like a war veteran. Benjamin Bunny was patched in four places, including a duct tape X over one eye. I tried telling her his days were numbered, but she refused to give up. She was currently on hold with the Cape May Police Department, where she had asked for a patrol officer to guard the house. I could just imagine the discussion they were having in the station.

Joanne had every surface in my kitchen covered with petits fours dipped in pastel white chocolate. She had decorated them with piped flowers, polka dots, and swirls, and she was working on Easter eggs and ladybugs.

"You've done a beautiful job."

She stopped decorating a pale-pink cake to glare at me. "What's that supposed to mean?"

"Just what I said. These are gorgeous. How come you don't do cake decorating professionally?"

She narrowed her eyes, trying to decide whether I was sincere or not, then went back to covering the little cakes with designs. "I did for a while. I was laid off when the bakery was sold to make room for condos."

Victory came into the kitchen and returned her cleaning supplies to the mudroom. "Fancey keitty has bed so verry expenseive. Eit cost more than some house ein my veillage." She washed her hands and reached for a petit four.

Joanne smacked her hand and Victory snatched it back. "Hey! I want teeny baby cake."

"Those are for afternoon tea."

Victory got herself a Dr Pepper and took a seat at the table to pout.

I was just glad I hadn't tried to take a petit four. Who knew Joanne was so protective with her desserts?

Aunt Ginny slammed the phone down and threw herself onto the banquette in a fit of pique. "They won't help. They said they can't spare anyone right now."

"Well, Amber is on administrative leave, which I think is some kind of suspension, and Officers Birkwell and Consuelos are on duty at Convention Hall, so that's probably true."

Aunt Ginny made a face and fished out a pack of green gummy bears from a pocket in her housedress. Figaro flew into the room when he heard the wrapper—I don't know who trained him to recognize the sound of cellophane—and jumped on the table across from her to beg.

I had set out my scone ingredients and was about to turn on the food processor to cut in my butter. "Aunt Ginny, why do you still have those?"

"I went back this morning and bought them. The more I eat the more I seem to want. They cost a fortune too."

Figaro sniffed the gummy bears and swatted the packet to the floor.

Joanne snickered and picked the packet up for Aunt Ginny. She examined it before handing it back. "I hear that CBD oil works wonders for anxiety."

Well, it's made mine worse. I pulsed the KitchenAid and brought my scone dough together. We had twenty tables booked for tea tomorrow, and a head count of fifty-one. I did some math and figured I needed ten dozen scones to have enough for everyone to have two, plus a little extra for my "little extra" who was having a fit over Rabbitzilla.

Victory slumped to the table fast asleep on a loaf of bread. The three of us looked to be sure she was still breathing. Figaro reared back and stood on his hind legs.

He gave her a tentative pat on the head that she slept through.

"At least she isn't in a guest room this time." I hit Pulse again, and Joanne moved her trays of petits fours away from the food processor.

"I didn't work on these all day to have you dust them in flour. I made your hot cross buns like you demanded— you're welcome—and the chicken salad and egg salad are in the refrigerator. You really need to think about getting a sheet pan rack."

I mixed the currants into the scone dough and patted it into a disc. "Why don't you find one you like and order it?"

"Because I don't work here. I freelance. Ordering is your job."

I sighed. All my kitchens had become hostile work environments.

Figaro swiped the gummy bear packet to the floor again and Aunt Ginny shook her fist at him.

Victory woke up like she hadn't missed anything, picked the packet up and handed it to Aunt Ginny, "Why are bears green?"

Aunt Ginny shrugged. "I think it's for Easter."

Joanne and I made the briefest of eye contact but said nothing.

Joanne removed her apron and grabbed her fanny pack from its peg. "I'm off. I'll be back in the morning." She gave me a dirty look. "Is that all right with you, Princess?"

Why am I "princess"? I'm elbow deep in scone dough. "Have a good night." *Don't forget to sanitize that nose ring.*

Victory went back to the boardinghouse for the night

and Aunt Ginny was in her room with Figaro watching some show starring Dick Van Dyke, who she insisted looked like Royce, except Dick didn't break into Shakespeare at random intervals.

I spent the night baking. Joanne was right. We did need a sheet pan rack. I had taken mine to the coffee shop when I'd started baking for La Dolce Vita months ago. Now I had twelve dozen scones, plus a dozen gluten-free scones, because who was I kidding? I was going to cheat on this keto diet and eat three of them before the tea was over tomorrow. Six loaves of chocolate bread plus all of Joanne's cakes. There wasn't a spare inch in my kitchen to make the cherry mascarpone filling for the chocolate sandwiches.

My pocket buzzed and I pulled out my phone. Amber had sent me a text. **Go 2 TC. Someone knows something.**

"TC? What does TC mean?"

A second text came in. **Brenda says bring cookies.**

Okay, TC means Teen Center in the Villas. I hadn't been there since I dropped off twelve dozen cookies for their Christmas fundraiser. I checked the time; they'd be closing in an hour. "Maybe I should go there tomorrow."

Another text came in. **Go Now!**

I looked around the kitchen, then pulled the lid off the cookie jar and yelled into it, "Amber! Do you have my house bugged?"

I didn't get a reply, but that didn't mean no either. *We'll be talking about this, blondie.*

I grabbed a tray of aloha chocolate chip cookies that was meant for the Expo tomorrow. Two dozen less would have to be okay. I got my purse and my keys and headed down the hall, but before I could get out the front door Dale Parker stopped me.

"Poppy, do you have another computer?"

I looked into the library, where Rita was on the one at the desk. "No, I'm sorry. That's the only one. Do you need something?"

"I wanted to check Portia's standings before tomorrow's event and she's been on that all day."

"Oh dear. Can you check from your cell phone?"

He shook his head. "I can't read the numbers on the screen. They're too small."

I cleared my throat. "Hello, Rita."

"Hey, Poppy. How was the Expo today?"

"It was good. Lots of people attended, that's for sure. By any chance will you be finished on the computer soon?"

Rita held up a finger. "I'm just about done. Five more minutes."

Dale Parker gave me a look. "She's been saying that for hours."

I fetched Dale my iPad and logged it in to the guest setting I'd made for emergencies. *Guests have a lot more Internet surfing emergencies than you could ever imagine.* "Just put it back on the front desk when you're finished."

Crisis averted and I was on my way. I couldn't imagine taking a beach vacation and staying inside on the Internet all day. Rita must really love online shopping.

CHAPTER 27

The drive off the island and through North Cape May didn't take long. In another month the time would double with beach traffic, so I'd count my blessings for the preseason. Bayshore Road ran through the heart of the Villas. It was neither on the bay nor the shore, but it split in half a small, sleepy neighborhood full of cracker-jack houses on postage-stamp lawns. The Teen Center was conveniently sandwiched in between two government buildings that most teens wanted nothing to do with: the public library and the Lower Township Police Station.

I parked in front of the brown-brick building by the bike rack. The skateboarding ramp was empty, but the outdoor basketball court was full of kids doing as much trash-talking as they were putting the ball through the hoop.

Four months ago, I was here to ask questions about the

founder, Brody Brandt, who'd won the Cape May County Humanitarian Award. That seemed like ages ago. Now the lime-green lobby had a new brass plaque inside the front door dedicating the building to him.

"Hey, girl! Amber said you might stop by." As wide as she was tall, Brenda was the Teen Center gatekeeper. She had short-cropped, spiky pink hair and wore funky, silver cat eyeglasses. Her red T-shirt announced that she had beaten anorexia. She was my kinda gal. It was her job to keep the teens safe while they were in the building, so you had to sign in before she'd let you pass. Sign in and bring snacks.

I held up my tray of cookies. "Here to bribe you for some information."

"Alright! Come on in. We haven't seen you since Christmas." Brenda took two of the offered cookies and daintily placed them on a napkin next to her Diet Coke.

"I know. I'm sorry. It's been one thing after another. This weekend I have a booth at the Convention Hall Beauty Expo. Have you been?"

She blew a raspberry. "No. That's not for me. Lots of snooty, expensive snake oil and empty promises. All my money goes here." She cast her eyes around the lobby. "I'll stick with the Oil of Olay. You look good, though. Did you lose weight?"

"Oh." I let out this embarrassing guffaw that I wished I could take back. "Maybe a little."

"Yeah, I can tell. Your boobs look smaller."

"Oh." *Well, that's definitely not what I was going for.*

She laughed when I looked down at my chest. "Don't worry. You've got plenty left. Now, what do you want to know?"

I need to buy a better push-up bra. I set the tray of

cookies down on the front table by a stack of pamphlets about after-school tutoring. "Do you know a boy named Temarius Jackson?"

Brenda smiled. "Yes, I know Temarius. I haven't seen him in a while, though. What's he up to?"

My throat started to close up and I felt the light go out of my eyes. "Well, I'm sorry to have to tell you, but he's passed away."

Tears filled Brenda's eyes and her hand flew up to her chest. "That's just . . . What happened?"

"It looks like he was murdered."

Brenda hung her head and shook it, speechless.

"I was wondering if you might know if he was having problems with anyone. What crowd did he hang out with?"

Brenda wiped her eyes and gave me a chin nod. "Here's who you need to ask. I know you've already met this handsome young man."

A tall, skinny boy with light-brown skin and fuzzy, brown hair shiny with sweat came down the hall spinning a basketball. He had a group of younger boys following behind him, all dressed in shorts and tank tops and smelling like outside. "Emilio."

A grin split his face and he came in to hug me. "I'm sorry I'm all sweaty."

"That's okay, hug me anyway. You look great."

"Yeah, I don't look like a PEZ dispenser anymore." He laughed. "I smell cookies."

Now it was my turn to laugh. I motioned to the tray. "Help yourself." The boys cleaned it out before I could mention the coconut.

Brenda wisely hid her two cookies inside her drawer.

"Emilio is our full-time activities director now. He's been coaching the boys' basketball team after school for weeks."

Emilio tossed the basketball from hand to hand. "We've been playing local private schools. We're looking for a national league to join."

"That's awesome."

Brenda took the ball from Emilio. "Poppy wants to talk to you about something important."

"Oh sure. Why don't we go to my office?"

He led me to a little beige room down the hall from the front desk. He had two folding chairs, and his metal desk was stacked high with uniform catalogs. He took a seat and tipped back in his chair. "What's up?"

"Do you know Temarius Jackson?"

"Yeah. We're in the program together. He's doing great."

"I'm so sorry, Emilio, but . . . Temarius is dead."

Emilio froze, stunned. Then his face twisted in rage. He picked up an empty Gatorade bottle and hurled it against the wall. He sat down hard and dropped his head to his hands. "How did it happen?"

"All we know is that he was shot. A friend of mine is trying to find out who might have been involved. Do you know anyone who would want to hurt him?"

Emilio leaned forward in his chair until it squeaked. "Man, he got into a bad scene, pulling these small-time jobs. B and E, petty theft, stuff like that. He wanted to go straight, but he said he couldn't get out."

"What did he mean, he couldn't get out?"

"I only know someone had something on him. He said he was working with a cop, so I thought he was finally getting help and stopped riding him about it."

"When was that?"

"I dunno. Like February maybe. The last meeting he was at, he said he was in trouble and this time he was going down hard. He lost something and he said it would cost him his life." Emilio's eyes teared up. "Man, I shoulda done something. I shoulda called someone."

My heart broke for him. "It's not your fault, hon. There was nothing you could have done. When was the last meeting?"

"Two days ago."

The day before he died. "Do you know what he lost? Like maybe drugs he was supposed to deliver?"

Emilio cocked his head. "That wouldn't be possible. Addicts don't make the best middlemen. They end up using all the product. But I don't know, he was doing so good. He got his GED, and he'd just gotten his ninety-day chip. We sabotage ourselves, but I have a hard time believing he was using again. I think whatever he was mixed up in, someone else was pulling the strings."

CHAPTER 28

I was so exhausted after my visit to the Teen Center that I fell asleep in my clothes on top of the bed. Figaro purred himself into a ball under my chin around four a.m., and I woke up long enough to whip the comforter over us. I would have slept right through the breakfast service if I hadn't smelled waffles. That, and Figaro springboarding off my face when he heard the can opener two flights down.

I got myself together and put on a minimal layer of makeup—enough so I didn't scare anyone—then headed down the back stairs to the kitchen.

Joanne was ordering Victory around with a spatula. Victory had been placed at the Belgian waffle iron, a position I was convinced would end with her going to the emergency room, and Joanne was at the stove stirring two saucepans and watching the KitchenAid beat something that looked like cheesecake.

Victory tried to peek at the waffle and Joanne slapped the spatula against the counter. "Did I say open the waffle iron?"

"But eet smell done."

"It's done when I say it's done."

I ventured into the kitchen a little afraid for my life. "What are we making?"

Joanne tossed me a look over her shoulder, then dismissed me.

Victory grinned. "Cannoli waffle."

"What the heck is a cannoli waffle?"

Victory kept on grinning. "I don't know." She tried to lift the waffle lid and Joanne smacked the counter again.

I looked around the empty kitchen. "Hey. Where are all the scones and breads I made last night?"

Aunt Ginny appeared from the mudroom door chewing, her cheeks bulging like a squirrel. She froze when she realized she'd been caught.

Joanne turned off the mixer. "Because you're underwhelmingly prepared here to do this much baking, I brought my six-foot sheet pan rack from home. All the pastries are layered up over in that corner, where Ginny has just mysteriously appeared with her mouth full and icing on her nose."

Aunt Ginny tried to shrug, but pink crumbs fell from her blouse.

Joanne smacked the counter by Victory. "Now!"

Victory startled and sprang into action to lift the lid on the ancient steel Belgian waffle iron. She peeled a perfect, golden-brown waffle off the top and held it up. "See, I tell you eet feenesh."

Joanne shook her head and huffed. "Just put it on the sheet pan in the oven like I showed you. And Ginny, so help me if those pink petits fours are missing, your head will roll."

I motioned for Aunt Ginny to wipe her cheek.

She wiped the dab of pink chocolate off her face and shrugged. "I have no idea what you're talking about, Joanne. I was eating my Grape-Nuts in the laundry room like I do every Saturday morning."

Joanne spun around and narrowed her eyes at me.

"What? I just got here." I grinned. "So. Cannoli waffles. That sounds amazing. What is it?"

Joanne pointed her spatula around the various stations. "Cinnamon Belgian waffles with ricotta-mascarpone cream, chocolate syrup, cherry compote, and garnished with crushed pistachios and mini chocolate chips. And I'm about to take the bacon out of the second oven."

My mouth was watering. "Joanne, if those waffles are gluten-free, I'll double your salary."

She made a face back at me. "Eww. No. I told you: I don't do your weird, hipster diet rules."

I started to protest but quickly decided it was more pointless than kissing a frog. "Well, save me a little of everything and I'll make a keto waffle later. Hey, you didn't use the mascarpone and cherries I had for the chocolate sandwich filling, did you?"

Joanne rolled into her go-to response: defensive. "If you don't want me using something, you need to write it down. And I only used a little bit. There's still some in there."

I opened the pantry to check on my cherry preserves, and Figaro and Portia came flying out of the closet. "What the!"

Aunt Ginny laughed. "Uh-oh. You might be having kittens soon."

I scooped Figaro into my arms. "Not without a medical miracle I won't. What did you do? Her mother is going to be looking for her."

On cue, Patsy's voice carried down the hall. "Porrr-tiaaa!"

I caught Victory feeding the green-eyed Persian a piece of bacon and my heart almost stopped beating. Patsy's Miss Piggy slippers were clicking closer and closer to the kitchen.

I waved a hand at my ditzy chambermaid. "Zsst zsst!"

Victory held the cat against her tiny frame and flipped her apron over her belly just as Patsy turned the corner and stood under the archway. "Have you seen my Portia? I don't know how she managed to get out of our room again."

We all looked around the kitchen at each other, hemming and hawing. Figaro stood on his hind legs and patted Victory on the thigh and meowed.

Victory's stomach hissed quietly.

Aunt Ginny cleared her throat and patted her chest. "Something caught."

I picked up a tea towel and shook it at Figaro from behind the island. "Um . . . have you checked the library, Patsy?"

Victory's belly wiggled and Patsy glanced at her. Victory put her hand on her apron. "Baby keick me."

Aunt Ginny took Patsy by the arm and led her back out into the hall. "Why don't you try calling her again? Maybe from down here, away from the kitchen."

Victory lifted her apron and held up the white cat, who was purring and smacking her lips, and passed her to me.

I smoothed her fur down and placed her on the other side of the dining-room door.

Patsy was coming around the corner into the sitting room. "Porrr-tiaaa!"

Portia was having a love affair with the bacon and pretended not to hear her owner, so I gave her a little push on the rump.

Joanne, Victory, and I stood in the kitchen on the other side of the door listening and heard Patsy say, "Here you are, you silly girl. Come with Mummy now. Daddy is ready to give you your bath. We have a big day." We breathed a collective sigh of relief.

Rita and Faelynn shuffled into the dining room, said good morning to Patsy, and took up their usual seats. The ladies were very subdued today. They both had red-rimmed eyes and flushed faces. I wondered if they'd had a falling-out. "Are you ladies enjoying your stay?"

Rita was taking her time pouring cream into her coffee. "Yes, it's lovely."

"Are you both feeling okay?"

Faelynn rolled her eyes to Rita. "It's the pollen. We have terrible allergies."

"Do you need some allergy medicine?"

Rita jumped in. "Oh no. We have some. That's okay. We did want to ask you something, though."

"What's that?"

Faelynn lifted her coffee cup and sighed, "We want to bring a group here for a tea in about a month. Could we get a reservation for that?"

"I'm sure we could work that out, as long as it isn't a holiday weekend. What's the group's name?"

Faelynn started to speak. "It's the uh . . ."

Rita cut her off. "The Real Housewives of New Jersey."

I chuckled. "How did you end up in a housewives of

New Jersey group when you live in New York and Faelynn lives in Connecticut?"

Rita's face went blank, so Faelynn took over. "Oh, I
was born in Egg Harbor. We thought it would be fun if we
both joined."

Now it was getting weird. "Just you were born in New
Jersey?"

Faelynn nodded. "Why?"

Rita gritted her teeth. "Because we're sisters."

Faelynn laughed and waved a hand. "Oh, well, our
parents divorced when we were young. Rita grew up in
New York with our father, and I moved to Connecticut
and lived with our mom."

"Like *The Parent Trap*."

Both women smiled and nodded. "Yes, exactly."

"Except they're twins."

Their faces fell. "Oh."

I didn't believe a word they were saying, but it also
wasn't any of my business. Whatever their reason for
telling them, their half-baked lies didn't affect me, so I
didn't dig any further. "I'll just go get your waffles."

The guests were served, and for about the millionth
time, I thought about Gia and wondered what he was
doing. I went to the rack of scones, grabbed two, and
dropped them into a sandwich baggie. "I'm going to
check on the Expo booth and pick up some more mascarpone and cherry preserves. I'll be back by the time breakfast is over and we can start making the custard tarts."

I parked the car in the Heritage Inn guest parking,
which was a no-no, by the way. Don't try this if you're in
town. I waved to the front-desk clerk and pointed at my

wrist, then flashed five fingers. She nodded and waved me on.

I crossed the street and flashed my vendor pass to get into the Expo. I was hoping Gia could make me a latte before I ran to the cheese shop. I pulled up short and almost knocked over a display of peel-and-stick eye masks. There was a beefy, dark, shifty-looking stranger manning the La Dolce Vita booth. Dressed in a slick, silver dress shirt and black leather jacket. He was handsome in a good-looking, hitman kind of way.

He gave me a chin nod. "Can I help you today, ma'am?"

Oops, I've stared too long. "Erm . . . I was just looking for Gia."

He looked me up and down. "Giampaolo has had to run an errand for the Scarduzio family. He'll be back soon. Would you be Poppy?"

I wanted to wrap my arms around myself and shrink away. "Yep. What kind of errand?" *And why is he running errands for Alex's father?*

He turned his gaze back to the milling crowd and ignored my question. "You have created quite a stir with the family. They don't like a stir. They like to live a quiet life. Maybe you would rather live a quiet life too."

What the crap? This was Gia's idea of a joke for asking all those thinly veiled questions about the Mob, wasn't it? I looked around and scanned the Expo hall to see where he was hiding, waiting for him to yell "Gotcha."

I went from stunned to amused to uneasy when it became obvious that Gia wasn't there. "Is that a threat?"

"No, ma'am. Just an observation. Giampaolo has been through a lot. Why not let him get his life back together instead of creating unnecessary drama?"

"Creating drama? You think I'm creating drama? I don't need this. You can tell Gia this isn't funny." I was so angry I slapped the scones to crumbs on the counter, hugged my purse tight, and spun around to storm off. I just wanted to get away from this goon as fast as possible.

I crashed through the door outside on the boardwalk while a voice in my head kept yelling *wait!* I rubbed my arms against the ocean breeze and calmed myself. Something was wrong. I mentally retraced my steps through my uncomfortable confrontation. *Eye masks, good-looking hitman, threat to be whacked* . . . Then I saw it.

Shayla Rose creeping out of Dr. Rubin's tent with something tucked under her arm. She saw me, then vanished before my eyes.

CHAPTER 29

I ran back inside through the hall with the stage where Dr. Rubin had given his inflammatory keynote speech and back onto the vendor floor from there. I didn't see Shayla anywhere. And her cousins were less than helpful today, pretending like they suddenly didn't speak English. "You're not funny, Jimmy. I know you were born in North Carolina. We just talked about Katy Perry yesterday."

He wasn't budging and I didn't have time to press him further. My five-minute parking at the Heritage Inn was over a half an hour ago.

I collected my car, which had an angry note on the windshield, and drove to the specialty cheese store, then headed home to make the cherry mascarpone filling.

I was getting the bags out of my car when a blue Jeep drove past the house. That's when I heard the *popffftppp!* I dropped to the ground on my belly. *Am I being shot at?* I held my breath and waited. All I heard was *shhhhhhhh*. I peeked through my hair and saw Rabbitzilla bowing down to sniff the daffodils. *Are we on some website of obnoxious Easter decorations to fire at?* I crawled to my knees and pushed the Speed Dial for Smitty.

He answered on the first ring. "I'll get the duct tape."

I didn't appreciate Joanne bullying me—not in high school, not at the reunion, and not while she was wearing my pink cupcake apron. But her custard tarts and chocolate passion fruit petits fours were so delicious that I just wanted to forgive and forget. Then she started making fun of me.

"So, are you trying to get the fat sucked out of your giant butt or your thighs?"

"What are you talking about?" *I hid that brochure in my underwear drawer. She couldn't possibly know about that.*

"I'm talking about you looking for a face-lifter to tackle those crow's feet. I saw the ad on your computer."

"You saw the ad for what?"

"Fraudster. Don't act dumb about it. If my boyfriend was that gorgeous stallion who picks you up, I'd get some work done too."

How did she get on my Facebook account? I stopped filling the chocolate bread with cherry mascarpone and put my knife down. "Where did you see the Fraudster ad?"

"On the tablet when I went to check my . . . stuff. Duh."

"And that has to do with getting liposuction how?"

Joanne's lip curled in distaste. "Gol—I wasn't expecting a tribunal. I just logged in to check my connections and it popped up."

I went out to the front desk and grabbed the iPad. "Here. Can you show me?"

Joanne huffed and snatched the device from me. She clicked the keys and flipped the iPad over. "See?"

"Whose Tinder account is this?"

"It's mine—shut up! Just look at the ad in the corner."

"'Fraudster. Saving your skin from cosmetic surgery blunders.'" I clicked the link. It was a website dedicated to complaints about plastic surgeons. Most of them were about Dr. Lance Rubin.

Joanne flipped the iPad back over. "You can do research on your own time. We have three hundred sandwiches to fill."

She stowed the tablet behind the cookie jar and I picked up my knife. "So . . . you're on Tinder. . . ."

She cut me off immediately. "We're not talking about it."

We worked in relative silence. Making sandwiches, filling bowls of Devonshire cream, lemon curd, and Aunt Ginny's homemade strawberry champagne preserves. We plated everything with the cakes and tarts on three-tiered stands that we'd bought or borrowed from the biddies and their Bingo besties.

Everyone had abandoned us after we'd set the tables up for the one o'clock seating. I was a little worried about Aunt Ginny, who would usually be underfoot right about now, but she had disappeared over an hour ago. That was a long time for her to plot something sneaky.

The kitchen eventually got so steamy from simmering water that Joanne had to open the windows. "Uh-oh. You'd better come see this."

It was still a quarter to one and a dozen ladies were milling about the wraparound porch, stalking the tables. "Where is Aunt Ginny? She's supposed to be checking people in and seating them."

"You better go rein them in or you'll have a riot on your hands."

I pushed through the dining room and found Aunt Ginny dressed like Queen Elizabeth on coronation day, and she was directing ladies to their tables by way of pointing a fancy wand. I sidled up to her and dropped my voice to a whisper. "What are you doing?"

She arched her eyebrows and stuck out her good hip. "What do you think I'm doing? I'm seating everyone."

"What is that in your hand?"

"My jeweled scepter."

I took a long look at the crown jewels and sighed. "That's the doorknob from my bathroom and a curtain pole, isn't it?"

Aunt Ginny looked at me like she was suffering through a conversation we'd had many times. "It had to be done."

"Why couldn't it be done with your doorknob?"

"Mine doesn't look like a giant sapphire."

This was an argument I would never win. "Are you checking people in against the list?"

"Of course I am."

I took one of the laminated guest lists off the sideboard and read the names. "Rita and Faelynn?"

"On the front porch."

I looked through the bay window in the sitting room and, sure enough, the ladies were seated at table one, right out front. "The Hortons?"

"Table five around the corner."

"The Shuttleworths?"

"Table eighteen around the back."

"The Lotts?"

"Right there in the tower."

Two ladies waved to me from the table in the circular tower section of the sitting room.

I handed Aunt Ginny the guest list. "Okay. I thought you were up to something."

Aunt Ginny's eyes drooped and her lower lip jutted out. "Would I be up to something? I know this is a big deal for us."

"I'm sorry. Joanne and I will start bringing around the pots of tea to those who are seated. Okay?"

Aunt Ginny gave me a prim nod. "Okay."

"And please put my doorknob back when we're done here."

"Fine."

"Fine." I went back to the kitchen and filled pots of tea. Joanne and I had made three kinds: English breakfast, Ipsahan—a black tea flavored with violet and rose—and an herbal infusion of oranges and berries that I thought tasted like sangria. I gave Joanne a nod. "Okay, let's do this."

We made our way from opposite ends of the porch, delivering tea and welcoming guests. Joanne started delivering the towers of sandwiches, scones, and sweets while I finished the tea service inside the house. I was delivering a pot of English breakfast to the Lotts at the tower table when I heard the tinkle of a little bell. I only had one room left to serve and I definitely hadn't put a bell in there. I slowly turned around to face the library across the hall.

There they were. The Four Horsemen of the Apocalypse. Dressed in Victorian splendor from their flowered hats and pearls to their lace hankies and feathered neck-lines. The biddies held their teacups in salute and Aunt Ginny snapped her fingers.

I smiled at the Lott party, tried to control the twitch in my eyebrow, and took a pot of violet rose across the hall. "Ladies. You know I'm fully booked for today."

Mrs. Dodson tapped her cane on the floor. "Of course we know. We'd never think of showing up without a reservation. What do you think we are? Barbarians?"

I picked up the laminated guest list in the library and checked it. "I don't see your names on here anywhere."

"Look under Lady Ashcroft." She held her nose high in the air and blinked twice.

"I see. And who is the Viscountess Lady Westbrooke?"

Mrs. Davis tittered and blew her feathers, the exact same shade of pink as her hair, away from her mouth.

I took the bell away from Aunt Ginny. "Uh-huh. I've met the queen here; Elizabeth Windsor, I presume." I turned to Mother Gibson. "And just who might you be?"

The grin she gave me was too devious for a Sunday school superintendent, so I knew they'd been planning this for weeks. "I'm Her Royal Majesty, Queen Sophia Charlotte, the first black queen of England."

"Of course you are."

The ladies leveled even stares at me. I could tell they'd fired their first round and had a rebuttal ready in the chamber. Joanne carried one of the towers laden with sa-vories and sweets for four into the room. "Are you going to help me or what?"

"I'm sorry, I was just trying to make sense of the reser-vation list, here."

Joanne put the tower in the middle of the table. "Don't look at me. Ginny handled most of the reservations."

Aunt Ginny grinned and motioned to the empty seat next to her. "We'll need another tower. As you can see, we have a fifth who's running late."

Mrs. Davis shook a lace hanky at me. "Oh, Poppy honey, before I forget, I heard about you finding that doctor who'd been killed at Convention Hall. That's a shame."

Mother Gibson's lips flattened and she shook her head. "Child . . . they say crazy Agnes killed him."

Aunt Ginny snorted. "Agnes Pfeister-Pinze is still waiting on that appeal that's never going to happen. She should have taken the deal."

I tapped the guest list against the table. "You all know about the lawsuit?"

Mrs. Dodson tilted her head back to look down her nose. "Honey, everyone knows about Agnes Pfeister-Pinze and her lawsuit. She took out a full-page ad in the *Herald* complaining that the Expo should be canceled due to the condition of her nostrils."

Aunt Ginny held up her scepter. "Protesting is not going to get her anywhere. Anyone with eyes can see she got a botched face-lift. But she signed a waiver absolving the doctor of blame if anything went wrong, then she refused to settle out of court like the attorneys wanted. Now he's dead and she's not getting anything."

The front door swung open and Victory ran in, face flushed and dressed in a lace wedding gown shaped like a bell with a bulbous appendage sticking out of her middle. She flopped down in the seat next to Aunt Ginny. "I am soory to be late. I had to feind materneity wedding dress at threift shop. There were so manee to choose from."

I scanned the guest list one last time. "And that would make you . . . ?"

Victory stuck her chin out and posed. "Princess Kate Middleton."

"Uh-huh. Why are you pregnant?"

Victory put her hand over her belly. "In case fancee cat ladee see me. I commeet to role."

God help me. "I don't understand why you're all in costume."

Mother Gibson adjusted her fur cape. "We've been looking for an excuse to dress up."

Mrs. Davis giggled. "Besides, a proper ladies' tea demands formal attire."

Aunt Ginny held her cup and saucer up to me. "Now, buxom housemaid, will you pour whilst we fill thee in about thy beau's incommodious wife?"

CHAPTER 30

If anyone in Cape May County would know about shady dealings and connections, it was these racketeers. I filled their cups with steaming Ipsahan. "Lay it on me, ladies."

Mrs. Dodson dabbed her mouth with a cloth napkin and cleared her throat. "I ran a background check on Alexandra Larusso."

Mrs. Davis tittered. "You mean your daughter Charlotte ran a background check."

Mrs. Dodson gave a reprimanding eye roll at her more lighthearted friend. "I told her what to type. Anyway. We discovered that Alexandra came to the country on a student visa. She didn't graduate from any college or university, and her visa was about to expire when she was fortunate enough to marry a US citizen."

Aunt Ginny held up a cucumber sandwich. "That

would be our Gia, who had gotten his citizenship a few years earlier."

Mrs. Davis giggled. "Lucky girl."

Mrs. Dodson continued her report. "Gia filed for a separation two and a half years into the marriage, so they didn't stay together long enough for Alexandra to get permanent resident status. While background information doesn't tell us what Alex did for the next few years, we do know that she moved around a lot. Charlotte found addresses in six states, and all of them were connected with different men's names on the utility bills."

Aunt Ginny rolled her eyes. "I'm sure that's just a friendly coincidence."

Mrs. Dodson snickered. "In addition, she has some minor traffic violations in Connecticut and she passed a couple bad checks in New York."

Mother Gibson added a few well-placed interjections: "Mmm-mm-mm."

Aunt Ginny adjusted her tiara. "But wait for the big one."

Mrs. Dodson paused for dramatic effect. "Two months ago she was picked up in Los Angeles and charged with indecent exposure and public intoxication on Rodeo Drive."

Mother Gibson helped herself to an egg salad triangle. "That's probably how the uncle found her."

Mrs. Dodson folded her hands over the top of her cane and looked around the room triumphantly.

"Well," I asked, "if she is in the US on a marriage green card, wouldn't she be a citizen by now? It's been six years or so."

Mrs. Dodson shook her head. "She's had her visa renewed, but no formal citizenship application is on record because she would need her husband's signature."

Mrs. Davis grinned. "Probably too busy running around. How did she get the money to afford trips to New York City and Los Angeles?"

Victory held up a chocolate cherry sandwich. "Theis is my favorite one."

Aunt Ginny ignored Victory. "Someone must be bank-rolling her."

"Well, that's something to think about, isn't it?" I said. "What about the arrests? Doesn't Immigration send you back when you break the law?"

Aunt Ginny put her bejeweled hand over mine. "They were all misdemeanors, honey. And she's still technically married to a US citizen."

A very peeved "ahem" sounded behind me. Joanne looked like she'd just done a vinegar colonic and wanted to share her disappointment. "The next time you want to have twenty tables for tea, you can serve them yourself."

"I'm so sorry. I'm coming right now."

Victory called after me as I was leaving the room, "Bring more candee sayndweich."

Joanne and I had served everyone and done a couple of hospitality laps. Now we were back in the kitchen re-filling teapots. I was staring at a lone custard tart on the tray and I could feel myself weakening.

Joanne snickered. "Those aren't gluten-free, you know."

"So, the only things we have that are gluten-free are the things I made?"

She handed me a rice cake from her pocket. "Here you go. Pour a cup of tea and knock yourself out."

Nope. I gave Joanne a dirty look and chucked the rice cake back at her. *See, this is why we called you "buffalo gal" in high school.*

Joanne was slapping herself on the back for that piece

of witty repartee when the back door flew open and Sawyer rushed in. "I'm sorry, I'm sorry, I'm sorry. I know I'm so late."

"Late for what?"

Sawyer looked from me to Joanne. "The tea. I thought you asked me to help."

"I did. You said you couldn't leave the bookstore."

We heard a tinkling bell coming from the library, then the intercom. "Serving wench, we require a fresh pot of Ipsahan and a few more scones posthaste."

Joanne picked up a plate of scones. "I thought you took that bell away from them."

"They had a backup."

While Joanne was serving their ladyships, I sat Sawyer down with tea and a scone. "So, what happened?"

"I don't know. I'm so confused lately. I can't seem to remember what I'm supposed to be doing day to day." She split her scone and slathered lemon curd on one half. "I forgot all about kids story time yesterday until they started showing up. I picked out *A Bargain for Frances*— one of my favorites—then realized halfway through I was reading about a badger's tea party to a room full of five-year-old boys."

I opened the secret Tupperware container I'd hidden behind the potatoes and took out a gluten-free scone. "How'd that go over?"

"Better than expected. The tea party had cake, and cake is a universal language."

I lifted my scone with clotted cream and strawberry jam. "Hear! Hear!"

She lifted her teacup to toast me, and my eyes caught something I hadn't seen in many years.

"Why are you wearing Kurt's ring?"

Sawyer's hand flew under the table.

"It's too late. I've already seen it."

She sighed and took a cucumber sandwich from her plate. "It's no big deal. I don't care if you see it."

Sure you don't; that's why you tried to hide it. "Then why are you wearing your ex-husband's class ring six months after the divorce was finalized?"

"I'm getting it appraised."

Joanne bustled back into the kitchen and frowned when she saw us sitting and eating scones.

Sawyer ignored Joanne's passive-aggressive deep sigh and poured herself some more tea. "I do have some news, though."

"What's that?"

"The Twilight Egg Hunt is back on for tonight."

Joanne snorted. "I thought all the glow sticks were stolen from Congress Hall."

Sawyer shrugged. "I heard some muckety-muck from Philly donated a few cases so the event could go on. They just announced on the radio that the band starts at six."

Joanne made herself a plate of tea sandwiches and stood alone at the counter to eat them. "That's a stupid event anyway. Grown adults hunting glow-in-the-dark, painted eggs."

I grinned at Sawyer. "What time do you want to walk over there?"

She grinned back. "I'll be here at seven."

Joanne grumbled in disgust and left the kitchen.

"I should probably go help her, although she gets to complain about me as part of her benefits package, so I may as well give her a good reason." My phone chimed a text alert and I checked the screen. "Geez, Amber. You'd think she had me on retainer the way she wants me to jump every time she calls."

"What does she want now?"

"She says she's set up a meeting for tonight."

"Meeting with who?"

"She didn't say."

"Why can't she tell you what she's walking you into? What if she's sending you in to another crime scene? Or to contaminate evidence? Are you sure she isn't guilty?"

"I'm not sure of anything except the trust is not going both ways."

"I wouldn't do another thing until she tells you everything. Is there anything else in the text?"

"All it says is 'I'll text you when I'm ready. Don't tell Sawyer.' Oops."

"Why don't tell me? What am I going to do?"

"I don't know. Should I ask her?"

Sawyer's eyes darted to the side. "No, don't ask her. I'm sure she has her reasons."

Okay. Weird. "Since when do we care about Amber's reasons?"

I had more questions, but Joanne busted through the dining-room door carrying three teapots. "A little help out there, please. Tables two, seven, and eight want more tea. We need to start sending this lot off soon if we're going to reset for three o'clock."

Sawyer jumped into action and took a teapot. We all refilled for the various tables. I took the front section and started with the tower table. I had just poured when a bell tinkled from the library.

"You rang?"

"Look!" Victory hoisted a fluffy white Persian over her head. "Kittee come to feind me."

I felt my eyes bug out, but all I could do was stare at Portia, who was licking strawberry jam off her whiskers.

Aunt Ginny pointed at Portia. "That. Plus, we need more lemon curd."

I nodded dumbly. "Okay. Just so you know, I have to prep the three o'clock seating in fifteen minutes."

Mrs. Dodson pressed her lips tight and gave me a slow nod. "We have the room until five."

I lifted the laminated reservations list from the mantel and flipped it over. They were all listed for both seatings. *Note to self: Aunt Ginny doesn't do the reservations anymore.* They would still show up wherever I was serving food, but at least they couldn't sneak in under royal identities.

Mrs. Davis held up the sandwich plate. "Since you're going back to the kitchen, could you also bring some more of the egg salad and cucumber sandwiches?"

Victory squealed, "Candee sayndweich!"

Mother Gibson nodded and her tiara bobbed back and forth. "And some more of those chicken salad in the hot cross buns. Mm-mmm!"

I took the empty tiers from the table to go refill everything—because they'd be asking for petits fours next—and was just about to leave the library when Figaro trotted in with something in his mouth.

I was trying to figure out what it was and whether or not I should be concerned, but he looked around until he spotted Portia in Victory's arms. He trotted over to the table and dropped a stunned chipmunk at Victory's feet. Figaro looked up adoringly into Portia's green eyes, but Mrs. Davis screamed, "Mouse!"

That, in turn, shocked the bejeezus out of the chipmunk, who sprang to its feet and started zipping from room to room, looking for an escape. It ran across the foyer into the sitting room, and one of the Lotts jumped on top of her chair and screamed, "Mouse!" and started a cascade event of women flying from the house in terror.

Figaro was quite pleased with his declaration of love and waited to be fawned over, but Portia only returned a cold hiss.

I was trying to calm the hysteria when Dale Parker came around the corner and into the library, hopping over the zipping chipmunk. "Have you seen Portia? Oh, there you are, darling. Come to Daddy." Dale took the white Persian in his arms and stroked her softly under the chin. "We won another blue ribbon today, didn't we, baby? Come on, let's get you a tuna treat."

Figaro heard the word "treat" and flopped over with a thud, which caused Portia to hiss again.

Dale cradled his cat and marched up the stairs, oblivious to the mayhem Portia had been a party to.

I had to do some quick damage control with the mass exodus while trying to explain that it wasn't a mouse but a cute little chipmunk, like in the cartoons. I picked Figaro up and looked into his bright-orange eyes. "Sorry, baby. I know you like her."

Figaro patted a paw against my lips, shushing me.

"We might have to accept that sometimes, despite our best efforts, it just isn't meant to be."

CHAPTER 31

Figaro's offering of love threw a damper on the one o'clock tea and the women evacuated like there was free money falling on the front lawn. On the plus side, that gave us plenty of time to prep for the three o'clock seating. That one was more chipmunk-friendly and chaos-free.

Joanne reset all the tables with clean linens, Sawyer washed all the dishes while I made fresh pots of tea and refilled the towers, and Aunt Ginny and the biddies used the intercom—since we had confiscated their bells—and demanded another bowl of cream for the scones.

Afternoon rolled into early evening, and Joanne declared that cleanup was my job and left with the biddies, while Sawyer said she had to run an errand but would be back in time to go to the Egg Hunt. The last few ladies were milling around, admiring the antique furniture, and

Aunt Ginny's royal duties were complete, so I asked her the question that had been on my mind all day. "What do you know about the Scarduzio family?"

Aunt Ginny's eyes grew as big as my doorknob and she shushed me. She grabbed my arm and dragged me into the kitchen. "Be careful where you say that."

"I'm in my own house. How much more careful does it get?"

"There are people here. The Scarduzios have ears everywhere."

"You think ninety-two-year-old Mrs. Pawlowski is going to rat on me?"

Aunt Ginny pinched me. "I'm serious. Now where did you hear that name?"

"Ow! That's Alex's family. Gia's wife's maiden name is Scarduzio."

The blood drained from Aunt Ginny's face, and she more fell than sat on the kitchen bench. "Edith didn't mention that as part of the background check. That's not good."

The nerves in my stomach were coming alive. "Why is that not good?"

"The Philly Scarduzios used to come down the shore every summer when I was a teenager to launder money in their Wildwood nightclub. You knew to keep your mouth shut, and whatever you did, you didn't get involved with any of them."

"Well, maybe she isn't one of those Scarduzios. Maybe Alex comes from philanthropic Scarduzios full of nuns and generous billionaires."

Aunt Ginny gave me a look that I usually gave to her when she voiced a half-baked scheme. "What happened?"

I sat across from her with my elbows on the table and

folded my hands under my chin. "I think Gia might be working for the Mob."

"Would that make a difference?"

I was really hoping for something more like "Don't be ridiculous," or "That's your imagination." "If he's been working for the Mob this whole time, I don't know him as well as I thought. And while I can forgive him for not being divorced, this would be one secret too many."

Aunt Ginny nodded, then got lost in her thoughts.

Victory rounded the corner, still wearing her wedding dress and carrying her tote of cleaning supplies. "Bed are turns down, meints are ein peillows, and I caught keitty opening door with her fluffy paw."

And here I was blaming Figaro. "I'll ask Smitty to check the latch on the Monarch Suite."

Victory dug around the refrigerator until she found the Fresca Aunt Ginny was hiding behind the beets. "Seister ladee bought manee things at Beauty Show. She has so manee box of face cream. Her room luuk leike store."

Aunt Ginny narrowed her eyes. "Which lady?"

Victory looked at the ceiling. "Seister in purple room. She eis verry good teipper."

Aunt Ginny sat back in her seat and crossed her arms. "Faelynn?"

I shook my head. "It's none of our business."

She fluttered her eyes. "What do we care that she went to the Expo? I'm sure she has a perfectly normal skin-care routine for a woman her age."

"Exactly. So what that she said she's not into that sort of thing."

Aunt Ginny shrugged. "It's just a coincidence that someone was murdered at the very Expo she said she hadn't been to?"

Victory took a swig of her Fresca. "What eis happening now?"

I shrugged. "I'm sure Faelynn's harmless."

Aunt Ginny and I jumped from the table and raced up the stairs to the Emperor Suite. Aunt Ginny reached around me and knocked on the door.

Victory had followed us and pulled out her key. "No one eis home."

I pushed the door and it squealed as it slowly creaked open, and the three of us craned our necks to look around from the hall. "We've got to stop doing this."

From the threshold we could see the many boxes and tubes and pots of skin-care products lined up on the dresser.

Victory pointed. "See. Eis a lot."

I tried to see what the different items were without crossing into the room. "I don't know. Is that a lot for a woman of her age?"

Aunt Ginny clicked her tongue. "Honey, you are her age. And that would be a lot even for Estée Lauder herself."

I squinted to see the boxes closer. "Maybe she's a distributor. What are the odds that everything would be from the Rubinesque line? See that logo? Those are all Dr. Rubin's products."

Victory kept looking in the room and back to us. "She have your jelleefeish one too."

I took a hesitant step into the room. "Are you serious? Those samples were never given out. They were stolen the night before."

Victory marched into the room to the dresser and held up the little black pot of Shayla Rose. "Eet right here next to Convention Hall teickets and map."

Aunt Ginny blew out her breath. "You know what this means, don't you?"

"What?"

"We're going to have to rename this room the Murderer Suite."

CHAPTER 32

"Maybe she stole them when she knocked the doctor off." Aunt Ginny craned her neck around the door.

"Have you lost your mind? Why would Faelynn murder Dr. Rubin? She doesn't have a botched face-lift."

Aunt Ginny pushed me aside to get a better look in the room. "Maybe he botched something you can't see with her clothes on."

"Well, I saw the crime scene. If it was a robbery, the thief left plenty behind." My back pocket buzzed and we all jumped. I pulled it out to check the screen. It was a message from Amber.

I'm out front.

I typed back: **Of what?**

Your house. Come on!!!

I sighed. This was not the heads-up I had expected from **I'll text you when I'm ready.** "I gotta go. Put that cream back where you found it. And don't say anything to Rita and Faelynn about this. And make sure you keep track of the time I'm leaving. I may need an alibi later."

I ran down the stairs and grabbed my purse from the front desk. Figaro was in the sitting-room window with his paws on the glass. Once outside I discovered the chipmunk parading back and forth on the front porch, flaunting its freedom. Smitty was performing patch surgery on Rabbitzilla and I paused to wave hello.

Wheet wheeeee! Amber leaned on the horn.

I gave her a what-is-your-rush look and she tapped her wrist.

I got to the little green rust bucket but hesitated. I didn't want to be anyone's patsy. "Where are we going?"

"Just get in!"

"No. I want to know who we're talking to first."

"A friend of mine in Woodbine. Now get in or we'll be late."

That was a terrible answer. The least she could have done was lie and say she was taking me for pizza. *I'd get in the car for pizza.* I climbed into Amber's death trap and dug around in between the seats for my missing alibi card from Dr. Rubin.

"What are you doing?"

I pulled out a sticky Whatchamacallit candy wrapper and added it to the pile behind her seat next to the fire extinguisher. "I lost something important when my purse was dumped the other night."

Amber blasted away from the curb and slammed me against the seat. "Yeah, sorry about that. That was Connor Simmons. He can be a real tool."

"He's the one who found the gun in the dumpster?" I

dug between the seat and the center console and found a limp, strawberry Charleston Chew. *Eww.*

"The same. Hey, I've been looking for that." She took the hot candy bar and ripped the wrapper to gnaw off a bite.

"So, what came of that?"

"The crime lab's running tests on the shell casings found in the apartment to compare to the gun they pulled from the dumpster and my service weapon. Then they'll run them through the national database and look for a match."

"That's good news, isn't it? If you're innocent, that should prove it."

Amber stopped chewing and slowly turned to face me. Her eyes had turned cold. "What do you mean, *if* I'm innocent?"

"Whoa! Watch the road!" I'd gone back and forth with my trust in Amber. I used to be a good judge of character. My instincts said she was telling the truth. My instincts had also been making a fool out of me since I drove off the ferry in North Cape May last September, so they'd lost the privilege of being consulted. "I'm just saying you have nothing to worry about, right?"

Amber didn't answer. She picked up a super Big Gulp from her cup holder and took a long drink.

"So . . . what's it like being a cop in Cape May?"

"It's fine."

"Do you have a lot of friends on the force?"

"It's not kindergarten, McAllister."

"I know, but is there any reason another cop would be out to get you? Do you have any enemies on the force? Why would someone want to frame you, specifically?"

Amber stared straight ahead. "Who knows why people do what they do?"

"How about Kieran Dunne? Have you ever worked with him before?"

Amber checked her blind spot, then changed lanes. "He investigated my partner for evidence tampering a few years ago. He accused me of covering for him and interfering with the investigation."

"Did you?"

Amber was silent.

So much for getting Amber's side of the story. We drove in awkward silence for the rest of the trip. I was starting to worry that Amber was taking me out to the Pine Barrens and leaving me for dead when she pulled into a complex of government buildings. The parking lot was nearly empty, and one pole light after another flickered to life as we cruised past. When she stopped in front of the Cape May County Medical Examiner's office, the muscles in my neck relaxed. "Why didn't you just say we were coming to a legit source this time?"

Amber flung her door open. "Either you trust me, or you don't, McAllister."

She slammed her door in my face. I had to crank my window down, reach my arm out, and heave my door from the outside while she waited with her back to me by the entrance.

Amber said something to the security guard on duty and we were buzzed in. Inside we were met by the same woman who had taken Dr. Rubin's body from the Expo. We stared at each other for a moment while I was trying to remember if I knew her name.

Amber cut through our momentary stare down, her words still biting with an edge. "Poppy McAllister, this is

Kat Hinkle. Kat is one of the county coroners. Kat, this is Poppy. She's . . . assisting me."

What was in that pause?

An uncomfortable flicker flashed behind Kat's eyes as she picked up on the tension between us. "Nice to meet you, Poppy. If you'll both follow me, please."

It was immediately obvious that the county government had not budgeted for color. Kat led me through the beige lobby, around a maze of beige walkways, past beige offices full of beige cubicles. I followed behind, silently listening to them chat.

"How are you holding up?"

"I'm hanging in there. I still have one friend on the force who hasn't turned their back on me."

"You know I'm here for you. I'm just sorry we have to do it like this. With your record, I can't believe that anyone would try to pin you with murder in the first. Who did you piss off?"

"When I find that out I'll let you know."

We reached the dead end of a well-lit hallway and stood at a door that said PRIVATE in black-and-white lettering on a beige plaque. Kat pulled out a ring of keys and unlocked the door. The interior looked like a scene from mad scientist theater. Everything was gray: the walls, the floors, the cabinets, the body on top of the stainless-steel table. All gray. I wished I had been nicer about the beige. The ceiling was high, and a giant exhaust fan hung in the center over the exam table. There was a nightmare set of tools on a tray next to the table—things that looked like they were designed in a Nazi medical facility. What was that? A razor? Screwdriver? Giant pliers? I looked down and wished I hadn't. The scariest thing in the room was the drain in the middle of the floor. *Oh God.* My stomach turned over. The room was cold, but the air was stifling.

"McAllister! Don't pass out in here. You'll contaminate the evidence."

I grabbed the counter by the sink and made the mistake of looking on the tray next to it. "What's that?"

Kat was pulling on latex gloves and glanced over at the tray. "That's a bone saw."

White prickles of light filled my vision and my mouth went dry. Amber jerked me up by my shoulder. "Get ahold of yourself. Look in my eyes. Think of this as a set on a TV show, got it?"

I tried to focus on her, but she was wavy, like someone needed to adjust her picture.

"All of these are props, and that's an actor getting paid to just lie there. Now just breathe normal in and out of your nose. That's it."

"It smells like ammonia and bad pickle juice."

Kat pulled on a lab coat. "That's the formalin. You get used to it."

Amber got something off a shelf behind me. It was a surgical mask. Then she took a vial of lemon essential oil out of her front jeans pocket. "Rub this under your nose. Now put this on. Pretend you're an extra on the set of *Bones.*"

I did as she said, and the thudding of my heart quieted down.

Kat picked up a laser pointer and started to go over the deceased body of Temarius Jackson.

I tried to blink back a couple of tears, but they escaped. I expected him to look like a dangerous street thug, maybe a gangbanger from the news, but he was so young. Just a child. Why are human beings so cruel to each other that his life was valued less than another's? I wished I could turn back the calendar and warn Emilio that Temarius was in trouble.

Amber shook something at me. She was eating a bag of Funyuns. "Hey, focus."

"Two gunshot wounds midchest. Based on apparent diameter, the wounds were made from a large-caliber handgun. The soot and stippling around the wound show that the gun was fired at very close range. The wound track traveling downward to the rear of the aorta."

I felt like a fifth-grade math student who got lost on the way to long division and ended up in advanced calculus.

Amber must have seen my dazed expression. "It confirms that the shooter shot him from above while he was sitting on the couch."

I nodded to Kat to continue.

"Exactly. I was able to remove two projectiles and the lab has them now. They are not consistent with a nine-millimeter from your semiautomatic, police-issue firearm."

Amber ate another Funyun. "What are all these marks?"

Kat turned her laser pointer to a reptilian-like pattern on the body. "Now, that is fascinating. It's postmortem bruising from the body being packed in ice cubes."

I raised my hand. "Why would somebody do that?"

Kat turned off her laser and put the device on the counter. "To mask the time of death. Somebody wanted to slow down decomposition, so it would appear like the victim was killed much later than he was."

"How much later?"

Kat replied, "Hours. I've rolled the time of death back to sometime early morning."

I thought back to the crime scene. "That's why the couch was all wet."

Amber paused with her Funyun halfway to her mouth. "You could have mentioned that sooner, McAllister."

"You got a text message from him at eight p.m., an hour before you found him. How did he pull that off?"

Amber shrugged. "I'm not tech savvy; I have no idea."

I looked back at Kat. "Can I ask another question?"

"Yes, of course."

"Did you test his blood to see if he was on anything?"

Kat nodded. "The routine toxicology screen came back negative."

"So he was clean. No drugs."

"That's right."

Amber balled up the empty bag and tossed it in a trash bin marked recyclable. "Thanks, Kat. I appreciate this."

"There is one more thing you need to see." Kat walked over toward the door and hit the light switch. We were immersed in darkness. Kat lifted the edge of the sheet, and we could see that all of Temarius's fingers were glowing a dull blue.

Amber leaned in closer. "What is that?"

Kat bent down with Amber. "Chemical luminescence. I'm still waiting on results from the lab as to what kind."

I recognized that color. "I saw this blue-glowing dye at his house the other day. Like something had leaked out of a box on the floor. Could it be from glow sticks?"

Both women looked at me like I'd just solved my first word problem.

"It's just that someone stole several cases of glow sticks from Congress Hall a few days ago and they were never caught."

Amber cocked an eyebrow. "You also didn't tell me you found evidence at the crime scene."

"You were kind of busy getting arrested."

Kat examined Temarius's left hand. "It could be chemiluminescence from cyalume in glow sticks, but he would have to have been exposed to a very high concentration to still glow days later."

"Did you find out what the glowing blue goo was in that mask that killed Dr. Lance Rubin?"

Kat pointed at me. "That's where I know you from."

Amber dropped her head back and groaned. "What did you get into now?"

"I'm sorry, which one of us is the murder suspect this time?"

Amber made a face at me and I matched it back to her, but it lost its significance behind the surgical mask.

Kat turned the lights back on. "Test results from the UV light mask should be here Monday morning. In the meantime I'll run another chem panel on your gunshot victim to see if there's a toxic level of phenyl oxalate ester in his blood to confirm the glow sticks theory. I have to warn you, though, even if we can prove there was a chemical agent in play, the cause of death was still catastrophic injury to the heart and blood vessels from the shooting."

I took one last look at the boy in front of me and made him a silent vow. *I can do very little to affect change in a broken system, but I will do all I can to bring justice for you.*

CHAPTER 33

"Who would kill a seventeen-year-old kid over a case of ninety-nine-cent party supplies?" I breathed deep in the fresh air. Anything to clear my senses from the smell of death and ammonia.

Amber slammed her door and one of the ceiling thumbtacks fell to my seat. "I don't suppose there's anything else you forgot to tell me about the crime scene?"

I stuck the tack back in while my mind went to the cell phone I found in Temarius's couch. If the time of death was early morning, whoever texted Temarius that they were on the way was probably the last person to see him alive. How much could I trust Amber that she wasn't using me to gather evidence for her to destroy? Maybe she brought me here to see if the shock would cause me to spill something. "Ah, no. Nope. Nothing else to report."

Amber frowned and turned the key in the ignition. The

Pinto coughed and sputtered like someone had bent the tube on its life support.

I yanked my seat belt on and felt like a traitor. I couldn't even look at her. What if I held the one piece of evidence that would exonerate her?

"I had no idea you would be such a baby in there."

"It was horrible. How can you stand it?"

Her voice was quiet and soft. "It's easier when you don't know the victim."

I could feel her sadness. Amber and I had a terrible history together, full of backstabbing and mistrust. I wanted to send an olive branch, but I didn't want it flung back in my face. Instead, I tried small talk. "How did you not notice the couch was all wet?"

Amber threw the car in Neutral and pumped the gas pedal while we rolled backward. It was like a time bomb that eventually groaned its way to a mediocre explosion. "I was too busy checking for a pulse. Then Simmons and Crabtree showed up with their guns blazing. I couldn't very well go around contaminating the crime scene while we waited for the coroner to arrive. My name's not Poppy."

That's the third person this week to call me Poppy and make it sound strange. I'm having a weird week. I pulled out my cell phone and texted Kim.

Can I program a text message to be delivered at a later date?

Yeah. Depending on your phone. You may need an app. Let's try it.

The Pinto sputtered and stalled. "You need a new car."

Amber gave me some side-eye. "Yeah, I'll move that up to the top of my priorities, right after 'get a good defense lawyer.'"

"Who did Temarius live with? There was a second bedroom."

"It's his grandmother's apartment. He'd been living with her since his mother died of a drug overdose when he was seven."

"Where's the grandmother now?"

"She's been visiting her sister in Tallahassee. I think the sister has cancer."

"So, she doesn't know about Temarius yet?"

Amber sipped her Big Gulp. "I don't know if the station has tracked her down. They'll coordinate with the Tallahassee Police to inform her of his death in person."

We got on the road and were lulled by the rhythmic *thump-thump, thump-thump* of Route 47.

My phone broke the silence between us with Bruno Mars singing "Count on Me." I dug it out of my pocket and answered. "I'm sorry, I'm running late. Why don't I meet you there in about thirty minutes? Ooh yes. Get me a fancy water."

I clicked off, and after a minute Amber asked, "Was that Sawyer?"

"Hm? Yeah."

"You two have plans?"

"Uh . . . yeah. Yep. We do."

A few more awkward seconds passed. "Where you going?"

"Twilight Egg Hunt."

Amber tapped a beat on her steering wheel, then took a drink of her flat Big Gulp. "Have a good time."

"Yeah, thanks."

She dropped me off at home and said she'd be in touch. The Pinto stalled again. She cranked the motor, then it belched a cloud of exhaust before driving off.

Dale and Patsy were sitting in rockers on the front porch drinking champagne. "Poppy, did you hear the news? Our little Portia took first place in the Pretty Kitty Cat Show."

"Congratulations. Portia is a beautiful girl."

Dale beamed. "Her fur was exceptionally soft this weekend."

Patsy leaned back in the rocker. "I think the salt air agrees with her."

That or the bacon. I picked the empty bird feeder up and rehung it on the pole. "That's fabulous. Are you going to the Twilight Egg Hunt at Congress Hall? I was just on my way over there."

Patsy picked up the champagne and refilled their glasses. "We saw that advertised at the Cat Show. It sounds like fun."

Dale waved me on. "I think we'll pass. We're exhausted from the day. We've already tucked Portia in for the night."

I could clearly see Portia behind them in the bay window, swatting at Figaro's tail, but I was already late enough, so I smiled and waved and told them to have a good night.

The streetlights twinkled against the purple and orange sky. Congress Hall was a short walk away. I faintly heard the band playing "All About That Bass" from down the street. There would be nowhere to park within blocks, so I set out on foot.

Congress Hall was a historic, seaside boardinghouse built in the late eighteen hundreds. Three stories high, with a mansard roof and covered colonnade, the beautiful yellow hotel was built like a giant L opening to a giant, grassy lawn with a swimming pool and a garden facing the ocean. The lawn was covered in neon Easter decorations and hiding one hundred luminescent dyed eggs. The bright lights were keeping the eggs hidden, but once they went out and the black lights were turned on, everything would glow.

I handed in my ticket and found Sawyer at the popcorn vendor, just like she said she'd be.

She had to shout to be heard over the band. "What took you so long?"

"Our appointment was all the way up in Woodbine. Did I miss anything?"

"Only the rules. They're going to start any minute. Follow me. I think I spot a yellow one in the knot of that tree."

We meandered over to our starting point and waited for the signal. I drank my flavored water and filled Sawyer in on the visit with the coroner. She made appropriate faces of disgust as I described the nuances of a room designated for removing and weighing organs.

Most people came to the Egg Hunt in the spirit of the event, wearing glow-in-the-dark bracelets and necklaces, glow sticks wound in their hair like curlers and around their waist like belts. Many of them had created designs on their faces that were coming alive the moment the black lights came on. I asked one girl, "How did you do that?" and circled my face.

"It's rave makeup; you can buy it on eBay."

The music stopped, and someone in charge blew an air horn, and chaos erupted.

I gave Sawyer a leg up to get whatever was in the knot in the tree. A painted duck. It was a clever ploy. There were decoys everywhere. I grabbed a neon-green tennis ball, then tossed it back under the azaleas where it came from.

Sawyer grabbed my arm. "There!" A glowing pink orb

barely sticking out of some boxwood hedges. We took off running, but some men tracked us and followed our path. I broke off to create a diversion and dove on a tuft of plastic tulips. Two of the men followed me and left one to chase down Sawyer.

I got to my feet and brushed off my jeans. "Sorry. I guess it was just the moon." When they had left on the scent of another prize, I caught something out of the corner of my eye. It was a tiny wooden egg glowing a soft orange, hidden in the cup of one of the tulips. I plucked it from the flower and held it tight. It had number 27 on the bottom in gold paint.

"You found one!"

I looked up and into the face of a woman who had gone full-on, glow-in-the-dark blue.

"Nice rave makeup."

She touched her face. "Makeup?"

I noticed her fingertips were slightly blue as well. I circled my face. "Your rave makeup. A lot of the girls are wearing it."

"I'm not wearing anything."

She looked confused so I took out my phone, turned off the flash, and took her picture to show her.

She gulped and started patting her face. "The only thing I'm wearing is the Shayla Rose antiaging concentrate I got at the Beauty Expo."

"Immortality? The little black pot with the pink writing? I thought they were all stolen."

She nodded. "I got a sample when we were setting up on Wednesday. I run the Kefir Everything booth."

Sawyer showed up next to me, panting and bending to work out a side stitch. The front of her body was covered in mud and she had a scratch on her cheek, but she victoriously held up a glowing, blue-painted egg. "That jack-weed tried to take it from me. He'll be limping when he gets up."

I took the egg from Sawyer and held it up to the woman's face. They were both glowing blue. I handed it back to Sawyer.

"What's wrong?"

The lady was trying to wipe the blue off her face with the corner of her shirt. "What if it's toxic? If I get skin cancer from this, I'll sue that Shayla Rose for every penny she's got. You don't think she put glow-stick chemicals in the concentrate, do you? I look like an idiot."

I remembered Shayla's words. The cream wasn't on the market. I kind of recalled her saying she wasn't *allowed* to sell it yet. Maybe something about it *was* toxic. I hadn't thought much about it then, but now I had to wonder.

Sawyer cocked her head from side to side, examining the woman's skin. "It's not coming off. Maybe it will be gone by morning."

The woman kept frantically scrubbing at her forehead. "She's lucky they were stolen. Can you imagine if she'd given out all of them?"

An announcement came over the speaker to report in when you were finished so they could see how many of the eggs had been found and how many were still out there.

Sawyer and I made eye contact and passed the message that we wanted to go register our eggs.

Sawyer reached out her hand toward the woman, who now looked like a character from Avatar. "I'm so sorry. I hope you are safe, and it all works out."

I added, "I'll stop by tomorrow and check on you."

She nodded, and we left to find out what our eggs

won. Apparently, I won a five-dollar gift card for Douglass Fudge—just what I needed. And Sawyer won a twenty-five-dollar gift card to Slap Yo Mamma! the Caribbean fusion restaurant on the mall.

Behind us, we heard a series of *whoop-whoops* as a group who had pooled their resources had found six eggs and won the grand prize: a five-hundred-dollar gift card for the Radiance Day Spa at the Chambers Mansion. They started swaying and singing "We Are the Champions."

Even though the group was covered in rave makeup and matching UV-painted T-shirts declaring them the Four Queens, I still recognized them. One of the queens tapped her cane on the ground and gave me a chin up, while the little redheaded one winked a glowing pink eyelid at me and grinned.

I shook my head and tried to take in just how lucky they were, but before I could congratulate them, my phone chimed that I'd missed a call and received a voice mail.

"Who is it?" Sawyer asked.

"I don't know. I don't recognize the number, but it's local." We walked a few steps away from the judges' table, where it was a little quieter, and I played the message on Speaker.

"'Hello? Hello? Are you there? Is this recording? You kids never answer your phones anymore. Always running the streets when you should be at home. This is Idel Rotnitzky. I told you I'd call. Your blonde is back. She just walked past my apartment. I think she's breaking in across the hall again. I'll call you back when she's leaving, but if you want to catch her, you'd better hurry."

CHAPTER 34

"I gotta go."

Sawyer mirrored the concern on my face. "What's wrong?"

"I have to run out to the Villas. Oh, I wish I'd brought my car."

"I'll drive you. I'm right across the street."

We started heading for the exit. "Are you sure you're free?"

Sawyer shoved her gift card in her front pocket. "Yeah. I don't have anything until midnight."

"Midnight? What do you have going on at midnight?"

Sawyer's eyes rolled up to the side. It was one of her tells. So was the fact that her cover stories were always poorly thought-out. "Bed. I have plans to go to bed. At midnight."

"Okay, don't tell me."

We crossed the street and climbed into Sawyer's car.

She pulled away from the meter, and a stack of papers fell from her visor.

"These are parking tickets. Good Lord, Sawyer. Where have you been parking? You walk to work!"

She snatched them up and stuffed them in a tote bag between the seats. Then she tossed the tote bag to the back. "Don't worry about that. That's nothing."

"Nothing? That must be a fortune in fines."

She shrugged it off. "We're going back to where I picked you up the other night, right?"

I settled back in my seat, concerned that she was having money problems. "The same."

"What are we doing there?"

"Trying to find out once and for all if Amber is using me as her scapegoat. She told me she wasn't allowed to go near Temarius's apartment and that's why she sent me in. But if she's there now like Mrs. Rotnitzky says she is, then I'll know she's been lying to me."

When we arrived at the Bay Vista apartments, I had her park in the back. "Do you see Amber's little green Pinto?"

"No. And none of the cars are on fire, so we can rule them out."

"I hope we haven't missed her."

We dove out of Sawyer's car and hit the ground running to enter the dark lobby. I flew up the three flights of stairs while Sawyer lagged behind. There was no one in the hall by Temarius's apartment, but one piece of the crime-scene tape had detached and was dangling. I heard a *ding* and spun around. Sawyer popped out from around the other corner. "Where'd you come from?"

"Elevator. I'm not climbing all those steps. Now, what are we looking for?"

Mrs. Rotnitzky's door opened a crack. She peeked out and the door closed again. Then it opened all the way and she dragged us inside. "Come on before she sees you."

The three of us stood in her apartment. Sawyer and me with our ears to the door and Mrs. Rotnitzky standing on a footstool with her eye pasted to the peephole.

"I see you brought Slim with you."

"She drove me."

"Good plan. That way the blonde won't notice your car."

"Have the police been back?" I asked.

"Once. An officer was here this morning, but he didn't stay long. I think he wanted to check the apartment to make sure no one had broken in again." She gave me a pointed look before going back to her peephole.

Sawyer caught my eye behind the old woman's back. Her eyes rolled down to the end table, where there was a full bottle of Jack Daniel's.

Mrs. Rotnitzky stayed glued to the peephole. "Yeah, I got more Jack. My check came, so I went shopping."

A few minutes went by and I was getting antsy. Sawyer was well past me. She was staring at the television behind us, which was playing some dating show.

I drew back and looked at Mrs. Rotnitzky. I was impressed that she was statue still looking through the peephole. "How much time do you spend doing this?"

"In a day or at a time?"

"At a time."

"Forty-five minutes is my personal best. That's about as long as I can hold my bladder."

We heard a door open and shut down the hall, and then voices.

Mrs. Rotnitzky threw back the chain. "This is it! Here she comes! Get ready, girls!"

Sawyer and I stepped away from the door and waited. My heart was pounding. I didn't want to look. I didn't want to know the truth. I'd be deeply disappointed if I caught Amber coming out of Temarius's apartment. It wouldn't be a surprise coming from high school Amber, but I realized I had come to respect adult Amber.

Mrs. Rotnitzky yanked the door open and jumped out into the hall. "Aha!"

We sprang out after her and found ourselves looking into the very surprised eyes of a man of slight build with long blond hair. To be fair, he could have passed for Amber's brother. If her brother were about sixty, partial to ribbed turtlenecks, and walking a corgi wearing a baby-blue bandanna.

The man pulled out a canister of Mace. "Stay back! I'm armed."

The corgi peed a little.

Mrs. Rotnitzky pointed at him. "There she is. The blonde I told you about."

I held my hands up in surrender. "I'm sorry. We were expecting someone else."

He recapped his canister and stuffed it back into the little pouch on his belt. "Now see what you've done? You've made Olivander piddle."

Mrs. Rotnitzky fast-waddled back into her apartment. "Doggone it. That was almost a new personal best."

Sawyer was no help at all. She doubled over with laughter.

It was up to me to apologize. "We didn't mean to startle you."

"Be glad I didn't Mace you. I'm a little jumpy. I moved in a few months ago with my girlfriend in four-sixteen. I didn't realize this was a high crime area." He tipped his head toward Temarius's apartment.

"I don't think it is. I'm sure you're very safe here."

"Really? How safe were we around this kid? Huh? The whole time Olivander and I were down the hall rolling sushi, this kid was here rolling joints and who knows what else."

"I heard he was a good kid. What would make you think he was doing drugs?"

"I could smell it. My first week here, I called 9-1-1 to report him. After that there were cop cars here all the time. Routine patrolling? I don't think so."

"Did you happen to see a cop here the day he died?"

"Are you kidding? First the one arrived, then within fifteen minutes they were all over the building. I overheard that one of the cops plugged him during the drug bust."

"Did you hear the gunshots?"

He considered that while Olivander lay down on Sawyer's foot and rolled his belly to her. "No. We only heard the commotion from the sirens when they came flying past our window."

I looked down the row. "So, you're across the hall from Mrs. Rotnitzky?"

He jingled Olivander's leash. "That's right. I bet it's a lot quieter on her side. We have to deal with the traffic on Bayshore. I'm sorry, we have to go for a walk before it gets too late. Come, Olivander. It's time for potty."

He picked up the corgi and disappeared around the corner by the elevator.

Sawyer looked at the puddle on the floor, "I think he's too late."

"I just want to know how Mrs. Rotnitzky, in her eighties, charged up on Jack and Coke, heard the gunshots from her apartment, but that guy and his girlfriend two doors down didn't hear a thing."

CHAPTER 35

Sawyer and I thanked Mrs. Rotnitzky for her watchful eyes over the hallway and the alert that "the blonde" was on the premises. Then we explained that the blonde with the corgi was, in fact, a man, and her new neighbor. She didn't care for that and started looking through her phone book for the apartment landlord to report a trespassing man with lady hair. So, we settled her into her stuffed rocking chair, handed her the remote, refreshed her ice, removed a cobweb that had been bothering her but she was too short to reach, watered a ficus on the other side of the living room, and promised to bring her a box of Tagalongs the next time we were in the neighborhood.

Once we'd extracted ourselves from our captor, we headed back to my house. The wind was picking up and it smelled like rain. Benjamin Bunny was bouncing around on his tether like a Macy's Parade disaster. "Looks like a storm is brewing. Are you coming in?"

Sawyer frowned. "I can't, I have to go by the bookstore to check on things."

"Check on what? You're closed."

"I have to . . . drop some stuff off and . . . make sure the lights are turned out."

"I can go with you."

"No! It's fine. You've had a long day. Just go in and get some rest."

Riiight. "Is this your midnight appointment?"

Sawyer blushed. "It's only ten o'clock."

"Okay. I'll talk to you tomorrow, then."

Sawyer's grin didn't meet her eyes.

I waved when I was in the house and she drove off. Figaro met me with his list of complaints. I scooped him up and nuzzled him. He rabbit-kicked my hand to express that he was too dignified for this display of emotion, but his purring told another story.

Faelynn and Rita were in the library. Rita was on the guest computer and Faelynn was reading her romance novel. They asked about the Expo and if there were any updates on the plastic surgeon's death. I told them no and chatted with them for a few minutes. They were both still in a somber mood and Figaro was flicking his tail with impatience, so I said good night.

We headed to the kitchen, as was our custom, and I stopped by the front desk to check my messages. My phone buzzed. It was Kim.

I sent this right after the last message for three hours in the future. Did it work?

Yep. Thanks.

So, apparently you can schedule texts in advance. I got

my laptop and headed to the kitchen. Fig and I shared a piece of cheese, then I had a snack. Fig had forgotten that he'd already had dinner, so he whined for me to open a can. I ignored him, so he swatted a bottle cap off the counter. Then a box of Claritin, a bottle of thyroid medicine, two pens, and a clip for my hair. Then Fig had a snack so he would stop acting out.

I was on my way upstairs when there was a knock at the front door. I opened it to see the stranger from the La Dolce Vita booth at the Expo. *He'd better not be here to make me an offer I can't refuse.*

I looked left and right to see if there were any witnesses about. Even Rita and Faelynn had gone up to bed. *Where are these nosy neighbors when you need them?* "What do you want?"

"Mrs. Larusso would like to remind you that church tomorrow morning starts at ten thirty."

What kind of maniac . . . It's after ten p.m. "I haven't forgotten."

"She would also like you to remember that dinner in her home follows the Mass. Dress appropriately."

I blinked a couple of times, stunned for a response.

He turned and walked down the sidewalk and disappeared into the night.

Figaro gave me a look that said he was just as surprised about it as I was, and what we needed was another snack to overcome the shock.

I took the laptop up to my room to shake off the uncomfortable encounter. I had some research to do, and I went in the bathroom to get my Shayla Rose Immortality concentrate. My doorknob had been replaced as promised. It was installed backward with the lock on the outside, but it was there.

I searched for the cream everywhere. I wanted to Google the ingredients listed on the label. It wasn't in my makeup bag or my medicine cabinet. I got on my hands and knees to see if it had rolled behind the toilet. It was missing.

I looked around the room, exasperated, and an idea struck me. I turned out the lights. A blue glow backlit the gauzy, white curtain in my bathroom window. Then I remembered the police chase a few nights ago. I had left the open container on the windowsill. The cream was glowing bright blue. It wasn't glowing the first time I'd used it, so something had changed.

I dabbed a tiny bit on my jaw to see what would happen. The spot lit up like Aunt Ginny's lava lamp. I jumped in the shower and quickly washed it off, along with all my makeup. After I toweled off I put on my night moisturizer and eye cream. I'd been at the Beauty Expo for three days and with all the drama it hadn't occurred to me once to go shopping for supplies.

I was seriously behind in my laundry duties and I'd reached the bottom of the underwear drawer. I put on an old pair that were a little tight and pulled over some raggedy yoga pants to hold them in place. My faded tank top was two sizes too small and made me look like a really low-class stripper who would be asked for change. *I really hope there aren't any guest emergencies in the middle of the night.*

I took the cream to the bedroom, swept Figaro off my laptop, and scolded him for trying to bite my hand. "What's gotten into you lately? Do I need to change your food?"

Figaro flopped on the bed and made a slight bounce.

I could no more see the list of ingredients on the tiny pot of antiaging concentrate than I could see the dust on the moon. I took a picture with my phone and sent it to myself in an email. Once I'd blown it up on my laptop screen, I started a deep dive into jellyfish venom essence and luciferin. Apparently, jellyfish toxins are supposed to make your skin look younger by making it hydrated and glowing. *That's a big check on the glowing.*

Shayla's website promised that jellyfish toxins numb the muscles that cause wrinkles just like Botox, only the jellyfish toxins absorb through the skin without the need for injections. There was a photo of the cream in the jar glowing bright blue and the caption said, "Your skin will glow from the inside out."

I had to look up a lot of words like "hyaluronic acid" and "retinol." Apparently, luciferin was what gave the cream its luminescence. The antiaging concentrate's list of benefits made it sound like a miracle drug that would take thirty years off your appearance and get you dates. Ironically, no mention of turning you into a Smurf—although there was a warning to keep it out of the light and only wear it at night.

Shayla's website also promised that Immortality would be on the market soon and to check back often. And, of course, there were a few other products you could buy in the meantime.

Figaro started galloping back and forth around the room for no apparent reason—his favorite reason to do things. I tried to Google Shayla Rose herself, and Figaro pranced across my laptop and Googled Shia LaBeouf. I picked him up and stared into his wild orange eyes. "Be have." I placed him on the bed, and he attacked my foot. "Ow. Knock it off."

My second attempt found a couple of articles about Shayla in cosmetic industry magazines. She was listed as a research scientist and marine extraction expert with a degree in biochemistry. A link to a cosmetic industry journal reported that two years earlier, Shayla was reprimanded by the board of dermatology for selling products before they were FDA approved.

Her Facebook page was the normal collection of memes and photos. Shayla and her friends eating at an Indian restaurant for her birthday. Shayla posting her list of favorite movies. Shayla and her friends posing at the Adele concert. Shayla posting that she wanted a Pomsky puppy more than anything, and her grandmother leaving a series of awkward comments on the post asking if Shayla was coming to dinner on Sunday and did she want dumplings or steamed buns? There was a post last year when Shayla started a new job at Shayla Rose Skin Care that had a lot of congratulations and well-wishes. She'd commented that she was on the verge of going big-time because of a discovery she'd made in her jellyfish toxin research.

A Fraudster pop-up took over my screen and I searched for Shayla on their website. No hits. I guess there wouldn't be. It was all plastic surgeon complaints and warnings. Figaro dove on my foot and bit me through the blanket. I jerked my foot away and he did a flip and a roll because one claw was stuck. "It serves you right." I extracted his claw and heard a quiet meow from the other side of my bedroom door.

Figaro's ears swiveled like a satellite dish and he jumped off the bed, taking up a position across from the door.

"Well, hello beautiful."

Little Miss Portia blinked her big green eyes and gave another little meow, as if asking to come in.

Figaro went through a complete transformation, suddenly graduating charm school in the next thirty seconds. He sat, very handsome and dignified, and waited for his lady friend to *entrez-vous*.

She placed a tentative paw over the threshold and Figaro's whiskers twitched. When she'd come all the way into the room, he dove under the bed and came back with some hideous, frayed toy chicken that I thought was long gone. He dropped it at her feet and awaited her approval.

She gave it a tentative pat and Figaro flopped with a thud.

Dale's voice floated up the stairs. "Portia honey . . . come to Daddy. Treat."

Portia shot out of the room like a kid who heard the ice cream truck coming down the block.

"I'm sorry, baby. You tried."

Figaro settled into loaf position in the middle of the floor to strategize his next move, and my cell phone rang.

"Amber?"

"I know it's late, McAllister. And I wouldn't ask if it wasn't important. But I just got a really big lead and I need someone to check it out with me."

"When?"

"I'm outside by the mailbox."

CHAPTER 36

"You know, the world wouldn't end if you gave me a fifteen-minute warning for a change."

"We have to go now before the evidence disappears."

An assault of leaves peppered the car and Mr. Winston's trash-can lid flopped around, beating a warning to go back inside. I crouched down and held my hair in place. "I have to change. I can't go anywhere like this. I'm in pajamas and flip-flops."

Amber scanned me. "If you had a toddler on your hip and a cigarette hanging out of your mouth, you'd be my last bust before I was put on leave. But we don't have time for you to change. Just get in. No one will see you but me anyway."

Against my better judgment I hopped in. The spring in the passenger seat poked me in the backside and I hit my head on the ceiling. "Ow! You need to get that fixed."

Amber pulled away from the curb. "My seat's fine."

"So, what is this about evidence disappearing? You're afraid someone is covering their tracks?"

"Well, yes. But in this case the rain is our enemy."

The seat belt had betrayed me and fused into place since our trip to the medical examiner's office. No matter how much I yanked, it wouldn't budge. I finally got it to come out far enough to click it into place, but if I breathed out, I would crack a rib. "Okay, where are we going?"

"What I'm about to say to you never leaves this car. Got it?"

"Absolutely." I'd hold my breath, but I didn't have any.

"I got a tip from Birkwell. He responded to a call that vandals were hitting an abandoned warehouse on the outskirts of Wildwood Crest. When he arrived on the scene it was just some kids skateboarding in the parking lot. He gave them a warning about trespassing, sent them off, and did a security walk around. He found this on the side of the building." She pulled up a screen on her cell phone and handed it to me. It was a picture of blue, glowing fingerprints by a door and on the security keypad. "He was able to scan them and run them through the police database. They're a match for Temarius."

"Did Officer Birkwell go inside the warehouse?"

"He can't go in without a search warrant."

"Oh yeah, that makes sense. . . ." My heart dropped an inch in my chest and I sighed. "That's why I'm here, isn't it?"

"Okay now, settle down. Nothing will happen if you don't get caught."

"Are you new here? Have you seen my luck with crime scenes? I've been home six months and I'm rack-ing up bodies like a Viking on a rampage. People are going to be afraid to come near me."

We passed Maxine's and all the lights were on. Tim and Gigi must have had a full house tonight.

Amber noticed me looking. Probably because I twisted my neck around like an exorcism candidate. "How are you doing with that?"

"With what?"

"You know. You finally made a decision and it bit you on the . . ."

I cut her off. "How do you know about that?"

"It's a small island. For what it's worth, I like Gia better. And I've never seen any indication that he's involved in anything criminal."

I felt like a two-hundred-pound gorilla had been lifted off my back. "It's probably ridiculous that I would even think there's Mob activity in Cape May, right?"

Amber didn't answer.

"Right?"

Amber gave me another long pause. "I'm just saying I don't think Gia is involved in anything like that. If he is, he's been very smart about staying under the radar."

Never mind. The gorilla's back.

We started passing low, aluminum industrial buildings and scrap yards. This was a part of town they don't put on the vacation brochures. We pulled into a gravel parking lot surrounded by a ten-foot-high chain-link fence. There were several nondescript, gray-blue metal buildings with wide garages. A couple had very industrial-sounding names on them like Shotcrete and Keen Canning and Fishery. We pulled up to one that looked like a perfect place to cook meth.

"Birkwell said the door was on the side, so I'm going to park around the back so we aren't seen from the road."

I followed the roofline of the buildings and the electrical poles for cameras. "What about the security system?"

Amber glanced up to where I was looking. "I don't see anything obvious. The warehouse is listed as abandoned, so there probably isn't anyone watching it from outside."

"Do you really believe that?"

"No."

We got out and scanned the parking lot. I pointed to a few beer bottles and empty cigarette packs and a yellow T-shirt or rag that had been ground into the mud. "It looks like the skateboard kids use the lot to party."

Amber stuck to the shadows and headed toward the door with the glowing blue marks. "Hopefully that's a good sign that there isn't a lot of traffic in or out."

We stood before a bare metal door with no signage. Only a nine-digit keypad. There were blue fingerprints and half a handprint near the keypad, and a smudge of faintly glowing blue halfway down the door. Amber put on a latex glove and handed one to me. She tried the knob and the door was locked.

I looked closer at the keypad. "Wait. Shift this way and block that little bit of streetlight. I think the code is these four numbers. They're the only ones with the blue glow to them."

Amber examined the buttons for a moment, then punched in 1-9-7-6. The lock released with a loud click.

"How'd you figure that out?"

"I pressed them in descending order of how strong they were glowing. If he used the same finger, he wiped a little bit off with each number." She held the door open for me to go in.

I felt like I was reliving my summer camp swim test. That did not go well, and I had similar expectations for this jump.

Amber pressed me on the back. "Get in there before someone spots us."

"It's dark."

She shoved a flashlight in my hand, pushed me through, and shut the door behind me. *Well, I just hit the bottom of the pool.* With a shaky hand, I turned on the beam and threw it around like I was hypnotizing a moth. Checking out this room would take all night at this rate. I took a breath and turned the flashlight off and waited for my eyes to adjust. Partial blue shoe prints tracked from the door to the middle of the room. I followed them to where a table was set up with boxes and canisters and changed back to the flashlight.

Amber opened the door a crack. "Well? Did you find anything?"

How could I describe what I was looking at? My hands were no longer shaking because my brain was working overtime. "You need to come see this."

The door closed and quick, irritated steps came toward me. "What?"

I shone the flashlight on the worktable covered with boxes of low-quality cold cream from the discount store, professional-looking containers that said Shayla Rose Skin Care, six cases of premium-grade glow sticks, and Shayla Rose's stolen, sample-size jars of Immortality. "Dear God, what have we walked into?"

CHAPTER 37

Neither of us spoke. I didn't think Amber understood all the pieces we were looking at. I pointed at the broken containers of Shayla's antiaging concentrate. "That's why there are glowing prints everywhere. He must have broken a couple and tried to clean them up. He didn't know it was going to glow in the dark."

Amber shook her head and poked her flashlight into the cold creams. "What exactly was he trying to do here?"

"Do you know what's been going on at Convention Hall with the death of the plastic surgeon?"

Amber shook her head. "I've been focused on Temarius."

I explained to her who Dr. Rubin was and how I had found him dead in one of his new UV masks with glowing blue goo inside it. I pointed my flashlight to the glow sticks. "Someone, presumably Temarius, stole these from

Congress Hall last week. Then these little black jars with the glowing blue goo in them were stolen from Convention Hall Wednesday night, also presumably by Temarius, considering all the evidence he tracked into his house and then here."

Amber sighed. "By Thursday morning he was dead in his apartment, and Thursday night I received a text from him to meet."

"Oh yeah. That checks out, by the way. Kim and I tested it."

She nodded. "An hour later I found his body. So how are they connected?"

I examined the table and asked myself what would Aunt Ginny do with all this. "What if someone was making a knockoff face cream to copycat Shayla Rose's new bioluminescent, antiaging concentrate? They stole her samples for what? To break down the formula?"

Amber looked dubious. "Do you see a laboratory in here?"

"No, but I see enough evidence that someone with no idea what they were doing thought they could use the chemicals in glow sticks to mimic the luciferin in the jellyfish to make dollar-store face cream glow."

Amber considered my proposal and nodded. "Or. What if there is no knockoff? What if this is where Shayla Rose makes her face cream? Maybe the whole bio-anti-whatever-you-said is fake. Those containers sure look professional."

"Those are her colors, but I don't think she ever intended for her cream to glow in the dark."

Amber strangled a chuckle. "I don't see how Temarius would be involved in this. He just got into mechanic school. And he was trying so hard to get his life together to make his grandmother proud of him. I can't see him masterminding a scheme to make fake wrinkle cream. And then do what with it?"

"Sell it on Amazon or eBay. Shayla told me the market is flooded with counterfeit products that might as well be mayonnaise."

Amber's face scrunched up on one side. "The timing of this is all wrong. Why would he do this now?"

I knew Temarius wasn't working alone, but I'd struggled with fears that Amber might be making me her scapegoat, so I'd kept silent. It was time for me to take a leap of faith and trust her. "Listen, there are a couple of things I haven't told you."

Amber's expression fell from confusion to frustration; even in the ghostly glow of the flashlights, I could see she was hurt. "This is going to piss me off, isn't it?"

"I found something in Temarius's couch. A cell phone. With only one unnamed contact. I think it's a burner. Whatever he was mixed up in, he wasn't working alone. And I spoke with some of his friends at the Teen Center. They said he was involved in something he didn't want to be a part of, but someone had leverage over him. He said he lost something important and he was going down hard because of it."

Amber's jaw dropped and she blinked a few times. "Oh my god, are you seriously just telling me all this now? Whoever was pushing Temarius to commit these crimes most likely killed him. He didn't have an accomplice; he had a handler. Why would you keep that from me?" Her expression changed to shock and she gasped. "Wait . . . you thought I was the handler."

"Well, I couldn't be sure yet."

Amber started to pace. "I don't believe it. Even when you were the prime suspect in a murder investigation, I still treated you with respect."

"I wouldn't say that. . . ."

She turned around fast. "I did! And I knew you were sneaking around, interviewing suspects to try to clear your name and I turned a blind eye."

"You did threaten to put me in jail a lot."

She threw her arms out. "For your own protection!"

"Uh . . . The word 'obstruction' was used many times."

"Because that's what it's called! I still gave you more than a little leeway. I even saved your life."

"The biddies were already . . . you know. That's not important."

Amber rattled off a few choice swear words, then stopped in front of me. "I came to you to help me clear my name."

I spoke to her like I was trying to calm a wounded possum because her eyes and her ponytail were both looking a little wild. "Okay, now, see . . . that's a good thing. So, let's do that. Let's just forget that I accused you of setting me up and move on from here. Maybe go get a smoothie sometime."

Amber held up a hand in my direction. "Baby steps."

"So, what do we need to do next?"

Amber took a beat to calm herself down. "We need to look into this Shayla Rose because I'm not convinced she isn't behind her own fake production. What I don't know is, what's her connection to Temarius?"

"I think we need to find out who owns this warehouse. Whoever that is, cop or criminal, they were handling Temarius, and I think they killed him when he became a liability."

Amber gave me a nod. "But why frame me?"

"That's the big question. Why you specifically? Who knew that Temarius was your CI and would want to take you down? Who knew they could get you to his apartment at the right time and place?"

The door flew open, followed by a loud bang. An impossibly white light pierced the room and I was blinded. The ringing in my ears was louder than anything I'd ever heard, and someone tackled me. I was dizzy and felt like I might vomit, but I just lay there praying it would be over soon. When the ringing died down to just excruciatingly annoying, I heard a man yell, "Hands behind your back. You have the right to remain silent . . ."

My hands were jerked together and zip tied. I knew Amber was getting the same treatment just a few feet away.

We were dragged outside and I was shoved down into the back of a police cruiser. The door was slammed shut, hitting me on the cheek. That would leave a bruise to match my hip. My pupils were starting to dilate again and I could just make out the flashing blue lights.

"Sit tight. We'll be at the station for processing in no time." It was a woman's voice. It came out garbled and faint, and I didn't recognize her.

"What was that?" I realized too late I was yelling.

"Small flash bang. The nausea will pass soon."

I looked out the window into the other cruiser. The suit was standing outside Amber's window talking on a cell phone, looking smug. Amber and I made eye contact just before the sirens blared and we pulled away.

CHAPTER 38

Amber and I were split up for booking. This may have been her first time on this side of the process, but I was familiar with the drill. First Miranda rights, then fingerprinting, then mug shot. Today's police photographer thought he was a comedian. He snickered at my frizzy, wind-whipped hair, blotchy skin, and three-day-bender tank top, and asked if I'd like copies for scrapbooking. "Sure. And maybe an eight by ten."

I was handed off to Officer Consuelos. He took one look at me and made a quick call home on his cell phone to say he would be late. "What happened?"

I tried to discreetly shift my underwear back in place through my yoga pants. "Amber said no one would see me but her."

"What were you two doing breaking into private property?"

"I can't say."

"You're only going to hurt yourself if you cover for her." He lowered his voice. "You tripped a silent alarm while trespassing on private property. If the owner presses charges, there will be additional fines and possibly jail time."

"I don't think the owner will do that."

"Why not?"

"I think the owner will want this to go away very quietly."

He gave me a deep sigh and pulled out the perfunctory paperwork. Most of the perp questions, like name, age, and address, he already knew, so he filled them in while I looked around in utter disbelief that I was arrested yet again. *If Amber had only given me that fifteen-minute warning, at least I'd be wearing a bra.* I caught sight of a folder marked Dr. Lance Rubin on top of his desk.

"What's going on with that investigation?"

He kept his head down but scanned the station to see who was around. "I can't talk about that."

"Well, I may have some information to trade."

He gave me a questioning eyebrow raise and I returned a cocky one. Officer Consuelos slid the folder my way and knocked it open with his pinkie. Then he bent down to tie his shoe.

Inside were copies of the death threats that Dr. Rubin had received. They were pasted together from magazine clippings. "You're a butcher and you deserve to die." "Your death will be slow and painful." "I will make sure you're scared for life."

"Well, I know who sent these."

He sat up quickly. "Who?"

"These are from Agnes Pfeister-Pinze. She called Dr. Rubin a butcher during his keynote speech right before she attacked him. Plus, see how she misspells 'scarred' as 'scared'? She spelled it like that on her protest sign too. She's been sending these threats for a year. She obviously has no intention of following through on them. Besides, if she really meant to kill him, he'd have been dead a long time ago. She got close enough to shock him with her pink-lady Taser before Convention security grabbed her. I think she really wanted to take him to court to humiliate him."

Officer Consuelos gave me an appraising nod. He pulled something small and red from the back of the stack and unfolded it. "Do you know anything about this?"

"Someone left these stickers all over the Expo. Fraudster's a website dedicated to negative reviews about plastic surgery in general, but most of the information is about Dr. Lance Rubin and the several open malpractice suits against him. I understand most of those lawsuits are anonymous."

"Do you know who's behind the Fraudster organization?"

"No idea."

Officer Consuelos pulled out a thick packet titled Cyber Forensics. "This is the investigative report on the Fraudster website and negative reviews left on four different surgical review forums. Dr. Rubin ordered the digital investigation late last February. One of his nurses just got the report last night and faxed it over. Almost all these reviews came from the same IP address and it's registered to Fraudster.org out of New York City."

I discreetly thumbed through the pages. The report was at least a LifeSavers width thick. "These were all left by the same person?"

"The same IP address."

"Isn't that the same thing?"

"Not if different people hop onto the same shared Wi-Fi, like at a library or a coffee shop. Of course, the address registered to this IP looks like it's in an upscale residential neighborhood in Manhattan. Do you have any ideas on this one?"

I checked the dates of the report. The last entry was from a week ago. "I might. See if you can get an update of postings over the last couple of days from the cybersecurity company."

He gathered up the papers and closed the file. "Done. And don't take long. The coroner is waiting on one more report before she rules Dr. Rubin's death a homicide, and the longer it takes to start the investigation the more time the murderer has to destroy evidence."

"Okay. Now I want something."

He nodded.

"Who reported the trespassing?"

He typed some info into the computer. His eyebrows scrunched together and he opened a new screen and typed something else. He glanced at me, then picked up his desk phone. "Gloria, did that ten-thirty-one in the Crest come through Dispatch? Thanks." Officer Consuelos made a face and hung up.

"Well?"

"Apparently, there's no record of the call."

"What does that mean?"

"That means it came from inside the station. Maybe someone got an anonymous tip on their cell." He saw someone approaching from behind me and his jaw tightened.

"Officer Ben, can I have a moment with the lady, please?" It was the suit I'd seen at both of Amber's crime scenes. He was a few inches shorter than me, but his dark hair and blue eyes were striking. I bet those supermodel eyelashes got him a lot of praise. He was very good-looking, even for someone so grim.

"Yes, of course sir." Officer Consuelos excused himself but passed me a silent warning over the man's head before disappearing.

The man took a small knife from his pants pocket and cut through my zip-ties. He returned the knife to his pocket, then sat on the edge of the desk opposite me and gave me a charming smile. "What's your name?"

"Poppy Blossom McAllister. One seven two–three nine—"

He chuckled and held up his hand. "It's just an introduction, Poppy—may I call you Poppy? I'm Kieran Dunn with Internal Affairs. Do you know why I'm here?"

"You're investigating Officer Fenton."

"That's right. And were you aware that eyewitnesses placed her at the scene where a young boy was shot in cold blood in his apartment last Thursday?"

"If you mean Idel Rotnitzky, she may not be the most reliable witness. Especially after she's been hitting the whiskey."

He grinned. It was friendly and warm but had an edge of patronizing. He was smug. On second thought, he wasn't that good-looking. This wasn't polite chitchat. He was trying to trick me into giving something away to incriminate Amber.

"I know that Amber is a friend of yours."

Then you obviously haven't looked into her past arrests.

"And you want to help her. But I must warn you, she

hasn't been truthful with you. She hasn't told you everything."

"Like what?"

"Did you know we found a handgun on the victim's premises?"

"Did you?"

"Well, that gun was confiscated in a domestic disturbance eight weeks ago. The officer who confiscated the weapon was Officer Amber Fenton."

I had the feeling in the pit of my stomach that you get right after you eat something, and the last bite tastes not quite right, and you know the day isn't going to end well.

"Officer Fenton filed a report on the incident and the handgun seizure, as an officer is required to do, but the gun was never logged into evidence, according to procedure. Now, what are the odds, do you suppose, that a bullet, pulled from the chest of the victim, would match that very handgun?"

"I wouldn't know."

"Well, I'll tell ya. About one in four hundred million."

I swallowed hard. "Did you check the gun for prints?"

He tapped me on the knee like he was proud of me for coming up with that question. "We sure did. And you know what? The gun had been wiped clean. Now, why do you suppose that is?"

"I would suppose that the killer wanted to frame a decorated officer of the law and didn't want his fingerprints on the weapon to mess up his plans."

Kieran Dunne kept smiling, but his eyes flashed anger. "Why are you helping her?"

"Who says I am? I'm only pointing out that your argument has holes in it."

He leaned down until we were practically nose to nose. "So, I guess we'll be putting you down as an accomplice, Poppy Blossom McAllister."

"You can put me down as whatever you want. It won't make me guilty of anything."

"Dunne!" An officer in a white dress shirt poked his head around the corner. "What are you doing?"

Kieran took out a pair of tortoiseshell glasses and slid them on. "Conducting my investigation, Chief. Surely you don't have a problem with that?"

The man came to stand beside Kieran Dunne. He was tall, probably my height. His mink-brown hair was graying at the sideburns. He had a medium build and a slim waist, with a badge hooked onto one side of his belt that said Chief of Police. His sleeves were rolled up and he was wearing a leather shoulder holster that was soft and faded, the brass buckles having lost the shine from their finish. I would have expected the police chief to look like he had a drawer full of punch cards for Dunkin' Donuts, but he was very fit. I sucked in my stomach.

"We have protocols here. You can't interrogate a witness on the floor of the station house. That's what the interview rooms are for. Besides." He turned and smiled at me. "Miss McAllister isn't fully processed yet." He put a hand on my chair. "I'll take it from here."

Kieran Dunne leaned down with his hands on the arms of my chair and growled a raspy threat. "I will prosecute Officer Fenton to the fullest extent of the law and I'll make sure you go down with her."

The chief's voice was gruff. "That's enough."

I glared at the IA officer. "What happened to innocent until proven guilty? Or do they only teach you how to make threats in Internal Affairs?"

With my head held high, I stood up. My underwear did not stand up with me. They rolled down in a twist of horror that made me appear to have a rope tied around the top of my thighs under my threadbare yoga pants. Chief Fischer had the decency to act like he hadn't noticed and led me across the room of police officers and perps being processed. With my eyes straight ahead and my knees together, I clenched and followed behind.

CHAPTER 39

"I'm sorry about that. Internal Affairs is the butt crack of the police force. You know they're necessary, but you never want to see one in your face." He flicked on the bright, overhead lights and motioned to a chair opposite his desk. "Please, sit." He leaned back in his chair till it bounced a little. "Officer Crabtree tells me you were with Officer Fenton while trespassing in an abandoned warehouse. Is that right?"

This might have been part of good cop/bad cop, but I was still mulling over the butt-crack analogy. I was also wondering if he'd noticed I'd hiked my underwear back up when he was turned around.

He picked up my arrest documents to review them. "Do you want something to drink? Some coffee, tea?"

I shook my head. "No thank you." I caught sight of a framed photo of a collie on his desk. "That's a beautiful dog."

He swiveled the photo toward me and smiled. "This is Clementine. She's my baby. It's my ex-wife's name, but I've had more loyalty and affection from the dog."

The tune from *Huckleberry Hound* invaded my mind and I giggled under my breath.

"So, what were you and Amber looking for?"

I shrugged. "I don't really know."

"Just tell me this. Did she find anything useful to prove her innocence? She's a good cop—maybe one of my best—and I trust her, but she's given me nothing to work with to defend her actions, and IA is breathing down my neck to prosecute. You met Kieran Dunne. He's a little dog with a big bark."

He had kind eyes, and he didn't look down on me the way Kieran Dunne had. But this wasn't my world in here. I didn't know who to trust. I barely trusted Amber and I'd known her for thirty-five years. So I was careful not to give him any evidence he didn't already have. "We know that Temarius Jackson was at the warehouse before he died because he left fingerprints on the keypad, but we didn't find anything that proves who killed him or why."

Chief Fischer sighed and folded his hands. "She's running out of time. As it is, I have to put her in a cell overnight for obstruction of justice and evidence tampering. She can bond out in the morning."

The officer who had pulled the gun from the dumpster walked past the office and the chief called him in. "Simmons. Come here."

This was the first time I'd seen Officer Simmons up close and not through a rearview mirror. He was young and pale blond, with pink skin and a broad forehead with brown eyes too close together. His lips were too pink, like he'd just eaten a cherry Popsicle. He glanced at me and held my tank top too long in his sight. Simmons was a smarmy-looking cop. The kind you'd expect to suspect you're hiding evidence so he'd have just cause to pat you down. "Yeah, Chief?"

"Hey, where's Fenton right now?"

"Pru's got her in a holding cell with that drunk and disorderly."

"No. Get her out of there. Tell Officer Crabtree to put Fenton in the overflow cage. We don't put cops in Gen Pop."

Simmons took off to rescue Amber. I felt sorry for her. She didn't hesitate to lock me up, but still. This had to be hard on her. I wished I had some Juicy Fruit gum to offer her.

Chief Fischer leaned forward in his chair and clasped his hands together. "I'm releasing you on your own recognizance. You'll have some paperwork to fill out and you'll get a notice in the mail advising you of your court date. In the meantime, stay away from Amber. It's for your own good. And don't worry, I've got her back. I've got my best cops working on finding the truth. We won't let her take the rap on this."

He stayed at his desk, but hollered through the door, "Consuelos!"

Officer Consuelos poked his head in the room and checked for me. "Yes, Chief?"

"Have Miss McAllister sign the OR papers and make sure she gets home safely."

Officer Consuelos waved his fingers for me to come with him. I stood and joined him at the door.

"And Ben, find out what Dunne is up to." The chief quirked an eyebrow.

Officer Consuelos nodded. "Understood." He walked

me back to his desk and gave me the paperwork to fill out. He also let me make a phone call for someone to pick me up.

While I waited an eternity for my ride to arrive, I watched the police come and go. Their wary eyes always checking me out to see if I was a threat. Officer Simmons returned with a box of coffees and doughnuts from Wawa, and the other officers swarmed his desk. Prudence Crabtree tried to take two and said one was for the chief. She was accused of being a kiss up and put the coffee back with a rude gesture. The chief eventually came out and got his own coffee and told Simmons to bring it directly to him next time.

A code came in over the loudspeaker and there was a sudden shift in mood. Cops started gathering their gear to go on patrol, and those who worked behind desks made themselves look busy. I heard a *squgg squgg squgg* come down the hallway issuing unsolicited advice. "Gladys, I love the new hair color. It matches the veins on your cheek. Mike, you've been hitting the doughnuts, I see. Those bad guys'll be able to outrun you if you're not careful. Ben, I didn't know you worked the graveyard shift. Weren't you at the Expo all day yesterday?" Aunt Ginny had arrived to take me home.

Officer Consuelos didn't get away fast enough. "Yes, Mrs. Frankowski. We're working rotating shifts until Memorial Day. I should have left at midnight."

Aunt Ginny took a look at me and her eyes popped. "Holy cow! Did you walk out of the house in that getup?"

I gave her a slow nod.

She doubled over laughing. "Tell Carl I want a copy of that mug shot."

Officer Consuelos, the rat, promised Aunt Ginny he

would let Carl know. I mouthed a warning to him, but it made him more amused.

Most of the cops had scattered to their corners, and I made a show of finishing my paperwork while Aunt Ginny slipped me something out of her girdle. "I hope this is what you're looking for. It took forever to charge on that USB cord on the computer."

"This is it." I took the burner phone and held it under Officer Consuelos's desk. I turned it on and prayed it wouldn't sing a song or anything.

A policewoman started heading toward us and Aunt Ginny sprang in front of me. "I want to file a complaint about a recent crime wave against my lawn ornaments."

She'll regret coming to work today. The call log screen came up; I hit Redial and held my breath. Across the room, I heard a phone vibrating on a metal desk but couldn't pinpoint its location. No one reached for anything. I was just about to hang up when a cop came around the corner carrying coffee and a sandwich. He heard the buzzing, went to the desk, put down the coffee and picked up the phone. "Yeah?"

I heard the "yeah" come through the burner. I disconnected and, as nonchalantly as I could, walked to the hallway where Aunt Ginny had cornered the policewoman. I grabbed Aunt Ginny by the arm. "She'll call it in later. We gotta go."

I dragged her to the front desk, afraid the burner phone would ring any second and we'd be discovered. I furiously tried to turn it off, but it had a will to live and refused to power down.

Aunt Ginny collected her purse and driver's license and we fast walked to her car, trying to avoid suspicion. "Who was it? Who's the handler?"

I kept looking behind me to see if we were being followed. I dove in the passenger side and shut the door. Once Aunt Ginny pulled out of the parking lot I could breathe again. "Your driving has really improved. You haven't come close to hitting anything yet."

She held up a pack of gummies with one green bear left. "I think I see better with the sugar rush."

Aunt Ginny had shown up at the police station to bail me out high on gummy bears.

"So? Get on with it! Who answered the burner?"

"The head of the Internal Affairs investigation, Kieran Dunne."

CHAPTER 40

"I know you don't like it when I come into your room when you're asleep, but we have to leave in twenty minutes to go to church with your potential future mother-in-law, so you may want to get up now."

My eyes popped open and my heart cranked to a sprint. I knocked my phone off the nightstand trying to check the time. I forgot to charge it. *Oh no.* I fell out of bed and ran to the bathroom. "Why did you wait so long to come and get me?"

Aunt Ginny was serenely sitting at my desk in a pink-floral ensemble and a coordinating spring hat. She even had on her Sunday heels. She'd apparently been up preening for hours. "Because you said not to sneak in here when you're sleeping anymore."

"Yeah, but you did it anyway. I'm just saying, why didn't you do it sooner?" I splashed cold water on my face and dabbed some depuff cream under my eyes.

"I started to get worried when you slept through break-fast. Don't panic; Joanne had it covered. She made the cutest little fruit salad Easter baskets out of cantaloupe halves. I only came to get you because this is the first family event we've been invited to and I don't want us to make a bad impression."

I didn't have time for the elaborate hairstyle I'd been planning for days. I brushed my hair out with a dab of styling oil and wound it into a French twist with one loose ringlet down the side. At least I'd gotten all the twigs and leaves out from last night's overzealous SWAT raid. "Did you save me a fruit salad?"

"No. Joanne said fruit wasn't keto, so she didn't make you one. But she left a protein bar on the counter with a sticky note that says, 'Happy Easter.' I thought that was nice of her."

That was passive-aggressive of her, and Joanne knew I would pick up on it. I blended in some color corrector to hide my sallowness and dark circles. "How much time do I have left?"

"Twelve minutes. We weren't supposed to take any-thing, were we?"

I stopped midswipe under my eye. "Oh crap. I don't know. I'm sure we at least need a hostess gift. What am I gonna do now?" I grabbed my cyeliner.

"I'll take care of it. You can't think of everything. You were up until past two trying to do a good deed for Amber. She always was a high-maintenance little thing. Remember when she went home early from that Hal-loween party because of a few peeled grapes?"

I came out of the bathroom and threw open my closet. "Yeah. She mentioned that she was still traumatized about that."

"Silly girl. She's lucky she didn't put her hand in the Jell-O. I had your great-grandfather's dentures in there."

I pulled on a pale-yellow sundress and turned so Aunt Ginny could zip me up. Figaro pushed his face against the door and wedged his way into the room. He was wearing a bright-pink bow tie and had a little tan top hat sticking off the side of his head. "Oh my Lord, just look at you. You are so handsome, Fig!" I wanted to pick him up, but I couldn't be covered in cat hair for lunch at Momma's house.

Figaro dropped to a roll and lifted his back leg for a special Easter wash.

Aunt Ginny nudged him with her foot. "That was a present from Dale and Patsy. Wait until you see Portia. They had a photo session before breakfast. I'm pretty sure there will be hell to pay later. Figaro looks irritated in every picture."

I grabbed my pale-yellow sweater and slipped on my chunky white heels. "Let's go."

Aunt Ginny held up her hand. "Not so fast. Where are your blue diamond earrings?"

"I can't."

"You need to make a statement that you're in this for keeps. He'll understand."

I opened my jewelry box and took out the gift I'd received for Valentine's Day. "Are you sure?"

"One hundred percent."

Portia lounged in between Patsy and Dale on the love seat in the sitting room, wearing a fuchsia tutu, a tiara clipped in the fur on top of her head. I stopped long enough to give a snort of delight. "You look adorable."

Dale held up his cell phone to show me the photo with Fig. "Here they are together."

Portia was clearly used to posing for publication. She looked like a *Cat Fancy* supermodel. Figaro, however, looked like he'd been given cold oatmeal for breakfast. His ears were pinned flat and he couldn't hold his head from the burden of the very heavy top hat. His orange eyes were slightly squinty, so I knew he was planning vengeance for later. "That's awesome."

Dale asked if he could put the picture on Portia's website, and I assured him that we would love that.

Aunt Ginny jerked her head toward the door in a we-gotta-go move. I told Dale and Patsy I'd see them this afternoon and we headed to my car.

Our Lady Star of the Sea was on the Washington Street Mall, two blocks down from La Dolce Vita. A beautiful gothic church built from gray granite and limestone with an eighty-foot-tall bell tower that was now ringing the call to Mass.

We stood on the front steps waiting for Gia, wondering what to do next.

"Poppy, over here." Karla waved us over from inside the Romanesque archway. "Gia has saved you and your aunt seats with the family."

Aunt Ginny and I followed Gia's sister up the aisle while trying not to gawk. The interior was cream and gold and beautiful in its own right—like cathedrals I'd visited in Rome years ago. But the real beauty was in the stunning, stained-glass windows. Sparkling jewel tones depicting scenes from the Bible that were even more beautiful from outside when all lit up at night.

Karla led us to a wooden pew at the front and indicated that we were to sit in the empty spots on the end. Farther down the pew in the middle was Oliva Larusso, Gia's momma. Dressed in her festive Easter blacks, she grimaced when she saw me and crossed herself.

I tried to encourage Aunt Ginny to climb in ahead of me, but she grunted and swiveled to my back. So I slid in toward Momma and left an empty spot between us for Gia, who still hadn't arrived. I repeatedly looked over my shoulder to see if he was coming up the aisle. I was still angry about that wiseguy stunt that was pulled at the Expo yesterday, and I was hoping to get a chance to speak to him about it before Mass began. I yawned, and Momma caught me. She did not look pleased that I wasn't giving full respect for the Lord's sacrifice even though I'd only had a few hours of sleep and the service hadn't begun yet.

Aunt Ginny leaned into me. "What are we supposed to be doing?"

"I think we're waiting for it to start."

"Are we supposed to go up there and light one of those candles?"

"I don't know." I looked around. "Wouldn't someone tell us if we had to do that?"

Momma cleared her throat. Apparently, it was quiet reflection time.

I was reflecting on how I ended up coming to Easter Mass with this sour woman in the first place. I repented of that uncharitable thought and shifted my mind to last night, and how someone on the police force had a little beauty cream side hustle and it appeared to be Kieran Dunne. I yawned again, and Aunt Ginny elbowed me in the ribs.

I checked the time. If Mass started in ten minutes, then why were so many people getting up and moving around? There were two little booths at the front of the room on the left. Maybe we were waiting for the priest to make his entrance from one of those. The little wooden door opened, and Tally exited one of the booths. I jabbed Aunt Ginny.

"Oof. What?"

"That's Tally. She works with Dr. Rubin. What's she doing here?"

"Going to confession, from the looks of it."

I watched her walk to the back row, cross herself, and sit down. *Were we supposed to cross ourselves when we got here?*

"Hello, hello." While I was watching Tally, Alex had snuck up behind us. Her voice was definitely above a whisper and no one gave her the evil eye. I'm just sayin'.

Momma lit up like she'd been plugged directly into the transformer. She waddled over to give Alex a hug. She stepped on my foot, and the black taffeta of her hat veil poked me in the eye.

Alex greeted Momma in Italian, then changed to English for my sake. "We're sorry we're late. You know how hard it is, trying to get a child out the door."

We?

Aunt Ginny looked behind me and slumped down in her seat with a groan.

Alex was wearing a beautiful, green silk dress covered in little embroidered rosebuds. Henry was behind her in a matching green sweater and khakis. His hair was slicked back and held into place with gel. And Gia was behind him, wearing an identical outfit to Henry's. The three of them had coordinated like it was family portrait day.

Aunt Ginny grabbed my wrist under her coat to keep me from escaping.

Momma ushered Alex and Henry past her so they would be on the far side, away from me. Then she sat on my hand to keep Gia from sitting next to me. *"Mi scusi."*

Gia started to protest, but a white-robed priest took the podium, and he was forced to move to the other side of his mother.

I had the distinct feeling that this orchestrated plan had begun from the moment my invitation to dinner was extended.

The service started, but my mind was on Gia and his nuclear family next to me. It took me fifteen minutes to realize everything being said was in Latin. Apparently that was the "special" in special Easter Mass. We were having a lot of position changes from sitting to standing to kneeling, then back to sitting.

Aunt Ginny and I were not Catholic, so we really didn't know what we were doing. By the time Aunt Ginny got on her knees, it was time to stand up again. I had to help pull her to her feet. Aunt Ginny had grown up Methodist. Methodists don't kneel.

"I hope all that praying was for healing, because I'm going to need it." We shared a look that said this was the last time we'd be doing this.

There were a lot of things the congregation had to repeat, and they were written in a little booklet in a pocket on the back of the pew. I tried to keep up, but I lost my place and said, "And also with you" to a dead-silent church. The priest glanced at me, then away.

Aunt Ginny whispered, "I don't think that was right."

"No."

Alex snickered, and Momma snorted her disapproval.

The priest called everyone up for Communion, where an altar boy held a little gold mirror under your chin. I started to get up, and Momma put her hand on my shoulder and muscled me back to the hard bench.

Alex explained as she passed us, "Catholics only."

Momma must have weighed out taking Communion versus losing her seat to keep me in check. Guarding the heathens on the bench won out.

All through the service I could feel Gia's eyes on me, but I refused to look at him. My agony was on full display and it wanted to hand him his diamond earrings and hit the bricks. Have a nice life. Tears welled in my eyes and I had to force myself to think about something else.

Tally. Why was she here? Other than it was Easter, and this was probably the closest church to her hotel. Was she devoutly Catholic or looking for absolution for Dr. Rubin's death? And if the latter, what did she do? And what was the Phoenix Protocol?

The priest gave a hand signal that the service was over.

I blew out my breath in relief and Aunt Ginny muttered, "Thank you, Jesus!"

When everyone started milling around and greeting each other I made a beeline away from Gia and his perfect little matchy-matchy family toward the back row. "Tally? Hey, Happy Easter."

"Oh, Poppy right? Yes, Happy Easter to you too. I was just on my way out."

"I'll walk with you."

Her face fell.

"I bet you miss being at your home church today. Especially with it being Easter Sunday."

Tally looked for the exit. "I don't really go to church much. I just needed to get some spiritual guidance this morning."

"Sure. I understand, with all that's been going on. But you must be feeling better to know you don't have to track down the cyber forensics company now."

She looked confused. "What do you mean?"

"The company Dr. Rubin hired to find out who was behind the online slander? You were worried because you didn't know how to contact them. The report is in."

"Are you sure? How do you know?"

"The police have it. I was there last night . . . helping with the investigation. . . . I saw it." I suspected that leaving out the arrest and booking part of my night was probably a sin. Maybe I should go sit in that booth at the front.

"Well, that is a relief." Her eyes told a different story. They shifted around like she was trying to recall some information. "Did the police say how they got the report?"

"They said one of the nurses faxed it down."

She nodded. "You know, I was going to leave, but on second thought, I'm going to go pray and light a candle for Lance."

Is that what those are for? I looked up to the front of the church, where the candles were lined up across a table. I caught the wooden door swing open, and Gia came out of one side of the booth. Out of the other side exited a man dressed all in black. Gia handed the man a fat wad of cash and they shook hands. *What in the world was that?*

"Especially after my unpleasant run-in last night," Tally droned on.

"Uh-huh."

"I caught a woman coming out of his hotel room."

"You caught a what?"

"A woman. Coming out of Lance's room. It got me so upset, it's why I came to the Mass today."

"A woman? Was she with housekeeping?"

"No. I think she was searching his room for valuables. I called out to her and asked her what she was doing there, but she ran off."

"It wasn't Agnes Pfeister-Pinze, was it?"

"No. But she was older. I know I've seen her before. She had on these designer red glasses and had hair like you, but with a blond streak across the front. If I see her again, I'll try to get a picture."

There was no need for a picture. I knew exactly who she was talking about, and I would see Faelynn Archer as soon as I returned to the B&B.

CHAPTER 41

"Don't leave me back there with those weirdos." Aunt Ginny grabbed my arm. "First you ran off like the priest was going to bring you on stage as a cautionary tale against dating, then Gia evaporated into thin air. What's gotten into you two?"

I tried to excuse myself from Tally, but she had already escaped. "Did you see where Gia went?"

"No. He just vanished. Not that I blame him . . ."

"I just saw him come out of the confessional. That's what that box is up there, isn't it?"

Aunt Ginny followed my stare. "Don't think too much about what he was confessing. That won't do you any good right now."

I was more concerned with what looked like a shady payoff. "Do people normally give sizable cash donations after confessing?"

Aunt Ginny shrugged. "Maybe it's a new type of penance to save on all those Hail Marys."

I felt a dark presence behind me and turned to see Momma glowering at my back. She handed me a folded piece of paper. "You come now." She waddled away.

Aunt Ginny's eyebrows shot up and disappeared under her hat. "You said she didn't speak English."

I opened the paper and read the address. "I swear, that is the first thing she's ever said to me that wasn't in Italian or a hand gesture. You don't think she overheard us talking about Gia, do you?"

Aunt Ginny adjusted her hat veil. "We'll find out soon enough. That address is just around the corner."

When we walked down the steps of the church, Mrs. Dodson and Mrs. Davis were waiting on a bench outside. They waved me over and handed me a gift bag. "It's a cut-glass olive-oil cruet. For the battle-ax."

I hugged them and fought back tears of relief. "Thank you. You're lifesavers."

Mrs. Davis patted me on the arm. "Lila would have been here, but she has a big Easter brunch with all her kids and grands after church today."

Mrs. Dodson gave a head nod toward the church. "How's it going so far?"

Aunt Ginny made a face. "See for yourself." She pointed to where Alex descended the steps of the church with Momma on her arm. They shared Easter greetings with the passing parishioners, while Gia and Henry followed behind in their coordinating scowls.

The biddies clucked their tongues and gave me sympathetic pats.

Mrs. Dodson gave me a nod. "Hold your head high

and knock 'em dead." I gave them a tremulous smile as they hefted themselves off the bench. "Now we're going to do a lap for more fudge samples. They just changed out the boy with the tray. The stingy one is on break."

We left them to their fudge shakedown and walked to the car. Oliva Larusso lived a few streets away from the church in a tiny, yellow, shingled cottage with yellow-and-white-striped awnings. It was a box bungalow that would fit inside our front sitting room. She had removed all the grass and replaced it with crushed seashells. Kneeling right in the middle of the yard was a praying ceramic angel. If I lived with Gia's mother, I'd be praying too.

The front door was open, and the storm door was fogged up with condensation from all the people and cooking inside. It was a lively bunch, but the conversation ground to complete silence the minute I knocked.

Karla answered the door. "Come on in." She whispered, "Be strong."

I was frozen in place, but Aunt Ginny prodded me in the behind with her pocketbook and pushed me into the packed living room.

Gia was immediately at my side. "We need to talk."

I swallowed hard, but Karla slapped him on the shoulder. "My God! Let her get inside first."

While Karla took my sweater and Aunt Ginny's coat, we looked around at eight pairs of eyes glued to us. I felt like an exotic exhibit at the zoo. "Hello."

Aunt Ginny was a little breathless from the attention as well. "Thank you for having us."

Momma must have been in the kitchen with Alex, but I recognized a few of the faces.

Gia took my hand. He said something in Italian with

an edge to it. Their eyes shifted to him, then back to me, without any change in their expressions. "Poppy, you've met my brothers, Piero and Luca. They helped set up our booth and brought the espresso machine. Luca's the oldest of us."

His brothers. I forced a smile and nodded. "Hello."

The men gave me silent chin raises.

"Then this is my baby sister, Stefania."

Karla leaned over my shoulder. "I'm the baby. Stefania is two years older."

Stefania smiled. "I'm older and wiser. It's nice to meet you both."

I said hello and Aunt Ginny gave a tiny wave.

"My other baby sister, Daniela, who's expecting her first."

Daniela placed her hands on her baby bump. "I'm older, but clearly not wiser. It's nice to finally meet you."

"And you know my sister Teresa from the Skype."

I smiled. "Hello again."

Teresa smacked her lips and looked away.

Oh. Okay.

"And this is Teresa's husband, Angelo."

I looked hard at Angelo, waiting for his reaction. When we'd met at the Expo, he all but threatened to whack me. Then he showed up unannounced at my house to tell me to dress appropriately for today. *So, this was Gia's brother-in-law.*

Angelo shifted in his seat and cleared his throat. "Nice to meet you."

Teresa slapped him on the back of the neck.

He jerked away from her. "What! What am I supposed to say?"

Gia slid his hand down my back. "My older sisters,

Francesca and Madalena. Their kids are in the backyard hunting the eggs."

Older sisters. Oh my god, they were gorgeous. All of them. Like celebrities. I wanted to shrink away and hide. "Hello."

The older women spoke in thick Italian accents. "So, we finally meet you." Madalena ran her eyes from my head to my feet. "You are the widow?"

"That's right." *Get me out of here.*

"Hm." She was not impressed with what she saw.

Francesca stood and offered me an awkward hug. "I am the divorced one. Until Daniela got knocked up, I was the black sheep."

Daniela gave me an eye roll. "But Gia will always be Momma's favorite."

Teresa cocked her head in my direction. "Not anymore."

The storm door opened, and a familiar, little Italian man walked in with a bouquet of daffodils and took off his fedora. *"Buona Pasqua, miei cari."*

Everyone responded, *"Buona Pasqua!"*

Gia rubbed his thumb in a circle on my shoulder blade. "And you know Zio Alfio."

Zio Alfio handed his coat and daffodils to Karla and kissed me on the cheek. "Ciao, Bella." Then he did the same to Aunt Ginny, who giggled and made me turn to look at her to see where that sound had come from.

Momma came into the living room wiping her hands on her apron, her face pink with exertion. She and Zio Alfio hugged and kissed like they hadn't seen each other since emigrating, when I knew for a fact they had just been together a couple of weeks ago.

Momma announced, *"Si mangia in trenta minuti."* We

eat in thirty minutes. This was the part of Italian I understood.

I handed her the gift the biddies had prepared. "Thank you for inviting us. Is there anything I can do to help?"

The room went silent again. I heard Aunt Ginny behind me. "Mmm."

Momma muttered something angrily with a hand gesture, then returned to the kitchen.

Stefania gave me an apologetic smile. "It isn't you. She won't let anyone help until it's time to clean up."

Daniela rubbed her baby bump. "She can't feel like a martyr unless she had to do everything by herself."

Luca, who they called Stubby, stood up and offered his seat to Aunt Ginny. "Please."

I know it galled her to feel like she was being treated like a senior citizen, but she swallowed her pride and thanked him for being a gentleman as she took the seat on the end of the couch. "And where is Alex?"

There was one collective eye roll that stopped at Teresa. Gia's hand froze on my shoulder blade and Zio Alfio muttered something dark.

Teresa answered, "She is in the kitchen learning to make tortellini, like a good daughter-in-law."

The younger sisters tsked and gave Teresa dirty looks.

A sigh caught in my throat that sounded like a sob. I tried measuring the distance from my body to the front door. *I bet I could make it to the car in thirty seconds.*

Henry appeared from the other side of the house. "Poppy!" He ran to me and flung his arms around my legs. "You're really here. I wanted to sit with you in church, but Nonna wouldn't let me."

I bent down and hugged him. "That's okay. I wouldn't miss having Easter with you."

Henry made an announcement to Gia's family that I had met all of five minutes ago. "Poppy is going to be my mommy."

I felt my cheeks get hot. The stony, uncomfortable faces that turned away from me were more than I could bear. Daniela looked like she might tear up, but Teresa's glare was pure hatred.

Gia put his hand on top of Henry's head. "Why don't you see if Nonna needs help setting the table? Poppy and I are going outside for a walk."

Henry tore off toward the kitchen. "I want to sit next to Poppy."

Gia pressed lightly against my back to lead me to the door. I looked at Aunt Ginny to see if she would be okay. She gave me a nod of steel that she could hold her own.

Gia wrapped my hand in his and led me down the steps. Once we were safely away from the house, he stopped walking. "First I am sorry about this stupid sweater. Momma gave them to us as presents and asked us to wear them today. I should have known it was a scheme. And we did not arrive with Alex. She waited for us by the door to come in at the same time, so you would see us together and assume." He took a half step toward me. "I could not pay attention in Mass with you so close to me. All I could think about was how much I love you, and how beautiful you look in those earrings." He kissed my fingers. "It means a lot to me that you would meet my family. I know they are not all accepting yet because of Alex, but they will come around."

I burst into tears. "I want to go home."

"Oh Bella, no. Do not cry." Gia's face twisted in pain.

"I can't do this anymore. Your mother hates me. Your sisters will never accept me. Your brother-in-law threatened me to leave you alone. I love you, but when I'm with you I feel like the other woman sneaking around, and that's not who I want to be. I'm sorry, but I'm done."

Gia touched his forehead to mine. "Please. Do not give up on me. It does not matter to me what my family thinks. I love you. I only care what you think. You are my family now. You and Henry." He pulled me to him and stroked my hair. "What do you mean, Angelo threatened you?"

I told Gia about the conversation at the Expo. His voice was light, but his eyes darkened nearly to black. "Do not pay attention to Angelo. Teresa has filled his head with nonsense. He thinks he is the Godfather. He's not even Italian. Their last name is Stankiewicz."

I pulled away to look Gia in the face. "Really?"

"*Sì*. He's been doing that Mafia act ever since the wedding. I think he is touched in the head. He works on the computers for a living." Gia tsked and shook his head.

I wiped my eyes. "What about you?"

Gia ran his thumb along my jaw. "What about me?"

"He said you were doing a job for the Scarduzio family."

Gia took my hand and we started walking slowly around the block. "Not a job. An errand."

"Is there a difference?"

"In this case, yes."

"What was it about?"

"I cannot tell you yet. Can you trust me a little longer?"

Out here I felt like I could trust him forever. It was once we got back in the house that I doubted myself. "Okay. What was with the stack of money I saw you hand over to that thug this morning? Was that a payoff?"

Gia's lips twitched into a crooked grin, but his smile was lacking its usual mirth. The day had been painful for both of us. "That *thug* was Father Seamus, and the payoff was a donation for new soccer uniforms. La Dolce Vita is sponsoring the Seahorses this year."

"Oh." I started crying again. I was messing everything up. I was so ashamed that I'd doubted him. Either he was the most patient man in the world and I was a fool or he was a complete sociopath. After meeting his family, I wasn't sure.

He pulled me closer. "I know this has been very hard on you. But please trust me. I won't do anything to hurt you."

We got back around to Oliva's house and stood there, silently regretting that we had to go inside.

Alex poked her head out the door and frowned. She marched down the steps and stood toe-to-toe with Gia. "We are still married and I won't have you out with another woman, cheating on me." Her words were much louder than they needed to be. I glanced at the house and saw a dozen faces pressed up against the screens. Some of the neighbors came out to water their rain-soaked lawns. "You abandoned me and took my child from me. Now I'm offering you forgiveness and the chance to start over and you throw her in my face!" Alex ran back into the house sobbing.

I was horrified. I felt dirty.

Gia's lips flattened. He rubbed a spot on his chin. "If you want to go home, I will take you."

Henry flew out the door and grabbed me around the legs. "Poppy! You're back!"

Break off another little piece of my heart. "I'll stay for Henry."

We went inside and caught everyone in full scatter

mode. They tried really hard to land in the right spots, but Stefania missed the chair completely and landed on the floor.

Momma called everyone through the kitchen to the backyard, where she had a long table set up in the garden next to the detached, two-story garage. She told everyone where to sit, and when at last she came to me, she had run out of chairs. She said something to Alex, who got up and handed me a plate and a fork. "There is a child table up on the deck where you can sit."

Gia sprang to his feet and the words were flying. All thirteen of them yelling in Italian at once. The only ones not involved were Aunt Ginny, Henry, and me.

Aunt Ginny had her elbows on the table, her chin resting on her folded hands. She looked at me and shook her head. "And people want to lock *me* up."

Henry got his plate and came over to me. He put his hand in mine. "I like the deck."

Alex reached across the table and picked up a bottle of expensive olive oil. "Basta!" She slammed the oil down with a thud, and they all sat. "Some of you are not part of the family. And you know who you are. You don't belong here." She gave me a withering glare.

I let Henry lead me to the deck, where we sat at a little white table with two chairs, talking in our own little world. We didn't have any food, but we had each other.

"And Mateo, that's my cousin, he found this pink egg with jellybeans in it. And Lorenzo, he's my cousin, he found a yellow one stuck inside the garage door where Zia Karla lives." Henry giggled hard. "And it broke in half and Christina, she's my cousin, she said chicken poops came out."

He was laughing so hard that I started laughing with him.

"And Mateo, he's my cousin, said the Easter chicken pooped in the egg."

This was the funniest story in the world to him, and it was the best thing I'd heard all day.

A shadow crossed over us and we squinted over my shoulder to see what it was. Gia had brought two plates of salad and some tortellini for Henry. He sat on the deck next to our little table. "Everything has gluten in it. Even the meat. What are you two laughing about?"

Henry and I started giggling again. "Apparently, chicken poop."

Henry fell off his chair and rolled backward laughing.

I didn't touch my salad. My appetite was long gone. The minute they were done with dessert, I found Aunt Ginny at the adult table and gave her the sign. Gia went to say something to his family while Karla retrieved our coat and sweater, and I kissed Henry goodbye. "I'll see you soon, sweet boy."

Angelo approached me, rubbing a rising welt on his jaw that was red and angry. "Giampaolo and I had a little talk. He said you are having problems with your Wi-Fi. I would like to come and fix it for you free of charge to make up for any unintentional threatening I may have done yesterday."

I gave a nod. "I'll let you know."

Gia was in a heated discussion with his mother and Alex. It wasn't going well. Zio Alfio slinked across the yard to me, like he thought he was being furtive. "I am sorry for my sister. She is no good with the change. She come to America when Karla was only baby. Giampaolo was the teenager. He love you very much. He tell me you might believe Alex. So, I show you." He took a folded document from his breast pocket and opened it for me. It was a separation agreement with intent to divorce. The reason for divorce was listed as abandonment by Alexandra Scarduzio, and Gia had signed it. I nodded at Zio Alfio.

"No, no. See." He pointed to the date and notary signature.

It had been notarized in Philly two months after Henry was born. My lip started to tremble and I bit down to keep it still.

"She is no good, but we can no find her. . . ." Zio Alfio shrugged, the apology in his eyes crossing the language barrier.

The family gathered in the living room, ready to send us off. Gia helped Aunt Ginny on with her coat. His eyes pleading with me to trust him.

Momma said something to Aunt Ginny in Italian and Teresa translated. "Momma say thank you for coming today. She sorry for any unpleasantness and she hope to see you again."

Aunt Ginny was very smooth. She gave Oliva a polite smile. "I seriously doubt that. After today you won't have to worry about us. After the deplorable way she's been treated Poppy won't ever want to come here again. So, all of her, and Gia, and Henry's holidays and family events will be with me. I should thank you. You may have pushed away a daughter, but I got your son." Aunt Ginny reached up and patted Gia affectionately on the cheek. He winked at her.

Momma's eyebrows knit and her face clouded in darkness before Teresa had a chance to translate.

Aunt Ginny smiled as she fixed her top button. "Good.

You do understand. Now we're all on the same page." She turned and walked out the front door.

Zio Alfio squeezed my hand. "Do not worry. It will all be over soon. Giampaolo, he fix it."

I squeezed his hand back and followed after the Queen of Awesome.

CHAPTER 42

I took Aunt Ginny home so we could change and head to the Expo. I had to check on our booth, and she wanted to redeem her free treatment she'd won in the raffle. I told her there was no way I wanted her putting on one of those death masks even it if was possible. "Dr. Rubin died by his own creation. There's no telling what could be wrong with them."

"If it starts melting my face, I'll just take it off. I won this fair and square."

Well, that remains to be seen. While I waited for Aunt Ginny to get her "spa duds" on, I called Amber to check in. I needed to tell her about Kieran Dunne answering that burner phone. She didn't answer her cell, so I called the police station to see if she'd been released yet. No one would give me any information, so I was stuck waiting for her to reach out to me.

Aunt Ginny emerged from her bedroom in a hot-pink velour tracksuit. "Come on, I'm not getting any younger."

Sierra texted me that she was running low on food, so we got in the car and drove to La Dolce Vita to pick up a few extra containers of brownies and chocolate-dipped shortbread, then on to Convention Hall. We had miraculous timing and showed up just as someone was pulling away from their parking spot out front. That would be my only moment of good luck all day.

Aunt Ginny split from me at the Kefir Everything booth. "When you see me next I'll look ten years younger."

"We could be sisters." I may as well save my words. Aunt Ginny would not be dissuaded from possible face melting if something free was on the line.

I checked on the Kefir lady, who no longer looked like a cartoon character. "Are you feeling better? How long did it take for the blue to wear off?"

"It hasn't yet. You can't see it under these lights, but you put me in the closet and I glow in the dark. I complained to that Shayla Rose and she wouldn't do a thing for me. She said it was my own fault and I must have kept the container in direct sunlight. But I didn't. It hasn't been out of my bathroom this whole time. I have half a mind to sue her for emotional distress."

"I'm sure it fades over time." Although if the prints outside the warehouse were any indication, she had at least a few more days before she'd fade.

"It can't happen soon enough. My husband wants me to wear a blond wig and a white dress to fulfill some Smurfette fantasy. I won't do it."

A little old lady with a pinched face had chosen that unfortunate moment to pick out a kefir salad dressing. "Gracious."

I backed away awkwardly while she apologized and left them to check on Sierra.

"Oh, thank God you're here. It's been nonstop since we opened."

I could tell from the disarray that she'd been busy. I restocked the pastry case, cleaned up the espresso machine, and refilled the cream and sugar station. When Sierra returned from her break I spotted Tim standing alone in the Paleo Diva booth. I wouldn't be at peace until I asked him why he'd ransacked my station, and with Gigi out of the way, now was a better time than any. Channeling my inner Aunt Ginny for courage, I marched over there and smacked the CIA button down on his counter. "Care to explain this?"

He shrugged. "What is that?"

"It's a button off a CIA chef coat. Is it yours or Gigi's?"

He ran his hand down his coat. "It's not mine. How did you get it?"

"I found it on the floor of my booth Friday morning after someone defaced it." I pointed to the banner that still had remnants of Paleo Fraud written across it.

Tim narrowed his eyes. "You think I did that?"

"You tell me. How else did a Culinary Institute of America button show up under my counter with a hailstorm of sugar packets?"

Gigi appeared and practically dropped her sample tray to leap behind the counter next to Tim, like she was afraid I was there to drag him away. "What's going on, honey?"

Tim didn't take his eyes off me. "Geeg, did you vandalize Poppy's boyfriend's booth?"

Gigi looked over at Sierra. "No. I just assumed it was an unhappy customer."

I scanned the buttons on Gigi's coat. They were all there, but this was a new day. I should have confronted them Friday, when it happened, instead of being distracted with Dr. Rubin's death and possibly being set up as Amber's scapegoat. I really did have a lot going on.

Tim nudged the button toward me. "It wasn't us. The fact that you think I would do something like that shows that you don't know me at all. Hurting people is your thing."

Gigi's eyebrows raised, but she said nothing. She took a fresh tray of samples from under her counter and re-filled her olive oil.

Tim leaned against his counter. "Please go."

I snatched up the button and tried to get back some of my dignity with it. I retreated to my own booth and disappeared into the coffee beans.

Sierra was cleaning the frothing wand when I returned. "What's wrong? You look like you're about to cry."

"If your high-school best friend ever asks you to go to a reunion with her, do yourself a favor and just say no."

Sierra patted me on the back. "Okay."

Eloise's assistant, Kevin, appeared at the counter. "Ma'am. We could use your assistance at the Rubinesque tent."

I sighed, pretty sure that I knew what kind of assistance they'd be looking for. "I'll be right there."

I bagged some Paleo brownies to take with me.

"What is that for?"

"A peace offering."

I entered the tent in the middle of a tirade.

"The raffle rules don't say the prize is invalid if someone murders the doctor."

Tally held up her hands. "Do they have to? And he wasn't murdered, it was accidental."

"Poppycock. And I don't believe for one minute that you believe that either."

"Well, the coroner hasn't ruled on his death yet, so as far as we're concerned it wasn't murder."

"Then there's no reason I can't have my free treatment."

I held up the bakery bag. "I brought you some brownies. Aunt Ginny, a minute, please?"

Tally let out a deep sigh and her shoulders dropped below her ears. Word had gotten out that one of the raffle winners was demanding their prize and a crowd had formed in the tent to jump on the bandwagon. She took Aunt Ginny by the back of the arm and nudged her toward Dr. Rubin's private office. "Why don't you ladies wait for me in here and I'll join you momentarily? We can get all this worked out in private."

Aunt Ginny and I were ushered into the office and Tally swung the hanging door shut. Aunt Ginny jerked her thumb toward the rippling canvas. "Like that's doing anything."

"Aunt Ginny, I think it may be insensitive for you to demand a free treatment when the doctor is dead."

Aunt Ginny poked through the papers on Dr. Rubin's desk. "Yeah, but you won't get anything if you don't make a fuss. I didn't kill him. The least they can do is give me some complimentary moisturizer. I'll take anything from this Phoenix Protocol."

"What did you just say?"

Aunt Ginny held up a slick display ad showing a fiery orange bird rising from the ashes on a lady's face. "The Phoenix Protocol."

I took the glossy photo she handed me. "Rubinesque announces their new spa line of rejuvenating skin-care solutions. Bring your skin back to life." The word "proof" was faintly printed in diagonal across the photo. Someone had written on the back, *run on all outlets starting May 2015.* That was next month.

Aunt Ginny held up a contract. "It looks like I'm in luck. Tally's listed as the Phoenix Protocol CEO. That means she has the authority to hand out free samples."

"I don't know if that's true, Aunt Ginny. That says it's a transfer of ownership contract and Dr. Rubin didn't sign it."

Aunt Ginny frowned. "Well, it's too late now."

"What do you think you're doing?"

That's the downside to a hanging door. There's no sound when someone opens it and catches you going through their desk.

I held up the ad. "We were just admiring the new product line."

Aunt Ginny pointed to the page. "I'll take a free wrinkle-erase cream if you can't fit me in for a treatment."

Tally sputtered and took the ad from me. "That . . . you shouldn't . . . That's top secret. It's not out yet. And I told you, I can't give you a treatment until we know the masks are safe. I could lose my license."

Aunt Ginny took out a pack of green gummy bears and ripped the corner off.

I felt my blood pressure rise a couple of notches. "When did you get more of those?"

"While you were talking to the yogurt lady." She popped one in her mouth and looked at Tally. "I'll be back. And I'm bringing reinforcements."

I knew who those reinforcements were. Aunt Ginny would own the whole practice by the time she was finished. I wanted to warn Tally, but a ruckus on the other side of the door drew us out.

Agnes Pfeister-Pinze was being detained by security again, and she was not going quietly. As they were dragging her through the tent opening, she arched her back and yelled, "Find Shayla Rose. She would do anything to keep news about her antiaging concentrate from getting out. She knows more than she's telling."

CHAPTER 43

Convention security dragged Agnes through the hall kicking and screaming and creating more disruption than if they'd just left her alone. She might be crazy, but she knew exactly what she was doing. Every eye was following her ejection. "Rubinesque Cosmetic Surgery is a sham! Lance Rubin never left the United States and he never worked with Doctors Without Borders. Check his passport! He's a fraud!"

Eloise shot through the room, wide-eyed and nervous. "Everything's fine. No need to stop what you're doing. Convention Hall would like to thank all our vendors for their patronage this weekend, and in appreciation, we're offering everyone ten-percent-off tickets for our next Expo, on security systems. Get your vouchers at the front office."

Shoppers went back to their browsing and sampling while vendors went back to their scalp massaging and eyebrow yanking. I caught sight of Shayla Rose trying to sneak out behind her own booth. "Hey! Not so fast."

I grabbed her arm and she frowned. "Let go of me! I don't have anything to say to you."

"You're acting awful guilty for someone who has nothing to hide."

"I heard Agnes accuse me before they carted her out of here. She's a nutjob. You can't believe anything she says." She wrenched out of my grip, which was much easier done than I'd like to admit, and ran behind Dr. Rubin's tent, where there was a door exiting to the boardwalk.

Her cousins, Leo and Jimmy, blocked my path, their arms across their chests and their faces set in scowls.

"Tell Shayla that unless she talks to me, I'm going to the media with everything I know about a warehouse full of glow-in-the-dark wrinkle cream, people walking around with blue alien faces, and the disciplinary action because of a lack of FDA approval. I know the hosts of *Wake Up South Jersey!* You don't want to push me." I gave them my fiercest scowl.

I stormed toward my booth and saw Sierra in the aisle, looking at me funny. Her eyes were as wide as they could get, and she was jabbing them to the side.

"What in the world are you doing?"

She jerked her head sideways and gritted her teeth. "Eds-fay."

"What?"

"Miss McAllister?"

I understood Sierra's warning too late. Two men in black suits and earpieces were going through our booth. "Can I help you gentlemen?"

They flashed badges so fast, for all I knew they were bought at Dellas 5 & 10. "Ma'am, we're investigating a local cell of organized crime. Are you aware of any incidents you may want to divulge?"

I could swear the planet slowed down to quarter speed on its axis. Even their words were coming out in slow motion. "Organized crime? No. I'm not aware of anything."

The men made eye contact and passed a silent nod to each other. One put his hand to his ear and whispered something into his shirt cuff. "This is not the time to withhold information, ma'am. You've recently been spotted with someone on the FBI watchlist."

Gia flashed in my mind, and I knew in that moment that if I knew anything, I would deny everything. *This must be the fear Al Capone's wife felt every day of her life.* "Really? Who?"

"We're not at liberty to say."

"Then how would I know what you're looking for?"

"We're just interested in anything you might have noticed or maybe overheard that might be unlawful."

"Well, I haven't seen or heard anything unlawful." *Other than two potential murders and one possible Internal Affairs cover-up. Plus, Aunt Ginny's getting high on CBD oil gummy bears.* "What do you think this person has done?"

They didn't answer the question. "Where is the owner of La Dolce Vita at this time?"

The air was getting thinner and my chest was feeling tight. "I haven't seen him."

The men gave me hard looks. One of them passed me a business card with a phone number on it. "In case you overhear anything."

They left the booth, and Sierra sucked in a gulp of air. "What was that all about?"

"I dunno, but don't talk to them if I'm not around." I tore up the card and threw it in the trash. When I looked up I caught Tim and Gigi watching me from across the room.

Tim had his arms crossed in front of him with an impassive look on his face. He wouldn't have come to help me even if I was the one being arrested. Gigi looped her arm in his and grinned triumphantly.

Maybe the feds being here wasn't an accident. Maybe someone called them with an anonymous tip. I couldn't go to Gia with this. If the feds were talking to me, they were probably watching me, and they would follow me when I left.

"Who was that?" Aunt Ginny hefted two shopping bags onto the counter. They bore the Rubinesque logo.

"Nobody. What did you do?"

"Got my free beauty creams."

"You wore them down."

"I won that free treatment fair and square."

I peeked in her bags. She must have had over five hundred dollars' worth of product. I shook my head. What could I say? This was always the inevitable conclusion.

"Can you drive me home? This is a lot to carry."

"I'll lose my parking spot."

"I could stay here and help you wait on customers until the Expo is over."

"I'll get my keys."

I took her bags and told Sierra I'd be back later. Aunt Ginny and I exited Convention Hall and ran into a group of people congregating on the boardwalk right outside. They were taking pictures of something down below that had created quite a stir. Aunt Ginny and I started down the ramp to the parking meters and the crowd grew quiet.

One man yelled, "Hey, lady, is that your car?"

That's when I saw it. My poor little Toyota. My windshield and headlights were smashed and shattered, and all four tires were slashed. Anger rose up from my belly like a volcano about to erupt.

The same man yelled, "I didn't see nuthin', but we called 9-1-1."

Aunt Ginny had a few choice words for whoever had done this.

There was a bright-pink paper stuck under my windshield wiper, flapping against the hood. On the front of it was Agnes Pfeister-Pinze's boycott-the-Expo notice. On the back someone had scrawled in black marker, "Mind your own business!"

CHAPTER 44

"Who did this?! When I find you, I will rip you in half! You won't be able to swing that bat again because I'm going to shove it so far up your . . ."

"Poppy!" Aunt Ginny cut me off, horrified. "Get ahold of yourself." Through gritted teeth, she growled, "They're filming us." She raised her eyebrows at the crowd hanging over the boardwalk railing, all pointing cell phones in our direction.

I tried to yoga breathe, but I felt like a bull who'd been branded one time too many. I called Sawyer and told her my car had been vandalized, and asked if she could come get Aunt Ginny and take her home for me.

Aunt Ginny was posing in front of the car, wringing her hands and looking forlorn. "Oh my. I'm just a poor little old lady on a fixed income. Whoever will repair my car from this brutal attack? If only there were a Good

Samaritan who could come to my rescue. You can donate funds to my Bitcoin account."

I snickered. "Okay, dial it back, Meryl Streep. Here comes the law."

The siren died to a pitiful whine as the police cruiser pulled over to my sad heap that was surely totaled, and Officer Consuelos got out of the vehicle. He took one look at me and threw his arms out to the side. "What did you do?!"

"It was like this when I found it." I filled him in on the little that I knew.

Hands on hips, he shook his head. "You have to have the worst luck of anyone I've ever met, and I know a man who lives in a dumpster. Stay here while I question the witnesses."

Aunt Ginny had started taking questions from the on-lookers. "Because she's very smart and she figures out things people don't want exposed . . . Her cleverness makes her a target . . . Probably by whoever killed the plastic surgeon . . ."

"What are you doing? Don't tell them that. They'll post it all over the Internet."

A mom with two kids brought us each a bottle of water. "I'm sorry about what happened."

"Thank you. You're very kind."

Sawyer ran up behind me and wrapped her arms around my neck. "I'm here. What can I do to help?"

"Take Aunt Ginny home, please."

Aunt Ginny hopped off the hood of the car. "What? I don't want to go home. My programs aren't even on for three more hours. I wanna stay here and watch."

Sawyer gave me a dry look. "How am I supposed to . . ."

She stopped in midsentence. She was staring at something over my shoulder. I turned around to see what it was, and Officer Consuelos was standing a few feet away, holding a clipboard. He appeared to be midtear on a tablet of paper. His eyes bore into Sawyer's, then flicked to me.

He finished ripping the yellow top sheet off the police report and handed it to me. "You'll need this for your insurance company."

"Thank you. What'd you find out?"

"Convention Hall has no outside security cameras. No one will admit to having seen your car being smashed in broad daylight. But a couple of kids came forward to show me a video they made." He pulled out his cell phone. "They're looking at the ocean, and you can hear metal smashing and glass breaking as your car is vandalized behind them. There's a large, white van behind your car, blocking the view across the street. As soon as the smashing stops, the van speeds off."

"Did you get a license plate or anything?"

"Nothing. I'm not even sure the person vandalizing your car got in the van." He looked at each one of us in turn. "Here comes your tow truck."

Sawyer remained oddly quiet while my car was hooked up. She kept to herself, off to the side. Aunt Ginny wanted to ride in the car while they towed it away, but the tow-truck driver said it was a liability and he wasn't allowed to let her do that.

She pouted all the way home about the loss of American freedoms until I suggested we order Chinese for dinner. Nothing brightens Aunt Ginny's mood like moo shu pork and dumplings. Ten minutes later there was a knock on the door. I picked up my wallet and went to pay Hunan Palace, only to find Gia standing on my porch, and he did not look happy.

"Why?! Why can you not call me when you are in trouble? Why do I have to find out through the rumor mill?"

"Who's the rumor mill?"

"It is not important. What is important is that I am here for you and you do not trust me!"

Aunt Ginny and Sawyer apparently felt that we needed to have a formal dinner in the dining room and started quietly setting out the good dishes within earshot.

Gia took a step toward me. "What do I need to do? How do I prove myself to you?"

Aunt Ginny muttered from the other room, "A divorce would be a good start."

Gia ran his hands through his hair and rattled off some complaints in Italian while pacing back and forth. "I do not like you always calling Sawyer when I could be there for you!"

Oh heck no. "Well, I don't like you keeping things from me. Not just a wife, but illegal activity that the feds are investigating! You want to know how to prove yourself to me? Start with being more honest! And I am a grown woman. I can call whoever I want."

Gia stood motionless, staring into my eyes. The heat was rolling off him like a sauna, but I didn't give up my ground.

"Hunan Palace. Forty-two thirty-five." A Chinese delivery boy stood in the doorway, holding out a large. greasy paper bag.

It's hard to maintain the high ground in an argument when you have to stop to ask about fortune cookies while there's a cat winding around your legs, purring. "Are you sure there's no gluten in my Mongolian beef?"

The delivery boy nodded. "Yes."

"I'm serious. I'm one disappointment away from throwing a fit."

He nodded again. "Yes."

Aunt Ginny sidled up behind me and took the bag. I handed him fifty and told him to keep the change.

"Yes. Thank you very much."

I shut the door and turned back to Gia, who had calmed down enough to look amused. "Don't smile at me. I'm really angry."

Gia came closer and took me in his arms. "You are right. I have not been able to trust in a very long time. I was so scared when I heard you were attacked. Will you forgive me?"

A lot of my anger had fizzled out. I wanted to still be angry; anger was a lot safer than what I was currently feeling because I couldn't do anything about that until Alex was out of the picture. "I wasn't attacked. My car was attacked."

Gia pulled me against his chest and stroked my hair. "I was not there for you."

"About that dishonesty I mentioned earlier—"

"What dishonesty? I have not been dishonest with you."

Aunt Ginny called us from the dining room. "Either come in here and have some dinner or kiss her already."

"Aunt Ginny!"

Sawyer giggled.

"You're not helping."

Sawyer answered from the dining room. "Well, Figaro and his girlfriend are going to eat your egg roll if you don't hurry up."

Gia looked like he thought kissing me was the way to go. I put my finger on his lips. "Are you divorced yet?"

He frowned.

"Then I'm eating my Mongolian beef."

We sat at the table and passed around the cartons. It was the first time I'd used china for Chinese food in my life and it felt wrong on many levels. I passed Gia the egg rolls. "I had a visit today from the feds. They were looking for you at the Expo."

Gia reared back and gave me an incredulous look. "Why would they look for me there?"

"They said they were investigating organized crime."

"And you think I'm involved in that?"

"You tell me. Why else would they be checking out La Dolce Vita?"

"Bella, there are other reasons."

"I would love to hear them."

Before he could give me any, there was another knock on the door. I wanted to throw something. I was this close to getting some answers and I didn't want anything to stop that. I looked at Aunt Ginny, silently begging her to answer it.

Her priorities lay elsewhere. "What? I have an egg roll."

I can feel that fit getting closer. I got up and went to the door. Gia's brother-in-law, Angelo, was standing on my porch again. The angry welt on his jaw had turned into an ugly bruise. I stared him down, willing him to challenge me.

"Begging your pardon, ma'am. I was hoping now might be a good time to take a look at your network." His eyes widened as he stared behind me. "Gia!"

Gia came to the door, wiping his mouth on a napkin.

Angelo blinked and tipped his head. "You are living dangerously, my friend."

Gia placed his hands on his hips. "And you need to stop listening to Teresa."

The men stared at each other for so long that I went and got the laptop. I figured I may as well give Angelo something to do to keep him from getting a bruise on the other side of his face.

Angelo took the laptop and followed me to the dining-room table, where he set up.

Gia gave me a questioning look, asking if I wanted to continue our conversation. I shook my head no and glanced at Angelo. No way was I going to talk about the feds' visit with him there.

"What is your password?"

"Password."

"Yes, what is it?"

"That's it. It's 'password.'"

Angelo gave me a droll look and typed it in while staring me down. "What is the problem you've been having?"

Aunt Ginny passed Gia the chicken fried rice. "It's too slow when I want to download free movies."

I shot Aunt Ginny a sassy look. "No, that's not the problem. And you have to stop doing that."

"Why? Everyone else is doing it."

I told Angelo about the Fraudster website pop-ups. "I originally thought it was a fluke, but now I'm worried it's a virus."

He typed for a solid two minutes. "Well, someone has accessed the Fraudster website in the past few days."

"I clicked on it a couple times to see what it was."

Aunt Ginny got up and got a plate for Angelo. "I may have clicked on it too. By accident."

Angelo took the plate and said thank you. "Do you think you've clicked on it about two hundred times?"

"What? No. Good Lord. No way."

Aunt Ginny thought about it. "Maybe three."

Angelo did some more typing. "Someone has logged into the Fraudster website through the admin portal on this laptop. The website has programed malware in their ads to spread them to every computer across a network."

Sawyer scrunched up her nose. "Who here would be logging into Fraudster?"

Angelo answered. "Whoever it was, they know all the site credentials and have made several updates in the past couple of days."

"Where else have people gone on the Internet this past week?" I asked.

Angelo showed me how to search the browsing history. "Google, Tinder, Top Docs, Yelp, Catster, Sexy Costumes for Seniors."

Aunt Ginny turned a shade of salmon. "That could have been anybody."

"A Facebook group called Wives of Plastic Surgeons."

"Stop. Show me the last one."

Angelo clicked on the link and it went to a Facebook login page. The sign-in had not been saved by the previous user.

Gia raised his eyebrows. "Who is the wife of a plastic surgeon?"

I opened my mouth to answer, and the front doorknob jiggled. Both cats ran to the foyer to see if the newcomer had brought anything exciting.

Rita opened the door, and she and Faelynn came through, holding restaurant leftover containers. Rita ambled toward the dining room. "Well, hello, everyone. You all look cozy in here."

I reached out and slapped the laptop shut. "We are. Did you all have a nice dinner?"

Faelynn held up a black plastic box. "Wonderful. Best blue crabs I've ever had."

"Oh?" A knot grew in the pit of my stomach.

Rita showed us the perky crab logo. "We went to Maxine's. Over by the marina. Do you know it?"

You could hear a pin drop in the dining room. Except for Angelo, who dragged the container of orange chicken to his plate and scraped out a scoopful. He looked at Gia with wide eyes, put the spoon down and folded his hands in front of him.

I put on my poker face. "I do, yes. I'm glad you had a good time."

Faelynn pulled out a coupon. "And look at this funny little thing they gave us. If you go to the Beauty Expo, stop at the La Dolce Vita booth to tell them Paleo Diva is better. Paleo Diva will give you a free item and twenty percent off your purchase. Isn't that funny?"

I looked from the coupon to Gia. "Aren't they a riot?"

Gia gave them a gracious smile. "Will you ladies be using your coupon?"

Rita shook her head. "Oh no. That's not for us. We just got a kick out of it."

Gia put his hand out. "Would you mind if I had it? I'd love to check out the Paleo Diva booth."

For just a moment I was kind of hoping Gia *was* in the Mob. I'd like to see him have "a little talk" with Gigi. I had to tell myself to snap out of it. You couldn't pick and choose acceptable Mob activity. Could you?

"Oh, of course." Faelynn handed the coupon over. "I'm sure it's all in good fun."

The four of us nodded and said in unison, "Mm-hmm. Sure."

Angelo ate a surreptitious forkful of his orange chicken.

The ladies said good night and started to climb the stairs. When I heard one door after another close, I said, "Well, one of them is your admin for Fraudster. So the other one must be the wife of a plastic surgeon."

Aunt Ginny passed around the fortune cookies. "How will we find out which is which?"

"Tomorrow, before they check out, we interrogate them."

CHAPTER 45

After we made a solid plan for the morning, and everyone had left, Angelo making sure that Gia was not alone with me to break any vows, I cleaned up and went to bed. I left Figaro and Portia in the foyer, playing soccer with my unwrapped fortune cookie. I didn't need to open it to know my fortune would be swelling and stomach pain if I ate the cookie.

I woke up to the sound of purring in stereo, followed by the shrill call of "Porrrtiaa!" Figaro had convinced the white Persian that my pillow was better than her fancy bed, and I had a fluffy cat on either side of my head. I picked the girl up and gently ushered her out of my room, and shut the door behind her.

Figaro jumped off the bed with a soft thud and scratched on the door.

"You can't follow her home. She's way too high maintenance for you anyway."

Patsy called up the stairs. "Porrrtiaa! Here, baby. Come to Mummy. It's time for your brushing."

Note to self: post quiet hours. I picked Fig up and looked into his smooshy face. "That would be your mother-in-law. Do you feel like wearing a bow tie every day?"

Figaro put two paws over my mouth and purred.

My mind shifted to what I had to do today, and the sting Aunt Ginny and I planned to carry out before breakfast. I did some yoga, then showered and dressed in jeans and a T-shirt. I hadn't worn these jeans in so long I couldn't believe they zipped. I was kind of regretting that I didn't have a scale anymore.

It was warm this morning, so I went downstairs to the empty guest rooms to air them out. I was in the Monarch Suite, cracking open the window, when I spotted the garbageman leave the curb in front of Mrs. Pritchard's house and roll toward mine. There was a hint of movement down below, and I saw eightyish-year-old Mrs. Pritchard come out on her porch in a full-length, white-cotton, prairie-style nightgown and foam curlers. I was about to holler a friendly hello when she hoisted a rifle to her shoulder and took aim through a sight at Benjamin Bunny. She fired off a shot, and Rabbitzilla began the slow wheeze to the ground once again. Mrs. Pritchard gave a nod to her handiwork and turned to go back in her house. I must have moved, because she spotted me in the second-floor window watching her in horror. Her hand flew up to cover her mouth, and she scurried back inside and slammed her door.

How was I supposed to tell Aunt Ginny that the woman who'd knitted my pink baby afghan had just performed a kill shot on her precious Benjamin Bunny? I had to find some way to shake the image from my mind because Rita and Faelynn would be down for coffee any minute and we had a plan to divide and conquer.

Aunt Ginny and Joanne had split the coffee service in two locations. Whoever came downstairs first, Aunt Ginny would direct them to the side porch to enjoy the morning view of what would now be a deflating lawn ornament. I waited in the kitchen until Aunt Ginny gave me the signal.

The dining-room door swung open. "They're in place."

That was my cue. I went across the hall to the library, where Rita was set up. "Good morning, Mrs. Bagshaw. How did you sleep?"

Rita was shaking two packets of Splenda, preparing to rip them open for her morning coffee. "Oh, like a baby. I'm almost sorry to go home today."

"Well, I'm glad I caught you alone. I need to warn you."

Her head jerked up and she stopped stirring. "Warn me? About what?"

"Two men from the FBI spoke with me yesterday. They said they were investigating criminal activity." *All true.*

She paled and nodded silently.

"It seems that someone on my network has been signing into a libelous website called Fraudster." *Also true.*

I watched the rest of the blood drain from Rita's face. I knew it was serious because she put the spoon down and abandoned her coffee. "Have you heard of it?" I didn't wait for her to answer. "It's dedicated to bad reviews and claims of malpractice against Dr. Lance Rubin, the cosmetic surgeon who died the other day."

"Why would federal agents be interested in a review website?"

"Dr. Rubin had been receiving death threats, and they think there might be a connection."

"There isn't. I know about the threats. They weren't going anywhere. But what do they have to do with this Fraudster website? Is that what you called it? Fraudster?"

When you have that much guilt written all over your face, it's too late to act coy. "Dr. Rubin thought the threat was serious enough that he hired an IT security company to run forensics on the website and many of his bad reviews. They've traced the IP address to your house in Manhattan. And, this week, to my house, while you've been here."

Rita's hand shook as she took out a Kleenex. She sighed. "Have you ever been married?"

Where is this going? "Yes."

"Some men will put you through hell."

I heard that, sister. I resisted the urge to give her a high five; I felt a confession coming on.

"The thing is, divorce is too expensive, and if he went to jail, I wouldn't get anything."

"Say what now?"

"Lance is—or was—my husband."

Well, I did not see that coming. "I'll be right back." I had to stop Aunt Ginny before she said too much.

Aunt Ginny was halfway through the sitting room, coming to get me. "She's his wife."

I stopped. "I know. She just told me."

"What?"

"Rita. She's married to Dr. Rubin."

Aunt Ginny frowned. "She can't be, because Faelynn is married to Dr. Rubin."

"What?"

We said in unison, "Switch."

I went out on the side porch, where Faelynn was sipping her coffee and halfway through a bagel. "Good Morning, Mrs. Archer. I was just talking to my aunt and I think she may have misunderstood something."

Faelynn shook her head. "No, she heard me right. Lance was my husband. He was married to me when he died."

"So, you were the one who's been logging into the Facebook group Wives of Plastic Surgeons?"

"I'm the admin. It's how Rita and I found each other and discovered that we were married to the same man."

"Currently married?"

"Yes. Lance was a bigamist."

"And you were okay with that?"

She gave me a look like I was insane for asking such a thing. "No. Why do you think we were trying to destroy him?"

"Okay . . . Did you consider turning him in to the authorities?"

"If I did that, he'd go to jail and I'd lose everything. Rita was married to him first; she's the only one with legal rights."

"So, you two started the Fraudster website to . . . ruin his practice?"

"I have nothing to do with Fraudster. That's Rita's baby."

"I'll be right back."

I ran into Aunt Ginny in the dining room this time. She was shaking her head and mumbling about scams. "They're both his wives."

"I know. And Rita is the one behind the Fraudster website."

Aunt Ginny leveled me with a dry look. "Because she had to destroy Dr. Rubin's name before Faelynn took all his money in fraudulent lawsuits."

"What? Switch."

I went back into the library, where Rita was dabbing her eyes. "So, you both knew you were married to the same man?"

Rita nodded.

"And to get back at him, you put up the Fraudster website, and Faelynn . . . ?"

"She's suing Lance under several aliases. She's started each one as an anonymous plaintiff based on his real-life cases where things didn't go well in surgery. His lawyers always try to settle out of court. If she won those lawsuits, Lance would have been bankrupt, and I'd be left penniless."

"So, you put up Fraudster to ruin his practice before she bled him dry?"

Rita snuffled. "I didn't want to destroy it entirely. Just enough so he'd turn over a controlling share to me. Fraudster was getting a lot of traffic and Rubinesque was losing clients. I was about to confront Lance and demand fifty percent of the practice to take it all down, but Fae said we should wait. She thought he was up to something even more unsavory than bigamy, and we could get more money out of him if we worked together. She said it was Blackmail 101. So, we came here to spy on him."

"Did you find anything?"

Rita nodded. "We think he stole another doctor's invention. He brought it here to debut for the press instead of in New York, where he would get national coverage but open himself up to harsher scrutiny. He never even mentioned working on a UV mask to either of us." She teared up. "I thought Lance was charming, and sexy, and kind. I guess I didn't know him at all."

"How'd you figure out where he was?"

"It wasn't easy. Lance stays off of all social media, so we never know where he'll be."

"Probably because he had two wives and didn't want you to find out about each other."

"We aren't supposed to call his office, but I did, and they let it slip that he'd be in Cape May for the Beauty Expo. We found the Expo website and saw him listed as the keynote speaker. Fae was reading the vendor bios, and you were listed as the owner of the Butterfly Wings Bed and Breakfast. We booked here to see if we could learn what was happening at the Expo without being discovered." A fat tear dripped on her leg. "But then Lance died."

"I'll be right back."

Aunt Ginny was in the hallway waiting for me. "Mine says she didn't kill him. She just wanted to take him for everything he was worth because he lied to her."

"I think mine really loved him. And the two of them have been upset since it happened. They told me at the tea that their eyes were red from allergies when they'd obviously been crying."

Aunt Ginny placed her hands on her hips. "Alright. Let's get them in the same room and see if they turn on each other."

Victory ran interference with the Parkers. She stuffed a pillow under her T-shirt and delivered breakfast to their room to keep them upstairs. We brought both ladies into the neutral zone or, as we called it, the sitting room. Faelynn didn't want to cooperate, but Rita convinced her that it was all about to come out now that Lance was dead.

"So, you were both trying to extort money anonymously out of your husband and ruin him instead of divorcing him or turning him in."

The women agreed.

Rita sniffled. "Please don't tell anyone."

"How in the world did you find out about each other?"

Faelynn took out her cell phone. "I started the Wives of Plastic Surgeons as a Facebook support group. It's hard to be married to a doctor. And Lance really is a very good cosmetic surgeon. He did my boobs. He's only had a couple legitimate malpractice suits. He was in constant demand. I was lucky to see him one weekend a month."

Rita had worked up the courage to take a sip of her coffee. "And I joined because I was lonely. Plus, I knew Lance was literally handling naked women all day, and I've never been tiny. No matter how little I eat or how much I exercise, I can't lose any weight. He made a fortune giving skinny women giant boobies. How could I compete with that? I thought he was having an affair. I never imagined he had another wife. I told my story to the members of the Facebook group and Faelynn sent me a private message that she thought we might be married to the same man."

Faelynn put her phone on the table. "We lived so close to each other, I suggested we meet in New York to share information. We were stunned to find out he'd been living a double life and somehow neither of us ever saw him."

I reached out for Joanne to hand me a cup of coffee. She made a rude gesture and left the room. "Dr. Rubin said he was traveling with Doctors Without Borders."

Both women snorted.

Rita answered. "We've compared notes, and we're not sure he ever worked with the charity. When he said he was in Africa he was with Fae."

"And when he said he was in South America he was with Rita. We have no idea where he was when he said he was in India. Probably Atlantic City." Faelynn handed me her cell phone. "Here's the group page. Our accounts are in our maiden names to protect our husbands' practices."

I scrolled through the site. Most of the members were women, but there were a couple of men. And a lot of the posts were of the missed-anniversary, ruined-dinner, you'll-never-guess-what-they-did-now variety.

Rita heaved a sigh. "This is the group we wanted to bring to tea next month. Fae and I thought we could have the support group meet here and we could get some closure on the horrible accident that took Lance's life."

"So, you think what happened was an accident?"

The women gave me startled looks. Faelynn said, "What else would it be? As far as I know, we are the only ones who could have wanted Lance dead."

"The police will eventually bring that up. Where will you say you were when he died?"

Rita pointed to the library. "I was on the Internet most of the night. You said that yourself. Fraudster is my alibi."

Faelynn picked at her muffin wrapper. "I snuck into his hotel room the night he died and checked his luggage for his passport. He was supposed to have been traveling abroad right before coming to New Jersey. I was going to use it to prove he was lying to us."

"Did anyone see you?"

"Just some woman coming down the hall. I pretended

like I didn't speak English and ran, but the front desk checked my ID when they gave me a key, so they'd have a record of it."

I scrolled down the Facebook page. "Was there anyone else who would have something against him? Something worth killing for?"

Aunt Ginny quirked an eyebrow.

I wasn't going to tell Rita and Faelynn for fear of what they would do next, but they weren't the only Mrs. Lance Rubins. I recognized one of the women in their Wives of Plastic Surgeons support group. And she had been within killing distance of the doctor all weekend.

CHAPTER 46

I grabbed my purse to head out the door. I tried Amber's cell phone again. Still no answer.

I didn't really care who killed Lance Rubin. I mean *I did*—only not as much as I wanted to help Amber and get justice for Temarius. Corporate espionage/bigamist Lance Rubin was not my problem. If somehow Temarius was involved with someone who was involved with Dr. Rubin, and both of them ended up dead, who was the puppet master?

I stopped by the La Dolce Vita booth to stare at Gia. He gave me a latte and a wink. I gave him a grin, grabbed some Paleo sugar cookies, and kept walking.

The Rubinesque booth had quieted down to a crawl. With no free treatments or famous plastic surgeon in residence, they may as well be a lemonade stand selling wheatgrass juice. Two of the bun heads were at the front desk, talking about plans to rebrand.

I cleared my throat.

The women looked at me with blank expressions.

"I'm looking for Tally."

They kept staring at me, unblinking.

I held up the bag. "I brought cookies."

One of the women whisper-whined, "No one here eats cookies."

I felt as deflated as Rabbitzilla.

Then she pointed to the hanging door. "But Tally's in the office."

I walked over and swung the door aside. Tally was sitting at the desk with her head in her hands, crying. On the desk in front of her was a gold wedding band. "Hey."

She looked up, surprised, and swept the ring into her lap.

"I already know." I stepped farther into the room and put the bag of cookies on the desk.

"You know what?"

"That you're married to Dr. Rubin."

She dabbed a tissue against her cheek. "I don't know what you're talking about."

"I read your posts in the Wives of Plastic Surgeons Facebook group. How you felt your husband didn't respect you. He referred to you as his nurse in front of other women to make himself look more important."

"How did you . . ." Tally's eyes drooped, and she blew out a defeated breath. "No one here can know. It was very important that our marriage be kept secret. Do you understand?"

Oh, I understand all right. He really did have a thing for redheads. "Why do *you* think he wanted it kept secret?"

"We'd only been married for three years. Lance said

the staff would respect us both less if they knew about us. I had to call him Dr. Rubin in the office. When we started dating he was worried it would look unprofessional, so he wouldn't allow any pictures of us together, and I wasn't allowed to mention him on social media. He insisted we elope to the Caribbean—just the two of us, to keep a modicum of privacy."

"And you didn't think that was strange?"

"It was a little strange, but he had a point. It's hard enough being a woman in a field dominated by men. I didn't need the other women on staff saying I slept my way to the top."

"Uh-huh." *I gotta give it to him. He found a good cover story.*

She set the ring back on the desk in front of her. "It doesn't matter anymore anyway. Things weren't working out between us and I'd told Lance I wanted a divorce. He was always off to Africa or South America with Doctors Without Borders. I felt like a part-time wife who only saw him when we went to our beach house in New Jersey."

"So, what does his death mean for Rubinesque?"

"We're trying to salvage our image. The press was here to do a story about the unveiling of the new UVaderm mask, but they ran the story about Lance's accidental death instead. Clients have been canceling their appointments left and right. We're all going to be out of work if we don't replace him."

"So, you think his death was accidental?"

"He was so determined to find the next big thing that he was taking unnecessary risks. He thought that stupid mask was going to be his claim to fame."

"It sure sounded like a breakthrough."

"You've been very nice. So, just between you and me, he found out a week ago that another doctor had filed a patent for the UV mask and was about to go public. It was just a matter of time before we were embroiled in another lawsuit."

"You knew he stole the mask from Dr. Hammerstein?"

She turned the wedding ring with her finger and raised her eyes to mine. "Lance didn't steal the mask. He had top electrical engineers develop that mask to his specifications. The problem was, he may have used Dr. Hammerstein's research to create those specifications. So, we *could* be sued for stealing intellectual property. Lance was working on a plan to upgrade the design so he could make it his own. He wanted to incorporate the use of my Phoenix serum to instantly regenerate the cells. Now he's dead, so you see where that got us."

She thinks she's having a bad day now. . . .

"I heard you on the phone the other day telling someone to enact the Phoenix Protocol. I thought it was some kind of corporate damage-control plan."

She tapped her finger on a stack of papers on her desk. "I was talking to my publicist. I wanted her to move forward with the advertising campaign we'd planned. My hope was to bury the story of Lance's death under the launch of our new spa line before the investors found out."

"I see the Phoenix Protocol contract was miraculously signed by Dr. Rubin after I left here with my aunt yesterday." *Dr. Rubin wasn't the only one in the family willing to break the law to succeed.*

Tally blushed to the roots of her strawberry-blond bun. She turned the contract over. "I really wish you hadn't seen that. I deserve this company. I run the cosmetic chemistry division of Rubinesque. That means I create the formulas for our exclusive skin-care line. I've been developing the Phoenix Protocol for two years. Lance was giving it to me in lieu of alimony to keep our divorce quiet. When he died before signing that contract I saw all my research and development being taken from me. I hope you're not going to make trouble for me over this. Especially after I gave your aunt hundreds of dollars' worth of products. Besides, it's not forgery if a wife signs for her husband with his permission."

"About that . . ."

"Wait a minute! You weren't having an affair with him, were you? That's why you keep asking me all these questions."

"Me?"

"I knew he was way too interested in those muffins for it to be natural."

"I was definitely *not* having an affair with Dr. Rubin. He was trying to solicit me to get liposuction."

"I saw the way he was flirting with you. You're just his type. First I caught him with that Shayla Rose and then you. Lance always was too charming for his own good."

"What do you mean, you caught him with Shayla Rose?"

"I caught him coming out of her booth the other night. He said he was talking to her about luciferin in skin care, but Lance didn't know anything about biochemistry. That was my job. He was just a surgeon. I knew he was planning on replacing me after we were divorced, but Shayla Rose? She's been slapped with fines from the FDA for rushing her products to market."

"That must have made you furious."

"You have no idea. I gave that man the best work of

my professional life and he was going to toss me over for that fraud with toxic ocean goo. My formulas are completely organic. I use biodynamic stem cells from fruits and plants. Every single ingredient in the Phoenix Protocol is natural."

I wanted to point out that arsenic, anthrax, and cyanide were all natural, and every one of them would kill you if you didn't know what you were doing. "Look, I wasn't having an affair with Dr. Rubin, okay? I'm just here to find out what really happened to him."

"What happened is, Lance accidentally electrocuted himself with that stupid mask."

"Let's say for a minute he did. How did it happen? Why not just take the mask off if it was starting to burn? Why not thrash around if you felt a shock? Dr. Rubin was just lying there peacefully on fire, like he'd fallen asleep."

Tally's mouth moved up and down, but no sounds came out. "I don't know. I didn't have those details. The UV masks have a built-in timer. They turn off automatically after twenty minutes so you can't do any damage to your skin from prolonged exposure."

"That didn't work because his power supply was crushed. Did that happen by accident? And what about the glowing blue goo? What the heck was that?"

Her eyes grew very wide. "I don't know. I just assumed Lance was running experiments with different products to see how they would react with the mask and one of them caused it to short out."

"I don't suppose you've ever heard of Temarius Jackson, have you?"

"Definitely not."

"Not a patient? Not someone who ran errands or did odd jobs for the practice?"

"No. And it's a name I would remember."

I was afraid of that.

One of the bun heads came to the door and swung it open. "Tally, your eleven o'clock is here."

Tally placed the wedding ring in her purse. "I'm sorry, I have to go. I'm interviewing a cosmetic surgeon to replace Lance. If we have any hope of Rubinesque moving forward, we need to be able to perform breast implants. I don't know the answers to any of your questions, but I'd sure love to hear them when you find out."

I picked a pen off her desk and wrote the names of Rita and Faelynn on a drug company promotional tablet. "Before I go, here are two ladies you need to talk to. And I mean tonight."

Tally took the tablet and read their names.

"Send them a message through your Facebook group, and tell them you're India. They'll know what it means. Trust me on this, you need to hear what they have to say. And be nice. One of them is very likely the new owner of Rubinesque."

CHAPTER 47

I walked past Shayla's booth, scanning to see if she was inside. Her cousins Jimmy and Leo guarded the front like stone sentries, their arms crossed to push out their biceps, their scowls following me. *I'm coming for you, Shayla.* One way or another, I was getting answers tonight.

I spotted Tim at the La Dolce Vita booth having a furious discussion with Gia. Gia slammed the coupon down and said, "This stops now!"

I spun around to head in the opposite direction but ran into Gigi at my tail.

"Not so fast. We have someone who needs to talk to you." She grabbed my arm and yanked me towards the fracas. "I got her."

Neither Tim nor Gia looked my way. They were too busy measuring up. I took their preoccupation with each other as my chance to escape again. "I'll come back later."

Tim called after me, "Poppy! You accused Gigi and me of vandalizing your boyfriend's booth the other day."

I slowly turned back around. *Was this going to be a fight? Did I have to take off my earrings?*

"I have someone who wants to tell you something. Chuck!"

Tim's sous chef had been standing a few feet away. I hadn't even noticed him before he squeaked and shuffled toward me. He hung his head, causing his glasses to slide down his nose. "Hey, Chef Poppy."

Gigi grumbled, "She's not a chef."

Tim held his hand up in her face.

Chuck lifted his eyes and pushed his glasses back up his nose. "I vandalized your booth. I was hoping you would leave the coffee shop and come back to Maxine's if this Paleo thing wasn't working out."

"How did you get in here?"

"I borrowed Chef Tim's pass and told the security guard I was a sub. It was stupid. I'm sorry."

I was feeling a mixture of compassion, flattery, and embarrassment for blaming Tim. "Aw, Chuck. That's so sweet and so foolish. Why would you do that?"

"Tim has been miserable. Plus, I miss you coming into Maxine's to make the desserts. You make the kitchen more fun. It's not the same without you." He flicked his eyes to Gigi and made a slight, reflexive jerk away from her.

Gigi clamped her jaw and narrowed her eyes at Chuck. "If you don't like it, you can always leave."

Tim ignored their exchange. "I noticed Chuck was missing a button last night when I showed up for closing and asked him about your booth. I had no idea he was going to do that. You can press charges if you want to, but Maxine's will pay for the damages to your stuff. And I have not been miserable."

Chuck breathed out a wobbly sigh and gave me a slight nod.

Gia gave Chuck a smile. "Do not worry about the damages. I will cover them. And I understand. I would go crazy if Poppy left me too. You cannot replace that kind of love so easily. She is far too precious."

That last bit was clearly for my benefit. I felt like my feet had left the floor. Gia gave me a look of such intensity, it was all I could do not to get lost in his eyes.

Gigi thrust her arm through Tim's.

Tim chewed his lip and looked at me. "As you wish . . . Come on, Chuck."

Chuck gave me a sad grin and a finger wave. "Bye, Poppy."

"Bye, Chuck. Drop in for coffee sometime."

His face lit up. "Yeah, that'd be great."

"Chuck!"

I squeezed Gia's hand. "Thank you."

Gia tipped my chin, and our eyes met. "Do you regret being here with me?"

"No. I regret that our timing is off."

"We are almost at the end."

"How do you know that?"

"I have a plan."

"Is this plan something I want to hear?"

"The only way to get rid of Alex is to give her what she wants."

"Yeah, but she wants *you*."

"Exactly."

Oh, I do not like the sound of this plan. "So, this is it? You and I are over before we even start?"

Gia kissed my forehead. "Do you trust me?"

I searched my heart for the answer. "I don't know. Every time I take a leap of faith, I fall."

"My love, if you leap, I promise to catch you."

"Then I will trust you."

CHAPTER 48

I left the Expo to clear my head. I walked home and told Aunt Ginny I needed the keys to Bessie, her 1958 red-and-white Corvette. I drove over the bridge into North Cape May and stopped at Destiny's Nails. There was a table set up on the sidewalk with stacks of Girl Scout cookies and a very aggressive after-school enterprise. Three Brownies ran the table like they were on the floor of the stock exchange. The pile of Thin Mints was shrinking fast and I was fourth in line. I was afraid they'd start a bidding war and I didn't bring my checkbook.

Thank God two of the moms were running late for karate practice and I was bumped up a couple of spaces. When a bossy nine-year-old in braces called me up to the table, I bought four boxes of Tagalongs and four boxes of Thin Mints. I also picked up two boxes of Do-si-Dos for Aunt Ginny. She had a sixth sense about peanut butter and I didn't want to face the firing squad if I came home empty-handed.

I drove into the Villas to see Mrs. Rotnitzky and parked in the back lot. *I don't know why they named this the Bay Vista Apartments. You couldn't see the bay from here if you used a telescope.* I found the elevator this time, but it smelled like pee, so I walked up the three flights of stairs to apartment 411. Temarius's apartment was still barred with police crime-scene tape. I rapped twice on Mrs. Rotnitzky's door.

"Who is it?"

I knew she was looking through the peephole, so I held up a box of cookies. "It's me."

"Hee-hee!"

I waited for her to click through the series of locks and finally open the door. I handed her the bag of cookies. "I just wanted to thank you again for all your help the other day."

"Of course, of course, anytime." She dug through the bag. "What? No S'mores?"

"You only said Tagalongs."

She hugged the bag to her chest and patted it. "Next time." She took the cookies to the kitchen counter and stashed them in a wooden breadbox. I could not help but notice that she didn't open a box to offer me any, which I believe is customary. I would have said no, but still . . .

"So, what are you here for? I know you didn't just come to bring me sweets."

She was a sharp one, even dressed in her purple, polyester, old-lady slacks and two different-colored shoes. Hopefully, she still believed I was a social worker. "I wanted to ask you a couple questions about Temarius."

She picked up a glass of something red and rocked in her chair. "Oh-kaaay."

"No Jack and Coke today?"

"Pssh. It's too early for Jack and Coke. I'm not an alcoholic. This is vodka and Hawaiian Punch. It's practically a vitamin. So, what do you want to know?"

"Did you ever meet any of Temarius's friends?"

"I don't think he had any. I know his nana was worried that he was running with the wrong crowd, but it's not like anyone came home with him after school."

"Did he ever mention working with someone? Maybe against his will? Anyone named Kieran Dunne from Internal Affairs? Or maybe a Chinese woman with pink hair?"

She thought so hard her curls vibrated. "No, I don't believe he did. And I woulda noticed the Chinese."

After the blonde-with-the-corgi false alarm, I had serious doubts that Mrs. Rotnitzky could have distinguished Shayla and her cousins from the Hunan Palace delivery driver, but I didn't push.

"I know he was working on getting his GED, but he did that on the computer at the library."

"Did you know Temarius had a drug problem?"

Mrs. Rotnitzky nodded. "He struggled for years. Losing a mother so young like that . . . His nana took him to a program in her church and got him off the stuff, but it didn't last. I know he was going to meetings again here recently because he showed me his ninety-day chip last week."

"I'm surprised his nana isn't home from Tallahassee yet. I would have thought the police would have broken the news to her by now, but the crime-scene tape is still up."

"Dead."

"I'm sorry?"

"She's dead. Orlena died a couple of years ago. She fell on the ice and hit her head down in the KMart parking lot. Died instantly."

"You're saying Temarius's grandmother died two years ago?"

Mrs. Rotnitzky nodded. "She and I used to walk down to the bay at sunset to watch the ferry come in. There's too many tourists there now."

"If his grandmother has passed, then who was Temarius living with?"

"No one."

"But he was seventeen. How had he been living all by himself for two years?"

Mrs. Rotnitzky sat forward in her chair and threw her hands up over her head. "You're the social worker; you tell me! That's why I told you you were too late the first time you came here."

"I thought you were just rambling."

"I expected someone to come around after Orlena passed to check on the boy, but no one did until you."

"How was he supporting himself?"

"Orlena's Social Security. Her checks were direct deposited, like mine. He never reported her death, so they kept coming."

"How'd he pay the bills?"

Mrs. Rotnitzky shrugged. "He used her debit card for groceries. I showed him how to write a check, but these kids pay everything on the computer nowadays. You do what you gotta do."

That's what they had on him. Whoever was threatening Temarius found out that he was a minor living on his own, committing Social Security fraud. They must have threatened to turn him in if he didn't do what they wanted. He had gotten away with fraud for two years. Why was he caught now?

Outside Mrs. Rotnitzky's door, we could hear that Olivander was going down to the yard for a piddle. "Thank you, Mrs. Rotnitzky. I have to go." I shot out of the apartment to catch the neighbor with the blond ponytail.

I turned the corner just as the elevator doors slid shut. I flew down the stairs and waited. The bell chimed and the door slid open. "Hi. Remember me?"

The man fell against the back of the car and reached for his belt.

"Please don't mace me."

"Oh, it's you. Stop jumping out at me. Olivander has a nervous bladder."

The evidence of that was in the elevator. "Remember when you told me you had to call 9-1-1 when you first moved in?"

"I remember. That boy was smoking pot."

"Did you happen to see the officers when they arrived?"

"Yes. I had to give a statement."

"What did they look like?"

"Oh, I don't know. One was a foxy little brunette and the other was a white male with nearly invisible eyebrows and a very pink mouth. Is it important?"

"Probably not. I'm sure it's fine. Hey, nice chatting with you. I gotta go."

"Okay. 'Bye?"

I could have warned him that Olivander no longer needed to potty, but he was about to find out on his own. I took out my cell phone and dialed a number I knew by heart. "Hey. I need you. Meet me by the back door of Convention Hall. I want you to help me trap Shayla Rose. She may be working with a dirty cop to frame Amber."

CHAPTER 49

"Final clearance. Everything must go." The Lolly sheet mask lady shoved a coupon in my face when I stepped on the vendor floor. Everyone was having a sale. It was the final three hours of the Beauty Expo, and if you could sell it on the cheap, you wouldn't have to carry it home with you.

I passed Aunt Ginny arguing with the guy at the CBD booth. "What do you mean, you're out?! Well, do you have a store somewhere? How do you not have a store? You don't have a website either? How will I find you to order more?"

Gia's brothers were loitering around the booth. Probably waiting to take the espresso machine back to wherever it came from. I didn't want to know. It was probably a Mafia hideout. I didn't have time to ask. I had Shayla in my sights and I was closing in.

She saw me coming and took off just like I'd expected

her to and disappeared around the back of the Rubinesque tent.

Leo and Jimmy tried to block me, and Sawyer popped out from the back of their booth. "Hey there, fellas. You are two good-looking guys. Do you work out?"

I gave her a grin as I passed.

Leo giggled. "Yeah, a little."

This was my chance. I picked up the pace and ducked behind the Rubinesque tent. I flapped my way between the glass windows and the canvas wall until I found the door, and Shayla. Sitting on a bench on the boardwalk, wearing her North Carolina Tar Heels sweatshirt, and pouting over a cinnamon latte. Gia had her caught.

"You play dirty, bringing pretty boy into this with free coffee."

I put my hand on Gia's back. "He's my secret weapon."

He gave me an intense look that felt like an electric charge move between us, then winked and went inside.

I turned my full attention to Shayla. "You've been running away from me for days. We could have been friends. The fact that you were trapped by a latte is proof of that."

"You know why I've been avoiding you. I'd rather not lie to your face."

"Give me one good reason why I shouldn't tell the cops you were in Dr. Rubin's tent the morning he was killed."

"Because I didn't kill him."

"You threw me down trying to get out of there. Even covered in a hoodie and sweatpants, I still knew it was you. Your signature scent gave it away."

Shayla looked out at the ocean. "I should have showered first. And I think Leo's been using my perfume. That was his hoodie." She scooted down on the bench for me to join her. "I was sure Lance Rubin had robbed me. I came early in the morning determined to get into his booth and steal my stuff back. I tried to sneak in the back door without security recording my arrival. When it was locked I almost went home. Then some skinny guy in glasses who worked for the Paleo Diva arrived. I grabbed an empty box and told the security guard we were together and he'd forgotten the muffins at the bakery. He let me in and I ran back here to search Lance's office before anyone arrived."

"Did you find anything?"

"Lance Rubin, dead and smoking under his own UV mask on one of his exam tables. I freaked out and was about to split when I saw two empty jars of Immortality on his counter in the middle of a bunch of other products. I was so angry that he'd taken my samples that I grabbed the containers and ran. Then I heard you calling for him and jumped behind that hanging door to wait for you to leave. I didn't have time to find the rest of my jars, but I know he stole them."

"To do what with them?"

"To have a biochemist break down the formula."

"He didn't have to steal them to do that. You were giving them out for free. And he already had two."

She sat back against the bench and crossed her legs. "Well, that's true."

I knew it was. I also had the benefit of knowing Temarius stole the samples, but I was trying to get a confession, so I didn't bring that up. "Do you know someone named Temarius Jackson?"

Her face was blank. "No. Should I?"

"How about Kieran Dunne?"

Her eyes squidged down. "I don't know what you're talking about."

"Where do you make your antiaging cream?"

She quirked an eyebrow. "In my lab. In North Carolina."

"You weren't married to Lance Rubin, were you?"

Shayla's face twisted in disgust. "Eww, no! Gross."

"Believe me, it's a fair question. You were spotted together after the Expo closed."

"Did you hurt yourself jumping to that conclusion? He cornered me in my booth and suggested a merger with Rubinesque. He wanted me to be his new cosmetic chemist. I told him I already had my own company. He even promised I could keep my name on the products if I shared the secret of my Immortality cream."

"How generous of him."

"Right? I was like, 'no way. I worked too hard to get my degree and research that jellyfish to hand it over to you.' When he didn't get what he wanted, he broke into my booth and stole my concentrate."

"The antiaging concentrate that isn't FDA approved for distribution and will probably get your license to make skin-care products revoked?"

Shayla frowned and looked away. "What do you want me to say? I effed up. It's why I couldn't go to the police. I should never have brought Immortality here before it was FDA approved. I just didn't want to be scooped again."

"You know it turns people blue? That can't be a good selling point."

Shayla cut me with a dry look. "It has a natural luminescence when it comes into contact with the skin, but the molecules can get hyperexcited if they're exposed to UV rays." She rolled her eyes. "And . . . then it can emit a bright-blue glow. It can be a real problem during firefly mating season. Look, I'd try to explain it, but you need to be a biochemist to understand."

"I understand that no one wants to glow in the dark. How long have you known about that?"

She pulled out her cell phone. "I discovered it by accident. I was presenting before the American Board of Dermatology. The jars had been under the UV lights at the lab all week and they activated the luciferin in the jellyfish proteins. Someone turned the lights out for my Power-Point and my face glowed in the dark." She showed me a video of herself wearing a lab coat with her face lit up, and people were pointing at her and laughing. "It was so embarrassing. I went back to my lab and ran hundreds of tests on the formula. It smooths out wrinkles like your face has been ironed, but it becomes a problem if you don't store it properly. That's why it says right on the container to only wear it at night. As long as it's kept in a cool, dark place, it's fine."

"I saw the Kefir lady at the Egg Hunt. It isn't fine."

"That's because those idiots Leo and Jimmy drove up here in a flatbed and left some of the containers exposed for hours. I told them to keep the crates inside the cab in the dark with the air-conditioning on, but they didn't want to take out their lacrosse gear. They didn't tell me what they'd done until that lady charged into my booth screaming. Now she's threatening to sue, and I've already gotten one reprimand from the FDA. I can't afford another. I'll never get investors. Thank God I only handed out a dozen samples before they were stolen. I just wish I could have found the rest of them in that office."

"You really believe Dr. Rubin stole your Immortality samples?"

"I know he did."

I kinda know he didn't.

"And my laptop. Which I found in the drawer of his desk under some contracts. He was using my research to run experiments on beauty products. You know what?" Shayla got up from the bench and grabbed my wrist. "Come with me. I'll show you."

She led me around to the front door. The Expo was starting to empty out. Many of the vendor booths were already broken down and gone, including La Dolce Vita. I felt so empty knowing Gia wasn't there. Losing him would be a rough adjustment. If his plan didn't work, I might have to get another cat. Or three. I could become that sad cat lady who lives alone that people talk about on the news.

Shayla marched me past both of her cousins, who were boxing up rose-scented exfoliant and vitamin serums. "Lance heard me speak on a cosmetic chemistry panel at Penn State a few months ago. He knew I was close to a breakthrough. That's why he cornered me here after his ridiculous keynote brag."

She pulled a laptop from her pink leather tote bag and placed it on the counter. "He managed to log in, although I have no idea how he got past my password."

"Was it 'password'? 'Cause I hear some people use that."

"No, Tar Heels. It's my college basketball team."

I looked at her sweatshirt. "Yeah, that may not have been as hard to crack as you think."

She opened the laptop, and there was a bright-pink Post-it Note next to the touch pad. "Don't touch that. It might have his fingerprints on it. When I got my laptop back to my bed and breakfast, my research documents had been opened and he had highlighted these passages about luciferin and ultraviolet light. And he left this."

I had no idea what *this* was. It sounded like something from a *Star Trek* science officer's log. *I added stronger UV power cells and combined the Immortal concentrate with the hyaluronic serum. Now to subject it to ultraviolet rays . . .* "What am I looking at?"

"These are his notes. He made adjustments to his UV mask and was trying to get it to work with a layer of anti-aging products. You can see here that he blended different acids, which is dangerous. And retinoids aren't stable in UV light. That's why the directions on my concentrate say 'Keep in a dark place.' Not everything that's natural is safe. He was a doctor. He should have known better."

He must have been desperate about that patent. "What would happen if you mixed Immortality with, say, discount-store cold cream?"

"Nothing. You'd destroy all the active ingredients in Immortality and clog your pores with petroleum. Why would anyone do that?"

"To make knockoff Immortality and sell it online."

"It would be cheaper to just repackage the cold cream and tell people it was Immortality. But it would have to look the part if they'd seen Immortality advertised. And all my products smell like roses, so they'd have to copy that to make it look authentic."

I thought about what I knew was sitting in the warehouse in Wildwood Crest, and how it was somehow tied to Shayla's robbery, Temarius's murder, and Amber being framed. Someone on the police force was at the center of it all. Only a cop would know Amber's schedule on the rotation. And only a cop would be able to set her up to arrive at the victim's house after some bogus gunshots that probably happened in the parking lot right before she arrived. But which cop would be involved in making knockoff wrinkle cream?

"What happened to your date the night your samples were stolen? Have you seen that guy again?"

Shayla wouldn't meet my eyes. "I think he's ghosting me."

"It's an odd coincidence that only you were robbed the night Convention Hall was broken into and you were on a date when it happened."

She cocked her head to the side. "What are you saying?"

"Tell me again what you and Mr. Perfect talked about."

"Uh . . . Pomskys, Indian food, biochemistry, Adele, working out . . ."

"Do you realize that you've posted about every one of those things on your Facebook page?"

"You looked me up on Facebook?"

"Mm-hmm. Did he ask you a lot of questions about your research?"

Shayla considered that. "Yeah. I thought he was really into me, but he hasn't called once since we went out to dinner."

"That's another thing. Why come all the way up here from North Carolina to take you to Stone Harbor for dinner? Stone Harbor is thirty more minutes away. There are great restaurants right here."

"He said the one in Stone Harbor was special."

"I think it was special because he'd be less likely to be recognized there."

"You think he was lying?"

"I think you were catfished. And I think the guy who catfished you had an accomplice who stole your samples while you were on that date."

"Son of a biscuit!"

"Was he a little guy with dark hair and very blue eyes?"

"I don't think he was that little. I'm kinda short, so it's all relative. And now that you mention it, his eyes were blue. He also had dark hair and tortoiseshell glasses. He was really good-looking."

"Do you have a picture?"

"He insisted we take all our pictures with his phone, so he had a reason to email them to me and get a second date."

"And?"

She frowned and shook her head. "Wait. I can show you his profile picture." She went to the Tinder website and signed in. She did some furious scrolling and muttering. "His profile has disappeared. He's gone."

CHAPTER 50

I sat in the car and tried Amber's cell again. Still no answer. I was irritated that I couldn't make the connection between Temarius and Dr. Rubin, but maybe there wasn't one. It looked like Lance Rubin may have accidentally killed himself trying to turn that creepy light mask into something he could claim was his own invention. But I was still having heartburn over the power supply.

According to Tally, if it hadn't been crushed, the mask would have turned off in twenty minutes. If Dr. Rubin had put the mask on himself, why didn't he at some point think, *hey, this is starting to burn, and I've been lying here a really long time. I wonder what time it is*, and get up? Maybe I'd been involved in too many murders, but my feeling was that something nefarious was involved.

I was missing Gia and feeling a little lonely and sorry for myself. So I texted Sawyer.

Where r u?
Home. Why?
Just checking.

I pulled away from the curb and headed for her condo. I was going to show up and surprise her. Maybe we could watch a movie tonight. We'd been talking about *The Breakfast Club* for weeks.

My cell rang its new *Dragnet* ringtone and I snickered to myself. "I've been trying to reach you all day. Are you okay?"

"I'm fine." Amber's voice was clipped. "I bonded out."

"Oh good. I was worried . . ."

She cut me off. "The tox screen is back on Temarius. It wasn't the chemical in glow sticks. It's definitely luciferin from the face creams."

I put her on Speaker. "Yeah, we figured."

"Okay, you don't always have to know everything."

Where is this coming from? "I know."

"One more thing. Kat told me something in confidence. I'm going to tell you, but you can't repeat it, okay?"

"I won't."

"That blue stuff in the doctor's mask and on his hands, that was the same stuff that was on Temarius."

"Yeah, I . . . oh really? Isn't that interesting."

There was silence for a moment. "You already knew, didn't you?"

"Well, I just confirmed it this afternoon. Shayla Rose has notes that the doctor was experimenting . . . it's a long story, but it looks like that's what killed him."

"It isn't entirely."

"What do you mean?"

She had victory in her tone. "Postmortem on your

plastic surgeon shows he had been bashed in the head. He had a skull fracture and a brain bleed. That incapacitated him enough for the blue goo to work on him for hours. Kat's ruling it homicide by blunt force trauma and chemical burns."

I nearly ran Bessie up on the curb. "What about the power supply?"

"She found carpet fibers in the power supply. Someone crushed it by stepping on it. Maybe intentionally, maybe during a struggle."

I knew it.

"What did you have to tell me?"

"Remember that burner I found in Temarius's couch?"

"Yeah?"

"When I called the contact Kieran Dunne answered."

"Are you sure it was him?"

"I watched him do it. I was still in the police station."

"Why would Kieran Dunne be Temarius's handler? He's from Trenton. He's only in town to investigate me."

"You don't think it was his phone?"

"How did he answer it? Did he act sneaky? Was he surprised to be getting a call from someone who he thought was dead?"

"No, he just picked it up from the desk and said hello."

"Either he has no idea it was Temarius's, or he knew the call was coming from you and he was trying to throw you off. He's very smart. It would be a mistake to underestimate him. But I wouldn't rule him out either."

"We know Temarius was killed by someone who knew you. Now we need to narrow the field. Kieran Dunne seems to have it in for you, and Prudence Crabtree and that pink little Simmons keep showing up every time you're doing something you could be arrested for. That can't be a coincidence."

"I'd love to find out how they're the only two to be dispatched every time the situation involves me."

I couldn't shake the smallest inkling of fear that one of the cops I had come to trust might be involved. Officers Birkwell and Consuelos gave me very different takes on Amber. How could two people have such different perspectives and both be right? "Is there anyone else I need to know about? Anyone who maybe questioned how you've been able to close so many cases lately?"

There was more silence; then her voice came in sharp. "Don't worry about my record. Just worry about keeping your ears open. It's the only reason I need you."

Holy cow, who peed in her Cheerios?

"I have someplace I want you to go tonight. If you don't run your mouth too much, you can get some answers. But I can't go in with you."

"Well, after the way you're talking to me, that doesn't sound like a bad thing."

"I'll pick you up at eight. Dress better than you did at the warehouse."

"Wait. I don't want to be stranded again. This time I want to take backup with me so at least I know I can get home."

"Understood." She hung up with an attitude that I tried to excuse as the postdetainment crankies.

I walked up the steps to the second floor of Sawyer's condo. *Change in plans. First the surprise, then I need her to go on a secret mission with me.* I knocked on the door and waited. After a few seconds it swung open to reveal a man wearing only a tiny towel around his waist.

My mood bottomed out. "Kurt? What are you doing here?"

"What do you mean? I live here."

"How do you live here?"

"Didn't Sawyer tell you?"

"Are you back together?"

"Now see? With that disgusted look on your face, how do you think that makes me feel?"

"You cheated on her with every one of her brides-maids. And your best man's wife. And half the waitresses at the Ugly Mug. It's why she divorced you. Then you brought a stripper to our high-school reunion."

"Exotic dancer. There's a difference."

"Is there?"

"I've changed. You've never given me a chance. Why don't you come in and we'll have a beer, and talk?"

I had no words. I turned around and *thunked* my way down the steps to the Corvette. *Oh Sawyer. I love you. I'll be here for you no matter what. But maybe you should just get cats with me.* I put the car in reverse and drove home.

Ally Sheedy was right. *When you grow up, your heart dies.*

CHAPTER 51

I sat on the porch, waiting for Amber. Rabbitzilla lay on the ground like a used parachute, one ear half puffed and limply waving. The only guests I had left were the Cat Show people, and they would leave in the morning. Aunt Ginny was out with Royce. She said Fiona had come along to chaperone, which meant Iggy was driving, which meant Aunt Ginny would come home precranked.

Figaro meowed through the window, and I let him out on the porch. He climbed up in my lap for some self-serving cuddles. "It's just you and me, baby." He pushed his face into mine, purring.

I'd come home and changed into jeans, a white T-shirt, and a red-plaid flannel. Since Amber never gave me advance info, I didn't know what to dress for. If Amber dropped me at a formal party looking like this, I would flip my lid.

The Pinto pulled up and I gave Fig a kiss and put him back in the house, then walked to the car.

"Get in."

"What is your problem with me today?" I clicked my seat belt into place.

Amber floored it and flung the car away from the curb. After a few blocks of silence she blurted out, "Why don't you think I'm a good cop?"

"Where is this coming from?"

"I heard the questions you were asking about me. Am I dirty? Do I take bribes? Do I plant evidence? My God, McAllister. Who do you think I am?"

I was rolling back my memory over the past week. None of this sounded right. The only time planting evidence came up was with Consuelos, and no one had used those words. "Who told you this?"

"It doesn't matter."

"Yes. It does. Because I didn't say any of those things. Not the way you're saying them."

"Word got around the station, okay? They said that my 'partner' rolled over on me."

"As in I gave them evidence about you?"

"You told them I'd been investigating Temarius's death even though I was on administrative leave. And you were worried I was planting evidence to implicate another officer."

"I can't believe you fell for that your-partner-gave-you-up bit. Cops do that to suspects all the time, Amber. I think *you* did it to *me*!"

We drove on for a few more minutes of silence. "It wasn't during my interview, McAllister. It was chatter around the holding tank."

"Okay. Chatter by who?"

"Prudence Crabtree, and some others."

"I've never even spoken to Prudence Crabtree."

"Well, it's too late to do anything about it now. The trespassing arrest has left me on full suspension." She pulled onto a gravel driveway near the entrance to the nature preserve that a long time ago was South Cape May, until a hurricane shaved off an entire town on the Jersey Shore. We parked in front of a two-story red barn in a sandy parking lot filled with police cars.

"Where are we?"

"Cop bar."

"I've never seen this place."

"You're not supposed to. And after tonight forget you know about it."

I spotted an angry, husky gal leaning against a porch pillar. She was wearing jeans and a leather vest over a gray T-shirt and chewing on a toothpick. "Then why is Joanne Junk here?"

"You said you needed backup."

Has it really come to this? "I meant *I* would get backup."

Amber leaned forward to look through the passenger window. "And who do you have?"

"I couldn't get anyone."

Amber snorted. "Joanne's been here with me before, and she knows how to act with this crowd, so you'll have no trouble there. You aren't here to make a scene. Try to blend in and keep your ears open for anything about the investigation. I'll be nearby if you get into trouble."

Officer Consuelos opened the barn door and stepped outside.

"That's your signal. Ben'll get you in. For once in your life just try to be cool."

I cranked the window down and stuck my arm out to open the door. I hefted myself out and bent over to look back inside. "I don't have to try to be cool, Amber. I am cool." I threw the door shut, and the corner of my plaid got caught in the crack.

I locked eyes with Amber. She raised her eyebrows and gave me a look like she was trying to be patient.

I opened the door, retrieved my plaid, and slammed it again.

"Hey, butt face."

"Joanne."

"Try not to embarrass me in here."

Officer Consuelos grinned and looked away. He opened the door, and we walked into a large barn with a polished wood-and-brass bar and an exposed-beam ceiling. The room smelled of Lemon Pledge and nachos. Top 40 hits played over speakers in the back, while two flat-screens behind the bar were playing basketball on one channel and golf on another. Only a few barstools were empty, but there were tables and booths scattered all over the room. The tables in the middle were all vacant.

"There are so many cops in here, I'm surprised there isn't a crime spree in town."

Officer Consuelos chuckled. "These aren't all cops. Some are badge bunnies, there are a couple of wives, and a few of these guys are retired."

The perimeter of the room was dimly lit, but the entry-way where we were was like an interrogation cell. The bartender gave us a chin up that was probably meant for Consuelos.

He moved in front of us. "Get a drink, get a table. Not in the middle of the room. And not right next to anyone else either. If you need me, I'll be at the bar. Don't need me."

I nodded.

He walked away, and Joanne and I wandered over to an empty section of the bar. Joanne took a seat and ordered a beer. I looked around. No windows. Only one way in or out. The main floor led into a smaller room off to the side, with video games and two pool tables. I thought I heard someone playing air hockey.

"What can I get you?" The bartender was an older black man, all tatted up, with a James Earl Jones voice and a silver hoop in one ear.

"Just an iced tea, please."

Joanne rolled her eyes at me when his back was turned. "Iced tea?"

"What? I'm really not a drinker. And this seems like a bad night to start."

Joanne pulled over a bowl of mixed nuts and scooped up a handful. She must have seen the look on my face. "What's the matter?"

I shook my head no and shrugged.

She looked away from me and tossed some nuts into her mouth.

"It's just that the news did a special on how those bowls of bar nuts are tainted with urine because people don't wash their hands when they go to the bathroom."

Joanne stopped chewing and slowly dropped the rest of the nuts back into the bowl.

The bartender delivered our drinks just as two men came in and took seats next to us. They had "cop" written all over them. I was the only one in the bar who tensed up. They ordered beers and started chatting about their day. After a couple minutes of silence they glanced our way, took their beers, and moved.

I leaned closer to Joanne. "I think we should be talking. We look suspicious, just sitting here listening."

Joanne huffed. "You're just going to suck every minute of fun out of this, aren't you?"

"Look, I don't even want to be here. I'm only here to help Amber."

"Well, why Amber would ask *you* is the bigger mystery."

"Amber trusts me. She said I have good instincts."

"Are you all talking about Officer Fenton?"

Joanne and I froze. Two women a few seats down were watching us intently. They were dressed for a sexy-night-out, not an unwind-from-the-shift.

I cleared my throat. "You know Amber?"

The brunette answered, "Oh yeah. She comes in here all the time when she gets off her shift."

Her friend with long, pink fingernails stirred a martini. "She usually sits alone in the back, though. I haven't seen her for a few days. I heard she got fired."

Joanne and I glanced at each other. Joanne said, "Oh? Fired for what?"

The brunette turned to her friend. "I don't remember. What did Pru say?"

"I think she killed a kid in his apartment."

"Wow." I shook the ice in my glass to mix my tea around. "And here I thought Amber was one of the good cops, you know?"

The ladies picked up their glasses and moved closer.

The brunette answered, "Most of these cops are good cops. But she wasn't very well-liked. At least not by the wives. I'm Karen, by the way."

Joanne and I said, "Hi."

The other one reached out her hand. "Jill."

"Hi."

"And what are your names?" Karen asked.

"Oh," I answered, "I'm . . . Blossom. And this is . . ."

Joanne put her hand out. "Jo."

"Did Pru say why Amber killed that kid?"

Karen took a sip of her drink. "I think he was about to go public that she was skimming."

Joanne crossed her arms on the bar. "You mean like keeping cash and drugs from busts?"

Jill nodded. "Mm-hmm, exactly."

I ran my finger around the rim of my glass. "Pru is pretty new to Cape May, isn't she? I heard she transferred from Upper. How is she liking it?"

Karen tilted her head and nodded. "She loves it. Pru was born to be a cop. She says Chief Fischer is the best. He's not afraid to put her out there just because she's a woman, you know? Some of the guys try to protect the women cops like they're fragile. I mean, not Amber. I hear she's kind of a ballbuster. But the other ladies have had problems."

Jill added, "Yeah. Not all the guys are superexcited about working with female cops."

Karen passed a look to Jill. "Well, that's because their wives don't like it."

Jill sucked the olive off her toothpick. "I wouldn't like it either. I don't want my husband driving around with another woman all day, telling her about our sex life."

I knocked back some of my tea. The ice shifted, and tea splashed on my shirt. I dabbed at it with my napkin. "Are you ladies married to cops?"

"No." Jill shook her head. "But I've dated a few." She pointed around the room. "Him. Him. Almost him. That one's a jerk, stay away from him."

Joanne looked over her shoulder and nodded toward Consuelos. "How about him?"

Karen grinned. "Oh, he's yummy. But I don't think he dates the girls from the bar. And we've all tried, believe me."

I smiled. "How about Pru's partner? The blond? What's his name?"

Karen scrunched her nose. "Connor Simmons. He's a creep. I overheard one of the guys say they thought he only made it on the force because his father built the Police Academy a fitness center."

Jill poked her toothpick at a floating olive. "There's something stalkery about him. I wouldn't stop the car if he was pulling me over."

Karen laughed. "That's how she meets most guys."

The door opened, and a couple of the cops raised their glasses.

Karen nudged me. "Here comes Pru now."

Oh no. I hopped off the barstool. "Actually, I have to use the ladies' room. Excuse me for a minute."

I skirted around the edge of the bar and hid my face from the door. If I walked slow, I could overhear pieces of conversation. Most of the cops were chatting about random things. Their girlfriends, their husbands, dreading tourist season, recent arrests.

I lingered by a booth with two burly men in sweats when I overheard them talking about the IA officer. "Dunne has never liked her. She made him look like a fool with Doyle."

"Doyle was innocent. Of course she'd fight back to prove it."

My red-plaid camouflage failed to hide me standing out in the open. The fact that I was gawking at their table probably didn't help either, and the men spotted me.

One of them narrowed his eyes and gave me a once-over. "Can I help you?"

I considered backing away quietly, but Prudence was still hovering around the bar. "Uh . . . just checking to see if everything is alright. Can I get you fellas anything?"

The other man's head tilted to the side. "Are you new?"

"Yep."

"How long have you been working here?"

"Would you believe this is my first night?"

The cop next to him gave me a slow nod. "Yeah, I think I would."

I tried a friendly, please-don't-report-me smile. "So, what'll it be?" *I hope it isn't against the law to impersonate a waitress.*

The first guy checked his phone. "Not for me, I gotta get goin'."

They both started to scoot out of the booth, so I grinned like a madwoman and stepped out of their way and turned into Flo from Mel's Diner. "Well, y'all have a good night, y'hear."

They gave me a nod on their way out.

That did not go great. I gotta blend in better. I crossed the room to an empty booth in the far corner and grabbed a couple of napkins. I tried to listen in on a table of policewomen in the booth next to mine while vigorously wiping down the clean table.

"I think they're setting her up."

"She should have been more careful. No one closes that many cases with no evidence."

"Well, the I-got-lucky excuse is bs. She can't keep using it."

"I think that waitress is listening to us."

Crap.

One of the women pointed an empty bottle at me. "Hey. You. What are you doing?"

I took a breath and tried to look more waitressey, like I could balance a tray of drinks with one hand if I had to. "Can I get you ladies another round?"

A heavily made-up, busty brunette scowled at me. "Since when does Jack have table service?"

"This is the first night."

She gave me an appraising scan. "Well, if you want to get some decent tips, don't hover around the empty tables trying to look busy."

I considered giving her my own tip that frosty peach lip gloss made her look like an undercover prostitute like Carla from *Cheers* would say, but everyone in here other than me probably had a gun on them, so instead I attempted a grateful smile. "Thank you. I'll do that."

The women ordered another round of drinks that they would never get because I wasn't going to tell anyone this ever happened, and I got away from them and practically ran into the video-game room to act like I was very interested in air hockey.

The same two young guys who were playing when we arrived were still battling it out. The one wearing a Flyers T-shirt didn't see me standing there. "At least if you're going to hold on to evidence, don't put it on your report."

The cop wearing a blue pullover noticed me watching. "Not that either of us would ever do that."

The Flyers T-shirt scored. "What? Not me. Fenton. Oh."

I gave him a smile. "I've always wanted to learn how to play this."

Judging from the distaste that registered on their faces,

my powers of seduction must have been on the fritz. They'd been on the fritz since the day I was born so I had no idea what they would look like if they ever surfaced.

The men gave me a once-over. Flyer's T-shirt said he was married and the pullover just said, "Not interested."

"Oh. Okay. Never mind, then." I picked up my dignity and slunk out of the room and back into the main bar area. One of the women I'd already talked to held up her glass, but I evaded her eyes and pretended I was being hailed by another table across the way.

I passed a man drinking alone and talking on his cell phone. "Of course I'm sorry. Just buy whatever you want and let's put this behind us."

Okay, that probably isn't about Amber. If it is, I don't know her at all. I didn't see Prudence at the bar anymore, so I started to head back to my seat.

Joanne caught my eye and shook me a panicked *no.*

Prudence stepped out from behind a larger officer and took a bottle of water offered by the bartender.

I spun on my heel and hid my face. I headed toward the farthest booth at the back of the room. The police-women tried to get my attention again. "It's coming right up. Jack said you were next." I had to find a way to get out of there before they complained to Jack about his waitress and the whole room realized I was just eavesdropping like Homeland Security. Amber would never forgive me for mucking this up.

I was going to do a discreet lap to kill some time waiting for Prudence to leave the bar when I overheard the name Simmons. I stopped at the far back table in the corner, where two older men were drinking something brown out of highball glasses. I stood against the wall with my back to them, like I was in line for the bathroom.

"That's why there's a chain of custody. To keep rats like Simmons honest."

"Pink little weasel."

"I don't think he's ever made an arrest. Fischer keeps him on traffic duty so he doesn't embarrass the department."

The bathroom door swung open and a woman ran into me. "There's no line. Go on in."

"Oh, thanks." Now that I was in the bathroom, I actually had to pee. I was taking care of business when I heard the door open, then footsteps. Then someone looked under my stall door. "Joanne? For all that is holy!"

"There's a problem. We gotta go."

I flushed and washed my hands. "What's the problem?"

"First of all, Sawyer just walked in."

I dropped my mouth and stared at Joanne.

"I know. It's hard for you when you don't know something."

"Who is she with?"

Joanne held up a palm. "None of my business."

"What's the other problem?"

"The forensics are in. The bullets that killed the kid are a match for the gun in the dumpster. Prudence Crabtree was here to gloat. Amber was just arrested for the murder of Temarius Jackson."

CHAPTER 52

"**I** feel like I'm letting her down." I climbed into Joanne Junk's tidy green pickup truck on the edge of
the lot. "I know she's innocent, but I don't know how to
prove it. I don't know who's framing her. There are too
many possibilities."

Joanne cranked the engine and put the truck in reverse.

"Kieran Dunne is clearly gunning for her, but he's had
the least amount of opportunity. He would have had to
drive down from Trenton several times to set things in
motion. And why would he keep his counterfeit beauty
cream operation in a warehouse near Wildwood Crest?
My God, what is that amazing smell?"

Joanne answered me with less enthusiasm than I have
for meeting Georgina at a seven a.m. networking breakfast. "Air freshener."

"It smells like strawberry shortcake." I inhaled deeply.
I wanted to have dreams about this smell later. "Kieran

sounds like the man Shayla Rose said she was on a date with, but I don't know if he was acting alone. It's so frustrating because the cops who respect Amber aren't standing up for her, and the cops who don't like her are willing to see her knocked down a few pegs whether she's guilty or not. I think maybe Prudence Crabtree and Connor Simmons are Kieran's accomplices." I looked at Joanne to see if she had any input.

She shook her head. "Do you always talk this much?"

"If I'm trying to work out a problem I do. Plus, I kinda think there might have been sugar in that iced tea, and I haven't had that much sugar in a long time."

"I just saw you eat a scone with half a jar of strawberry preserves on it."

"Well, yeah. But that was all."

"No wonder Sawyer wanted to go out without you."

"Now you're just being mean. Although I don't know why I'd expect anything less."

She gave me no answer.

"So, you have nothing? No thoughts on who could be framing Amber?"

After a minute Joanne said, "You need to see if those fake products are on the market. Then trace who the seller is."

"That's a good idea. I'll check Amazon and eBay to see if anyone is selling Shayla Rose. Immortality doesn't come out until later this fall, and that's if Shayla can get it to stop turning people blue and get it approved by the FDA. So anyone selling it now is selling counterfeit goods."

Joanne pulled to a stop in front of my house. I said thank you and got out. I heard her door shut behind me and turned around to see her walking up the sidewalk. "What are you doing?"

"I'm coming inside to check for counterfeit face cream on the Internet."

"Are you actually helping me?"

"No, moron. I'm helping Amber. You need a different kind of help that I can't give."

I was willing to let that slide because I'd lost my regular sidekick earlier in a cop bar and I was hoping Joanne would make me those petits fours again.

Joanne took the guest laptop and I went upstairs to get mine.

Figaro and Portia were curled up on top of my bed. Figaro scooted closer to Portia. Portia got up, spun around, and lay back down farther away from him. Figaro's eyes squinted and he lay his head on his paws.

By the time I'd returned to the kitchen Aunt Ginny had joined Joanne at the kitchen table and was complaining about running out of her green gummies from the CBD booth. "They don't even have a website, and I just learned how to find websites."

"I don't want you taking those anyway, Aunt Ginny. Even if you do drive better when you're on them."

Aunt Ginny rested her elbows on the table and her head in her hands. "It's just as well. I somehow gained seven pounds this week. Maybe it was the sugar."

Or the mountain of snacks you went through with the munchies. I patted Aunt Ginny on the back. "Maybe it was."

I joined them at the table and pulled out my cell phone to dial Connie, one of my high-school girlfriends who used to be a Realtor.

"Hello?"

"Oh good, you're still up."

"Are you kidding me? Emmilee has a book report due in the morning that she just told me about TWO HOURS AGO!" Those last three words were yelled away from the mouthpiece for Emmilee's benefit. "So, yeah. I'll be up for a while. What do yooze need?"

"Can you still get into the Multiple Listings database?"

"Yeah."

"If I send you an address, can you find out who owns it?"

"I can do my best. What is it?"

"I don't know. I'm going to have to use Google Earth to find it again."

"Alright. Send it over when you're ready. GET IN THAT ROOM AND FINISH THAT BOOK!"

I clicked off and Googled the names I remembered seeing on buildings nearby. Then I plugged them into Google Earth and changed to street view.

Figaro trotted into the kitchen, followed by Portia. He jumped on the table and proceeded to parade back and forth across my keyboard. It may have looked affectionate, but he was shaking me down for a snack. I picked him up around his middle and placed him on the floor. "Not now, Fig."

Joanne stopped typing. "I think I found something."

"What is it?"

Joanne read the description. "'Shayla Rose new Immortality antiaging concentrate. With bioluminescent jellyfish toxins to iron out wrinkles better than BOTOX. Your skin will glow from the inside out. New miracle breakthrough, as seen in *ELLE* magazine.'"

Aunt Ginny made a face. "Was it featured in a magazine? I thought it wasn't for sale yet."

Joanne spun the laptop around for me to see the screen.

"That reads like it was copied right from her brochure, except for the *ELLE* magazine bit. And that photo is the same one from her website."

Figaro jumped on the table between the laptops and let out a demanding meow. I scooped him up and gently placed him on the floor again.

"Who does it say the seller is?"

Joanne spun it back around and squinted at the monitor. "Beauty Supply Warehouse."

Aunt Ginny tapped the top of the monitor. "What else do they sell from Shayla Rose?"

It took Joanne a minute of searching before she answered. "Nothing else on eBay or Amazon."

Aunt Ginny shook her head. "See. That ain't right. That booth had half-a-dozen products displayed. I almost bought the rose-scented eye cream, but I already got some of that Phoenix stuff."

I drummed my fingers on the table. "Can you get any more information about the seller?" I heard a *thunk* from over by the toaster. Figaro was sitting pretty on the counter and a box of crackers was on the floor. I sighed. He was getting really naughty. *I think he's showing off for Portia.*

Joanne shook her head. "There isn't much about the seller, but in the last month they have a few five-star reviews and one one-star."

"What does the one-star review say?"

Joanne checked. "'This stuff smells awful. I have the Shayla Rose facial scrub and it smells like roses. This new antiaging concentrate smells like diaper rash cream. And it made my face breakout.'"

Another *thunk* sounded from across the room. Figaro

had one paw aloft and his eyes on me. My spice jar of cinnamon lay on the floor. I walked over and scooped him off the counter. "Quit acting up."

Aunt Ginny asked Joanne, "What do the good reviews say?"

Joanne blinked and squinted at the screen again. "Regular stuff. Fast shipping, great product. They could be fake reviews."

I narrowed down the address of the warehouse to two possibilities and texted them to Connie. There was another *thunk* from behind my head. I jumped up and spun around. "Figaro!"

Two bright-green eyes stared back, and a dainty white paw gently placed itself back on the counter. The can of cat treats rolled slowly across the kitchen floor. I think Portia may have smiled.

Aunt Ginny belly laughed. "I see Figaro has taught her a new trick. Just wait until she tries that at home."

Joanne smiled. "I'd give them each a treat just for being smarter than you."

I shook out two small piles of treats on the floor. I told Fig, "She goes home in the morning and you'll still live with me. So choose your allies wisely."

Fig flopped over and hit the floor with a thud. Portia edged over and finished the rest of his treats.

Joanne looked up from the laptop. "I don't guess you got any evidence of this counterfeit face cream scam while you were at the warehouse, did you?"

"We didn't have a chance before they threw in some kind of light grenade and we were on the floor."

Aunt Ginny tsked. "That's too bad, honey. If you could prove who is behind the counterfeit beauty scheme, you'd have Amber's dirty cop right where you want them."

It was risky, but Aunt Ginny was right. "It could be all of them."

Joanne grabbed her keys. "Alright, then. Come on."

"Come on where?"

"We're going to the warehouse."

"What if it's been cleaned out by now? Amber and I set off some silent alarm."

"There's only one way to find out."

Aunt Ginny handed me my cell phone. "Are you wearing good underwear this time?"

"Yes."

"Okay. I'll come bail you out in a few hours."

I led Joanne to Warehouse Row by memory. I didn't know the street names, but I knew Keen Canning was a landmark.

The chain-link gate was still open; either we were very lucky or about to walk into a trap. We turned into the parking lot and I told Joanne to drive around to the side of the building.

"The last time it took about ten minutes for the police to arrive after we tripped the silent alarm. I can be in and out in five. You stay in the truck and be ready to go. There's no reason for us both to get arrested."

I grabbed my flashlight and got out, approached the door, and punched 1-9-7-6 into the keypad. Hot breath was on the back of my neck and I flinched to smack it away.

"Hey, quit it!"

I turned my head and found Joanne right behind me. "I told you to wait in the truck."

"Amber will never forgive me if you go in there and

get shot and I didn't back you up, or at least try to save you."

"Wow. I was expecting you to be snarky."

"If I see a gun or an angry dog, you're on your own."

There it is.

I turned the handle and pushed the door open.

Joanne felt around for a switch. She flicked something, and the room was flooded with industrial-strength lights.

"Dude! Why don't you just call the cops and tell them we're here?" My eyes took a moment to adjust, but they went right to where the folding tables had been. The stacks of products we had seen two nights ago were gone. The tables were empty. "We're too late."

"I was wondering when you'd stop by."

My breath bottomed out. Connor Simmons was sitting on a metal folding chair ten feet away with a gun resting on his knee.

"Now, hands behind your back. You're under arrest."

CHAPTER 53

I put my wrists together and tried to memorize every inch of the warehouse while Officer Pink Weasel cuffed me. Against the back wall were half-a-dozen small, cardboard boxes stacked up like they were ready to ship. Next to them were shipping supplies, markers, labels, a postage scale. I also spotted an old box monitor on top of an ancient computer with a CD-ROM drive. "Nice place you have here."

Connor Simmons yanked the cuffs hard and pulled my arms behind me. My shoulders gave a spasm of protest. Joanne cried out in pain, and a shudder went right through me. I felt my heart grip in my chest. "No light grenade tonight?"

He chuckled. "Flash-bangs and zip-ties are only for special ops. This is just routine guard duty. We knew you'd return once Amber was arrested. And look, here you are."

"So, this is your warehouse?"

"Nope."

I caught Joanne's eyes as he pushed her past me toward the door. "If it isn't yours, who does it belong to?"

He shoved me through the door behind Joanne. "I dunno." He led us around back, where his police cruiser was hidden behind the Shotcrete warehouse.

Joanne asked him, "Do you know what that warehouse is being used for?"

"Not my problem."

I tried to egg him on. "What if it's a meth lab? Wouldn't you be concerned about a meth lab?"

"It's above my pay grade."

He shoved me in the back of the car, then shoved Joanne on top of me.

He got behind the wheel and cranked the engine. I noticed he didn't report to Dispatch that he was bringing us in. That was a bad sign. No accountability. Once he pulled through the fence, Joanne gave a subtle head jerk in his direction.

I wiggled in my seat to get sight of him through the rearview mirror. "How'd you know we would return?"

"I'm not exactly a rookie."

Joanne softened her voice to sound less Joanney. "Oh, how long have you been on the force?"

"Three years."

I jumped in. "That long? Have you done any work with Officer Amber in that time?"

His eyes flicked up to the mirror and held mine for a moment. "Fenton has considerably more seniority than me, so no."

Joanne put a disapproving tone in her voice toward

me. "You know Amber doesn't work with a partner. She thinks they slow her down."

"You're right. No one else is competent enough."

The back of Simmons's neck darkened. "Fenton doesn't work with a partner because no one wants to be anchored to a dirty cop."

I flipped my hair to appear casual. "Really? I thought she was the station's shining star. Didn't she just solve five high-profile murders recently?"

Simmons looked in the rearview mirror again. "Pssh. Yeah, but with what methods? She's made the entire squad look like no one else knows what they're doing but her. She lists an anonymous CI on the report, but we all know that's just a cover."

"Then how's she doing it?"

Joanne turned her head to make a face at me. Under her breath, I barely heard her say, "Really?"

I mouthed, *What?*

She gave me a piercing look in response.

Simmons continued, "Fenton's not that smart. Someone's helping her. Maybe she figured out the high-school murder on her own—she did know those people, but no way she just got lucky with that Senior Center theater. It takes longer to fill out the paperwork for a search warrant than it took her to apprehend the killer. She said the evidence just dropped in her lap. And the murder at the winery? That one was genius, and she ain't no genius. There had to be some unauthorized searching going on there."

Oh . . . no . . . I had a really bad feeling about this. "What other high-profile murders has she solved?"

He shrugged. "One was some chef thing. I'm pretty sure she planted evidence for that one. And that dude who won the humanitarian award? He was a local hero. You better believe that got her some good press. I think she has someone on the inside."

"The inside of a murder?" I tried not to laugh. "How exactly would that work?"

"I think the kid she killed set up some illegal wiretaps and video surveillance for her and was feeding her information."

"Then why would she kill him?"

"He was about to go public and blow the whole thing."

Joanne rolled her eyes. "What about the murder weapon? Did you find that?"

We stopped at a red light and Simmons looked over his shoulder and grinned. "She stashed it in a dumpster out back behind the kid's apartment."

I leaned forward a little. "Did you check the woods and the building first?"

"Naw. I knew it was in the dumpster. Got an anonymous tip."

Joanne snorted. "Wow. That was really lucky." Her sarcasm was not noticed.

Simmons pulled through a fence that said Authorized Personnel Only. "Yeah. Same with that warehouse raid the other night. Got a call that trespassers were on the property, so we went and rounded you up." He looked over his shoulder and laughed. "Maybe I'll be up for promotion next."

He got out and opened my door. My cell phone rang in my back pocket.

I softened my eyes. "Do you think I could answer that? I live with my eighty-two-year-old great-aunt and she's going to be worried sick. Her heart might not be able to take it that you've caught me twice in one week."

He chewed the inside of his mouth. "Yeah. I guess that would be okay. As long as I can take it out of your pocket for you. But be quick."

His hands did a lot of roving, considering my jeans had shrunk so tight after the sugar in the iced tea that my cell phone was popping out like the timer on a Thanksgiving turkey. I couldn't squeeze a dime down the waistband, yet he felt around like a blind man trying to memorize my assets.

"Here you go." It was Connie. He hit the Answer button and held it up to my ear.

"Thanks." *Uck.* "Short and sweet, I'm being arrested."

There was a moment of stunned silence. "The warehouse was purchased nine years ago by Clementine Newsome."

Holy crap.

CHAPTER 54

"Are you kidding me?" Officer Birkwell picked me up from the mug-shot room. "I've only been on duty fifteen minutes. I just saw Amber in the tank, and Joanne Junk's being fingerprinted. I had to trade Simmons my next day off to process you. What have you done now?"

He dropped my file on his desk and I took a seat.

"Forget about that for a second. I need your help proving Amber didn't kill Temarius Jackson, and we need to move fast before the evidence disappears."

He gave me a wary look under lidded eyes. "I can't get involved with that."

"You know she's a good cop and someone here is setting her up. I just need some information."

He picked up a pen like he was taking notes. "Like what, for instance?"

"What happens when a cop confiscates a gun from a crime scene?"

His eyes scanned the room. "There's a chain of custody. They write it on their report, log it into the system, then turn it into evidence."

"So, if Amber turned a gun into evidence eight weeks ago, what kind of record would there be for that?"

"She would have her copy of the report and a case number. And there would be a record of her logging the gun into the evidence file on the computer. Plus, she'd have signed the logbook when she put it in the evidence locker."

"Would she, like, go put it in a box in the evidence room herself?"

"After-hours she could. If she got the key from the watch commander. If she turned it in during the day, she'd sign it in with the property clerk." The tone of his voice changed. "Spell your full name."

"You already know that."

Kieran Dunne approached the desk and gave me a look of contempt. "Welcome back. As soon as you're processed, I'll be conducting your interview."

I stared him down. "I can't wait."

He gave me a haughty look down his perfect nose. "Neither can I."

He started walking away and I called after him, "Shayla Rose told me that she knows you've been ghosting her."

His eyebrows dipped slightly and he looked up to his hairline. "Who?"

"Shayla Rose, the biochemist you've been dating."

Only his eyes moved, and they shifted slightly to the right. Then his lip curled and he blew me off.

Officer Birkwell's eyebrows shot up and his eyes grew wide. "What was that all about?"

I said, more to myself than to him, "Just checking something. What if a dirty cop wanted to keep some evidence for themself?"

"I don't know anyone who has ever done that."

"But what if they wanted to?"

"They wouldn't put it on the report, that's for sure."

"Can you look up Amber's report from eight weeks ago? The one where she confiscated the gun?"

He gave me a frustrated look and sighed. After some keystrokes he pulled up a database. "What was the call for?"

"Domestic disturbance."

He paged through a few records. "Here's the only domestic reported by Amber in the past three months where a weapon was seized. The wife refused to press charges, so Amber confiscated a thirty-eight at the scene for the wife's protection."

"Okay. Where is the evidence report that gets turned in with the gun?"

He clicked a link and an error message popped up. "No report with that number. Huh. That's not right. Let me check the evidence log." He typed some more and opened a new screen. He sat up very straight and ran his eyes around the room, then looked over his shoulder, then back at the screen. "There's a report missing. See these numbers? They're sequential: 115-818, 115-819, then it goes to 115-821. Amber's evidence record from the domestic was 820. It appears to have been deleted."

I immediately felt vindicated.

An officer passed the desk and her radio crackled. I stretched to release some of my tension before it snapped my neck like a rubber band. "So, someone deleted the evidence file from Amber's report?"

Officer Birkwell tabbed back over to the database. "That's what it looks like. Everyone has a unique ID code for signing into the evidence log. Here, you can see my code was entered four minutes ago. If I enter or delete a record, it leaves a trace."

"Who's been in there recently?"

"In the past two weeks Carter, Consuelos, Crabtree, and McBride have logged in. And now me."

"Does that mean one of them deleted the record?"

He squeezed his eyes half shut and shook his head. "We don't know when the record was deleted. I think that's a question for IT. But there's also a written log that everyone has to sign when they turn in evidence. I can check to see if Amber signed the logbook, but I'll need a little time to get in there." Officer Birkwell's eyes darkened and his expression changed.

Kieran Dunne grabbed me under the armpit and jerked me to my feet. Well, he jerked me halfway to my feet. I was several inches taller than him and he couldn't reach high enough to get me all the way to my feet, so I had to help him. "Let's go."

I passed one last look to Officer Birkwell. "You need to call IT to fix that virus before it spreads."

CHAPTER 55

Kieran Dunne led me down the hall to an interrogation room with a table and two benches that had been bolted to the floor. A window made out of a one-way mirror was on the wall next to the door. I knew who was on the other side.

"Have a seat." Kieran dropped a file folder on the table between us that said *Jackson, Temarius—Homicide* on the tab. "So, tell me what happened the night of April the first."

"I went back to my home after a long day setting up for the Beauty Expo at Convention Hall, where I met Shayla Rose."

"And who is Shayla Rose?"

"She's the woman who was catfished through her Facebook page so her antiaging concentrates could be stolen while she was on a date."

He looked up and blinked. "Uh-huh. Now, tell me what happened at the home of Temarius Jackson."

I looked Kieran Dunne dead in the eyes, then I looked at the one-way mirror on the wall. "I went to the home of Temarius Jackson and found a burner phone in the couch. There was only one contact."

Kieran scribbled some notes on the file. "What time was this?"

The door opened, and Chief Fischer entered the room. "I'll take it from here, Dunne."

Bingo.

Kieran began to protest. "I just got started."

The chief put his hand on Kieran's shoulder. "I got it."

Kieran Dunne stood in a huff and straightened his tie. "This isn't finished, Fischer."

Before he could shut the door, the chief said, "Dunne. Go get the other one and take her back down to finger-printing. Stay with her and make sure she cooperates. She smudged the prints the last time."

Kieran ground his teeth like he was trying to get his temper in check. "I don't work for you." He left and shut the door behind him.

I locked eyes with the chief. "Didn't want him on the other side of the glass, did you?"

Chief Fischer smiled. "We like to thwart Internal Affairs whenever we can. Cops should look after their own. Not investigate them."

"But you don't have any problem framing one for murder."

He didn't blink.

I examined his face. "I bet you are really good-looking with glasses on. Do you actually wear them, or were you just Clark Kenting? And did you specifically pick glasses that look like Kieran's, or was that a coincidence?"

"I have no idea what you're talking about. Now, I'm going to ignore for a minute that you broke into a crime scene that was sealed. Tell me about this cell phone you found. Why didn't you turn it in to the police?"

"I didn't know who I could trust."

"You can trust me. I'm in charge of the station. We'll need that cell phone for evidence."

"You're in charge of the shift assignments too, aren't you?"

His eyes flicked with impatience. "I am."

"Did you plan to frame Amber from the start, or was it a last-minute decision because she had a gun in evidence?"

He tapped his finger on the folder in front of him. "Amber has arrested both you and your aunt for murder this past year. This is your chance to help me put her away."

"Why didn't you frame someone who was off-duty? Then you wouldn't have had to use the ice cubes to mask the time of death until you could get Amber over there. Unless you were setting up your alibi."

His eyes narrowed slightly and his lip curled, but his voice was perfectly calm. "Miss McAllister, Poppy. You're in way over your head here. You have no idea what you're talking about. I would hate to have to charge you as an accessory to murder because you didn't cooperate. What would happen to your aunt if you weren't there to take care of her? She could fall down the stairs and break her neck. You don't want that on your conscience, do you?"

My veins felt like they were pumping ice water. "Are you threatening to hurt Aunt Ginny? Because my neighbors won't be as easy to fool with gunshots outside their windows as Mrs. Rotnitzky was."

He sprang to his feet, his face flushed and his nostrils flaring. He pounded his fists on the table. "Where's the damn cell phone!"

I leaned back so far I almost fell off the bench. "I'll tell you everything if you give me immunity. But first I need to know that there's really no one in that room who can burn me with the information later."

He sat down with a cocky grin. "Go knock on the glass and see if anyone knocks back."

I got up and walked to the mirror. I could see the reflection of the chief, watching me. I held up my hands, still cuffed together, and made a fist. His hands moved to the edge of the table and his back arched like a loaded spring. I pretended to knock on the glass, but instead reached over and slapped the light switch off. The room went dark and silent. I spun around and caught Chief Fischer's fingertips glowing bright blue.

He flew off the bench and slammed the lights back on. His face was twisted in rage.

My eyes locked on his. "Clementine is a really unusual name. You had to know I'd remember it from the picture of your dog."

His brow furrowed and he pulled his gun. He grabbed me by the throat and pushed me into the glass. "You think you're so clever, don't you?"

He covered my mouth with his hand and dug the nose of his gun into my ribs. Then he opened the door a crack and looked out. He threw it open all the way and prodded me. "Move!"

He pushed me through the door and dragged me farther down the hall.

My blood was thudding in my ears and the gun bit into my ribs, but all I could think was how much I loved Gia and Henry and Aunt Ginny. Also, I was really glad that I'd worn good underwear.

He opened a metal door that led to the stairwell and shoved me through. I tripped and cracked my knee on the concrete step. "What are you going to do? Shoot me here in the police station? IT has already found where you logged into the evidence log and deleted Amber's record." *I hope.*

"There are no cameras in this part of the building. My report will say you tried to escape and grabbed my gun."

"Even if you kill me, they'll still know it was you. Shayla Rose can ID you. How much of a disguise is a pair of glasses? And that blue glow will last a couple of days."

He grabbed my wrist and pulled me to my feet. He used his gun to corral me down the steps. "Go!"

"How could you kill that kid? Do you have no decency in you at all? I understand that he'd become a liability. He made a mess with Shayla's face cream, and he tracked that stuff everywhere, including your warehouse. And I'm sure he was being a nuisance, complaining about doing your dirty work when he wanted to go straight, but you killed him like his life didn't matter. Losing the burner phone that could be tracked to you was the last straw, wasn't it? What? Is it registered to you? Does it have your fingerprints on it? A voice mail? Cell tower records?"

Chief Fischer said nothing. He poked me in the back with his gun and prodded me through a door into the basement under the police station.

"But why'd you kill Lance Rubin? As far as I can tell,

he didn't know anything about you. He was busy trying to create some miracle cure for aging."

We reached a dark hallway and the chief's fingertips lit up brightly.

"It was the glow, wasn't it? His fingers were glowing the same blue from mixing Shayla's creams. I bet he took one look at you and knew you had stolen her samples. And since your face wasn't glowing, he knew you weren't just putting it on. He figured out exactly what you were doing, didn't he? All he had to do was report it to the right person and your career would be over. But when did you see each other in the dark?"

"If you don't shut up, I'm going to crack you in the head and drag you down the hall by your hair."

Come on, give me something. All the other bad guys love to monologue. "I bet you were looking for that burner phone in Shayla's booth after the Expo closed. No wonder you agreed to patrol Convention Hall overnight for security. Did you catch the doctor mixing beauty creams and experimenting with the mask?"

He pushed his gun into my neck. "You don't know anything."

"That's it, isn't it?" His eyes bore into mine and I saw a mixture of fear and wrath. It was a lethal combination. He would surely kill me before tonight was over. "I bet he confronted you, and you killed him in a panic because you were about to be exposed. You fought with him and stepped on the power supply. Then you hit him in the head with your nightstick. It's not on your belt anymore. Where'd you stash it?"

He dragged me to a door, and I could see through a tiny window that it was a dimly lit parking garage. *He can't kill me in here. It would leave too much evidence.*

He must be planning to drive me somewhere and dump my body.

He threw me against the door. "For god's sake, shut up!"

"I get why you tossed the place and threw a bunch of Agnes Pfeister-Pinze's flyers around to make it look like she'd finally snapped. That wouldn't be hard to prove since Dr. Rubin had just been down to the station to press charges against her. But why did you put him on the exam bed and cover him with the mask? You'd already knocked him out. Why not shoot him?"

He flung the door to the garage open and threw me against the wall. My head slammed against the cinder block and I saw stars. He threw his body into mine and put the gun to my head. "I had no idea he would be there or that that creepy mask was deadly. But I'm going to do to you exactly what I did to him if you don't stop talking. I'm going to bash you in the head and force that mask on you until I see it eat the skin off your face. Is that what you want?"

"No."

"Then shut up!"

He dragged me across the parking lot, and I saw my window to escape closing. "Why in the world are you making counterfeit face cream to sell online? There has to be an easier way to get rich. Why don't you just sell the cocaine you confiscate like all the other dirty cops?"

"You can't sell cocaine anonymously on the Internet." He grabbed my wrist and twisted hard. He started pulling me toward an unmarked black SUV.

"Well, just so you know, Shayla Rose's Immortality wasn't supposed to glow in the dark. You went to all the trouble to mix the glow sticks into the cold cream for nothing. It's not even approved for sale by the FDA."

He threw me against the SUV and clocked me on the side of the temple with his gun. "I warned you."

Blood trickled down the side of my face. I knew no one was coming. I would die tonight, so I had nothing left to lose. "Just tell me one thing. Was it personal with Amber, or was she just the most convenient?"

"I'd like to know that too." Amber stepped out from behind a police SUV with her gun pointed at the chief.

Chief Fischer yanked me in front of him and pointed his gun at my temple. "Drop your weapon or I'll shoot her in the head. I've been wanting to for twenty minutes. Just give me a reason."

Amber kept her aim. "Why'd you frame me, Clayton?"

"You know why."

"I wasn't a threat to you."

"It was just a matter of time. I needed someone to take the fall, and I didn't think anyone would look too hard to prove your innocence, hotshot."

"All this for wrinkle cream? You killed two people."

Fischer's breathing was getting erratic. "It's not about the wrinkle cream. It's my retirement. It's what I'm due. I'll make more money selling fake Shayla Rose than I have in my 401(k) And there's no way I'm letting you, or her, or a rich plastic surgeon pull it out from under me."

I managed to get a breath and squeaked out, "What about Temarius? Did he have to die?"

"No punk kid in the system is going to destroy my career and my reputation because he suddenly wants to go straight and confess."

Amber took a step closer, and Chief Fischer's arm tightened around me. I was getting a little dizzy and knew I might pass out soon. "What were you going to do if

Amber had an emergency and got stuck at another crime scene when she was supposed to be caught standing over him?"

Amber cocked her head but held her arm steady. "Were Crabtree and Simmons your plan B?"

The chief snarled, "I had more contingency plans than you can imagine. Now get out of my way or you're going down with your friend. It would be easy to prove you killed each other when she turned on you. I laid the groundwork for that yesterday."

"You're a stench, Clayton. You promised to protect and serve these people. You used Temarius, then got rid of him like he was expendable. How dare you wear that uniform?"

"No one will give another thought to the loss of one more disadvantaged kid in the system."

"That's where you're wrong. Now. Drop. Your. Gun."

Chief Fischer pushed the gun deeper into my temple. "You're killing her."

"Then why don't you let her go and take me instead?"

Chief Fischer laughed. "That's your problem, Amber. You always have to be a hero."

Amber removed her aim and held both her hands over her head. "You know what to do."

The chief moved his gun away from my temple and took aim at Amber. I flung my body against his arm, and a loud shot echoed throughout the underground garage. Amber dropped to the ground.

I screamed, "No!"

I felt the chief pull away from me and I rushed to Amber's side. I knelt on the ground next to her. "Oh Amber, I'm so sorry."

She looked up at me. "Would you relax? I'm fine. He just clipped my arm."

Kieran Dunne stepped out from behind a concrete pylon with his gun aimed at the chief of police, who lay in a crumpled heap on the ground. A red pool flowing from his chest.

A chill ran down my arms and I shuddered.

Kieran holstered his firearm and came toward us. "My God, I thought you two would never stop talking." He put his hand down to Amber. She stared at him for a beat, then put her hand in his, and he helped her up.

"I guess I'll get myself up. I was just the hostage for the last hour while you were doing God knows what."

I struggled to my feet, but before I could dust off my jeans, Amber wrapped me in a hug and whispered, "Thank you."

I hugged her back. "You're welcome."

"Never tell anyone about this."

"Okay, but now we're even for the grapes "

"Not even close."

CHAPTER 56

"When will we all learn that the quality of a man is not in the color of his skin?" I started to sob. Somehow uncovering the identity of Temarius's killer had left me feeling empty and sick inside.

Officer Birkwell handed me a cup of coffee. He put his hand on my shoulder and squeezed.

I had to give my statement about fifty times in between receiving updates about what had happened while I was being dragged to my death in the parking garage.

While I was being interrogated by Kieran Dunne, Officer Birkwell had discovered that the written evidence log had a page missing. Joanne Junk had used her one phone call from the station to call Sawyer, so Sawyer could tell Consuelos that we were in trouble and the owner of the warehouse was Clementine Newsome. Consuelos called Birkwell, who reported his suspicions to Kieran Dunne, then, at Kieran Dunne's direction, called the department IT officer to print out an emergency log report from the backups. Based on the login information in the file, it appeared that Prudence Crabtree had signed in and deleted Amber's entry in the evidence log.

Amber came and sat next to me. "How's your head?"

I shrugged. "It's fine. My best plaid is ruined. So how did you get out of your cell?"

"When Kieran found out the evidence log had been tampered with, he finally believed that I'd been framed. He let me out and mentioned that intel had just surfaced that the warehouse was owned by Clementine Newsome. He wanted to know why that was significant."

"You told him about the collie?"

"Everyone knows the chief named that dog after his ex-wife out of spite."

"I really thought Kieran was the handler. Why would he answer that cell phone if it wasn't his?"

Amber snorted. "He said he answered the burner phone by accident because it looked like the one Fischer had given him to use during the investigation. The chief bought them by the case for department use. Apparently, they have sequential serial numbers."

"So the one he gave Temarius could be tracked back to him."

Kieran led Prudence Crabtree to the desk across from where Amber and I were sitting. She had just arrived back at the station and was doing a perp walk with Big Shirley for her third drunk and disorderly this year.

Prudence appeared to be in a panic. "But I didn't delete the record."

"It's your username and password."

Prudence pulled out a notebook with shaking hands. "Look at my call log. I couldn't have done it. I was in court all day."

Kieran shouted across the room to the IT officer. "Find out if that login was hacked."

Kieran folded his arms and perched on the edge of the desk to look down at Prudence. "If it wasn't, we'll be moving this conversation to the interrogation room. Now, who sent you to Jackson's apartment?"

She squirmed in her seat. "Chief Fischer directly, sir."

"And the warehouse?"

"There too."

"Didn't you think it was strange the calls didn't come through Dispatch?"

Prudence twisted her hands. "He said they were top level, off-book missions based on anonymous intel. I didn't question him. He'd been grooming me for promotion to detective, so I figured it was a test. Am I in trouble?"

Kieran replied sweetly, "Absolutely. I'm just trying to determine exactly how much trouble you're in."

Prudence whimpered.

I whispered to Amber, "Wow, she is cracking like a Christmas walnut."

Amber whispered back, "Oh, she is nowhere close to being ready for detective."

Birkwell approached Kieran with his notebook open. "Apparently Simmons was assigned by Chief Fischer to perform surveillance inside the warehouse to wait for the next break-in. He was told to keep the incident off the radio and not to write up a report about it. He said he was just happy to have something to do other than issue parking tickets for a change."

Kieran shook his head. "God help us if that boy ever

has to fire his weapon. Birkwell, take Crabtree here down to the holding tank until I'm ready to interview her formally."

Prudence Crabtree held Amber's gaze as Shane Birkwell led her off the station floor.

I called after her, "If Big Shirley charges you, make sure you plant your feet."

She whimpered again, and Amber snickered under her breath.

The IT officer eventually brought over a printout and handed it to Kieran. "I was able to trace the login by the end user's IP address to the PC in the chief's office. Either she logged in from his computer or he used Officer Crabtree's username and password to make the deletion himself."

"Good work, Edgar." He looked over at me sitting at the desk with a giant bandage wrapped around my head. "I'm sending you to Cape Regional to get checked out."

I tried to protest. "I don't want to go to the hospital. I just want to go home."

He held up his hand. "I insist."

He called the paramedics to transport me to be sure I was safe. I thought it was more likely to ensure I wouldn't sue the department for reckless endangerment. I felt like an idiot sitting in the emergency room with Amber, wrapped in a huge sheet of tinfoil, waiting for my blood pressure to return to normal. When I was finally released to go home, it was nearly seven a.m. Amber drove me, and I had her drop me off at Sawyer's bookstore on the Mall. She had texted me hours ago that we needed to talk as soon as I could get there.

* * *

Sawyer was ready for me when I knocked. The door opened, and the smell of coffee made me a little less miserable than I'd been before I arrived. She handed me a cup and made a fuss over the butterfly bandage that was pasted to my temple.

"You should see the other guy."

We went to her back office. A sofa bed was closed up with a folded blanket and two pillows resting on one side.

"So?" I plugged my cell phone into her charger. "What's going on?"

"I'm living here. I've been here for weeks. The lights you keep seeing on are from me."

"You're not back together with Kurt?"

"Eww, no. Why would you think that?"

"Because I ran into him at your condo and he led me to believe that you'd reconciled."

"Did he say that? Uck. He's such a liar."

"Then why is he there?"

"That's what I didn't want to tell you. Kurt is living in my condo temporarily because he's homeless."

I took a long sip of coffee and tried to keep my mouth shut.

"He lost his job a few months ago, and the house a few months after that."

"Okay. So why do you need to be the one to help him get back on his feet?"

"Because I can't afford the rent on the condo without his alimony, and he can't pay alimony plus rent on an apartment. I was letting him sleep on the couch, but it became . . . problematic . . . and I moved out. It's only temporary. He has one month to find a place and get out, even if that means I have to get a loan."

Sawyer's heart had always been two sizes too big for her own good. I wanted to hug her and shake her at the same time. "You know, you could have stayed with me. I have empty guest rooms. Plus, Joanne can make us breakfast."

She nodded.

"So why isn't Kurt the one sleeping on the pullout sofa while you live in the condo?"

"Because she's moving in with me." Officer Consuelos appeared in the doorway, wiping shaving cream from his face. "At least until we can get him out of there."

Sawyer gave me a tiny smile, but the light in her eyes was jumping for joy. "That was the other thing I didn't want to tell you. Ben and I have been dating since the winery."

Ben came over and stood behind Sawyer.

"Why wouldn't you want to tell me that? You know I'm thrilled for you . . . as long as it isn't Kurt. And why am I the last to know? Both Amber and Joanne have hinted about you two, and I was too dense to catch on sooner."

Sawyer took his hand in hers. "At first I kept it a secret because you had so much going on with Tim and Gia. Then, just as I was about to tell you, Alex showed up, and I didn't want to rub it in your face." A tear slid down her cheek.

I put my coffee down and pulled her into a hug. "You're ridiculous, you know that? Your happiness means far more to me."

She nodded against my shoulder.

"But if you're dating a cop, why do you have all those parking tickets? There ought to be some perks."

Sawyer blushed and looked up at Officer Consuelos. "Those aren't parking tickets." She giggled. "Ben leaves little notes for me when he patrols."

I gave Officer Consuelos a look that said *aww, aren't you cute*. He cleared his throat and looked away.

I got to my feet. "I'm going to go home and make sure Victory isn't asleep in a closet somewhere, check out my Cat Show people, mend Figaro's broken heart with tuna, then sleep until next weekend."

My cell phone chimed that I had a voice mail, and I took it off the charger. It was from Gia. Sawyer walked me to the door, and I hit Play.

"Bella, I did not want to leave this in a message. Please come by the coffee shop tonight at six so I can explain in person."

Sawyer's eyes doubled in size. "What is that about?"

I looked across the courtyard at La Dolce Vita. Alex was out front in a pretty little flowered dress, casually sweeping the sidewalk. "I guess the plan is in motion."

CHAPTER 57

"I hope you had a wonderful stay with us."

Dale Parker held up his empty cat carrier. "Everything was lovely. And breakfast in bed was such a nice treat."

"I'm so glad you enjoyed it. And congratulations again to Portia for winning first place in the Pretty Kitty Cat Show."

Dale smiled, then looked in his empty cat carrier with a grimace. "I hope Patsy finds her soon. We need to get on the road."

The entire household had been nervously looking for the green-eyed girl since breakfast. I gave Dale a supportive smile that I hoped hid my fear that Figaro was somehow involved in Portia's disappearance.

Patsy came down the hall empty-handed, shaking her head. "I just can't find her anywhere. It's not like her to hide."

"You know what, she's been venturing up to the third floor with Fig. I'm going to go do another sweep." I stopped in the kitchen and dug around the refrigerator. I took out a package of bacon and microwaved a piece.

Aunt Ginny came in from the mudroom. "Not in there. What are you doing?"

I held up the bacon. "Bait."

Aunt Ginny nodded her approval. "It should at least work on Fig."

I climbed the back stairs to the third floor, calling, "Portia, here kitty. Treat." No soft thud. No meow of begging. I checked my room and two of the old servants' rooms. No cats. I was about to give up and eat the bacon myself when I noticed the door to the storage room was slightly ajar.

I crept in the room and moved aside the mink coats and Christmas tree. In the very back corner, curled up together like yin and yang, I found Figaro and Portia. Snuggled down in a box of mittens and scarves.

I sighed. "It's time for Portia to go home, baby."

Fig opened one eye to a slit and closed it again. I was dismissed.

"Portia, I have bacon."

Her green eyes popped open and she licked her mouth. Portia stretched and sat tall, the call of the bacon was more appealing than the lure of a boyfriend. *I know where your priorities lie.*

I broke off a piece and fed it to her. Then I picked up the white Persian and carried her down the stairs. "I found her."

Dale let out a sigh of relief and reached for the kitty. "Oh thank goodness. You naughty girl." They put her in the carrier and prepared to go.

Figaro appeared at my ankles and let out a long meow to declare his thoughts on Portia leaving.

Portia returned her customary cold hiss. She had moved on. Figaro sat in loaf position, looking out the window for the rest of the day. He wouldn't even eat the bacon.

CHAPTER 58

I brought Aunt Ginny with me to La Dolce Vita. She had been my rock these past six months and I didn't think I could face tonight without her. Gia had asked me to wait in the alley until he was ready to let us in.

Aunt Ginny humphed and gave me a look that said she was not pleased with him right now.

About five after six he opened the door and put his finger to his lips. He led us into his small office, where a laptop was set up with a view of the dining room. He indicated for us to take our seats, then he kissed me on the forehead and shut us in.

Aunt Ginny and I looked at each other, both confused but waiting to see how this played out.

I had to fight back the fear that Gia would return any minute to tell me we were over. Alex and he had worked things out and they were going to try again. *No. I can trust him.*

The screen in front of us showed that two tables in the dining room were occupied. Two men in Hawaiian shirts sat, casually having coffee and talking about fishing. A woman in the corner was reading a book and occasionally sipping a cappuccino.

Gia hummed a tune while he cleaned the bar. I recognized it immediately. *He's humming "Unchained Melody."* I tried to swallow, but a sob caught in my throat. It was the song he'd played for me on Valentine's Day, when we had our first date.

The front door opened and the bell jingled. Momma came in with Alex and they both gave Gia a kiss.

Aunt Ginny patted me on the leg.

He sat them at a table right in front of the camera and made them each espressos.

A couple of minutes later Zio Alfio entered the shop with his briefcase and took off his fedora. They greeted one another with cheek kisses, and Gia joined them at the table.

Gia took Alex's hand and said to her, "I have given it a lot of thought; you are right. We should try again. You say you have never stopped loving me, so I think we should renew our vows."

A little part of me went dead inside hearing Gia say those words to another woman.

Alex squealed and threw her arms around Gia's neck, planting kisses all over his face. "*Mio caro.* I am so excited. There is so much I want us to do. Let's renew our vows in Montepulciano. They have the cutest little church. And I saw this cozy beach house in Monterrey that would be perfect for us."

Gia held up his hand. "Whoa. *Tesoro mio.* As much as

I want you to have everything your heart desires, I do not have money for those things."

Alex brightened with a smile. "Don't worry, we can spend some of the inheritance. It won't be that much."

Gia gently pushed Alex off him. "What do you mean, spend the inheritance? What inheritance?"

Alex's smile lost a touch of its confidence. "The inheritance your father left you. Papa said the family property in Italy was sold for millions and you would inherit most of it." She looked from Gia to Zio Alfio.

Zio Alfio raised both his palms and muttered something in Italian that no one understood.

Momma smacked him on the back of the head and said some things that everyone understood, including me and Aunt Ginny.

Gia asked, "Zio Alfio, what did you do?"

"I may have put out some . . . how you say . . . *informazioni false* with my contacts in Roma for Vincenzo Scarduzio to hear in the wind. I suspect the scent of money would get Alexandra to return."

Gia made a fist and pointed at Zio Alfio. "You mean you lied."

Alex's face froze in confusion, but her eyelids fluttered. "So, there is no money?"

Gia put his hand on her back. "It is okay, *tesoro mio*. We can start over in Philly by your cousins. Maybe you can get your job back at Marco's Pizzeria."

Alex's face turned three shades of pink.

Aunt Ginny snickered. "Liars do not like to be lied to."

Alex shook her head for a long time before the words came out of her mouth. "No. No. I will not move back to Philly. I want us to stay here and run La Dolce Vita."

I felt a scrap of fear begin to flutter to the surface.

Gia took Alex's hands in his. "*Mia cara*, I cannot stay here by Poppy. If we are to be together, I have to start over away from her. I never thought you would return to me and I let myself fall in love again."

Alex crossed her arms over her chest and leaned away from Gia. "No. This is no good for me."

Momma grabbed Alex's wrist, and she appeared to be pleading with her, but Alex would only shake her head no.

Zio Alfio threw his hands in the air. "Then what you want, eh? You got *marito*! You got *bambino*! What is problem?"

Alex threw her hand in the air like double karate chops. "I want the inheritance I was promised!"

Gia yelled, "There is no inheritance! My father is dead thirty years—he leave nothing!"

Everyone was yelling now. I was impressed that the men in Hawaiian shirts were able to ignore the chaos and eat their biscotti like it was any other day. The woman probably hadn't read a word in ten minutes.

Zio Alfio picked up his briefcase and slammed it on the table to silence everyone.

Aunt Ginny looked at me and nodded her approval. "That's how you do that."

Zio Alfio leaned toward Alex. "What, you want to walk away? Eh?"

I held my breath.

"I want La Dolce Vita and I want you to sign my citizenship form saying we have been married seven years."

Zio Alfio opened his briefcase and pulled out some papers. He handed Alex a pen.

She perused the documents. "This is permanent resident form? It says we have been together the whole time?"

Zio Alfio nodded. "*Sì.*"

Alex signed it and handed the pen to Gia.

He stared at her for a moment with hurt on his face, then signed it.

She flipped through the papers. "This one is for divorce?"

Zio Alfio nodded again and fluttered his fingers. *"Sì, sì, sì."*

I grabbed Aunt Ginny's hand and squeezed.

Alex put the pen down. "I will only sign if La Dolce Vita is one hundred percent mine."

Zio Alfio pulled out another document. "Transfer of ownership. I prepare just in case."

Alex nodded and picked the pen back up.

Gia stood and paced back and forth. "You do not love me?"

"No, Giampaolo. I do not."

"Then why do you come to break my heart again?"

Alex signed and turned the paper to Gia. "Sign over your business to me and you are free."

Oh my god. Gia couldn't possibly . . . the price is too high.

Gia's face twisted in pain and frustration. He ran his hand through his hair. "This is all I have, Alex. You even take Henry. You will leave me with nothing."

Alex thought for a minute. "I will sign over parental rights. You can have Henry for La Dolce Vita."

I started to get up to go out there and tear her hair out by the roots for not wanting the world's sweetest little boy, but Aunt Ginny held tight on my hand. "No. Just wait."

Gia made a lot of complaints in Italian, then he begrudgingly signed the contracts. "They are of no use to you until they are witnessed and notarized."

The woman in the corner spoke up. "I'm a notary."

Zio Alfio shouted, "Eh! *Dolce signora, per favore!*" He waved his hand toward the document. *"Giusto qui. Sì."*

The woman took her bag to the table and brought out her notary seal. "I need some witnesses to sign, though."

"We can witness." The tourists in Hawaiian shirts stood and went to the table. Gia got so upset he had to walk away.

The tourists returned to their table and Alex smiled approvingly at her copies of the documents.

Zio Alfio put his copies in his briefcase and nodded at Gia. *"Va bene."*

Gia went back to the table. "Why do you do this, Alex? Why do you come back only to make trouble? Why do you not stay with me?"

Alex folded her papers and put them in her purse. "I want more than this." She nodded her head toward the espresso machine.

Gia placed his palms on the table and leaned to face her. "Then why do you want La Dolce Vita?"

Alex coolly crossed her legs, and one side of her mouth grinned. "Papa wants to expand the Morello DiSanto distribution in the United States, and La Dolce Vita will be his home base."

The look on Gia's face was incredulous. "This is about the fake olive oil your father sends through this country?"

Alex's mask came all the way off and she leveled a look of contempt at Gia. "So what if it's mostly soybean? That fake olive oil has kept your family in money for years. If it were not for Papa laundering Morello DiSanto through Momma's ristorante and giving her a cut of the profit, do you think Mia Famiglia would have survived this long? Your family needs Vincenzo Scarduzio."

Aunt Ginny gasped.

I whispered, "What is happening?"

Aunt Ginny whispered back, "Gia's mother is the Mob connection."

Momma smacked the table. "No! Basta!"

Alex laughed bitterly. "I told you months ago, Oliva, it's too late for that now. No one turns their back on the family. If you dishonor Papa, it might get out that Luca has been smuggling the olive oil for you through his imports business. I don't believe he has ever turned in those customs forms, has he? Your son got his precious divorce that you asked for. Let's just leave it at that and be happy. Now, everyone needs to get out of my shop so I can call Papa and tell him the news."

One of the men in a Hawaiian shirt spoke into his watch. "We're a go." He approached Alex and put his hand on her elbow. "Alexandra Scarduzio, I'm going to need you to come with me, please."

Alex jerked her arm away from him. "What? I'm not going anywhere. Who are you?"

"Agent Scott with US Customs and Border Patrol. My partner, Agent Robinson. Ma'am, we're placing you under arrest."

Alex stamped her foot. "No. I am not a US citizen; I demand to be taken to the Italian consulate!"

Agent Scott cocked his head. "I'm afraid it's too late for that. I personally witnessed your citizenship application. You'll be spending a few years in a good old United States prison."

He started to lead Alex from the coffee shop, and she called over her shoulder, "You all think you're so smart, but this isn't over. La Dolce Vita is still mine."

Zio Alfio crossed his arms and threw them out like an umpire. "No. Is no good."

Alex narrowed her eyes and her forehead crinkled in tiny lines. "What are you talking about, old man?"

Gia crossed his arms in front of his broad chest. "He means you should have read the contract closer. There is a clause in the transfer of ownership that if you get arrested in the first year of business, the contract is void and the property reverts back to me."

Alex's entire countenance drooped. "Are you serious?"

Gia nodded. "You had one year to mess up and you did not last one hour."

"You will regret this. When I talk to Vincenzo Scarduzio, he will make you pay."

The customs agents removed Alex from the building and Zio Alfio cheered.

Gia disappeared from the screen and a moment later threw open the door to the office.

I leapt into his arms and kissed him with a thousand kisses that I'd been holding on to from the moment Alex appeared. "Is it really over?"

His eyes sparkled with emotion. "It is over. I am all yours."

EPILOGUE

One Week Later

My house had been taken over by pink streamers and gold mylar. When I'd agreed to let Smitty throw Georgina's birthday party here, I didn't realize he was going to fill enough helium balloons to launch an old codger in a lawn chair into space.

Figaro was in cat ninja heaven. Prowling and performing sneak attacks on the curly ribbons dangling enticingly throughout the house. A few times the ribbons got the upper hand, and he had to retreat to the sunroom to re-group. It had taken a few cans of tuna to heal his broken heart from Portia's absence, but I think the last two days he'd just been milking it. If he had any idea about the Internet sensation he'd become since the Parkers posted his photo on Instagram, he would be insufferable. His squished face was made into a dozen memes overnight. All of them crabby.

Georgina's pink Louboutins clacked down the dark, wood-plank hallway from the foyer. "Poppy! Did you make that strawberry tiramisu that I love?" She poked her head into the kitchen and reared back. "Oh, sorry. There's nowhere to knock before coming in here."

I giggled, and Gia reluctantly released me from the embrace my pretty-in-pink, former mother-in-law had just walked in on. "I made it."

"Oh good. I told my little Smitty I would take care of all the food."

When Georgina says she will take care of all the food, what she means is she will order me to take care of all the food. "Don't worry. I've got everything under control."

The doorbell rang, and I left Gia in charge of the coffee to go answer it. It was Mrs. Pritchard, shamefaced and holding a banana cream pie. "I've come to apologize."

I took the pie she held out and gave her a little smile. "I never told Aunt Ginny it was you. Mostly because I didn't know how to explain it."

She wrung her hands and looked everywhere but at me. "He blocks the afternoon sun from Mr. Lincoln."

"You've been shooting our giant, inflatable rabbit because he casts shade on your roses?"

"They won't bloom if they don't get enough sun. Mr. Lincoln has won very prestigious awards. He takes first place in the Cape May Flower Show every year. I need to defend his title."

I gave the older woman in orthopedic shoes and knee-high stockings a chastising stare down. "You could have really hurt someone, you know that?"

She gave me a meek nod. "It's just a pellet gun. They aren't real bullets."

"It's still dangerous. We thought it was drive-by shooters."

Mrs. Pritchard turned gentle eyes up to mine. "I had to wait for the cars to go by to cover the sound of the shot, like that sniper said on *Dateline*."

"Well, if you promise never to shoot that pellet gun toward anyone's yard again, I won't tell Aunt Ginny."

Mrs. Pritchard gave me a genuine smile. "Deal."

"And next time just come talk to me. Don't pick off the lawn ornaments in your nightgown, okay?"

She agreed and promised to keep me posted on Mr. Lincoln's standings this summer.

The biddies pulled into the driveway and Mrs. Dodson honked twice. Gia went out to unload the car and bring in their packages.

Henry flew down the hall from helping Aunt Ginny wrap Georgina's presents and passed me to help carry in the groceries. He returned with a giant bag of potato chips. Smitty had not been totally hands off with the menu. Georgina didn't become the model of high-society soirees in the Waterford elite set by serving potato chips and onion dip.

Smitty was right behind Henry with a case of some funky-weird sassafras soda that I knew wasn't sanctioned either. "Oi, wise guy. Nyuck, nyuck, nyuck."

Henry threw his head back and belly laughed. "Guh nuh yuck."

A police car pulled up in front of the house and Sawyer climbed out. She kissed Ben Consuelos goodbye and he gave me a wave before taking off. "He's sorry he can't stay, but he's on duty. And oh my gosh, I have the most hilarious thing to tell you."

"What is it?"

"Lance Rubin's funeral was this morning. Six widows

showed up to sit in the front row and started a riot in the funeral home."

"Get out!"

"I'm serious! It's all over local news. And guess who sent a touching tribute for the eulogy?"

I thought. "Doctors Without Borders?"

Sawyer nodded. "He actually did three tours in Somalia."

We walked to the kitchen together, laughing. "How are things going at Casa Consuelos?"

Sawyer blushed. "I hope Kurt never moves out."

The biddies were in the living room sneaking hors d'oeuvres and Georgina and Smitty were pretending not to notice. I had just taken a pan of onion cheese tarts from the oven when the doorbell rang again.

Figaro galloped ahead and tried to trip me, as was his custom. I dodged and threatened to punt him next time, as was mine.

"Hey, Amber. How was the memorial?"

Amber stood on my porch in her police uniform, her hat in her hands. "I bet there were a hundred people packed into that little church. Temarius touched a lot more lives than Fischer ever imagined."

"I'm so sorry I had to leave early, but I'm thrilled that you've been reinstated. Come in."

She entered the foyer and looked around at the balloons and the party in the next room. "I just wanted to let you know that Clayton Fischer pulled through, and he's been charged in the murder of Temarius Jackson and Lance Rubin."

"How are you doing? I know you looked up to him."

She shifted her feet. "Yeah, well. I don't think I really knew him after all. We have a new chief now. A transfer from Trenton."

My mouth dropped open and I gasped. "No."

She nodded. "Yep. Kieran Dunne is the new Cape May chief of police. And he's already making threats to give me a partner *for accountability*."

"Holy cow."

"He impressed the right people."

Speaking of . . . "Amber. I'm sorry if I've somehow made you look bad. . . ."

She cut me off. "Please. I don't care what anyone thinks. And if they had any idea about how little you know what you're doing, and how many times I've had to save your sorry behind, I'd start getting hazard pay."

"You are a really good cop."

Amber took a step back and cleared her throat. "So, I just stopped by to say thank you, and to let you know I'm working on my next case."

Aunt Ginny walked into the foyer to offer Amber a glass of punch.

"I'm investigating illegal marijuana distribution dis- guised as CBD gummies. Officer Birkwell picked up a packet of MyTHiC Teddies at the Expo that have been laced with cannabis. Do you know anything about that?"

Aunt Ginny said, "Nope." She spun around without giving Amber the punch and left the foyer.

I smiled. "I'll keep my eyes open."

She put her hat on and turned to reach for the door. "You do that."

"Amber?"

"What?"

"Would you like to stay? We're having a party for my former mother-in-law, who's dating my handyman. . . . I have potato chips and M&M's."

Amber blinked twice. Then she smiled. "Sure. If you want, I can stay for a little while."

Amber went to join the others and I went to the kitchen to pour the potato chips in a bowl. Mrs. Dodson came in and took a look around. "So, my girl did a good job for you?"

Aunt Ginny brought in an empty tray to be refilled with grapes and cheese. "She was great. You should have seen her in there. Cool as a cucumber."

I took the tray from Aunt Ginny. "No grapes this time. And who are we talking about?"

Mrs. Dodson tapped her cane on the ground and flashed a full set of dentures. "You didn't recognize her?"

"Recognize who?"

Gia returned from Wawa carrying two twenty-pound bags of ice, one on each shoulder.

Mrs. Dodson motioned to Gia. "Your man there asked for a notary to seal his divorce. That was my Charlotte in the coffee shop."

Aunt Ginny nudged me. "I can't believe you didn't recognize her."

"I was just trying to hold it together. I didn't pay any attention to anyone not at that table." *Look at him carry that ice.*

Aunt Ginny brought the ice bucket out of the mudroom and placed it on the counter. "Yes, we've all noticed your tunnel vision."

Gia's eyes softened and he put the ice in the sink. He came closer and kissed me.

Aunt Ginny and Mrs. Dodson both made *yuck* noises and left the kitchen.

I didn't care.

He looked into my eyes. "Why don't we run away together and tell no one?"

"What about Henry?"

"We will take him. We can homeschool. You teach him English and cooking and I will teach him Italian and how to tell the difference between good olive oil and fake."

"Oh yeah, that'll come in handy. Especially with your family."

"Maybe Momma can visit once in a while, when she's not doing community service."

"All this time she hated me because you were still married, and your divorce threatened her business with the Mob. I can't believe you turned her in to the feds."

"*Amore mio*, the Mob is not what it used to be. Momma will lose a lot of money from not working with Vincenzo Scarduzio, but she was going to be caught soon anyway. The agents looking for me at the Expo were already investigating her. They were on to Signor Scarduzio for months. I made sure we had a signed immunity agreement before I told them anything."

"I thought they were looking to arrest you."

He chuckled and shook his head. "I am not now and have never been in the Mafia."

I snuggled into him. "Why didn't you just tell me that before?"

"Because you were so funny, trying to catch me in all your beat-around-the-bush questions."

"Is there anything else I need to know about you? Any other secrets?"

His face became very serious. "There is one. But you will find out eventually."

"Uh-oh. What is it?"

"I snore."

ACKNOWLEDGMENTS

Special thanks to Steven Haddock, PhD, of the Monterey Bay Aquarium Research Institute for his invaluable information on jellyfish toxins.

And to Allie Marie, retired police chief and author of the True Colors Series, Mark Bergin, retired officer and author of *Apprehension*, and retired Officer and FBI Agent Mayme Boyd for their assistance with police procedure and Internal Affairs protocols.

Special thanks also to Rossana Tarantini for fixing my Italian translations. Gia's family talks so fast, I can barely understand them.

And to my writers' group for their fabulous insights and critique. Jerry, Peter, Mandy, and Kathy—a million thanks for making Poppy as great as she can be!

Lastly, to Convention Hall for being a good sport. I'm sure your security is top-notch and the Beauty Expo was just a fluke. And Congress Hall—tell me that Twilight Egg Hunt isn't a great idea! I totally want to do that!

Butterfly Wings Bed and Breakfast
Afternoon Tea

Traditional Cucumber Cream Cheese Triangles
Grandma Emmy's Egg Salad on Wheat
Poppy's Chicken Salad in Hot Cross Buns
Chocolate Cherry Mascarpone Dessert Sandwiches

English Scones with
Devonshire Cream
Strawberry Champagne Preserves
Lemon Curd

Fresh Strawberries
Custard Tarts
Joanne's Petits Fours in chocolate passionfruit,
raspberry rose, and black vanilla

RECIPES

Poppy's Chicken Salad

I usually use a rotisserie chicken, but you can start by cooking and cooling three chicken breasts if you'd rather. You're going to cut all the ingredients in cubes roughly the size of dice. This makes about 4-5 cups of Chicken salad.

Ingredients

2 cups cooked and cooled chicken cut into cubes
3 ribs of celery, chopped chunky
2–3 scallions, white ends removed, chopped chunky
1 apple, peel left on, cored, and chopped chunky
1 cup dried cherries
1 cup roasted, shelled pistachios
1–1½ cups mayonnaise
1 teaspoon salt
1 teaspoon pepper

Directions

Combine the first six ingredients in a mixing bowl. It will make a very loose, chunky salad. But we aren't finished yet.

Add 1 cup of mayonnaise, salt, and pepper and mix well.

Now we're going to pulse the chicken salad in the food processor. The goal is to have a spreadable filling with some small pieces of cherries and nuts. Not to make pâté. So don't just turn it on and let it go.

I had to pulse it in two batches, and I pulsed each batch ten times. If you cut your pieces very small, you may only need 8 pulses. If you cut them very large, you may need 12–14 pulses. You can tell by the way each pulse sounds that the pistachios are getting smaller. Do as many pulses as you like to make your finished chicken salad the right consistency. Just don't get carried away.

At this point you can add more mayonnaise if you feel it is too dry.

This is wonderful filled in a Gluten-Free Hot Cross Bun.

Gluten-Free Hot Cross Buns

Yield 12-18 buns

Ingredients

½ cup rum, water, or apple juice

½ cup dried fruit (I used orange peel)

1 cup mixed raisins

1 tablespoon orange zest

1¼ cups milk, room temperature

2 large eggs, plus 1 egg yolk (save the white for the wash)

8 tablespoons butter, melted

4½ cups Gluten Free Flour Blend

1 tablespoon instant yeast

½ cup brown sugar, packed

1½ teaspoon cinnamon

½ teaspoon cloves

½ teaspoon allspice

½ teaspoon nutmeg

2 teaspoons salt

1 tablespoon baking powder

1 large egg white reserved from above

1 tablespoon milk

*Icing for the crosses

1 cup confectioners' sugar

½ teaspoon clear vanilla

Pinch salt

4 teaspoons milk, give or take

*I didn't make the icing crosses for the chicken salad sandwiches, but I wanted you to have the entire recipe in case you just want to make the buns by themselves.

Directions

If you've ever made bread before, be sure to read through these directions first. We aren't doing things the usual way. For gluten-free bread we'll only get one rise, so we have to go straight to forming the buns and letting them rise.

Line your sheet pan with parchment paper. Turn on your oven to 200 degrees Fahrenheit. Place a 9 x 13 pan of hot water on the bottom rack.

Mix the rum, water, or apple juice with the dried fruit, raisins, and orange zest in a glass bowl. Cover with plastic wrap and microwave for a minute or two until hot. Set aside to cool to room temperature.

Mix together all the dry ingredients

Drain the excess liquid off the fruit. Set it aside.

Add the eggs, butter, and milk to the dry ingredients. Start mixing (I do it by hand) and add the room-temperature, rehydrated dry fruit. If the dough is too dry, add a little of the reserved liquid from the fruit. If it is too wet, add a little more flour. Once the dough comes together, form into balls the size of small oranges right away. They will rise, but not as much as regular yeast rolls. Arrange them on the parchment-lined pan.

Cover the pan with an oiled sheet of parchment (you can spray a sheet of parchment with PAM if you want). Then cover that with a light kitchen towel. Nothing too heavy. Let's not make the rolls have to work any harder than they have to.

Put the pan in the oven and TURN IT OFF. Let the rolls rise in the oven for an hour. They will only puff up a little. Take them out of the oven and increase the temperature to 375 degrees.

While the oven comes up to heat, whisk the reserved egg white with the tablespoon of milk. Brush the tops of the rolls with the egg wash. Bake for 20 minutes until golden brown.

Take the buns' temperature. Insert an instant-read thermometer to the center of the bun. The temperature should be 205–210° F when fully baked. Transfer finished buns to a rack to cool.

If you're making the icing crosses, mix half the milk into the confectioners' sugar with the salt and the vanilla. Add milk a little at a time until you get a thick paste. If it's too thin, the icing crosses will run all over.

Gluten-Free Chocolate Loaf*

Makes one loaf

Ingredients
1¾ cups gluten-free flour
½ cup unsweetened cocoa
½ teaspoon baking powder
½ teaspoon baking soda
½ teaspoon salt
¼ teaspoon xanthan gum *omit this if it is already in the
     flour blend
1 cup sugar
½ cup butter, softened
2 eggs
1 cup heavy cream
1 cup small or mini chocolate chips

Directions
Heat oven to 350 degrees. Grease bottom only of a 9 x 5-inch loaf pan.

Combine flour, cocoa, baking powder, baking soda, and salt in a small bowl. Mix together.

In a large bowl, beat together sugar and butter. Add eggs; blend well. Stir in cream.

Add the dry ingredients and stir until the batter comes together. Do not overmix.

Fold in chocolate chips.

Pour into the greased loaf pan. Bake at 350 degrees for 50 minutes or until toothpick inserted in center comes out

*adapted from the paleo chocolate loaf recipe in *Restaurant Weeks Are Murder* clean. Cool 15 minutes, then remove from the pan to cool completely.

After the loaf has cooled, wrap tightly and store in refrigerator. This will cut in half-inch slices much better if it is refrigerated. Cut with a serrated knife and fill with Cherry Mascarpone filling.

Cherry Mascarpone Filling

This makes about a cup and a half of spread.

1 cup mascarpone cheese, room temperature.
½ cup Morello Cherry Preserves, room temperature

Beat mascarpone with hand mixer to loosen it up. Add cherry preserves and combine well. This spreads best if it is whipped up right before it's needed and used right away.

Gluten-Free Cream Tea Scones

This makes about a dozen scones

Ingredients
3 cups gluten-free flour
1 tablespoon baking powder
1 teaspoon salt
$\frac{1}{3}$ cup sugar
8 tablespoons butter, cold
$1\frac{1}{2}$ teaspoons vanilla extract
$1\frac{1}{4}$ cups heavy whipping cream
Additional heavy cream, to brush on top of scones before baking

Directions
Preheat oven to 425 degrees. Line a baking sheet with parchment.

Into a food processor bowl, combine gluten-free flour, baking powder, salt, and sugar. Pulse until well combined.

Add cold butter by the tablespoon and pulse until combined.

Add the vanilla extract to the heavy cream. Pour in a little at a time while pulsing.

You should form a lovely, cohesive dough. Not sticky, but no flour left in the bottom of the bowl either. Lightly dust your counter with gluten-free flour. Turn the dough out and let it rest for a minute.

Form the dough into a ball and flatten it with your hands. Roll out to a thickness of about ¾-inch thick. Cut into rounds with a biscuit cutter.

Place rounds on prepared baking sheet close together, but not touching. As they rise, they will help each other.

Brush the tops with heavy cream.

Bake for 15 minutes and check for doneness. I usually cut that last ugly one I mashed together with leftover dough in half to see if the middle is baked all the way. If they need a little more time, put the pan back in the oven for 5 minutes. If the tops are getting too brown, turn the oven down to 350 degrees for the last 5 minutes.

Remove from oven and let cool until you won't burn your mouth. Serve warm and spread with Devonshire cream and jam or lemon curd. Or all three. I'm not judging.

Joanne's Extreme Vanilla and Raspberry Rose Petits Fours

Extreme Vanilla Cake

Ingredients
1½ cups gluten-free flour blend
½ teaspoon baking powder
½ teaspoon salt
2 sticks butter, softened
1 cup sugar
1 tablespoon light corn syrup
3 large eggs, room temperature
2 tablespoons sour cream
2 fat vanilla beans or 1 tablespoon vanilla bean paste*
1 tablespoon vanilla extract

Directions
Preheat oven to 350 degrees. Spray a 9 x 13 pan with nonstick baking spray or line with parchment.

In a mixing bowl, add gluten-free flour blend, baking powder, and salt. Whisk to combine.

In a separate bowl, cream the butter and sugar until light and fluffy. Add corn syrup and whip a little more. Add eggs one at a time and whip until each one disappears into the batter. Add sour cream, vanilla bean paste, and vanilla extract.

Whip some more to combine fully. Be sure to scrape the sides and bottom of the bowl to get everything whipped together.

*If you scraped your own vanilla beans, be sure to put the empty husks in a bottle of rum or vodka to start your own vanilla extract.

Now add your dry ingredients in two batches and mix on low speed. Do not overmix here. Sometimes I stop the mixer before the flour is completely incorporated and I finish by hand with a rubber spatula.

Spread the batter evenly in the prepared pan. It will not be a high cake, and because it is so dense it shouldn't rise as much as cakes usually do. Bake for 15 minutes and check for doneness. If it needs a little more time, give it 5 more minutes and check again.

Let the cake cool completely on a wire rack before turning out on your work surface. I use a cutting board. When the cake is completely cool, wrap it in plastic and chill several hours or overnight. At this point I have enough mess in the kitchen to keep me busy cleaning until that cake is cold.

The first step in making petits fours is to level and layer your cake. If you have a cake leveler, the job is a snap. If you don't, a long knife works well when cut at eye level. Trim off the top dome of the cake so you have a flat surface, then cut through the cake at the halfway point, making two thin 9 x 13 layers. Wrap in plastic and freeze until you have your filling ready.

Extreme Vanilla Ganache

Ingredients
2 cups of white chocolate chips, or a white chocolate
    bar, chopped
¾ cup of heavy whipping cream
2 fat vanilla beans, scraped
1 tablespoon vanilla extract

Directions

Place white chocolate in a glass mixing bowl. Heat heavy cream on top of the stove until it just starts to simmer. You can see it bubbling around the edges. Pour hot cream over the white chocolate and walk away. Give it a minute to work on its own.

Come back after a minute and whisk until you have a smooth, creamy consistency with no lumps. On the off chance that you did not get your cream hot enough and the white chocolate is not melting, put the bowl in the microwave on high for 30 seconds and try whisking again.

Add in your vanilla bean goo and your vanilla extract. Whisk until you can see all the little flecks of beans spread out throughout the ganache. Cover with plastic wrap right on the surface of the ganache. Refrigerate until cold and thick.

Spread the ganache between the layers of frozen cake. Rewrap in plastic and refreeze until the glaze is ready.

Rose Ganache

Ingredients

340 grams of white chocolate chips, or a white chocolate bar, chopped
200 grams of heavy whipping cream
1 teaspoon of rose extract

Directions

Follow all the directions above, adding in the rose extract instead of vanilla bean and vanilla extract. Add a little more extract if you want the rose to come through stronger. It should be a light taste, like an afterthought. Not a strong flavor like perfume.

Spread the ganache between the layers of frozen cake.

Add a thin layer of ½ cup seedless raspberry jam on top of ganache. Rewrap in plastic and refreeze until the glaze is ready.

White Chocolate Glaze

Ingredients
13.47 ounces (1 bag) white chocolate chips or a white
   chocolate bar, chopped
⅔ cup heavy cream

Directions
Place white chocolate in a glass mixing bowl. Heat heavy cream on top of the stove until it just starts to simmer. You can see it bubbling around the edges. Pour hot cream over the white chocolate and let it sit for a minute. Whisk until smooth. Let it cool a bit.

Cutting and Glazing the Petits Fours

Take your cake out of the freezer and, using a sharp, straight edge knife, trim off the edges to make very clean sides. Cut cake into squares (or use a small round cutter if you want circles).

You'll need two forks, and a wire cooling rack on top of a sheet pan lined with parchment. You want the glaze around 85 degrees for dipping. That's warm, but not hot. If it is too hot, it will be very thin and sheer. If it's too cool, it will be thick and lumpy. Keep a pan of very hot water on the stove in case you need to warm up the glaze a few degrees. I find it is a lot easier to pour some glaze into a small working bowl for dipping. Small and deep is better than wide and shallow.

Using two forks, plunge and submerge your cake square.

Try to keep it sitting on the lifting fork in the right direction. When you bite into the petit four you want the filling horizontal between layers, not vertical splitting the cakes into two sides. Pull the cake square out of the glaze and tap the lifting fork it's sitting on with the other fork. You're tapping off excess glaze. Scrape the bottom of the lifting fork with the tapping fork to clean the bottom edge of the cake and gently slide off the fork and onto the wire rack.

If you are decorating the tops with something like sprinkles, *dragées*, sparkling sugar, or other toppings, you'll want to sprinkle it on before the glaze fully sets. If you're piping designs with royal icing, you'll want to make sure it fully sets before you begin decorating.

These look so pretty in little fluted papers. Store in the refrigerator for up to two weeks.